EXCEL

(2nd Edition)
by Jasper T. Scott

http://www.JasperTscott.com
@JasperTscott

Cover design by Tom Edwards
(http://tomedwardsdmuga.blogspot.co.uk)

This book is a work of fiction. All names, places, and incidents described are products of the writer's imagination and any resemblance to real people or life events is purely coincidental.

OTHER BOOKS BY JASPER T. SCOTT:

Dark Space
Dark Space 2: The Invisible War
Dark Space 3: Origin
Dark Space 4: Revenge
Dark Space 5: Avilon
Dark Space 6: Armageddon

Escape
Mrythdom

Coming Soon…
Mindscape (December 2016)

RECOMMENDED BOOKS BY OTHER AUTHORS:

Home Front: Portal Wars III by Jay Allen
The Ember War by Richard Fox
The Synchronity War by Dietmar Wehr
The Star Cross by Raymond L. Weil

TABLE OF CONTENTS

COPYRIGHT PAGE 1

OTHER BOOKS BY JASPER T. SCOTT: 2

ACKNOWLEDGEMENTS 6

DEDICATION 7

DRAMATIS PERSONAE 8

PART ONE: OPERATION ALICE 10

CHAPTER 1 11

CHAPTER 2 31

CHAPTER 3 47

CHAPTER 4 67

CHAPTER 5 78

CHAPTER 6 85

CHAPTER 7 93

CHAPTER 8 100

CHAPTER 9 109

CHAPTER 10 116

CHAPTER 11 122

CHAPTER 12 129

CHAPTER 13 134

PART TWO: WONDERLAND 144

CHAPTER 14 145

CHAPTER 15 152

CHAPTER 16 157

CHAPTER 17 170

CHAPTER 18 181

CHAPTER 19 ..... *188*
CHAPTER 20 ..... *195*
CHAPTER 21 ..... *202*
CHAPTER 22 ..... *212*
CHAPTER 23 ..... *220*
CHAPTER 24 ..... *231*
CHAPTER 25 ..... *244*
CHAPTER 26 ..... *249*
CHAPTER 27 ..... *259*
CHAPTER 28 ..... *264*
CHAPTER 29 ..... *271*
CHAPTER 30 ..... *278*
CHAPTER 31 ..... *286*
CHAPTER 32 ..... *295*
CHAPTER 33 ..... *309*
PART THREE: THE LAST WAR *313*
CHAPTER 34 ..... *314*
CHAPTER 35 ..... *321*
CHAPTER 36 ..... *325*
CHAPTER 37 ..... *335*
CHAPTER 38 ..... *339*
CHAPTER 39 ..... *347*
CHAPTER 40 ..... *357*
CHAPTER 41 ..... *363*
CHAPTER 42 ..... *369*
CHAPTER 43 ..... *374*

CHAPTER 44 381

CHAPTER 45 386

CHAPTER 46 391

CHAPTER 47 400

CHAPTER 48 408

CHAPTER 49 413

CHAPTER 50 419

CHAPTER 51 427

CHAPTER 52 433

EPILOGUE 443

READ ON FOR A SNEAK PEEK OF THE SEQUEL 452

CHAPTER 1 453

FREE OFFER 465

KEEP IN TOUCH 466

ABOUT THE AUTHOR 467

ACKNOWLEDGEMENTS

A big thank you to my wife for her support, and to my fans, who've read and reviewed my previous books. Thanks go out to my editor, Aaron Sikes, and to my volunteer editor, Dave Cantrell. Their feedback was crucial to polishing this book. Also special credit goes to William Schmidt for reading through an early draft at an inhumanly fast pace, and to Ian F. Jedlica (pen name, Dani J. Caile), who has eyes like an eagle when it comes to typos. Oh—and the cover—that delicious piece of art is thanks to Tom Edwards. He took my concept and made it better than I had imagined. Really amazing work.

Finally, thank you to all of my beta readers who read and gave me feedback on the advance reader copy of this book—Betty Hoffner, Damon Trent, Daniel Eloff, Dave Topan, David Smith, Davis Shellabarger, Dwight Hall, Gage Linville, Gary Watts, Gregor Hinckley, Henry Clerval, H. Huyler, Ian Seccombe, Iain Gold, Jay Gehringer, Jeff Moore, Jim Meinen, Jim Thrash, Joe Kane, KB Jolley, Paul Burch, Rose Getch, Wade Whitaker, and William Schmidt—your feedback was crucial to the final stages of editing. As always, I am in your debt.

Thank you, all of you!

DEDICATION

For my wife and all the other women who have shared Catalina's struggles. And for all the veterans and the soldiers on active duty who know what it is to leave loved ones behind to fight a war you hate for a country that you love.

DRAMATIS PERSONAE

The Crew of the *Lincoln*

Bridge Crew (White Deck)

O-6 CAPT - Captain Alexander de Leon

O-5 CDR - Commander Sirena Korbin

Ship's Executive Officer (XO), Mission Counselor, Medic

O-4 LCDR - Lieutenant Commander Eduardo Stone

Starfighter and Drone Command, Mission Geologist, Head of Security

O-3 LT - Lieutenant Rogelio Williams

Sensor Operator, Mission Meteorologist, Quartermaster

O-3 LT - Lieutenant Luis Hayes

Comms Operator, Mission Technical Specialist, Senior Information Systems Techician

O-3 LT - Lieutenant David Davorian

Helmsman, Mission Astrophysicist

O-3 LT - Lieutenant Guillermo Cardinal

Weapons Chief, Mission Botanist

O-2 LTJG - Junior Lieutenant Viviana McAdams

Chief Engineer, Mission Biologist

O-2 LTJG - Junior Lieutenant Sofia Vasquez

Other Crew

O-4 LCDR - Lieutenant Commander Dr. Diego Crespin

Head of Ship's Medical Corps (Blue Deck), Mission Microbiologist and Pathologist

O-3 LT - Lieutenant Seth Ryder

CAG, Commander of the 61st Rapier Squadron

O-3 LT - Lieutenant Julio Fernandez

Executive Officer of the 61st Rapier Squadron

Enlisted

E-6 PO1 - Petty Officer First Class Pedro Suarez

E-5 PO2 - Petty Officer Second Class Carlos Ramos

Civilian

Ambassador Maximillian Carter

Mission First Contact Specialist, Mission Documentarian, Minister Plenipotentiary

Alliance Leaders

President Ryan Baker

O-11 FADM - Fleet Admiral John Wilson

O-9 VADM - Vice Admiral Gaulle

O-8 RADM - Rear Admiral Leona Flores

Confederate Leaders

Chancellor Wang Ping

Minister Wang Jun

Admiral Chiangul

Admiral Zhang

Civilian Characters on Earth

Catalina de Leon

David Porras

Dorian Porras

PART ONE: OPERATION ALICE

"Such then is the human condition, that to wish greatness for one's country is to wish harm to one's neighbors."

—Voltaire

CHAPTER 1

"Don't go, Alex."

"I don't have a choice, Caty. I go where they send me, remember? That was the deal. Move up North and pay for our upgrades with two terms of service."

"But you're almost done! Ten years was the deal. They can't ask you to serve longer than that!"

"We're at war."

"It's a cold war. No one's shooting at you up there."

"Fleet Command doesn't see the difference."

"It isn't fair." Caty wiped her eyes and shook her head. She looked away, out to Anchor Station's launch platform. Alexander followed her gaze. One of the climber cars sat waiting on the platform, big enough to be a skyscraper. Two more just like it could be seen rising one below the other on the opposite side of the elevator ribbon. The higher of the two was a mere glinting speck against the broad blue sky.

Alexander turned back to his wife. Her lower lip was trembling. As he watched, a tear ran down her cheek and landed on her lips. He leaned in and kissed it away.

"Don't cry," he whispered.

"How can you ask me not to cry? I don't even know when you're coming back—or if."

"Shhh." Alexander pressed his forehead against hers. "I will come back. Do you hear me? I promise."

"Don't make promises you can't keep, Alex."

"I don't, Caty, you know that. I promised I'd get us out of the South, and I did. Life's better now."

"No, it's not. Not if I don't have you. It wasn't supposed to be like this. You signed up for the oceanic navy, then they transferred you to space, and now they're sending you away indefinitely! They won't tell me how long you'll be gone, or where you're going… They tricked us, Alex! They're sending you because your service is almost up. They don't want to let you go."

"Caty…"

"We should have stayed in the South."

Alexander shook his head. "No. Even if I don't come back, at least I was able to save you."

"For what? So that I'll live long enough to die alone when World War III breaks out?"

"That won't happen. Neither the Alliance nor the Confederacy is that stupid. It's all just posturing." Alexander took a few steps forward and cupped Caty's beautiful face in his hands. "Listen to me. Time is nothing to us now. If anything we've got too much of it. If you can wait for me, I'll find you. The maximum period they can send me away for is another ten years. That's how long I would have been on reserve."

Caty shook her head. "I'm only twenty-nine. Ten years is a third of my life! That's not nothing."

"Maybe not yet, but it will be."

"You really think we can last that long without seeing each other? How do I know you'll wait for me?"

"I can. I will. I'll message you every day. It might take a long time for the messages to reach you, but they will. Count on it."

Caty gave him a pleading look. "What about children, Alex? We said we'd have three. A girl and two boys. We even had names picked out!"

"None of that has changed! It's just delayed, and you don't have to worry about your biological clock anymore."

"That's not the point. I don't want you to leave me a widow, Alex!"

He shook his head. "I won't." He felt a knot forming in his throat, tied so tight he could barely speak. "I love you, Caty."

Her face crumpled, and she broke down in tears. She rushed in for a hug and he held her, stroking her head, and offering more empty reassurances. Ten minutes went by like that and then came the final boarding call, booming out from the launch platform.

A pair of petty officers walked up to them, their spotless black uniforms shining indigo in the sun. One of them cleared his throat and stepped forward. He snapped to attention and saluted. "Captain de Leon! By your leave, sir… we are at T-minus thirty minutes and counting."

Alexander nodded and kissed his wife goodbye.

"Wait, I have something for you…" Caty said, reaching into her pocket.

Alexander watched as she produced a shiny golden locket on a chain and handed it to him. There was an engraving on one side that read—

"Time is an illusion."

-Albert Einstein

—and another engraving on the other side that read—

"Love is the only truth. Let mine be yours."

-Caty

Alexander's mouth curved into a sad smile, and his eyes grew warm and blurry as he turned the locket over and over in his hand.

"Aren't you going to open it?"

He looked up and nodded quickly, blinking away tears. He depressed the catch at the top of the locket and it sprang open, revealing that it was actually an old mechanical pocket watch with a real photograph—not a hologram—of him and Caty on the inside front of the case. It was all so anachronistic, a kind of physical proof for Einstein's side of the watch—*Time is an illusion.* The kiss Caty was planting on his cheek in that photograph was the proof of her side—*Love is the only truth. Let mine be yours.*

"I can't believe you did this," he said, shaking his head. More tears fell as he stared at her gift.

"It was hard to find a mechanical watch that had the date as well as the time. I thought you might like to count the days or something."

Alexander looked up, feeling suddenly miserable. "I didn't think to get you anything."

"That's okay. Maybe you'll find a souvenir to bring back for me from wherever you're going."

Alexander nodded and shut the watch. He slipped it into his pocket and leaned in for another kiss. It went on and on, but not nearly long enough.

A tap on his shoulder interrupted them. "Sir, we're out of time…"

Alexander broke away reluctantly. "Don't forget to message me," he said while their fingertips were still touching, one hand slipping away from the other.

"Don't you forget either," Caty sniffed.

Alexander shook his head and waved as he walked away, smiling reassuringly as he went. "Every day. I'll be back before you know it!" he called out.

"Don't make me wait forever!"

"I won't."

* * *

Forty minutes later, Captain Alexander de Leon sat in the front row of the climber car's viewing gallery, watching as Earth fell away below the bubble-shaped canopy. The giant equatorial anchor at the base of the elevator had been reduced to a thumb-sized speck. All around, the ocean shone a deep, stunning blue in the morning sun. Hundreds of small gray dots floated there—cargo ships and warships alike. The Alliance wasn't in a state of open war, but it would be foolhardy to leave their space elevator undefended. Far off in the hazy distance, he thought he saw the island of Curaçao, the Southern State closest to Anchor Station.

Alexander reached into his pocket and withdrew the gift Caty had given him. He read the engravings once more, opened the watch, stared at the photo of him and his wife, and remembered the past month he'd spent with her. The prospect of being apart for as much as a decade weighed heavy on his mind. Even immortals could get tired of waiting, and he and Caty had grown apart as it was. Bi-annual leave wasn't nearly enough to keep a marriage alive. Staying together had always been the plan, but his primary goal had been to save her, and he'd already done that.

Life in the Southern States was a death sentence. Alexander remembered learning about it in school. In the South people were born naturally and they died naturally. Mother nature at its best. The circle of death. They were the so-called *degenerates* or *natural-born* humans.

Up North, medical science had found ways around old age

and dying. People were genetically-engineered from birth to live forever and never to age. Geners all looked and acted just as perfect as their parents could make them, but all of that engineering came at a price, and that kind of money... you were either born with it or you weren't. Most people down South weren't, so they stayed down there and they died down there.

Alexander's family was no different. His parents struggled just to pay rent and put food on the table, let alone pay for over a hundred thousand sols of implants and genetic treatments for their son to become immortal.

Fortunately, there was another way. The war with the Confederacy meant that the Alliance needed soldiers, and the wealthy members of its population were all already immortal, so they would never willingly risk their lives in war. The poor, however, could be easily persuaded. One five-year term of service would save a life. Two terms would save two lives. Alexander had served his two already, saving both his wife and himself.

At the time, joining the navy had seemed like an easy way to get out of the South and escape the human condition. But he and Caty hadn't counted on the navy choosing him for Operation Alice.

From what he'd been allowed to know of it, Operation Alice was a mission to another planet, code-named Wonderland. Mission planners believed it could be another Earth. Alexander didn't know where it was, or how the Alliance proposed traveling there when manned missions had yet to make it beyond the solar system. Maybe the Alliance had finally developed a working FTL drive? Either way, the mission would keep him away from Earth for an indefinite period of time, so he'd been sent down to the surface to say goodbye to his loved ones.

Alexander sighed and reclined his chair. He felt restless and heart-sore, but despite the former condition, he was also intensely curious about the mission. He had a feeling he was going to lose a lot of sleep guessing about it over the next two days of travel from Anchor Station to Orbital One, the Alliance's counter-weighting space station at the top end of the elevator.

As the climber car continued racing up, Alexander came to eye level with a thin golden crust of cirrus clouds. They gleamed bright on the horizon, slowly baking to a crisp in the heat of the rising equatorial sun. Then, all of a few minutes later, Alexander was staring at a deep indigo sky with a multitude of stars pricking through.

He was leaving *terra firma* behind, and this time, he was going to be gone a lot longer than six months. Alexander blew out another sigh. He had the war to thank for that. People erroneously thought if they could just get away from Earth, then they could leave its problems behind, too. Operation Alice was just the latest initiative in a race to colonize the stars. There were already colonies on the Moon, Mars, Titan, and Europa, but that wasn't good enough. The panacea would be to find another planet like Earth, and according to the mission planners, Wonderland was it.

Alexander shook his head. It was ridiculous that space exploration and extra-terrestrial colonization had been fueled by the threat of self-extinction, but at the same time, it made a sick kind of sense. The human race had always been its own worst enemy. *Problem is you can't run from yourself.*

There came a sharp intake of air, followed by a young woman's voice: "Captain de Leon!"

Alexander saw a woman come skidding to a stop in front of him, blocking his view. She stood at attention and saluted. The single silver bar she wore marked her as a lieutenant junior grade, while the glowing white stripe below it indicated she was a member of the bridge crew of a starship.

A junior lieutenant made bridge crew? Alexander wondered, looking her up and down carefully. The woman was not ugly by any means, and not all natural-borns were, but something about the lieutenant set him off. Her eyes were a rare turquoise; her hair looked like liquid gold, not one strand out of place; her complexion was too perfect, and her bosom—Alexander stopped his analysis there.

It was rare to find a gener in the navy—or in any other branch of the service, for that matter—but not impossible; he'd met a few of them warming seats in OCS. They had their own government incentives, financial ones to match the cost of what the navy offered to natural-borns. Maybe this lieutenant had been born a gener child, but then her family had run out of money and she'd signed up to save someone else. A baby, perhaps…?

No, he decided. Northerners had implants to prevent pregnancy, and giving birth to degenerates was illegal in the Northern States. She must have had other reasons for joining the service.

"Something on your mind, Lieutenant?" Alexander asked, frowning up at her.

"Sir, Junior Lieutenant McAdams, reporting for duty, sir!"

Alexander's frown deepened. "You're assigned to the *W.A.S. Lincoln?*"

"Yes, sir!"

"I know my entire crew from White Deck to Blue, and I don't recognize you."

"I'm a recent transfer, sir. I have my orders if you'd like to see them."

"Please."

The young woman held out her arm. Her sleeve rode up, revealing her comm band. She used her other hand to activate the holo display and then navigated by touching holographic buttons and making gestures. Once she found the right document, she made a circle in the air with her finger, and the display rotated to face him. He scanned her orders. Everything checked out. McAdams was to replace Lieutenant Ramirez as the *Lincoln's* chief engineer.

Alexander's eyebrows floated up as he read that. "You're a junior lieutenant. According to fleet regulations, a ship's chief engineer must be at least a full lieutenant."

"Admiral Flores waived the requirement for me, sir."

"And what happened to Lieutenant Ramirez?"

McAdams gave him a dumb look.

"My previous chief. He was supposed to be aboard this climber. Where is he?"

"I don't know, sir."

"Never mind. I assume you've been through the training for this mission and that you've been adequately briefed?"

"Yes, sir. I was one of the reserves."

"And you've served on a Hunter-class destroyer before?"

McAdams shook her head. "Not on active duty, sir, but the reserves were all trained on one, and I've been studying the operational manuals."

Alexander grunted. "It'll have to do, I suppose. Carry on, Lieutenant. I'll see you on deck."

"Aye-aye, sir." McAdams saluted once more and went on her way.

Alexander went back to watching the view. Earth could now be seen curving away below him, the upper edge of the atmosphere glowing bright blue against the black of space. The sun peered over the horizon at him, dazzling his eyes and making him see spots when he looked away. Alexander's stomach grumbled, reminding him that he hadn't eaten breakfast yet. He unbuckled and rose stiff-legged from his chair.

It was time to get to the mess hall, and while he was at it, to check the Lincoln's roster. His crew was like family; he hoped he hadn't lost anyone else. Ramirez had left the mission without so much as a goodbye. Maybe he'd thought it would be too painful to see them off, but that still left the question of why he wasn't on the mission. Assignments weren't optional, so it had to be something serious. Alexander hoped it wasn't because Ramirez had gone AWOL, but if he had, maybe he could escape a court-martial for a while by hiding out in the South.

Suerte hermano, Alexander thought, and while he was at it—*Good luck to the rest of us, too.*

* * *

As it happened Ramirez wasn't the only one who'd left the mission. Almost a third of Alexander's crew had been detached from the *W.A.S. Lincoln* with little or no notice, and the reserves had been called up instead.

Now Alexander's heart was sore for more reasons than he could count. He didn't understand it. Why hadn't he been told? Why had no one come to say goodbye?

No sooner did Alexander arrive on Orbital One than he received orders via his comm band to report to Admiral Flores in the auxiliary briefing room on deck nine. He walked there, once again enjoying the effects of gravity.

The station's gravity was artificially generated by its rotation around the Earth and its location above GEO (Geostationary Earth Orbit), such that "down" was actually facing outer space and "up" was facing Earth.

Alexander reached the auxiliary briefing room, and a pair of petty officers guarding the entrance scanned him with wands. Neither of them moved to open the doors for him. Instead, one of them raised a hand to his ear and said, "Call Admiral Flores." The man's earpiece recognized the command, activated his communicator, and placed the call. When the call went through, the petty officer announced to the admiral that Captain de Leon was waiting outside the briefing room for her.

Moments later, the doors swished open to reveal Admiral Flores herself. Her white admiral's uniform contrasted sharply with her ebony skin. Alexander stood at attention and saluted. Flores returned the salute.

"At ease, Captain," she said, stepping aside so he could enter the room.

Once inside, the admiral shut the doors with a gesture and locked them with another. From there she turned and strode down the aisle to the speaker's podium. Alexander followed, and noted with a growing frown that they were the only ones in the room.

"I must be early," he said.

"Actually, you're late," Flores replied.

That gave him pause. "Where are the others, then?" They reached the speaker's podium, and the admiral stepped up while he sat down in the front row.

"What others?" Flores asked, turning back to face him.

"I'm not sure I understand, ma'am..." Alexander replied slowly. "How many people know about this mission?"

"Five hundred, give or take."

Alexander's eyes widened. "Then why am I the only one being briefed?"

"They already know everything they need to. They're with mission control on Lewis Station."

"Lewis Station? I've never heard of it."

Admiral Flores' cheeks dimpled with rare amusement. "Nor should you have. Operation Alice is highly classified. If you were to breach operational security, even accidentally, you would be looking at a dishonorable discharge and a firing squad. In order to spare everyone that unpleasantness, we've told you as little as possible up till now."

Alexander's pulse began jumping in his temples. "I see."

"No, you don't, but you will."

Flores walked up to the far wall and began making gestures. A series of holo displays glowed to life, showing star maps and flight plans.

Flores pointed to the first hologram, a flight plan, and began to explain: the *Lincoln* was to detach from Orbital One and fly straight to Venus, where it would get a gravity assist and fly on toward the Alliance colony on Titan.

But Titan wasn't their real destination. The *Lincoln* was to fly to a set range of a hundred million klicks from Venus, where no Confederate eyes were likely to be watching, and then they would deviate from their course and head for coordinates another fifty-seven million klicks away from Earth.

Flores gestured to another hologram. This one showed deep space, and it was marked with two icons. One of them was labeled *Lewis Station,* and the other was labeled the *Looking Glass.* That rang a bell. Alexander was beginning to recognize the nomenclature.

Flores appeared to notice his distraction. "Something on your mind, Captain?"

"The *Looking Glass*—what is that?" The icon on the map looked like a perfectly clear marble floating in space, distorting the star field behind its spherical shape. He couldn't even guess at what it might represent. "The names are all vaguely familiar—Alice, Wonderland, The Looking Glass."

"Operation Alice was named after a pair of books by Lewis Caroll, hence *Lewis Station.* The names are all metaphors for what Operation Alice is about. For example, in one of the books a girl named Alice travels through a mirror or *Looking Glass* to another world."

"So the Looking Glass is..." Alexander felt his heart begin to pound as wild ideas flew through his head. "Some kind of gateway?"

Admiral Flores pointed to the map, and the hologram zoomed in.

"The Looking Glass is a Lorentzian wormhole, otherwise known as a *Schwarzschild wormhole* or an *Einstein–Rosen bridge,*" she said, pointing to it on the map. "In layman's terms, it's a traversable tunnel from one point in spacetime to another."

Alexander grinned wildly and leaned suddenly forward in his chair. "We managed to create one? Where does it go?"

"We're not entirely sure where it goes. We keep losing contact with our probes soon after they arrive in the Wonderland System. From what little data we've managed to receive, our best guess is that the wormhole leads to another galaxy entirely. And as for how it got there... We didn't create it. We found it."

"You mean the wormhole is naturally occurring?"

"We don't know if it is or isn't naturally occurring. What we do know is that it's occupying a stable orbit around our sun, at a mean distance of two hundred eighty-nine million klicks. That puts it relatively close to Earth, depending on what time of year you choose to travel. Right now it's actually at its most proximal point, at just over a hundred million klicks away, but we're taking a circuitous route via Venus so that we don't attract any unwanted Confederate attention."

Alexander frowned. "If the wormhole is just a hundred million klicks from Earth, surely the Confederates have already spotted it."

Flores shrugged. "Wormholes are surprisingly hard to detect. They'd have to know exactly where to look. Let's hope they don't, but if they have spotted something, it's squarely in our territory, and we have Lewis Station to prove it. We can even claim that we built the wormhole. That might just scare the socialism out of them and put an end to this stupid war once and for all."

"Or scare them enough to attack us before we develop any more of a technological edge."

"Let's hope not. Meanwhile..." Flores turned back to her holo displays and gestured for a new screen to appear. It was a map of a solar system. "This is the Wonderland System. It has a G-type star, or yellow dwarf, the same as us. There are ten planets in all." Flores pointed to one in particular and zoomed in on it. "The third one from the sun appears to have all the same characteristics as Earth. That's Wonderland herself. From our current data we suspect the planet has a lot more surface water than ours, but otherwise it could be a perfect sister planet for Earth, right down to its mass, which will produce a tolerable one point one times Earth's gravity."

Alexander was shocked. After a long, silent moment, he said, "People have been dreaming about this for centuries, ever since we put the first man in space. What's the catch?"

"There's more than one, actually," the admiral replied. "The overriding concern—which has been repeatedly put forward by Dr. Thales, the head of our astrophysics department on Lewis Station—is that there's no way this wormhole could be a natural phenomenon. If he's right, then we might be looking at a first contact situation on the other end. But we have to ask ourselves: if the wormhole was created, then the race that created it must have intended to use it to get to our solar system. So where are they, and why haven't we met them yet? It would appear that they built the gateway just for us, which doesn't seem likely. To be safe, we are sending an Alliance diplomat aboard the *Lincoln* as the president's official representative should you meet intelligent alien life."

Alexander nodded. He couldn't help but agree: first contact was unlikely. That so-called first contact specialist was going to be a lot of dead weight.

"So what's the other catch?" he asked.

"The probes. None of them ever made it back. The popular theory is that the wormhole is only open on our side. By traveling through it we force it open in Wonderland for a few minutes, and then the Wonderland side collapses to an infinitesimal width, making a return trip and ongoing transmissions impossible."

Alexander paled and he gaped at the admiral. "That's the popular theory? Then why are we sending a manned mission?"

"The probe data is inconclusive, and even though the Collapsing Gateway Theory is the most popular one, the other theories are still valid—space time distortion, equipment failure, radiation damage, alien interference, etc. A Hunter-class destroyer is much larger than any probe, so it is infinitely better equipped to run the necessary scans of the area and help us narrow down the list of possibilities.

"In case you're wondering, we have sent probes with live animal subjects and confirmed that they made it to the Wonderland System alive and well."

Alexander blew out a breath. "But they still didn't make it back. You're basically telling me that this is a one-way trip."

"Not at all, Captain. We should be able to force the wormhole open for you by sending another probe. You'll have some time to investigate Wonderland before then, but that is one of your mission objectives, regardless. Rest assured, we aren't planning to abandon the *Lincoln,* Captain."

"You said the wormhole stays open for just a few minutes. That's an incredibly tight window. Even if you can force it open for us, that doesn't explain why you didn't try this method to rescue one of the probes."

"As I said, a ship like the *Lincoln* is better equipped. The same goes for her crew versus the limited intelligence of a probe. We've set your clocks to coincide with pre-planned launch times for future missions. As soon as you arrive in Wonderland, the *Lincoln* will send us her nav and sensor data from the trip, and we'll use that to make adjustments on our end.

"We've factored in time dilation and checked the math a thousand times. It *is* a tight window, but you'll have a chance, Captain, and if you don't make it the first time, we'll keep sending probes until you do. The nav data from each failed attempt will be used to make adjustments on both our ends. Through an iterative process of trial and error, we *will* get you home. You have my word on that."

"How long will it take us to get to Wonderland?" Alexander asked.

"Around seventy days."

"So ten weeks. That's twenty weeks there and back. Plus the time spent waiting for a rescue..."

The admiral nodded. "Correct, although, you won't notice the time passing until you arrive. Traversing the wormhole calls for you and your crew to spend the entire trip in a medically-induced coma."

Alexander blinked. "What? Why?"

"The wormhole is roughly 0.07 light years from end to end. You'll spend the first eighteen days accelerating at a constant ten Gs until you've reached half the speed of light. After cruising for just over a month you'll spend the same amount of time decelerating."

"Ten *G*s for eighteen days? We'll be dead long before we get up to speed, Admiral."

She just smiled and shook her head. "You'll be spending the duration of the trip in *G*-tanks, and to answer your first question, putting you in a coma isn't strictly necessary, but mission planners decided that it would be better for your mental health. Ten weeks is a long time to spend floating in a fish bowl with nothing to do but sleep and listen to your heart beating."

Alexander's brow furrowed. "So why not wake us and bring us out of the tanks once we've reached cruising speed? We could spend that month preparing for our mission in Wonderland, and stretch our legs while we're at it."

"The 10 *G*s generated by the *Lincoln's* engines while accelerating and decelerating is actually a fraction of what the wormhole itself will subject you to. Anyone who spends the trip outside of a *G*-tank would be turned to jelly."

"Point taken. I'm assuming any rescue missions you send will take just as long to reach us as we spent getting there."

Admiral Flores looked sheepish. She tried to say something, but stopped herself.

"What aren't you telling me?"

"Time dilation."

"Yeah, at half the speed of light we'll be running a few days faster than Earth time—what's the problem?"

"Time dilation isn't just affected by speed, Captain. It's also affected by the geometry of space-time which is anything but flat inside a wormhole."

Alexander was beginning to feel nervous. "So... what are we talking about here? A month?"

"Almost fourteen months."

Alexander blinked. "So seventy days becomes... over four hundred?"

The admiral nodded.

Alexander went on, thinking out loud, "Two times that is two years and four months. That's how long it'll take for us to get home, even if we turn around as soon as we get there. Except that we won't be able to do that. We'll be trapped until a rescue mission can come for us, and if you have to wait to receive our signal before you even send that rescue mission..." Alexander shook his head. "Please tell me the signal doesn't experience the same time dilation that we do."

"It does, but the time it will take for a comm signal to travel the point oh seven light years inside the wormhole is a little under five months from Earth's perspective."

Alexander felt a headache encroaching as he tried to add up all the various time frames. He unconsciously squeezed the bridge of his nose between forefinger and thumb. "Five months to receive our signal plus fourteen more to get to us... that's almost two years spent waiting in Wonderland for a rescue."

"Yes."

"And you don't even know how many rescue missions you'll need to send before one of them succeeds. With two year turnaround times between missions..."

"You might not need rescuing, Captain. Once you've analyzed all the data for yourselves, you'll know why we've been losing contact with our probes, and maybe you'll be able to solve the problem from that end."

Alexander stroked his chin—smooth as a baby's bottom thanks to the depilatory treatments he'd received in preparation for the mission back on Earth. He didn't like the qualifying language the admiral was using—*might, maybe...* "All right, but if not, we could be away for a very long time."

"That is a possibility, but we've packed you with enough supplies to account for an extended stay on Wonderland, and we'll be sending additional supplies aboard each probe, just in case."

Alexander shook his head and gave the admiral a narrow-eyed look. "Maybe after the first decade or two we'll just settle down in Wonderland and forget all about being rescued."

"You'd be abandoning the mission and going AWOL—not that I expect we would be able to conduct a court-martial—but you'll have to think about your families back on Earth. Settling on Wonderland, if that is in fact possible, will mean never seeing any of your loved ones again."

That was when it hit him. Alexander bounced to his feet, his eyes wide, his pulse pounding, blood roaring in his ears. "That's why you picked me, isn't it?"

"Settle down, Captain."

"That's also why you made all of those last-minute changes to my crew."

Admiral Flores remained silent.

"You cherry-picked us to make sure we all had strong emotional ties to Earth! My engineer, Ramirez—he was the only one with no family back on Earth. And me—how many other captains could you have sent? Divorced ones, single ones, unhappily married ones? Any one of them would have made a better choice, but no, you wanted people with a reason to come home. You took what I'd shared in confidence with you about my personal life, and used it against me!"

"Don't take this personally, Captain."

"How else should I take it?"

Suddenly the station's emergency klaxons started screaming. The lights dimmed to a bloody red, a siren sounded, and the PA system boomed, "This is not a drill! This is not a drill! General quarters, general quarters! All hands to battle stations!"

Admiral Flores' eyes flew wide. "Go!" she said.

CHAPTER 2

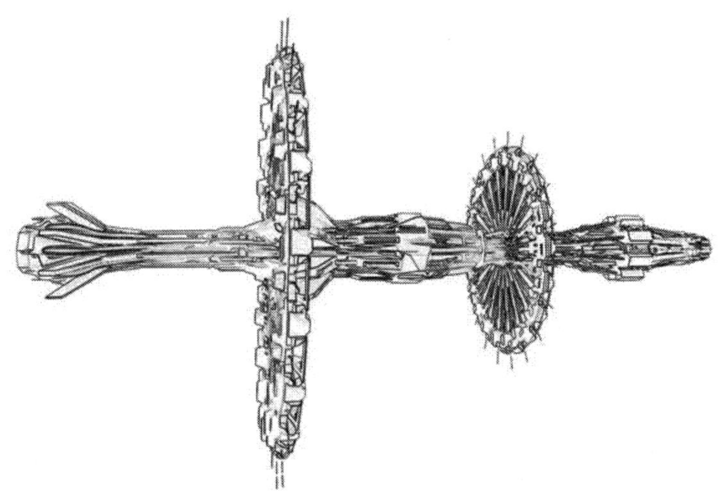

Alexander rode the elevator down through Orbital One to the station's space-facing docking arm. As the elevator raced down, he hurried to put on one of the emergency combat suits stored inside the elevator. He skipped the helmet, since a more sophisticated version would be waiting for him on the bridge of the *Lincoln*. When the elevator stopped, the floor opened up, revealing a ladder leading down into his ship's airlock. Inside that airlock was another elevator that ran all the way down the central shaft of the *W.A.S. Lincoln*.

Alexander climbed down the ladder into the *Lincoln's* elevator and selected the glowing white button labeled *Bridge (10)* from the color-coded control panel. The airlock cycled shut overhead, and the elevator raced down. When it opened again, he walked out onto the bridge just as normally as if the *Lincoln* were sitting on Earth with her engines on the ground and her bow facing the sky. The reverse was actually true.

Despite the artificial gravity, Alexander's perspective

changed as soon as he walked onto the bridge. Dead ahead, the bridge control stations were mounted at varying heights along the far wall, all of them facing the ceiling. Ladders crawled up the wall, allowing the crew to access their control stations while the ship was simulating normal gravity.

The ship's acceleration couches all faced the bow, so that any excess *G*-forces generated by active thrust would pin the crew against their seats.

"Sensors, report!" Alexander called out as he stopped in front of the captain's and executive officer's couches. He took a moment to still his racing heart, leaning on his couch as he did so. His station was located in the rearmost position, so there was no need for him to climb up a ladder to get there. *The perks of being the Captain.*

"Sensors show forty-seven Confederate warships leaving orbit, sir!" Lieutenant Williams reported from the sensors station. "Their trajectory lines up with our own mission destination."

Alexander grabbed the rails along the front of his couch to lower himself into his seat. He let go of the rails and dropped the last few centimeters into his chair, provoking a *whuff* of air escaping from the cushion. His XO, Commander Korbin, was already seated beside him. He nodded to her and she flashed a tight-lipped smile that never reached her warm, watery brown eyes. Between those eyes and her motherly features, she was a natural fit for her secondary role as the ship's counselor.

Alexander turned back to the fore. Now he felt like he was lying on the deck, gazing up at the ceiling, but the bridge's layout managed to convince him that he was actually sitting on the deck at zero-*G* inside a ship that was being accelerated at just over one *G* through space. He shook his head to clear away his growing disorientation and fumbled with the buckles of his safety harness. Relief tubes snaked out from his couch and attached themselves to the front and back of his suit. Both tubes would transmit waste away from his body as needed without him ever having to get up. Food and hydration were handled by a nutrient line, which he manually attached to the catheter implanted in his left wrist. Combat could last a long time in space, and the need to maneuver was unpredictable, so crew had to be able to remain seated and strapped in for extended periods of time.

Reaching up, Alexander found the helmet clipped to his headrest. He pulled it down and slipped it over his head. Air *hissed* out around his neck as the helmet formed an airtight seal with the collar of his combat suit. Alexander heard his breathing reverberate inside the helmet. The pace was too fast.

I'm anxious, he thought, trying to control his breathing. Slow, deep breaths. Being a soldier was one thing. Going to war was another.

A heads-up display flickered to life, projected on the inside of his visor in bright blues and greens. Alexander began making mental selections from the HUD in order to check the *Lincoln's* readiness. Mental interaction with the HUD was the ship's primary control interface, but there were also secondary, hands-on controls located in the armrests of each crewman's couch.

Commander Korbin quieted the ship's general quarters siren and killed the flashing red lights, bringing everything back to a calm, crisp whiteness. That bit of normalcy was deceptive, but necessary to keep the crew's frayed nerves in check.

Dead ahead, the ship's three main forward viewports glowed to life, relaying the view from the *Lincoln's* bow cameras. Right now all they could see was a close-up of the dark, solar-energy-collecting underside of Orbital One.

"Captain! Admiral Flores is requesting to speak with you!" Lieutenant Hayes reported from the comms station.

"Put her through. Full screen."

All three of the ship's main holo displays faded from a black canvas of stars to a larger-than-life visual of the admiral herself. She appeared dead center of the main holo display, taking up almost the entire thing while the mad bustle of activity going on around her inside the command center of Orbital One appeared on the left and right holo displays.

"Your orders have changed, Captain." The fire glinting in the admiral's green eyes and the tightness of her cheeks spoke volumes. *This could be it,* he thought, *the thawing out of a century-long cold war.* "You are to act as a comm relay to help us communicate with the Confederate Fleet while we try to dissuade them from their current flight path. Meanwhile, you will fly with all possible speed direct to Lewis Station and prepare to hold off Confederate forces if it comes to that. The Third Fleet will meet you there as soon as they can."

"Yes, ma'am."

"Updated nav data is being downloaded to the *Lincoln* now. Please confirm."

"Confirmed, Captain!" Lieutenant Davorian replied from the helm at the foremost/uppermost control station.

Alexander nodded. "We're ready to go, Admiral."

"Good luck, Captain. You are at T-minus ten minutes to launch. Flores out."

The admiral's face disappeared, and back was the underside of Orbital One. "Helm! Set the clock and alert the crew! T-minus ten."

"Aye-aye, Captain!" Davorian replied.

A green launch timer appeared at the top of the ship's main holo display, counting down from ten minutes.

Alexander's gaze slid away to regard his XO. "Commander Korbin—" She turned to him, her pale blue eyes wide and unfocused. He frowned and snapped his fingers. "Wake up, Commander!"

Korbin shook herself, as if waking from a dream—*More like a nightmare,* he thought—and then she said, "Yes, sir!"

"Double-check everyone's launch checklists. We can't afford to have any mistakes."

"Aye, sir," Korbin said, already consulting her holo displays.

"Lieutenant Stone!" Alexander called out, keeping half an eye on the launch timer as he directed his attention to the *Lincoln's* starfighter and drone command station. "What's the status of 61st Squadron?"

"They're getting suited up, sir."

"Tell them to pick up the pace! I don't want anyone plastered to the bulkheads when we fire up the mains."

"Yes, sir. They've drilled for this. Five minutes to suit, four more to hit their cockpits and strap in. That leaves one for margin of error."

"I'm going to trust you on that, Stone."

Due to comm latency (speed-of-light restricted), manned fighters still had their place. At a distance of just three hundred thousand klicks, a remote pilot would be reacting a full two seconds after everything had already happened. To get around that, manned fighters followed drones into combat and commanded them from behind.

"Gunnery! Engineering! What's our status?"

"All gunners standing by, weapons hot," Lieutenant Cardinal replied from the gunnery station.

"Good. Engineering?"

"All systems green, sir," Junior Lieutenant McAdams replied.

"T-minus five!" Lieutenant Hayes called out from the comms.

Alexander nodded. "Safety harness check!"

Everyone tugged on their buckles and tightened their belts. Alexander pulled his own straps taut. He looked up at the main holo display, his eyes idly tracing constellations while he waited for the launch timer to run down. As the minutes slipped by, his thoughts turned to his wife. He hoped things would calm down and that she wouldn't be affected by this latest power struggle. If open war broke out and something happened to her…

"61st Squadron is strapped in and waiting, Captain!" Stone reported from starfighter command.

Alexander noted the launch timer was down to fifteen seconds. That was close. "Good. Let's hope they were the last ones. Commander Korbin, crew safety check!"

"All hands securely strapped in and waiting for launch."

"T-minus ten seconds!" Davorian said from the helm. "Nine, eight… three, two, one, zero! Docking clamps detached!"

Suddenly Alexander was weightless and watching Orbital One drift away. It was an opaque black disc with weapon emplacements sprouting like barnacles from its outer hull. Seconds later, Earth appeared behind the station, silhouetting it with a dazzling white and blue halo.

The rest of the Alliance armada was nowhere to be seen, but Alexander knew they would still be at GEO, and much too far away to see without magnification.

"Brace for maneuvering thrust," Davorian reported from the helm.

Alexander felt the ship turn. His view panned away from Orbital One and Earth to face the vast starry darkness of outer space.

"Helm, what's our ETA to reach Lewis Station?"

"Just under a week, Captain," Davorian replied.

"And the Confederates?"

"They'll be about six hours behind us, assuming regulation rates of acceleration and deceleration."

"We may have to push past regulation limits on this one."

"Yes, sir… I don't have Lewis Station marked on my star maps," Davorian said.

"It's at our final mission waypoint, and you can't see it because the very existence of that station is classified. Head for the waypoint. You'll find Lewis Station when we get close enough."

"Yes, sir… thrusters going hot in five, four, three, two, one!"

Alexander braced himself. Then came a deafening roar, and the *Lincoln* shuddered all around them. A gut-wrenching boost shoved them against their couches, and the *Lincoln* shot away from Orbital One. Acceleration rose swiftly, pressing Alexander against the back of his couch with terrifying force. His cheeks threatened to peel back from his face, and he had to force himself to breathe. The combat suit helped to keep him breathing and to make sure blood didn't pool where it shouldn't, but it wasn't nearly enough. Alexander felt like he weighed a thousand pounds. He clutched the armrests of his couch, knuckles turning white, elbows pinned to the padded backing. His heart labored in his chest. His vision dimmed and narrowed.

A blackout was coming.

Then, suddenly, the acceleration eased, and he gasped collectively with the crew. "Davorian! What the hell was that?" Alexander demanded, his voice hoarse from the strain of so many Gs. "That couldn't have been regulation thrust."

"Sorry, sir… That was 20 Gs. I don't know what happened. We had a malfunction with the thruster controls, but I'm using the computer to compensate. Acceleration is set to a steady three point five Gs now, but we'll be backing off to two in a moment."

"McAdams, what caused that malfunction, and why didn't you see it? Another few Gs and we'd all be unconscious right now."

"I don't know, sir..." McAdams replied. "I'm looking into it."

Alexander grunted. *Rookie.*

"Time to reach cruising speed?"

"One hour fifty eight minutes," Davorian replied. "Speed set to one hundred and sixty klicks per second."

Alexander tried to nod, but he found his head was still pinned to his headrest. Likewise, his chest still felt heavy and his heartbeat was irregular. He struggled to imagine spending the next two hours like that. His stomach rolled just thinking about it.

"Acceleration dropping to two *G*s," Davorian reported.

Alexander felt the weight on his chest ease, and he took a deep breath. Now he weighed about 300 pounds.

"Sir!" Hayes called out from the comms station. "Admiral Flores is ordering us to relay her transmission to the Confederates."

"Are we cleared to watch?"

"Yes, sir."

"Put them on the secondary holo displays then, Hayes."

The ship's right and left holo displays faded from space to their respective video transmissions. Admiral Flores appeared on the right, and on the left, an unfamiliar man appeared. He was strapped into an acceleration couch. Above the holo display a bar of text identified him as Admiral Chiangul. He looked to be of Chinese descent, but there was no way of knowing with Confederates, who were all geners from birth. Chiangul's tangerine eyes were a dead giveaway that he was not natural-born.

The wonders of socialism, Alexander thought—*everyone gets to live forever and pick exotic eye colors for their children. Perfect equality.* It was a tried-and-failed system made to work by tampering with human nature itself.

"Admiral Flores," Chiangul said. "The Confederacy is not on speaking terms with the Alliance, so I trust that you will make this brief." The Confederate Admiral spoke to them in English rather than Chinese—a not-so-subtle way of proving his superiority. He'd learned his enemy's tongue, but the same could not be said for the majority of Alliance officers.

Admiral Flores smiled and inclined her head to him. "Nín hǎo, Admiral," she replied. "I'll keep it very brief, don't worry. We couldn't help but notice that your fleet's current heading will ultimately bring it into restricted Alliance space."

Chiangul's tangerine eyes narrowed to paper-thin slits. "We are investigating a spacial anomaly. There are no known Alliance stations along our flight path—unless you're trying to tell me that you have an unregistered territorial claim somewhere in deep space?"

"That is exactly what I am saying, Mr. Chiangul. In about one hundred million kilometers you will stumble straight into Lewis Station. It's a deep-space research post."

"Ah, research. That is interesting. Then you must be studying the wormhole phenomenon?"

Alexander heard a few of his crew gasp, and he noticed Commander Korbin glance his way. *A wormhole?* she mouthed to him.

He gave no reply. She wasn't authorized to know about the Looking Glass yet, although something told him operational security was about to be blown wide open.

There was a distinct several-second pause on Admiral Flores' end of the comm. It looked as though her transmission had frozen, but Alexander suspected the delay was deliberate. Flores had to be conferring with someone, and she didn't want the Confederates to see or overhear.

"Admiral Flores?" Chiangul asked, looking impatient. "If you are having technical difficulties, please do not waste our time."

The video transmission unfroze a moment later, with Flores standing a few inches to the left of where she had been before. She shook her head. "My apologies, Mr. Chiangul, we were indeed having technical difficulties. As for the wormhole phenomenon you mentioned, we created it, and that is in fact the nature of our research at Lewis Station."

More gasps rose from the *Lincoln's* crew. This was all highly classified information, but the part about creating the wormhole was a lie.

"You have created a stable wormhole?"

"Yes, though it is not yet traversable."

"I do not believe you," Chiangul replied. "Your technology is not sufficiently advanced to create such a thing. We know what the Alliance can and cannot do. This is one of the cannots."

"I'm sorry to disappoint you, but you have been misled. Regardless, the Alliance is filing a retroactive territorial claim as we speak. That claim will be effective long before you arrive, and as per the terms of the Space and Extra-Terrestrial Colonies Treaty, section four, sub-section D, the Alliance is formally requesting that you turn your fleet around, or at least alter its trajectory to avoid passing through registered Alliance space. We will happily send you the coordinates of our claim prior to its official registry in order to facilitate your course corrections."

It was Admiral Chiangul's turn for technical difficulties, and fully thirty seconds passed before his image unfroze. When it did, he was gone. The man who took his place was none other than the Confederacy's head of state, Chancellor Wang Ping himself. Alexander recognized the control room where the Chancellor was standing as being aboard Tianlong (Heavenly

Dragon) Station, which was the Confederate equivalent of Orbital One.

"Admiral Flores," Wang Ping began.

"Your Excellency," she replied.

"If your government has access to a wormhole, then we regret to inform you that the Space and Extra-Terrestrial Colonies Treaty, which you cited for the Alliance's territorial claim, will need to be renegotiated. The Confederacy sees wormhole technology as a threat to our sovereignty, and if your government has developed such technology, then they would do well to resolve this threat by sharing their discoveries with us."

"In exchange for what, Your Excellency?" Admiral Flores looked furious, but Alexander could see she was trying hard to keep a lid on it.

Wang ping offered a smug smile. "We would be more than happy to share our advances in anti-gravity in exchange for your understanding of wormhole technology."

Alexander smirked. *One fictitious technology for another.*

"One moment please, Chancellor. It would be better if you were to discuss this directly with my government."

"I think so too, yes."

Flores' transmission froze once more, but this time it was replaced by a waiting screen with the Alliance flag. Soon after that, the Confederate transmission also went to a waiting screen with their flag. Minutes passed. Alexander distracted himself by studying the two flags—the Alliance's was essentially a map of their half of the Earth, with their member states shown in white on a dark blue backdrop. The Americas and Europe were marked, along with a few dozen islands at larger-than-life scale. Each member state had a gold star in its center, for a total of sixty-seven stars.

The Confederate flag, on the other hand, was solid red with

a yellow dragon in the top-left corner, which signified Tianlong Station and the Confederacy's claim to having built the world's first space elevator. The rest of the flag was made up of yellow stars. Just like the Alliance flag, there was one for each member state, but their stars were laid out in a hammer-and-sickle pattern.

The waiting screens remained in place. How long had it been? Five minutes? Ten? Maybe they weren't allowed to see the negotiations going forward.

But then, to his surprise, the waiting screens disappeared, and rather than Admiral Flores on the right, this time they saw President Ryan Baker of the Alliance.

"Chancellor Wang Ping," Baker said, nodding. The chancellor's transmission returned a few seconds later, and President Baker smiled. "It's a pleasure to speak with you again, Your Excellency."

"Yes," Wang Ping agreed after a slight transmission delay.

President Baker went on, "Our intelligence suggests that your government has not achieved any more understanding of the technology you are offering us than what we have of the same. Therefore, you have nothing to trade us for our wormhole technology."

"Ah, yes, just as our intelligence suggests that the Alliance does not have the technology to create stable wormholes."

"And we haven't. Not a traversable one, anyway."

"Do not lie to me, Baker. We have watched you send your probes."

If he was surprised the Confederates knew about that, to his credit, President Baker didn't show it. "None of those probes returned," he explained.

"Yet they transmitted data from the other side," Wang Ping replied.

Alexander frowned. He was about to order his comms officer to cut off the transmission. There was no way they had the clearance to watch this. There had to be some mistake. Then again—Flores had given them permission.

Baker appeared to confer with someone off-screen. They didn't hear the conversation, but a moment later he turned back to face the camera. He looked apologetic. "I'm sorry, Chancellor. I've just confirmed that we received no such data. I'm not sure what you are talking about."

Wang Ping's unsmiling face disappeared, and a few seconds later a slow parade of star maps, sensor scans, and other data replaced his hologram. Alexander recognized fully half of those images from his briefing with Admiral Flores. The jig was up. Operation Alice had been blown wide open.

The Chancellor's face reappeared, and this time he was smiling. "Did you recognize any of that, President Baker?"

"Where did you get those images?"

"Do you think we are blind?"

The president's lips formed a grim line. "If you want to begin a peaceful exchange of information, then you need to start by telling us how you have access to our classified documents."

"We are enemies, President Baker, and enemies do not disclose their secrets lightly."

"Then you will understand when I say we cannot share our knowledge of wormholes with you."

Wang Ping shrugged. "You do not have such knowledge, so it does not matter."

"We do have it," the president insisted, "and that wormhole is Alliance property, in Alliance space. If you continue on your present course, you will be in direct violation of our sovereignty, and that will be a declaration of war. Is that what you are threatening, Ping?"

"We leave that up to you, Baker. Our fleet merely goes to emphasize our equal rights to a unique and naturally occurring part of the cosmos. What you do about that is for you to decide."

"At the risk of repeating myself, that wormhole is not a naturally occurring—"

"Save your lies for someone who believes them, Baker. We are no fools."

President Baker looked ready to say something else, but he stopped himself. "Then you will not recall your fleet?"

"That is correct."

"Earth won't survive this war," the president warned.

"War requires violence. We will not fire the first shot. If you are wise, then neither will you. Good day, Mr. Baker."

With that, the transmission ended on the Confederacy's end. President Baker scowled, and his face disappeared a split second later. Silence fell on the bridge. The implications of what they'd witnessed were staggering.

"Admiral Flores is on the comm, Captain!"

Alexander blinked. "Put her through."

The admiral appeared back on screen looking even more furious than before. "Damn those red ants!" she spat. "Operation Alice is compromised."

Alexander nodded. "It would seem so, ma'am," he croaked, his tongue rasping like sandpaper against the roof of his mouth.

"Look alive, Captain! We are at DEFCON One, and I need all my captains in this with their eyes wide open! The Confederacy is threatening to take control of the Looking Glass. We can't allow that to happen. The President sent you the recording of his negotiations with the Confederate Chancellor because you and your crew are the only ones who can beat them to Lewis Station, and you need to know the score."

Alexander blinked. So it hadn't been a mistake. That also explained the long delay with the Alliance and Confederate waiting screens. The transmissions had been sent to them after the fact, not during.

Admiral Flores went on. "Captain, you are to get to Lewis Station with all possible speed and join their defensive screen. The Reds planned their launch at just the right moment. Our fleet is still half an orbit away, and it's going to take a while before we can catch up."

"I understand. We'll be ready, ma'am."

"I doubt that, Captain. Odds are forty-seven to one against you being ready."

Alexander set his jaw. "Then we'll slow them down."

"Fleet Command thinks you can do better than that. We're going to fire a warning shot across their bows. You are to fly ahead of the Confederates along their trajectory and dead drop as much ordnance as you can in their way."

Alexander's eyes widened. Dead-dropping meant firing missiles with zero thrust from rail launchers to avoid enemy detection. They wouldn't see the missiles coming until it was too late.

"If all goes according to plan, we'll take out half a dozen Confederate ships before they even know what hit them."

Such an attack was sure to provoke World War III. It was really happening. Alexander couldn't believe it.

Caty...

"Captain, did you hear me?"

"Yes, ma'am," he managed.

"I'll be in touch. Good luck. Flores out."

Alexander nodded stiffly, and the holo display faded back to the black of space.

World War III was about to start. He watched the stars twinkle, like so many eyes watching him—judging him. His mouth was bone dry. Between the Alliance and the Confederacy, there were millions of megatons in orbit, not to mention what they had on the ground. Admiral Flores was asking him to start a war that could kill billions of people—including his wife.

"Captain…? Captain!"

Alexander turned to see his XO staring at him. He had a vague feeling that she'd been talking to him for a while. "I'm sorry, Commander, what was that?"

"I said if someone doesn't do something about this fast, then we're all going to hell in a hurry."

Alexander's lips twitched into a grim smile. "It's too late for that, Commander. The Second Cold War is over, and this next war is going to get hot enough to make hell look balmy."

CHAPTER 3

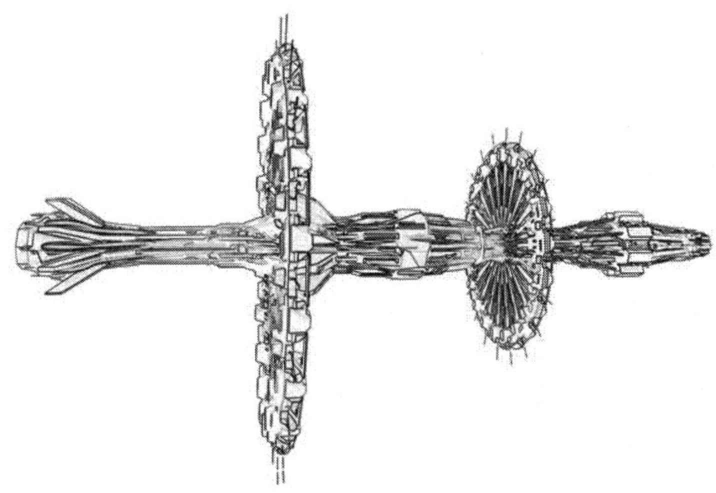

"**O**rdnance is ready, Captain. Standing by," Commander Korbin said.

Alexander hesitated. Six days had passed since they'd received their orders to start World War III. During that time President Baker had done his best to negotiate a peaceful resolution to the conflict, but the Confederates insisted that they had a right to have access to the wormhole, and the Alliance insisted that they didn't. Negotiations were at an impasse, and Alexander had just received clearance from Orbital One to open fire. In this case, that meant dead-dropping every nuke they had and letting the Confederates barrel straight into them.

It wasn't his place to question orders, but he couldn't help it. The fate of humanity hung in the balance, and there would be no going back from this. Alexander's thoughts went to his wife, Caty, back on Earth, and he grimaced.

This was it.

"Sir?"

Alexander took a deep breath and let it out again. "Gunnery—" he said.

"Yes, sir?" Lieutenant Cardinal replied.

"Commence dead-dropping."

"Aye-aye... The first dozen are away."

"Williams, what's the Confederate reaction?"

"Nothing so far," Lieutenant Williams reported from the sensor station.

"Good. Let's hope they don't see it coming. Gunnery, please proceed."

"Yes, sir."

They dropped another nine waves of warheads, staggered enough to prevent simultaneous detonations.

Once all one hundred and twenty nukes were drifting away behind them, and the *Lincoln's* rail-launchers were empty, Alexander felt a shortness of breath that had nothing to do with the ship's current rate of deceleration. Under the guise of slowing down to join Lewis Station's orbit around the sun, they had bled off more momentum than they needed to in order to allow the drifting warheads to reach their targets before the Confederates could reach Lewis Station.

That left the Confederates much closer now than they should have been, putting the *Lincoln* in danger of a retaliatory barrage.

"Davorian, decrease deceleration to point five *G*s. Let's try not to have the Confederates breathing down our necks by the time those nukes hit."

"Yes, sir."

Silence fell on the bridge. Beside him, Commander Korbin shook her head. "How long do we have?"

Alexander mentally summoned a tactical map from the holo projector between him and his XO. The *Lincoln* and her trajectory appeared on the map as a green icon with a line and an arrow pointing toward Lewis Station. Then came one hundred and twenty green dots with hair-thin vectors pointing in the opposite direction, each dot and vector corresponding to one of the nukes they'd dead-dropped. Finally, behind all of that, were the red icons of the Confederate fleet and the arrows of their trajectories.

Alexander drew a circle around the first wave of nukes, then he selected the leading Confederate warship. Giving a verbal command this time, he said, "Calculate time to nearest intersect."

A new vector line appeared, connecting the wave of nukes to the Confederate warship. The difference in velocities was ten point six klicks per second in favor of the Confederate ship. Range between the targets was 697,562 klicks. Time to intersect—eighteen hours, sixteen minutes, and forty-seven seconds.

Forty-six seconds. Forty-five...

"So we have eighteen hours before World War III begins," Korbin said.

Alexander grimaced. He had to try really hard not to see his guilt in the matter. He had given the order to drop the nukes, even if that order had ultimately come from someone else.

The minutes ticked away with agonizing slowness. Apart from the sound of life support cycling the *Lincoln's* air, the steady drone of her thrusters, and the hushed verbal commands of her crew, Alexander could hear nothing but the sound of his own heart thudding relentlessly in his chest.

"Captain!"

Thud!

Alexander recognized Williams' voice a second before he saw the man sit suddenly bolt upright at his station.

"What is it, Williams?"

"We're detecting the Confederate Fleet slowing down."

Alexander felt ice creeping through his veins. They couldn't have spotted the nukes at this range. "How fast?"

"Three *G*s deceleration, sir. They're slamming on the brakes."

"They must have caught on to our strategy. Do we still have remote access to those warheads?"

"Yes, sir."

"We may have to bring them online."

"If we do that, they'll be detected immediately, and the enemy's point defenses will have plenty of time to shoot them down," Lieutenant Cardinal said from gunnery.

"One or two might still get through. That's still enough for the purposes of a warning shot. Comms! Get me Lewis Station on the line."

"Yes, sir."

A moment later, a man with a shiny scalp and a nest of wrinkles around his eyes appeared on the right-hand holo display. Text above his transmission read *Admiral Gaulle*. Going by the admiral's appearance, he'd clearly waited too long to begin his gener treatments. Either that or he'd opted to take the incentives as a credit to his savings account instead.

"Admiral, the enemy is decelerating. It would appear they're on to us. Please advise."

"We see it, Captain, but it's unlikely they've detected your warheads."

"Then they suspected that we might try something like this and they're taking measures to evade."

"Even so..." The admiral shook his head. "In half an hour I want you to alter your trajectory. Make it look like you're heading straight for the Looking Glass."

Alexander's brow furrowed in confusion. "Our orders are to join your defensive screen, sir."

"And you will, but while you're still a day away from us we

don't need you getting hit by a bundle of dead-dropped nukes."

Alexander's eyes widened. The enemy might have slowed down to dead-drop their own missiles. But if that was the case, the *Lincoln* wasn't the most significant Alliance target in the area. She was just over 300 meters long, while Lewis Station was a wheel-shaped megastructure with an outer ring that was over three kilometers in diameter.

"Sir, they might not have dropped nukes along *our* trajectory. They may have dropped them on yours."

"There's no way of knowing that yet, and it would take us the better part of a week to alter our heading enough to evade any missiles, so for now let's just keep our eyes open, shall we? Let us know if you spot anything out there, Captain."

Alexander swallowed thickly and nodded once. "What about our missiles?"

"Leave them alone for now. You can always fire them up later."

"Yes, sir,"

"Lewis Station out."

"This is a mess!" Korbin said, turning to him. "For all we know the Reds just dropped a few thousand nukes; we've already dropped more than a hundred of our own, and everyone's still pretending like no one has fired a shot! Lewis Station should be evacuating right now."

Alexander shook his head. "And give up the Looking Glass? We'd be playing right into their hands. The station has fighters and drones to watch their backs. They also have us. That should be good enough."

Korbin turned to him with a dubious look. "I hope you're right, sir."

* * *

Over the last day of the *Lincoln's* approach, tensions reached an all-time high. They had managed to avoid any dead-dropped nukes that might have been heading their way by changing their trajectory multiple times during their approach. The Confederates had done likewise, and the *Lincoln's* dead-dropped warheads would never reach them now.

The opportunity for a surprise attack was gone, and now the Confederate Fleet was just fifty minutes from effective laser range (ELR) with Lewis Station. Meanwhile, the Alliance's Third Fleet was racing up fast behind them with an ETA of just twenty minutes to ELR with the Confederates. All of the respective forces were well within missile range and projectile range of each other, but so far no one had been seen to fire anything.

The *Lincoln* now sat in a stable orbit beside Lewis Station. Over twelve hours ago, while still on approach, they'd launched both the 61st Squadron and a full squadron of accompanying drones to join Lewis Station's fighter screen and help them scan for incoming dead-dropped missiles. Unfortunately, the only way to detect a piece of dead-dropped ordnance was to set it off. In this case, setting a missile off meant successfully bouncing active sensors off the missile's EM-absorbing armor.

Once detected, missiles would split into a dozen or more pieces, most of them armed with lasers rather than explosives, making them deadly long before they reached their targets. Standard sweeping procedure was to send drones ahead of manned fighters, giving them more time to intercept before the lasers started zapping.

Tactics in space were all about jinking around and trying to hit each other with projectile weapons and missiles before getting into effective laser range, because once that happened, engagements typically ended in a matter of minutes.

Alexander watched the squadrons of Rapier fighters at high magnification on the *Lincoln's* main holo display (MHD). The red-hot glow of their thrusters at full burn made them look like a swarm of fireflies in space.

"Nothing yet," Commander Korbin whispered, her eyes on the Rapiers.

Alexander shook his head. "Maybe the Chancellor meant it when he said they wouldn't fire the first shot."

"And I was born a gener," Korbin replied.

A few of the bridge crew chuckled at that. McAdams wasn't one of them. She was the only gener on deck.

A crackle of static hissed over the bridge speakers, followed by the sound of the fighter group's wing commander reporting in—Lieutenant Hayes had set the comms to the Alliance's command channel and left it open so they could hear the updates.

"Lewis Station, we're entering engagement zone sixty-five now… stand by…"

Mission Control had pre-calculated a hundred different hypothetical engagement zones, each of them 5,000 klicks deep and as wide as the enemy formation. Drones led the fighter group by 30,000 klicks.

"We're clear. Moving on to—strike that! Contact confirmed! Incoming missiles at 24,000 klicks. Five hundred plus detected."

Admiral Gaulle replied, "That's behind the drones, how did missiles get past them?"

"I don't know, sir."

"Never mind, open fire!"

"Engaging…"

Alexander glanced at the tactical map between him and Korbin in time to see the enemy missiles react to detection. Hundreds of red dots suddenly split into ten times as many smaller ones, all of them now going evasive and accelerating toward the

Rapiers at full burn.

"Increase magnification on the MHD," Alexander said as he looked up from the tactical map. Their visual of the Rapiers swelled, and Alexander watched the bright red glows of the fighters' engines winking out of sight as they turned tail and accelerated away from the incoming ordnance. Their survival depended on staying out of ELR with the laser-armed fragments for as long as possible.

The Rapiers opened fire and so did the drones. Golden lines of hypervelocity rounds stuttered out, tracking the enemy missiles from both sides. After just a few seconds, a pinprick of light flashed—one of the enemy warheads detonating as the Rapiers' fire found it. The explosion shouldn't have been visible, nor the weapons fire, but the *Lincoln's* combat computer did a good job of simulating visual and aural feedback. More pinpricks of fire appeared, dozens with every passing second.

Alexander checked the tactical map, comparing the vectors of the enemy missiles and the fighter group. ETA to laser range was a matter of seconds. Almost all of the enemy missiles would still be intact by then. Thirteen squadrons of twelve Rapier fighters was just over a hundred and fifty, and there were thousands of laser-armed missiles incoming.

The Rapiers didn't stand a chance. Unless...

"Lieutenant Stone! Get me the wing commander on the comms."

"Yes, sir."

Korbin glanced at him. "We're not authorized to give orders to the fighter group."

"I'm not going to give them orders. I'm going to give them a suggestion, and there's no time to get Admiral Gaulle's input."

The comms crackled. "*Lincoln,* Wing Commander Archer here."

"Commander, listen up. Flip back around and dead-drop your own missiles. Target the enemy's ordnance with yours and have your missiles go live just before they reach ELR."

"Our missiles are not armed with lasers, *Lincoln*. Going live at the enemy's ELR will just get them shot down."

"Exactly. Every laser they fire at one of your missiles is a laser they won't be firing at you. The more missiles you can put out there the better."

"Shit—roger that, *Lincoln*."

A moment later they heard Commander Archer relay Alexander's suggestion to the other squadrons like it was his own.

Korbin frowned. "Why didn't Commander Archer think of that?"

"It's hard to think straight while you're pulling six Gs to get away from certain death. The better question is why Admiral Gaulle didn't think of it."

"Maybe he was promoted for technical expertise rather than tactical," Korbin suggested.

"Maybe..." Alexander replied while zooming out the tactical map to look for the missiles the *Lincoln* had dead-dropped a day ago. They were millions of klicks past Lewis Station. Too late to fire them up now. Alexander had requested clearance to bring the ordnance online several times over the past day, but Admiral Gaulle had repeatedly denied his request—presumably to avoid provoking the Confederacy, although that concern was now moot.

Alexander watched the range between the enemy warheads and the fighter group tick down. ELR for the fighters was 2,000 klicks. The enemy's laser-armed missiles were shorter-ranged at just over 1,000 klicks.

The Rapiers finished dead-dropping their missiles, and then turned tail once more. As soon as the enemy ordnance reached

2,000 klicks, the Rapiers opened fire. Bright blue laser beams shot out, simulated on the *Lincoln's* MHD.

Pinprick-sized explosions flared once more, this time at least fifty at a time. Roughly one in every four laser beams hit its mark. Not bad considering the enemy missiles were accelerating at hundreds of *G*s on randomly varying trajectories. Unfortunately, fighters couldn't get anywhere near the kind of acceleration required to evade a laser, so they were bound to fare a lot worse once the enemy's ordnance started firing back.

Range dropped to 1,500 klicks and suddenly the fighter group's warheads went live, popping up out of nowhere and splitting into dozens of fragments, all of them tracking toward the enemy missiles.

In the next instant, thousands of Confederate laser-armed warheads opened fire all at once. Hundreds of friendly missiles went *boom*, lighting up the tactical map with simulated explosions that echoed softly through the speakers in Alexander's helmet.

The Rapiers kept firing, their aim getting better and better as range decreased. Then they came into the enemy's ELR and soon they were drawing fire, too. Rapiers were better armored than missiles, so it took several direct hits to take one out, but the enemy had more than enough firepower for that.

Alexander watched the number of Rapiers drop from over 150 to just 76 in a matter of seconds. Then the missiles and fighters flew past one another, and the Rapiers rotated their guns to the fore, firing on the missiles from behind. Enemy ordnance dropped from over 6,000 to just under 5,000. All of the Rapiers' own missiles had been intercepted, but they'd drawn enough fire to save fully half of the fighter group.

Not that any of that would matter to Lewis Station. There were still 5,000 missiles incoming.

Alexander grimaced. "Williams! How long until those missiles reach Lewis Station?"

"Twenty minutes, twenty-seven seconds, sir!"

Alexander did the math and shook his head. Soon those missiles would be out of ELR, and the fighter group would be back to intercepting them with hypervelocity rounds. Odds were there would still be several thousand missiles left by the time they reached laser range with Lewis Station and the *Lincoln,* not to mention what would happen when missiles carrying nuclear warheads slammed into the station at over 200 klicks per second. The kinetic energy alone would be enough to take out the station.

Talk about overkill, Alexander thought.

Beside him, Korbin whistled and pointed to the tactical map still hovering between their chairs. The Alliance had just opened fire on the Confederate Fleet with thousands of hot-fired missiles. The Confederates returned fire with their own missiles and deployed a fighter screen behind them. The Alliance already had their own fighters deployed. Then streams of hypervelocity rounds went streaking out from fighters and capital ships alike, trying to intercept each other's missiles. Soon lasers lanced between missiles, drones, and fighters. Explosions peppered the map. Capital ships began hitting each other at extreme range with projectiles fired from rail guns and coil guns at better than 20 klicks per second. A Confederate battleship got caught in multiple streams of fire, and Alexander watched it burst open at the seams like an overripe piece of fruit. Crewmen and debris went streaming out into space. A few seconds later the ship's engines went dark. Glancing around the map Alexander picked out at least six more ships already derelict on both sides of the conflict.

Missiles skipped past fighter screens and came into ELR

with capital ships. The capital ships opened fire with dazzling barrages of lasers. Then it was the missiles' turn. Laser-armed ordnance fired back, specifically targeting the big ships' lasers to decrease the firepower arrayed against them.

Only a handful of nukes actually made it to their targets, but each of them was a one-hit-kill that painted a dramatic explosion on the map, leaving nothing but a drifting cloud of debris in its wake.

Then the capital ships reached ELR and they began firing lasers at each other in a deadly light show—Alliance blue, Confederate red. Missiles and hypervelocity cannons went on firing, but lasers made the battle a simple point-and-shoot war of attrition. The side with the most guns and the strongest armor won.

In a matter of minutes, that side turned out to be the Alliance, but not by much. They had ten ships out of sixty still firing and maneuvering under active thrust by the time the Confederate fleet was derelict and drifting.

It took a few extra seconds to mop up Confederate fighters and drones, and then the Alliance's remaining starships launched repair ships and space marines, the former to aid repairs aboard their own derelict vessels, and the latter to board and capture enemy ones.

At the far end of the engagement a few squadrons of Confederate fighters were fleeing desperately toward Earth with Alliance drones in hot pursuit. Drones could pull higher *G*s so they caught up fast. Lasers flashed between them, and explosions flared, bringing the engagement to a decisive end.

It was over. Horror and disbelief settled in. From the simulated bird's-eye view of the tactical map, everything looked like a holo game. It couldn't be real.

"Sir!" Williams called out from the comms. "Lewis Station is busy evacuating. We've been advised to withdraw to a safe distance so we don't get caught by shrapnel when enemy ordnance hits."

Alexander looked up from the tactical map, mentally switching focus back to his side of the conflict. "Helm! Get us away!"

"Already ahead of you, sir! Brace for maximum thrust!"

There came a deafening roar, and then a train ran over him. The weight was unbearable. Alexander's lips parted in a grimace, and his heart felt like it actually stopped. Maximum regulation thrust for short periods was ten *G*s. Acceleration eased after just a few seconds, and Alexander's head lolled. He blinked spots from his eyes and fought a sudden urge to vomit.

"We're out of the blast radius, sir!" Davorian reported from the helm.

Alexander panned the tactical map over to his side of the conflict and watched the wave of enemy missiles drawing near to Lewis station. Alliance Rapiers were still in hot pursuit, firing at extreme range with bright golden streams of highly inaccurate projectiles.

The number of ordnance incoming had dropped to less than 4,000 missiles. Alexander grimaced, hoping that between the *Lincoln* and Lewis Station they could intercept the rest.

"Sensors! Are any of those missiles tracking us?"

"It's tough to tell at this range, sir."

They weren't far enough from the station to distinguish incoming missile trajectories. "Davorian, put some more distance between us and the station. Four *G*s thrust; keep that up until we identify incoming missiles."

"Aye-aye, sir."

Acceleration intensified once more, not nearly as bad as before, but still enough to make breathing labored and talking a chore.

"Sensors… track missiles whose vectors shift with ours. Highlight them on the tactical. Gunnery—as soon as you spot those missiles, start firing."

"At this range, sir? Odds are—"

"Still better than nothing, Lieutenant!" Alexander gritted out between gasps for air.

"Yes, sir."

Finally, Williams reported from the sensors station. "Incoming missiles detected!"

Davorian killed thrust and Alexander took a quick gulp of air. "How many?"

"Over one thousand."

"ETA?"

"Ten minutes."

"Gunnery, how many can we shoot down before they reach us? Best case scenario, please."

"Best case… we'll have fifteen seconds to intercept after they reach our ELR. We might do it, but when their laser-armed fragments start targeting our guns, interception rates are going to drop fast."

"In other words we're fucked."

A few heads turned at the expletive, but no one was going to cite code-of-conduct regulations to him at a time like this. Alexander thought about his dead-dropped ordnance with a pang of regret. If he still had those missiles he could have fired them to intercept the enemy's ordnance and evened the odds.

"Captain! We have a transmission incoming from Orbital One!"

"Full screen. I'll watch—everyone else, keep eyes on your stations!"

A chorus of *aye-ayes* echoed from the crew, and then Admiral Flores' face appeared on the MHD. She looked haggard. Her face was drawn, and her eyes were wide and staring. Officers yelled at each other in the background behind her.

"Captain de Leon," the admiral said. "I hope I've reached you in time."

Alexander frowned. With the distance between them being what it was, there was no sense in him replying. The transmission had to have been sent over five minutes ago.

"The Confederates have launched a sneak attack in orbit," Flores went on.

Suddenly the lights went out on the admiral's end of the transmission. Holo displays running on battery backups glowed bright blue behind her. Golden sparks flew, and then the lights were back, but much dimmer than before. One of the bulkheads belched a gout of flame, and Admiral Flores yelled for someone to put it out.

She faced the camera once more. "They tricked us, Captain. This was never about a wormhole. It was about drawing our forces away from Earth so they could launch an attack on our space elevator. Orbital One has been cut free of Earth with enemy ordnance in hot pursuit. It's only a matter of time before the nukes start flying back on Earth, and that means our green planet is headed for a nuclear winter. Now reaching Wonderland is more important than ever. Operation Alice is a go, Captain. Your job is to assess the planet for habitability. We'll come get you as planned if we still can, and if we can't, then—"

A sudden roar interrupted her, followed by a dazzling flare of light. Flores turned toward it just before the brightness consumed both her and her transmission.

It took a moment for reality to sink in. Orbital One was gone.

"Davorian! What's our ETA to the wormhole under maximum thrust? Can we make it before those missiles hit?"

"No, sir."

"Can we get back to Lewis Station?"

"Yes, sir."

"Do it. Comms, get me Admiral Gaulle!"

The Admiral's face appeared on-screen a moment later. He was strapped into an acceleration couch aboard a cramped-looking lifeboat with row upon row of crew strapped in behind him. His teeth were gritted and his lips were peeled back in a G-force-induced grimace.

"What can I... do for you... Captain?" Gaulle said between gasps for air.

"Do you have remote access to the station's defenses?"

"We do."

"Did you see Admiral Flores' last transmission?"

"Yes..."

"We need your help if we're going to make it to Wonderland, Admiral. Can you prioritize interception of the missiles tracking us?"

"Send me the... targets, and I'll see... what I can do."

Alexander nodded. "Thank you." A thought occurred to him then. "Do you have any missiles of your own on the station?"

"Why?"

Alexander blinked. Admiral Gaulle couldn't be that stupid. "You can use them to intercept!"

Gaulle shook his head. "Fired them all days ago. Earth-bound."

Alexander's jaw dropped. Lewis Station was about to be obliterated because the upper echelons had decided that Earth needed more missiles.

"I hope it was worth it."

"So do I. Good luck, Captain."

The transmission ended.

"Comms! Send Admiral Gaulle the target data for the missiles tracking us."

"Already sent, sir."

"Good. Lieutenant Stone, get our fighters and drones to focus on the same targets."

"Aye, Captain."

Alexander watched the incoming missiles on the tactical map. They were just five minutes away. Lewis Station and the *Lincoln* poured steady streams of projectiles at them, intercepting a couple of missiles with every passing second.

Time dragged by at the speed of sloth. Minutes felt like hours. The number of incoming ordnance dropped below 3000. ETA hit thirty seconds.

Alexander sat up straighter in his chair. "Start firing lasers!"

"We still have fifteen seconds to ELR," Lieutenant Cardinal objected.

"Concentrate your fire! We'll kill a few."

"Yes, sir."

There were still over 800 warheads aimed at the *Lincoln*.

Bright blue lasers lanced out in streams of twos and threes. Sure enough, a few extra missiles winked off the grid. Then enemy ordnance reached ELR, and both Lewis Station and the *Lincoln* began shooting them down in earnest. Incoming missiles winked off the grid by the hundreds. Alexander breathed a sigh of relief. Then he noticed that the number of missiles heading for the *Lincoln* wasn't dropping as fast as the overall count.

That was wrong. A closer look at the tactical map revealed that Lewis Station had devoted only a small fraction of its guns to covering the *Lincoln*. Admiral Gaulle was still determined to save his station.

Alexander cursed under his breath.

The enemy's laser-armed ordnance opened fire next. The ship shuddered and a muffled *bang* reached Alexander's ears.

He froze. That sound hadn't been simulated.

"Taking fire!" McAdams reported. "We're venting atmosphere on decks four, five, and six!"

The ship's storage. They were venting valuable supplies into space.

"Lock it down!" Alexander roared.

"Deploying repair drones..."

The number of incoming ordnance dropped below 400. ETA five seconds.

"Brace for impact!" Hayes warned.

"Helm! Set thrust to 50 *G*s!"

There was no time to hesitate, and Davorian didn't.

Alexander felt himself slam into a brick wall. That wall was the back of his acceleration couch. Conscious thought ceased. His chest stopped moving, and his heart froze.

After an indeterminate period of time, the acceleration stopped. It took a second for Alexander's lungs to remember how to breathe. As his heart went back to beating, a searing headache stabbed him behind his eyes. If that burst of acceleration had been anything but brief, they'd all be dead right now.

A quick look at the tactical map revealed that all of the incoming missiles had been intercepted. That last-ditch evasive maneuver had bought them the time they needed.

The station had not been so lucky.

"Multiple impacts on Lewis Station!" Lieutenant Williams reported.

"On-screen!"

The MHD switched to a view from the *Lincoln's* rear cameras, and they saw Lewis Station drifting in three pieces. The bones of the station's superstructure were showing, hull plates clinging here and there, charred black and looking like torn bits of paper.

Then the rest of the missiles hit those remains and blotted

out the tactical map with a wash of EM interference. When things came back into focus, Lewis Station was gone.

Alexander sighed. "Davorian, get us through the Looking Glass."

"Yes, sir."

Commander Korbin turned to him, her blue eyes wide and glassy. "What about Earth?"

Alexander shook his head. "Our orders are clear, Commander. We are to get to Wonderland and assess the planet for habitability."

"You have a wife on Earth, Captain. I have two children."

"And I have to believe that they'll be waiting for us when we get back."

"The odds of that are—"

"Better than nothing," Alexander replied. "McAdams, how are repairs coming along?"

"The hull breach is sealed, sir…"

"But?"

"We lost a lot of supplies."

"Then we have no choice. We have to go back," Korbin said.

Alexander shot her a look. "Williams! How long can we last with what's left? Do we still have enough supplies to get us to Wonderland and back?" Besides being the ship's sensors operator, Lieutenant Williams was also the ship's quartermaster, so he would know.

"The supplies closest to the outer hull were mostly non-essential equipment, and they were all locked down before launch. In terms of food and other critical supplies, we should still have everything we need."

"Then our mission stands. Lieutenant Stone—"

"Sir?"

"Recall our fighters and drones. Coordinate your efforts

with the helm to make sure they're all docked before we enter the wormhole."

"Yes, sir."

The MHD showed stars panning by as the *Lincoln* rotated. The Looking Glass came into view, a clear glass marble floating in a sea of stars. It was hard to imagine that through there lay humanity's only hope for survival—a planet that only probes had ever seen, and even then, just for a few minutes at a time. There was no way to be sure that it really was habitable, or even that its ecology wouldn't be completely hostile to humans. What if all the planet's water was poisonous? Or if the air wasn't breathable? Toxic? The planet could also be home to a host of deadly pathogens. Or maybe it was plagued by high surface winds that would make growing food next to impossible.

The list of possibilities was endless.

Chances were it would be easier to colonize than the Moon, Mars, Titan, or Europa, but it would likely still be a far cry from Earth. Alexander couldn't believe that this was what humanity had come to. *What have we done?* he wondered.

He was still wondering that long after the remainder of the 61st Squadron was aboard and the *Lincoln* passed through the wormhole.

What.

Have.

We.

Done?

CHAPTER 4

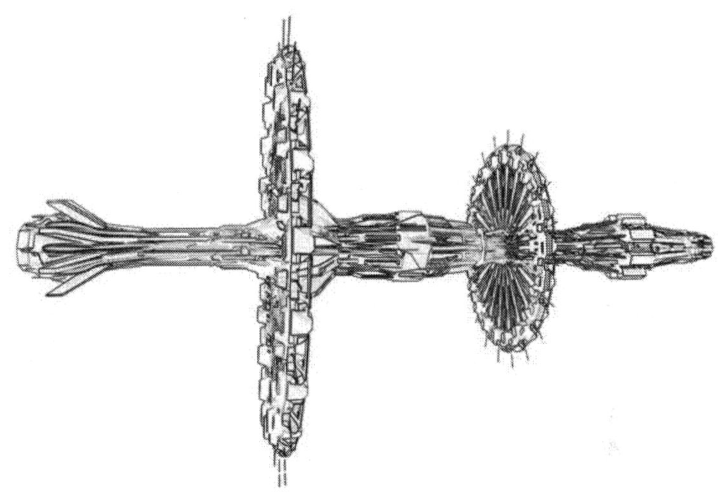

"Setting acceleration to point five *Gs*," Lieutenant Davorian said.

Alexander swallowed thickly and nodded. "Lieutenant Williams, confirm no hostiles inbound."

"We're clear, sir."

Alexander turned to look at the comms station. "Hayes, set condition green."

"Yes, sir."

"Now what?" Korbin asked, turning to him.

"Now we stretch our legs."

The bridge came alive with the sound of seat harnesses unbuckling. Alexander unbuckled his own harness and mentally disconnected his relief tubes. That done, he manually withdrew his nutrient line. Finally, he reached up and twisted his helmet, breaking the air-tight seal with a squeal of escaping air. He pulled off the helmet and attached it to the magnetic rack behind his headrest. The HUD disappeared, and his mental interface to the ship went with it, but they'd have plenty of warning if something happened to change their alert status. The nearest possible hostiles were back on Earth, and that was at least a week away.

"Williams, you have the conn and the deck."

"Yes, sir," Williams said, sighing as he sunk back into the sensors station.

"Everyone else, come with me. Hayes, before you leave your station, alert the rest of the crew report to the Officer's Lounge."

"Aye, sir."

Alexander reached up to the rails on the front of his armrests and pulled himself up out of the captain's couch. At point five *Gs*, it was easy to suspend his weight above the chair and swing himself backward to land on the deck behind the headrest. Commander Korbin landed beside him. She'd also removed her helmet.

Looking up, Alexander saw the rest of the crew climbing down the ladders from their stations. Some of them simply jumped down and landed with muffled thuds around him. Alexander frowned. That was against regulations, even in low gravity, but he wasn't going to reprimand them now. They all had bigger problems to deal with.

Once everyone except Williams was standing on the deck, Alexander headed for the elevators at the back of the bridge. He felt light and bouncy in the ship's half gravity, and he had to consciously watch his steps to avoid walking too fast and tripping over his own feet. After spending a week seated in their chairs with nothing but a few mandatory breaks to stretch their legs, walking felt like a strange new luxury.

They reached the elevators and Alexander gestured for the doors of the nearest lift to open. The control panel tracked his gesture and the elevator opened with a whisper. Alexander walked in and selected one of the glowing green buttons, the one labeled *Officer's Lounge (12).*

The doors slid shut and the lift went up two floors to the lounge on deck twelve. The doors opened to reveal a circular room with a wraparound vista of space. Furnishings and decorations were sparse and utilitarian, since everything had to be bolted to the deck.

Around the circumference of the room holoscreens reproduced feeds from cameras mounted on the outer hull, providing a dazzling, panoramic view of space. Alexander noticed that the geometry of space-time inside the wormhole subtly warped that view, as if they were looking out through a fisheye lens.

"Go make yourselves comfortable. Once everyone's here, we'll begin." Alexander walked over to the bar and took a seat on one of the stools. He idly glanced around the naked bar, wishing sorely for a drink, but they were all still on duty, and everything was still locked down in the cabinets. Couldn't have whiskey bottles cracking together at 10 *G*s.

That'd be a waste of perfectly good Scotch.

Damaging sensitive equipment inside the lounge was a secondary concern.

After a few minutes Commander Korbin came and sat down beside him. "Sir," she said.

"You can call me Alex. We're going to be off duty for a while, Sirena."

"I see. What's this about, Alex?"

"Morale. We lost half of the 61st Squadron out there." He couldn't bring himself to mention Earth.

Korbin swallowed visibly. "So this is a funeral."

"A memorial." One of the elevators arrived, and out spilled a group of non-coms. "Come in and take your seats," Alexander called out to them.

Another three lifts full of crew arrived before everyone was assembled and waiting. Alexander turned to them from the bar and cleared his throat.

"Everyone, gather around." He waited as the crew came together. Seth Ryder, the *CAG*—commander of the ship's fighters and drones—pushed through to the front of the group to stand beside Lieutenant Stone of starfighter command. Ryder and Stone could have been brothers, both big, burly men with dark hair and plenty of laugh lines to herald their mutual sense of humor, though Stone had a lumpy, don't-mess-with-me kind of face, so he was the less approachable of the two. Neither of them was laughing now, however. Ryder's gray eyes looked glassy and haunted, while Stone's gaze may as well have been named after him. Alexander scanned the rest of the crew and saw those expressions mirrored on dozens of other faces.

These people were like family to one another. With the exception of recent transfers, they'd all spent more time together than they'd spent with their real families. Alexander didn't even need to do a roll call to know who was missing. There were gaping holes where their faces should have been. Even without bodies, a ceremonial funeral was called for, but they hadn't had time to organize one yet, and Alexander wasn't sure it would be a good idea to encourage mourning—not with Earth's fate still so uncertain.

Making a snap decision, he nodded to the crew and said, "We lost five brothers and sisters today. That's enough reason to mourn without thinking about who else we might have lost. The truth is, we don't know, and without Lewis Station to act as a comm relay between us and Earth, we're not likely to find out until we re-establish contact.

"By now some of you have probably already figured out what's going on, and since operational security is already blown, I'm free to tell you what Operation Alice is all about.

"We're busy traveling through a wormhole to an earth-type planet called Wonderland. In light of the recent conflict back on Earth, our mission is more important than ever. We need to find out if Wonderland is really habitable, and report back to the Alliance with our findings so that we can establish a colony there before the Confederacy does."

Alexander let that news sink in before he went on. "If you have any questions about the mission specifics, please hold them until later. I'll be issuing a proper mission brief before the next sleep cycle that should answer all of your questions.

"But for the moment, we're going to stop and honor our fallen brothers and sisters-in-arms by doing something unconventional. We're going to celebrate their lives, not focus on their deaths. This is a wake, not a funeral. It's a time to share memories of the deceased. We'll have a few drinks, make a toast, and swap stories. For the next four hours, we're all officially off duty. Stone, Ryder, would you please see that everyone gets a drink?"

Lieutenant Stone nodded and started toward the bar. Ryder followed a few steps behind.

"That's all for now. Dismissed."

Hushed murmurs bubbled from the group as everyone dispersed back to couches and chairs. One man remained where he was. Alexander didn't recognize him, but from his lack of insignia and overly genteel appearance, he could guess who it might be.

"Can I help you, Mr. Ambassador?"

"Your orders are to get to Wonderland with all possible speed, Captain," the man said, approaching the bar like a snake slithering in for the kill.

"I'm sorry, I don't believe we've met," Alexander said, holding out a gloved hand.

The ambassador shook hands with him. "Maximilian Carter, Ambassador extraordinary and plenipotentiary to the Alliance."

"*Plenty-potenty-ary*... That's quite a mouthful, Max." Korbin glanced sharply at him, and Alexander offered a brisk smile to cover his contempt.

"*Pleni*-potentiary," Max corrected.

"That's what I said," Alexander replied.

"We're on a strict timeline here, Captain. Now more than ever."

"A few hours downtime won't make a lot of difference to our mission parameters, but it will to my crew's morale."

Alexander felt someone tap him on the shoulder.

"Here you are, sir."

He swiveled his chair to see Lieutenant Stone holding out an acrylic tumbler full of Scotch. He accepted the drink with a nod of thanks and swiveled back to face the ambassador once more. Alexander sat sipping away under Maximilian's watchful blue gaze. The man's wavy blond hair, long, aquiline nose, too-perfect face, and tall, trim figure gave him an aristocratic air. He was probably meant to look erudite and sophisticated to geners, but Alexander thought he looked pompous and disingenuous instead.

"What if the Confederacy follows us to Wonderland?" Max asked.

"That's a valid question. I have another one. What if a sea monster eats us?"

"Your attitude will be noted in my report."

"Well, the truth is, Max, I don't give a flying fuck what you write up in your report. I just lost five family members, and I have a paper-shuffling bureaucrat in my face, trying to tell me not to grieve for them. I'm sure you can understand how that might make me grumpy."

Max scowled and walked away.

"That's tellin' him, sir," Ryder said from behind the bar.

Alexander drained his glass and slammed it on the bar. "Hit me again. For some reason I have bad taste in my mouth."

"Coming right up, sir," Stone said, and then poured him another two thumbs of Scotch.

"You sure have a way with people," Korbin said, while accepting a beer from Ryder.

"I know. Maybe I should go into the foreign service? Become a professional snot like Max."

Korbin snorted. "You'd start a war."

Alexander froze in mid-sip of his second drink. Stone winced and Ryder spilled a precious ounce of Scotch on the bar counter.

"I'm sorry, Captain, I wasn't…"

"It's all right. We had our orders, and the shots we fired didn't start anything. Those missiles are well on their way to the Oort Cloud by now."

Korbin nodded and silence stretched between them.

"Well, shit," Ryder said. "Is this a wake or a wallow? I need to get drunk."

"I'm pretty sure a traditional wake doesn't involve getting drunk," Korbin replied.

"I believe in the *Irish* wake, not the Hispanic one."

"But you are Hispanic."

"Jewish Hispanic."

"Doesn't Jewish tradition call for designated mourners that don't shave, shower, or change their clothes for a week? You're the ones who invented sackcloth."

"All right, that's enough," Alexander said. "We're getting off topic. This is a memorial plain and simple. Grieve or remember however you like, so long it's in honor of the dead. You get drunk, you pop a pill to get sober, and get back to your stations as soon as the designated four hours are up."

Korbin nodded. "Sorry. I'm not sure what's got into me today."

Alexander studied his XO. He had an idea about what had gotten into her. Same thing that had her practically demanding they turn the ship around and head back to Earth. Her kids. "They're fine, Commander."

"How do you know?"

"Because if they aren't, there's nothing you can do about it, so worrying is a waste of time."

"That still doesn't mean they're fine."

"It doesn't mean they aren't either."

"Easy for you to say."

"Is it? My wife lives in LA. Out of the top ten cities to target with nukes, LA is number two."

Korbin took a deep breath and let it out again. "I guess we'll find out when we make contact with Earth again."

Alexander nodded agreeably. "Right." What he really meant was, *not likely.* Fleet Command wasn't going to tell them how bad things were on Earth, or even allow two-way contact with their families—unless nothing had actually happened back on Earth. It would be too bad for morale if half the crew suddenly realized their loved ones were all dead.

Hell, they pulled a third of the crew and called up the mission reserves instead just to make sure that everyone would have plenty of reasons to go back home. With a sigh Alexander put it out of his mind and turned to Lieutenant Stone.

"Everyone has a drink?"

"Everyone who wanted one."

"Good." Swiveling to face the rest of the room, Alexander knocked his knuckles on the bar behind him and whistled for attention. Heads turned. Eyes blinked, most of them red with grief. There were more than a few tear-streaked faces in the room.

"Listen up! Tonight we're celebrating the lives of exactly five people. As far as we're concerned, everyone else is still alive. For those of you who are new here, the deceased are: Junior Lieutenant Sara Martinez, Lieutenant Diana Rojas de Chacon, Lieutenant Eduardo Ortiz, Lieutenant Erika Fabrega, and Junior Lieutenant Angel Montero." Alexander raised his glass. "To their safe passage from this world to the next. May their sacrifice not have been in vain. *Salud!*"

"Salud!" the crew echoed back.

Alexander threw back the dregs of Scotch in his tumbler.

"Cheers," someone said quietly beside him.

Alexander saw that it was McAdams. She downed a martini in one gulp and waved to Lieutenant Stone for another.

Alexander nodded to her. "Where are you from?" he asked.

"Down South, same as you."

"Then you'd have said *salud,* not cheers."

"Not if my family is originally from up North."

"Your parents emigrated?"

"Grandparents."

"Walking up stream. I like it. Probably a smart move considering the war. They were rich geners I'm guessing."

"Geners, yes, rich no," McAdams replied as Stone passed her another martini.

"Then how come you're... you are a gener, right?"

"Yes. My grandparents moved down South to invest and live off their investments. Competition in the North is too fierce, and everything's too expensive. But things didn't work out and they became casualties of the crime rate. My dad was sixteen and had to fend for himself so he dropped school. He met my mom, they got married, and ended up working seventy hours a week to pay for me to be born a gener."

"So you joined the service to save your parents?"

McAdams nodded.

"Admirable."

She winced and looked down at her feet. "It was."

"Was? You got them moved up North in exchange for service to your country. That's doubly self-sacrificing. Downright noble."

When McAdams looked up from her feet, there were tears in her eyes. "I killed them, Captain."

Alexander shook his head. "They're not dead, Lieutenant. Ever heard of Schroedinger's cat?"

She shook her head.

"Ask Davorian sometime. The point is, you don't know that they're dead."

"I don't know that they're alive, either."

"But both are possibilities as far as we know, so which would you rather believe—the negative outcome or the positive one? Let me rephrase that: which outcome would you rather be true?"

"The positive one, of course."

"Then focus on that."

McAdams frowned and nodded. "Yes, sir."

"Call me Alex. You have a first name, McAdams?"

"Viviana," she said, flashing a brief smile and brushing a stray lock of blond hair out of her face.

"Nice to meet you, Viviana."

"Likewise, sir—Alex."

"Sir Alex. Has a nice ring to it."

She smiled wryly at that and turned to leave the bar.

He watched her walk away, sipping her martini as she went.

"I thought *I* was supposed to be the ship's counselor," Korbin said. "Or was that just your way of being friendly to the new *boot*."

"She's not technically a boot, but you're welcome."

"For?"

"When I send out those briefs, you're going to have the entire crew come filing through your office, each of them looking for some shred of hope and chipping away at your own reserves with all their doubts. The more hope they have to start with, the easier it'll be for you."

Korbin's brow beetled, dropping a shadow over her eyes. "What haven't they told us, Alex?"

He fixed her with a grim look. "Everything."

CHAPTER 5

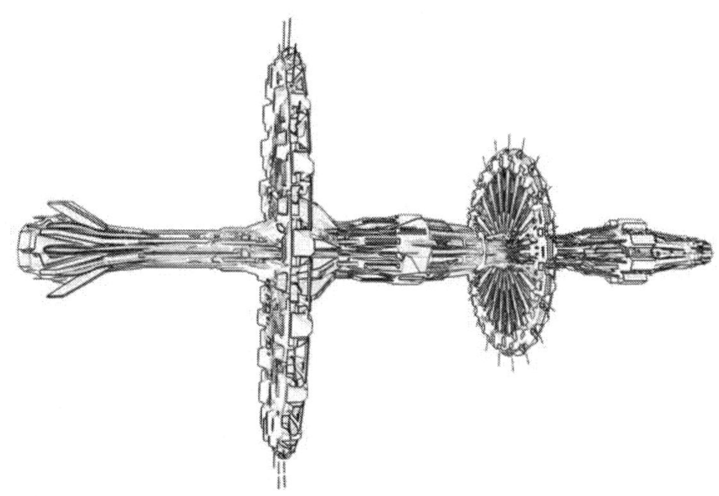

Two hours later Alexander sat in the office attached to his quarters, nursing the after effects of about twenty fingers of Scotch. He tore open a sachet of hydrating vitamins and stirred them into a cup of water. After letting the solution settle for a moment, he used it to wash down an over-the-counter alcohol metabolizer, courtesy of the ship's doctor. Doctor Crespin had been passing them around like candy before people had started pairing off to leave the lounge.

Fraternization wasn't technically against fleet regulations, and Alexander didn't believe in playing chaperone for his crew. They were grown-ups, and all was fair in love and war—unless it interfered with the crew's performance or shipboard duties.

Alexander laid his head back against his chair and closed his eyes for a minute. His head throbbed and spun, and his throat felt cut with grief. Nothing to do about his throat, but his head soon stopped spinning thanks to the metabolizer.

Sobriety made an unwelcome entrance, but she was a necessary muse. It was time to put together the mission brief. Thankfully, someone had thought to leave a locked archive on his computer with all the details of the mission. He used his clearance code to unlock it and then made judicious use of copy-paste to assemble his brief.

Once he was satisfied with his plagiarism, he wrote the summary himself: *We're going to be gone a long time due to time dilation and wormhole geometry. The G-tanks will make our seventy days travel time go by in a blink, but once we get to Wonderland, we'll be stuck waiting a year or more for a rescue. In a nutshell…*

Relativity's a bitch.

He scratched that last line, but then he imagined the look on Max Carter's face as he read the brief, and he wrote it back.

We'll be sending a comm probe to re-establish contact with Earth at 1930 hours, so take a break from whatever you're doing and record a message for your loved ones back home. Don't mention any mission specifics unless you want your message censored. Soon as you're done, forward your messages to Lieutenant Hayes, and he'll have them loaded onto the probe.

When he was finished, Alexander punched the *send* key on his keyboard, and the brief went out to all of the crew simultaneously. Soon they'd be reading it on their comm bands, assuming they weren't all too busy fraternizing.

Next order of business was to record a message for his wife.

He turned on the holocomm at his desk and stared into the lens of the camera, wondering what to say. How did he look? Pale? Disheveled? Drunk?

He stopped the recording and ran a hand through his hair to straighten it out. No sense giving his wife the idea that he'd been doing some fraternizing of his own. She knew better, but he'd rather not sow any doubt—especially now that he knew more about Operation Alice. Caty would have to suffer a lot of silence over the next few years, so this message had to be good if he expected her to wait for him.

Satisfied that his hair probably looked combed, he started recording again.

"Caty..."

That was as far as he got. What could he possibly say? Desperate for inspiration, he looked around his office. Nothing but gray walls, exposed conduits overhead, and the holoscreen viewport behind him showing a warped version of space.

Then he remembered the pocket watch she'd given him. He felt for it through the thick material of his combat suit. He'd zipped it up in one of the suit's outer pockets. Now he unzipped the pocket and withdrew the watch to read the inscriptions once more. *Time is an illusion. Love is the only truth. Let mine be yours.*

Nodding to himself, Alexander looked up once more and started the recording.

"Caty, by now you know more about what's happened than I do. I hope to God you're somewhere safe. As for me, I'm okay. The *Lincoln* is well on her way to her destination, but there's a lot they didn't tell us about this mission. I don't think I can say much without this message getting edited all to hell before it reaches you, but due to reasons I can't discuss, I'm not going to be able to keep contact with you. I'll still record messages every day that I can, but you probably won't get them for a long time. It's going to be years before we see each other, Caty—at best. I'll wait for you, just as I promised, but if you can't..." Alexander swallowed and managed to smile for the camera. "Above all, I want you to be happy. Whatever that means, I won't hold it against you, okay? Keep yourself safe. I love you, Caty. *Te amo,*" he added, repeating himself in their native tongue for emphasis.

Alexander stopped the recording and played it back to watch, trying to imagine how Caty would react when she saw it.

She'd cry when she saw how sad he looked and sounded. She'd also probably throw something at her holoscreen when she got to the part about him giving her permission to move on. That part made him wince, but it had to be said. Maybe she wouldn't like to hear it now, but in five years or ten… it might just ease her conscience.

He meant what he'd said about waiting for her, though. If he hadn't cheated in the last ten years that he'd spent in OCS and guarding Earth from orbit, then he wasn't about to give into temptation now. Besides, if their love was meant to last, it would, but not if he preemptively sabotaged it.

Alexander sighed and sent his recording to Hayes. As he did so, he heard the door chime. *Probably Korbin,* he thought.

"Come in!" he said.

The door slid open, and McAdams appeared standing there. She took a few steps forward, crossing the threshold. "Hello, Captain," she said, smiling brokenly at him and swaying on her feet.

Alexander took one look at her and hurried to assist. She looked terrible. She may as well have written *damsel in distress* on her forehead.

"What's wrong, Lieutenant?" He could smell the liquor on her breath as he drew near. *I should have set a two-drink limit,* he thought. "Come, sit down," he said, taking her by the arm to guide her through his office to the attached sitting room in his quarters.

She stumbled and fell against him. Before he realized what was happening, her lips smacked straight into his, wet and cold, and tasting like martini. He pushed her away a second later.

"Lieutenant! What do you think you're doing?"

McAdams had a dreamy look on her face, but it vanished promptly with his rebuke. "I—I thought—" she shook her head.

"Never mind. I'm sorry, sir!" she replied, saluting awkwardly and turning to leave. Alexander watched her stumble toward the door, his eyes wide with shock.

"Hold on, McAdams. Not so fast."

She stopped, and reluctantly turned back to face him. "Sir?"

"What is it exactly that you thought?"

"That you were flirting, sir."

Was I? He wondered as a frown hardened his lips. "I'm sorry if I gave you that impression, Lieutenant. I was just being friendly."

"Yes, sir. I apologize, sir," McAdams replied, hiding behind a blank expression. "May I go, sir?"

"Where's your metabolizer?"

"I… lost it."

"Go get another one from storage on Blue Deck and get some sleep. Also, I want you to schedule a meeting with Commander Korbin. We're all struggling to cope, but there are some things you can do to make that easier. Above all, stay positive, and don't forget to send a message to your family via Lieutenant Hayes. You read the mission brief?"

McAdams nodded.

That depressing news was probably what had brought her to his office in the first place. Maybe she'd thought he would be equally depressed from writing the brief. "Dismissed, Lieutenant," Alexander said.

"Yes, sir," McAdams replied, saluting once more.

Alexander watched her go. He chided himself for noticing the provocative way her hips swayed as she left. His manhood rebuked him for turning her away, but his heart and mind gave a silent cheer.

With a sigh, he made a swiping gesture to shut the door, and then headed back through his office to his quarters. It was time to get cleaned up and hit the rack for a few hours' sleep.

He needed to be back on the bridge soon to see if Earth had responded to their probe, and then it would be off to the G-tanks and seventy days of forced rest.

Come to think of it, that was probably what had pushed McAdams over the edge of proper conduct and into his arms. There was a sizable risk that some of them either wouldn't wake from the coma, or that something would happen to them and their ship while they were traveling through the wormhole. That was enough to make anyone behave recklessly, let alone a born gener like her, who'd grown up knowing that the only way she could die was by some unforeseen accident.

Alexander breezed through his sitting room and sleeping area to the attached wash station. He was just about to peel out of his combat suit (finally!) when his comm band vibrated against his wrist and trilled at him. He raised the band to eye level and accepted the call.

Lieutenant Davorian's face appeared projected above the band. His lean features, pale, baby-smooth skin and unnaturally bright, silver eyes gave him an erudite, almost alien appearance. Some of those features—like the eyes and skin tone—were elective, things he'd decided to change about himself after moving up North and accepting gener treatments. Alexander had refused to waste his money on cosmetic treatments, but each to their own.

"Sir," Davorian said.

Alexander nodded to him. "Is something wrong, Lieutenant?"

"I've been reviewing the mission logs, sir. There's something you need to see." Davorian had taken over from Williams as the *Officer of the Deck* (OOD) so that Williams could join the latter half of the memorial in the lounge.

"I'll be right there," Alexander replied, already heading for the exit.

After just a few minutes, Alexander was clinging to the ladder beside the helm, some twenty feet above the bridge deck. Davorian pointed up to a system diagnostic report that he had brought up on the ship's main holo display. Alexander craned his neck to study it.

"What am I looking at, Davorian?"

"You remember the faulty controls that made us leave Orbital One at greater than regulation thrust?"

Alexander nodded.

"I've isolated the cause. Someone altered the ship's engine code."

"What? How did they do that?"

"They included it as part of a firmware update. You see those two lines? They're not supposed to be there. Based on the code, I'd say the intention wasn't to destroy the ship, just cripple it with competing thrust vectors. That didn't happen because I caught the problem early and reset the entire navigation system to the last known safe settings."

"So someone tried to sabotage the *Lincoln*."

"That, or it was a serious oversight."

"Who's in charge of firmware updates for the nav systems?"

"The chief engineer."

"McAdams," Alexander said, his eyes widening suddenly.

CHAPTER 6

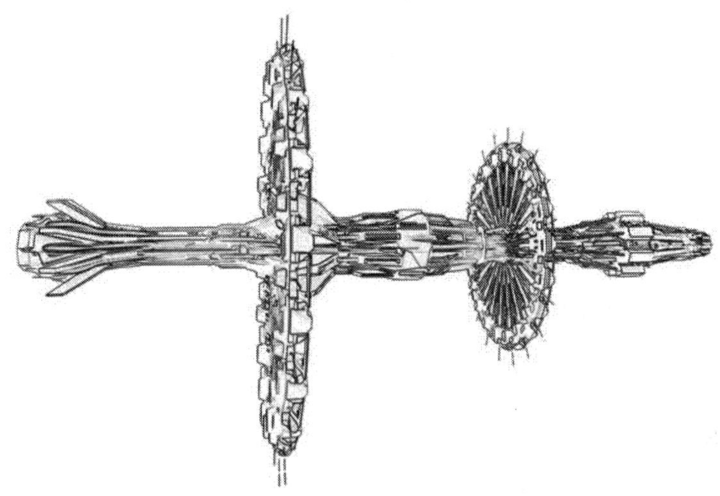

"So my new chief engineer is a spy. Is that what you're telling me?"

"Not necessarily. She isn't supposed to write the code, but she does have to give it a final check. She might have missed seeing the problem."

"What are the odds of that?"

"With an experienced chief, it's not likely, but she's new and she's a *junior* lieutenant, so it's a definite possibility. Someone might have simply taken advantage of her inexperience."

"So if we have a saboteur on board, it could be any one of the ship's engineers."

"Or someone else with the security clearance to make ad-hoc changes to the ship's code."

"Like who?"

"You. Commander Korbin. Me. Anyone else on the bridge."

"No one else had the necessary clearance?"

"Not that I know of."

"When was that firmware update initiated?"

"About an hour before launch."

"And who was on board at the time?"

"Everyone but you, sir."

Alexander blew out a breath. "Great."

"What do we do?"

"Well, we don't want the saboteur to know we're on to him."

"Or *her*," Davorian replied.

McAdams. It was tempting to blame the gener, but statistically she was a lot less likely to be involved in deviant behavior. Unless she was a Confederate spy, in which case it made plenty of sense. Confederates were all geners to begin with, so it would explain why one of them was hanging out on his ship.

"Right—or her," Alexander agreed. "We're going to have to lay a trap."

"How's that, sir?"

"Opportunity. Give the saboteur the perfect chance to do something else, but this time make sure we're watching for it."

"What makes you think they'll try again?"

"Now that the whole crew knows we're going to spend the trip in G-tanks, the only way to stop us from reaching our destination is to try something again before the good doctor turns us into sleeping goldfish."

"What do you suggest?"

"Have McAdams join Lieutenant Hayes on the bridge for the next watch. That's in..." Alexander checked the time on his comm band. "Fifteen minutes. Have her get the entire engineering staff on that shift with her. Tell her I want her to check over all the *Lincoln's* critical systems before we hop in the tanks. Meanwhile, you're going to set up the *Lincoln* to block and sandbox any further software or firmware updates until we've both had a chance to look at them."

"Yes, sir."

"Keep me posted."

"I will, sir."

As Alexander descended the access ladder back to the bridge deck, he thought about the possibility that Davorian was the saboteur. If so, leaving him alone at the helm was a very bad idea. Then again, if he were the saboteur, he hardly needed to feed bad code to the engines in order to cripple the ship. He could have done that long ago just by misfiring the engines.

That meant he could scratch two off the suspect list—himself (obviously), and Davorian. *No, three,* he decided. Williams had the first watch after setting condition green. Left all alone on the bridge for a couple hours, he could have destroyed the ship by now, too. That left the remaining five members of the bridge crew and a dozen engineers as suspects.

Alexander frowned. It was hard to suspect any of them when he knew them all so well, but there were a bunch of recent transfers—McAdams being one of them, and no doubt some of the enlisted engineers, too. He gestured for the bridge doors to open and then walked back down to his quarters.

Once there, he headed back to his wash station, sighing as he went. As if they didn't have enough concerns, what with traveling through a wormhole to another galaxy, open war back on Earth, and the survival of the human race resting on a successful outcome of their mission.

Alexander thought about all of that as he stripped out of his combat suit, shaved, and showered. The more he thought about it, the less sense it made. Why would the Confederacy even want to sabotage their mission? Not like their survival wasn't equally at stake. It would make a whole lot more sense for them to simply steal information from the mission and use it for their own purposes.

Who else might have had a motive to stop the *Lincoln* from reaching Wonderland?

Assuming the purpose of that code wasn't to destroy the ship, but just to damage it, then any one of the crew would have had a good motive. They'd all been chosen to make sure they had strong ties to Earth, so none of them really wanted to go. Hell, even *he* had a good motive for that kind of sabotage.

Hopefully whoever it was would fall into the trap he'd laid, but if they weren't trying to destroy the *Lincoln,* then sabotaging the engines wasn't a good idea now that they were so far from Earth and flying down a wormhole with who-knew-what kinds of navigational hazards.

A part of him couldn't help but hope whoever it was would find some way to turn the ship around, but the duty-bound captain in him won out and forced him to think about alternative forms of sabotage.

What would force them to turn the ship around?

Something Commander Korbin had said after the battle came to mind. She'd been talking about the supplies they'd lost and that they had no choice but to turn around. That was before she or anyone else had realized just how critical those supplies were. Now that the crew knew they going to be gone for *years,* supplies were more important than ever. Especially food.

Alexander felt his jaw tighten and a muscle twitch. Bringing his comm band up to his lips, he said, "Call Lieutenant Stone." As the ship's chief master-at-arms, Stone was in charge of shipboard security and the ship's master-at-arms force.

"Sir?" Stone answered.

"Get a detail of MAs down to the storage decks. I want at least one man on each deck. Have them check over the supplies and make sure everything is in order."

"Yes, sir. What should I tell them to look for?"

Alexander debated telling Stone anything. He was also a suspect, but if he was responsible for the sabotage then even ordering him to post guards on the supply decks would be enough warning for him to lie low. Likewise for his MAs. "Tell them to look for sabotage, but keep quiet about it. I don't want the whole ship to know what we're up to."

"Yes, sir…"

"Soon as you're done, meet me in the CIC."

"Not the bridge?"

"No." He didn't want McAdams or her engineers to find out what he and Stone were doing, just in case his hunch was wrong and they were busy sabotaging the ship's engines again.

"See you there, Captain," Stone replied.

Alexander nodded. "See you."

* * *

A dim blue glow radiated from the CIC's main holo display, which was currently displaying seven separate holo feeds from the MAs' helmet cams. It was hard to watch all the feeds at once, since he and Lieutenant Stone were the only ones in the CIC.

"Why would anyone want to sabotage our supplies?" Stone asked.

"I'm hoping they wouldn't," Alexander replied.

"But?"

Alexander turned to Stone with a frown, debating whether or not he should reveal what Davorian had found in the ship's engine code.

The room's PA system crackled, interrupting them before Alexander could say anything. "Ramos here. I think I might have something…"

"What is it, Ramos?" Stone asked.

Alexander's heart thudded in his chest as he scanned the associated feed. He squinted at the small window, trying to pick out details. Then Stone enlarged the feed, temporarily minimizing the others. The petty officer who'd reported was looking down the sights of his rifle, the barrel swinging back and forth as he scanned everything in sight, checking points of cover where there might be an ambush waiting. Every now and then his viewpoint strayed to one of the food crates at the back of the room. Alexander could see that the lid was cracked open. That had to have happened after the battle around Lewis Station or else the *Lincoln's* combat maneuvers would have distributed the contents of the crate all over the place by now.

Ramos crept up to that crate and reached out to lift the lid.

"Watch for booby-traps," Stone warned.

"Yes, sir."

Moving slower now, Ramos pressed his helmet to the crack between the lid and the crate and activated his helmet lamp to get a better look.

Alexander caught a glimpse of a group of metallic cylinders lying beside each other at the top of the crate. There didn't appear to be any wires running between the lid of the crate and those cylinders, so it hadn't been rigged to blow when opened.

Withdrawing, the MA lifted the lid and peered in again for a closer look.

Stone took a sharp breath. "Those are hypervelocity rounds. They're all wired together with detcord."

"It's a bomb, sir," Ramos confirmed.

"Whoever planted it had to have access to munitions storage on red deck," Alexander decided.

"Think you can disarm it?" Stone asked.

"I don't know. Let me take a look…"

"Careful."

"Yes, sir."

Alexander watched as Ramos removed the lid and scanned the contents of the crate. There was no timer, at least not one that they could see, but there was a comm band wired to the munitions.

"Looks like it's rigged for remote detonation," Ramos said. "I should be able to disable it by turning off the comm unit."

"Assuming the comm band isn't booby-trapped," Alexander said. "Hold on, Ramos." Turning to Stone he said, "We might be able to find out who the saboteur is if we leave that comm unit on."

"Time is critical here, Captain," Stone said. "We don't know when our saboteur is going to detonate."

"No, but we can't afford to detonate his bomb for him, either. And even if it's not rigged to blow, he could just plant another one later."

"We don't have time to inspect the comm unit's code and find out if it's rigged."

"Maybe, maybe not, but I have a better idea. What would you say the odds are that bomb was designed to destroy the *Lincoln?*"

"Slim to none, if the bomber knows something about the size of the payload he's working with."

"So if it goes off, what kind of damage are we looking at?"

"We'll lose most of our food stores to space, and those decks will be torn wide open, but that's about it."

"Then the bomber isn't looking to get himself killed. He probably just wants to turn this ship around and go home."

Stone blinked. "So…"

"So, let's get the crew together. We never did organize a proper funeral service for the pilots we lost."

Stone's eyebrows drew together in confusion. "Sir, I don't think this is the time to be discussing—"

Alexander held up a hand. "Let me stop you there, Lieutenant. I have a plan to catch our deviant crewman, but if it's going to work, we need everyone to be present. The funeral is a good excuse that won't tip anyone off."

"What are your orders, sir?" Ramos asked.

Alexander looked back to the feed. "Take that food crate to the amidships cargo-loading airlock and wait for us there."

"Too heavy for me to move it alone, sir."

"Get your squad mates to help," Alexander said.

"Aye-aye, Captain."

Lieutenant Stone muted the channel. "This plan of yours better not get more of our people killed."

"Danger is the spice of life, Lieutenant."

"Variety."

"I'm sorry?"

"Variety is the spice of life, sir."

"Well, I've never been very good with English idioms."

CHAPTER 7

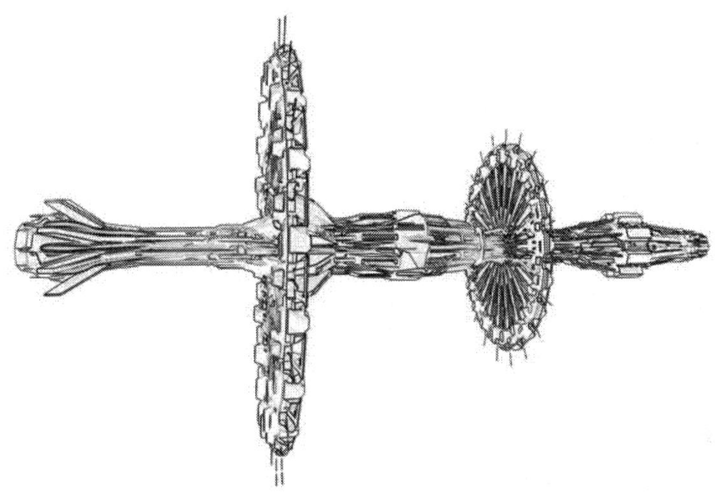

It was standing room only in the cargo bay at the amidships airlock—everyone except for Lieutenant Davorian was there. Since he had reported the bad engine code, Alexander had decided that he was probably above reproach, so Davorian was back on the bridge as the Officer of the Deck until Hayes and McAdams returned from the funeral.

Alexander stared dead ahead, through the thick palladium glass at the top of the inner airlock door. The symbolic casket sitting inside the airlock was actually the food crate they'd found rigged with a bomb. Alexander hoped the bomber would notice and start to get nervous, but so far he hadn't seen any adverse reactions from the crew.

Alexander stood beside the ship's chaplain as he read a passage from the Bible.

"Death has been swallowed up in victory. Where, O death, is your victory? Where, O death, is your sting?"

The chaplain went on reading, but Alexander tuned him out.

Being an agnostic, he found it ironic that even the chaplain had accepted gener treatments in exchange for his years of service with the navy. Alexander was pretty sure that constituted some kind of hypocrisy—preaching about immortality in the life to come, yet accepting it now in this one.

Hedging your bets? Alexander wondered.

Since the advent of medical immortality, the religions of the world had been relegated to promising life eternal to those who had yet to become immortal, and to those who were afraid they might still die of unnatural causes. If the current service was any indication, Alexander supposed that made some degree of sense. The chances of dying from unnatural causes over the course of an infinite lifespan were a hundred percent. Death was still a certainty, but not from old age.

Alexander scanned his crew, looking for someone who seemed particularly edgy. Time was ticking. With everyone here and suitably distracted, it was the perfect moment for the bomber to trigger his device, but if he was smart, he'd already recognized his bomb sitting in the airlock. The saboteur would know that detonating his bomb would actually kill the entire crew—himself included—*if* he was smart.

Alexander was counting on that. As soon as the chaplain finished reading, Alexander stepped up to a makeshift podium, saying, "Thank you, Chaplain. Now I'd like to share a few of my own words of comfort."

The chaplain looked bemused, but he nodded and stepped down.

Alexander surveyed his crew, studying each of their faces in turn. The ship's MAs were scattered around, guarding the entrances and exits, just in case the saboteur tried to make a run for it.

"Ladies and gentlemen, as far as I'm concerned we already

mourned our losses. I've actually brought you all here for another reason." Puzzlement flickered across several people's faces. Alexander smiled grimly and went on, "Less than an hour ago a bomb was discovered in the ship's food supply." People gasped. Faces paled. Crew traded looks of shock and betrayal. "Yes, I know—unconscionable. But don't worry, our food supply is safe. We've relocated the bomb to the amidships cargo airlock."

It took a moment for that to sink in, and then all eyes turned to the airlock they were standing next to. People began backing away. Murmurs of discontent filled the air.

Alexander made a *settle down* gesture with his hands. "There's no need to be alarmed! We brought the bomb here because one of you planted it, and we need that same person to step forward now so we can disable it without any loss of life."

"You brought a bomb here?" Max Carter demanded, pointing an accusing finger at Alexander. "Are you out of your mind?"

"Yes, I am, Max. Now, unless you have something to confess to, please keep quiet so the bomber can speak up."

The ambassador's eyes flashed. "Let us out of here right now, Captain!"

"Can't do that, sorry."

Commander Korbin spoke up next. "What are you waiting for? Just blow it out the airlock!"

"We could, but then we'd never find out who our bomber is, and he or she might just find a deadlier way to sabotage this ship at some later date."

"He could also blow all of us up, right here and now!" Korbin insisted.

"True, but if that was the bomber's intention, then the bomb should have been planted on Red Deck with the ship's munitions, or next to the fusion reactor. Since this bomb was planted with the ship's food stores, we believe the intention was to make us turn around, not to destroy the ship or cause any harm to its crew."

"You're willing to stake all of our lives on that?" Max demanded.

"Yes, I am. In fact, I'll bet that whoever planted this bomb will rather confess than allow it to go off and kill us all."

"That's a court-martial and a summary execution," Korbin said. "Where's the incentive to confess?"

"Good point, Commander. Tell you what, I promise I won't execute the saboteur," Alexander said, placing a hand over his chest and another one in the air, as if he were about to give sworn testimony. "I'll also make sure that they never see a court-martial." Alexander searched the room, but no one spoke up. Everyone was busy looking at one another accusingly. Promised leniency notwithstanding, the saboteur was still better off to disown his handiwork and keep his lips zipped.

Time to up the ante.

"All right. Let's do something," Alexander said, stepping down from the podium and striding toward the airlock. He snapped his fingers at the nearest MA. "You, Ramos, open the door."

"Sir?"

"You heard me. Open sesame."

"Yes, sir..." The security officer opened the airlock with a *hiss* of equalizing pressure and an accompanying *whoosh* of wind as the heavy door slid aside.

Alexander walked in, right up to the rigged crate. "This bomb is a bunch of jury-rigged munitions from Red Deck. That gives us some idea about who it might be. We found some other clues, too. Turns out the bomb has a remote detonator. It's wired to a comm band. So all it'll take is a whisper from our secret friend, and *boom*—we all get to see first-hand what the chaplain has spent his life preaching about.

"Naturally, we should have disarmed it on the spot, but just prior to discovering the bomb, we found signs of sabotage in the ship's engine code. That means that our saboteur knows how to use a computer, so he may have also tampered with the comm band's code and rigged it to blow the bomb if we try to disarm it. That's just a guess, mind you. We don't know for sure." Alexander went down on his haunches beside the crate. "I suppose there's an easy way to find out. Any bets it's rigged?" Alexander reached for the crate's lid and removed it, revealing the bomb inside.

The murmurs of discontent were back and growing louder by the second. Suddenly Max Carter stepped forward. "That's enough! It was me. I did it. Now stop this nonsense before you get us all killed."

"Really? You know how to tamper with the ship's engine code and rig a bomb using hypervelocity rounds and a comm band? How did you get access to Red Deck? Or the engine code? Or even to the storage levels where we found the food crate? You have a civilian clearance on this ship. That means you're barely authorized to wipe your own ass."

Max sneered. "I'll explain how later, Captain. You have your confession. Don't be stupid. Arrest me."

"I would love to, but there's just one problem, Max… I don't believe a word you said."

The ambassador's eyes widened, and he looked genuinely scared. "I said *enough*, Captain!"

"Sorry, I'm not done yet. Anyone else? Last chance before I pull the plug on this thing." Alexander scanned the crew one more time. No one else said a word. Alexander shrugged. "Fine. Have it your way." He looked up to the chaplain. The man looked paler than Frosty the snowman. "Say a prayer for us, minister." Alexander reached into the crate and lifted the comm band from the bomb assembly. It was trailing wires and detcord. "Red or blue? Hmmmm… Well, I'm no expert, so I guess I'll just have to cut them all…"

"Wait!" the voice was shrill, but not feminine. Alexander turned, and so did everyone else. Alexander couldn't believe who it was.

"Williams? Why?" Alexander asked, feeling genuinely confused. Then again it made sense, as the ship's quartermaster and a member of the bridge crew, he had all the clearance he needed to do just about anything.

Problem was, Alexander had known Williams for years, and sabotage was the last thing he would have expected from the man.

Williams looked stricken, and his entire body was trembling. "If you disconnect that, it'll kill us all. I'm going to hold you to your word, Captain. No court-martial. No execution."

Alexander returned the detonator to the crate and rose to his feet. "I'm a man of my word, Lieutenant, but there will still be consequences."

"I understand."

"Stone, arrest Lieutenant Williams and take him to the brig. Commander Korbin please accompany them and speak with the prisoner. See if you can establish a motive for this insanity."

"Yes, sir," Korbin said.

"What about the motive for your insanity, Captain?" Max asked. The diplomat's normally equanimous face had flushed red with fury. "You may have promised amnesty to this criminal—however illegal that might be—but no one's promised you anything yet. Give me one good reason why I shouldn't have you arrested and court-martialed."

Alexander smiled. "All right." He dropped to his haunches beside the crate once more and lifted the detonator.

"Captain!" Williams screamed.

"Stop him!" Max roared.

People screamed and dived for cover, and Ramos lunged toward him, but he wasn't fast enough. Alexander ripped the comm band free, and held it out to the crew. *"Boom,"* he said.

CHAPTER 8

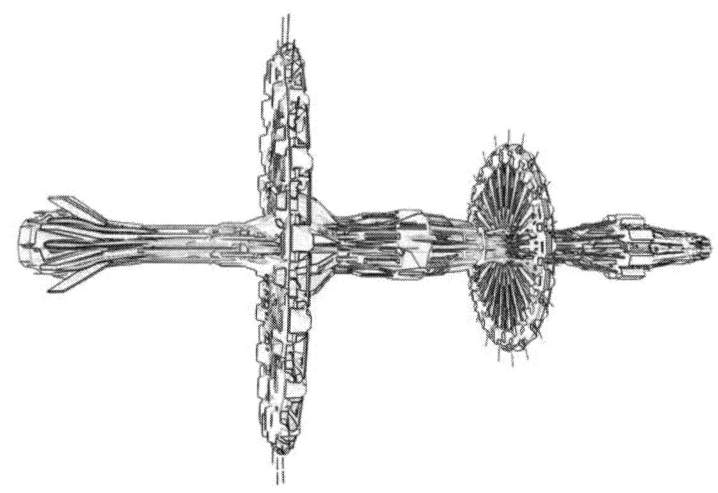

*"**B**oom?"* Lieutenant Williams echoed, incredulous.

Alexander nodded. "You thought it was real. That's why you confessed. Only the one who planted this bomb knew for sure that it was rigged to blow with tampering, so threatening to disarm it was a good way to get you to confess. Assuming that your real goal wasn't actually to kill everyone on this ship, that is."

Williams shook his head. "I don't understand. It *should* have blown."

"Disappointed?"

"No, sir!"

"You took a big risk disarming that bomb here with all of us in the blast radius, Captain!" Max Carter said. "Arrest him!" Max snapped his fingers at the nearest MA, Petty Officer Ramos, but Ramos made no move to obey the order.

"I'm afraid he's right, Captain," Commander Korbin said.

Alexander frowned. "You don't really think I'd subject my

entire crew to that kind of risk, do you? We jettisoned the real bomb out the airlock before any of you arrived." Alexander regarded the ambassador once more. "This one is just a fake that we put together to make you wet your pants, Max."

Alexander didn't think the ambassador's face could get any redder, but he turned a nice shade of lobster with that retort. *If looks could kill…*

"You tricked me," Williams said.

"You sabotaged my ship," Alexander replied, aiming a finger at the man's chest. "We're not even close to even yet. Why'd you do it?" Williams' lower lip trembled, but he said nothing. "Never mind. Tell it to Korbin. Get him out of here, Stone."

"Yes, sir."

"The rest of you, back to your stations."

A collective sigh rose from the cargo bay as people filed for the exits. Alexander lingered, frowning as he watched Williams being escorted away with his hands cuffed behind his back.

Commander Korbin came to stand beside him and blew out a breath. "Williams, a saboteur," she said, shaking her head. "I didn't see that coming."

"Neither did I."

"He's a romantic at heart. Usually romantics are peaceful souls."

"Or tortured ones," Alexander suggested.

"He has a wife and daughter back on Earth. Why would he risk a court-martial?"

"Maybe he thinks they're dead, or he's just desperate to turn the ship around and find out what happened to them. Go talk to him. See if you can get a full confession. When you're done I want you to schedule one-on-one's with all the rest of the crew. We need to make sure we don't have any more saboteurs on board."

"What are the odds of that?" Korbin asked, frowning.

Alexander arched an eyebrow at her. "You wanted to turn around and go home before we even entered the Looking Glass, even though that would have meant disobeying a direct order."

"Are you accusing me of something, sir?"

"No, but if even *you* wanted to turn the ship around, and Williams was willing to resort to sabotage, chances are there are plenty of others who aren't happy about leaving Earth behind. Besides, we still have one act of sabotage that's unaccounted for."

"And that is?"

"The bad engine code that almost stopped us cold before we even left Earth's orbit."

Korbin's brow furrowed. "I really doubt we have two saboteurs on board. It must have been Williams. Either that or it was an honest mistake between McAdams and her engineers."

Alexander held Korbin's gaze for a long moment. "Like I said, go talk to Williams and see if you can get a confession. If he didn't touch the engine code, then we need to find out who did before we end up stranded on Wonderland with them."

"Yes, sir." Korbin saluted and hurried off.

Alexander watched her go, thinking to himself that all of this was a bad omen. The start of World War III followed by two counts of shipboard sabotage made for an inauspicious start to their mission.

Hopefully, once their comm probe made contact with Earth there'd be good news.

* * *

"Message incoming, Captain."

"On-screen, Lieutenant Hayes."

An image appeared, full of snow and glitching distortion. The image stabilized and a familiar face appeared. It was President Ryan Baker of the Alliance. He appeared to be sitting in his office in the presidential palace, which was a good sign, but he looked grim and haggard, as if he hadn't slept in days.

"Hello, Captain de Leon. I'm glad to hear that you and your crew are already well on their way. Due to the risk of the enemy intercepting this transmission I'll keep it short. In response to your requested update on Earth's situation, I am happy to inform you that the conflict was amicably resolved and a global catastrophe avoided." President Baker smiled, but Alexander noted that the smile didn't reach Baker's eyes.

"With respect to your mission, everything remains the same. Your messages to your loved ones will be forwarded as requested, but unfortunately we cannot get their messages to you until you either arrive at or return from your destination, due to the aforementioned risks of interception for longer messages. Also for that reason, this must be our last contact until then. Don't reply to this message unless it is an emergency. Also, be advised that the *Looking Glass* is back under Alliance control, but in case that changes, keep watch for enemy probes and warships following you through. Good luck, *Lincoln,* and rest assured that your loved ones are all safe and well." President Baker saluted and smiled another half-smile.

The transmission ended and Alexander shifted nervously in his acceleration couch. "That was vague," he muttered.

"Should we reply with an update on our situation, sir?" Hayes asked from the comms station.

"The president said not to reply."

"Unless it's an emergency. Sabotage would qualify as an emergency, sir."

"We caught the saboteur, and nothing happened. Besides,

what are they going to do, turn us around so that the saboteur gets his way? Let's keep it to ourselves for now."

"Yes, sir."

Alexander didn't mention the possibility of there being *two* saboteurs, which if true, would constitute an ongoing emergency. "I'm going to the brig to see what progress has been made with Williams. You have the conn until I get back, Hayes."

"Yes, sir," Hayes replied as Alexander used the rails on his armrests to lift himself out of his couch. He glanced at the back of McAdams' head as he did so, his eyes narrowing thoughtfully. She was busy performing systems checks and updates as ordered, but none of those updates would be applied until they were thoroughly reviewed by himself and Lieutenant Davorian. If she or one of her engineers had sabotaged the engine code and they planned to do it again now, then they were about to get caught.

Alexander swung backward and landed on the deck behind his couch. Turning on his heel, he headed for the elevators and gestured for the nearest one to open. Once inside, he selected the button near the top of the panel, the one labeled *Brig (59)*. It was a small and often-ignored deck right behind the forward airlock on level 60. Under normal circumstances it wasn't supposed to be an active-duty deck, but circumstances were far from normal.

As the elevator shot up from level 10 to 59, Alexander steeled himself to face Lieutenant Williams once more. He was still furious with his sensors operator. He had yet to select Williams' replacement from the ship's enlisted personnel. Whoever he chose, they were bound to be under-qualified at best, and incompetent at worst. Williams had also been the ship's quartermaster and meteorologist, and replacing all of those roles was not going to be easy. The logical choice was to promote Williams' apprentice and emergency reserve, Chief Petty Officer

Vasquez—assuming Vasquez didn't know about and had nothing to do with the sabotage.

"What a mess," Alexander sighed as the elevator doors slid open and he stepped out onto the brig. He walked up to the security doors and nodded to the pair of MAs standing there. One of the two opened the door for him, and then Alexander walked through and stopped before a second door. The first door slid shut and then a green light came on above the second one and it slid open.

In the observation room on the other side he encountered Commander Korbin and Lieutenant Stone both standing in front of a one-way mirror, watching Lieutenant Williams through the glass. Williams sat in a brightly-lit interrogation room with nothing but two chairs, a table, and the beady red eye of a mobile security camera watching him from the ceiling. The sensor operator's shoulders were hunched and his head was bowed, studying his hands.

"Report, Commander," Alexander said as he approached.

Both officers turned and saluted before Korbin spoke. "Sir, Williams has confessed to everything except tampering with the engine code."

"I see. Go on."

"He insists he didn't want anyone to get hurt and that compromising the ship's engines like that would have resulted in injuries."

Stone snorted. "And planting a bomb wouldn't?"

Korbin's gaze darted sideways to Lieutenant Stone and she nodded. "I agree. It's a poor excuse."

"What about the bomb? Did he explain how he did it?"

"He claims that he sabotaged that food crate while we were all in the officer's lounge."

Stone began nodding. "While we were busy mourning our

losses he was taking advantage of our absence to compromise the mission. We should jettison him out the nearest airlock like the piece of garbage he is. One less mouth to feed."

Alexander gave Stone a hard look. "I promised no executions. I'm going to stand by that, Lieutenant."

"Yes, sir."

"What do the security cameras show?"

"There was a global systems malfunction at the time that Williams was supposed to be on the bridge. He admits to disabling the cameras," Stone replied.

Alexander shook his head. "He had to know he'd get caught. Why go to all that trouble? We've all known Williams a long time. He's not that stupid."

"Stupid, no, but desperate maybe," Korbin said. "When his wife said goodbye to him on Earth, she announced that she was leaving him for her lover. His three-year-old daughter probably wouldn't even remember him by the time he got back, and the new husband would have become her father. Williams couldn't stand the idea of his wife *and* daughter moving on without him, and he felt like he had nothing left to lose."

Alexander studied Williams through the one-way glass. He could sympathize with some of that, but not to the point of wanting to sabotage his own ship. "Why try to get back to Earth if he'd already lost everything there? He had to know he might be executed for his crime. What could he possibly gain from that?"

Korbin shrugged. "Like you, he was near the end of his term of service when he was assigned to Operation Alice. He saw the Alliance and the fleet as responsible for him losing his family. Sabotaging the ship wasn't just a way for him to return home early, it was about revenge."

Alexander sighed. "Well, I suppose that adds up. All right,

Stone, lock him up and keep a guard posted. We don't want him getting out, or someone *letting* him out. Until we have proof of who was responsible for the engines malfunction, we can't entirely rule out the possibility of there being another saboteur aboard."

"Yes, sir."

"Keep that to yourselves for now—and Korbin, start interviewing the rest of the crew for possible suspects. I'm sure Williams isn't the only one harboring feelings of resentment and latent aggression toward the Alliance because of this mission. You've got a little less than twenty-four hours before we're supposed to enter the G-tanks, so I suggest you get started."

"That's not enough time to interview everyone, even if I work around the clock."

"You have an assistant. Use him. If you both schedule half-hour appointments and only sleep for six hours you should have enough time."

"Yes, sir," Korbin replied.

"Let me know when it's my turn to be interviewed. Until then, if either of you need me, I'll be on the bridge."

"You don't want to speak with Williams before you go, sir?" Stone asked.

Alexander looked into the brightly-lit interrogation room one last time. Williams was still staring at his hands. Alexander grimaced. "No, I'm afraid I won't be able to control myself if I go in there right now," he said. "Lock him up."

"Yes, sir," Stone replied, heading for the interrogation room.

Alexander nodded to Korbin and turned to leave. The truth was, he didn't want to see Williams because he was afraid he might end up sympathizing too much with him. Admiral Flores had made a big mistake ensuring that everyone assigned to the *Lincoln* had strong emotional ties to Earth. No one wanted to be here. Especially not now that they knew how long they'd be gone, and that Earth's fate was uncertain. President Baker's insistence that their loved ones were all *safe and well* just made Alexander more suspicious.

What else could the president say? That they were all dead? That would undermine the crew's morale and their motivation to come home. Even if Earth was a radioactive ball of ash, no one aboard the *Lincoln* could be allowed to know that until they returned home.

Alexander shut his eyes as he rode the elevator back down to the bridge, and prayed to a god he'd long since stopped believing in that Caty was among the survivors.

CHAPTER 9

Los Angeles, Eight Hours Earlier

Catalina sat glued to her holoscreen, watching a breaking news story on WANN (World Alliance News Network). A trio of WANN reporters came on, all of them sitting before a table, looking pale and stricken. The woman in the middle of the three spoke first, "We have a very tragic alert for you right now. Live footage of the World Alliance Space Elevator collapsing in what's believed—speculation at this point—to be a Confederate sneak attack in orbit."

The scene cut to show cottony white streaks of cloud against an electric blue sky. A large black cylinder was speeding down, wreathed in a blanket of orange flame. The camera zoomed in on the falling object until it snapped into focus. It was a climber car from the Alliance's Space Elevator. The elevator ribbon was a tangled mess of glinting silver bunching up below the car as it fell.

In the background the woman from WANN went on describing the situation, but Caty tuned her out. She didn't need anyone to explain what was happening.

The feed zoomed out and panned down to show the elevator ribbon hitting Anchor Station at high speed, striking sparks from the deck. The ribbon was light, so there wasn't a lot of damage. The rest of it came crashing down in the ocean, and water splashed up in a snaking line. The camera tracked that line, revealing that the cameraman was standing on the deck of a civilian supply ship a few kilometers away from Anchor Station.

The camera tracked up to find the falling elevator car once more. It was moving at a wicked speed, heading for the ocean, just a few seconds from impact. Caty heard people screaming in the background of the recording. The camera bobbed and weaved as whoever was holding it ran for higher ground.

BOOM!

The elevator car hit with a sound like a thousand thunderclaps. Water roared with deafening fury as it sprayed up in a cone-shaped plume of vapor and liquid tall as any skyscraper. More screaming. The camera shook urgently as the person holding it ran to get away. Then the shock wave hit, and the camera went flying amidst a violent stream of mist and spray. Just before the feed cut out, Caty glimpsed people tumbling over the side of the ship, screaming as they fell.

The scene cut to a second camera, this one much farther out. From a distance the shock wave looked like a savage storm, a living thing racing across the surface of the ocean, spreading fast in all directions. In all of a second that storm wall hit, *roaring* and buffeting the camera with gale force winds. A blurry curtain of spray blotted out the camera. The wind died down, and Caty heard the man cursing about how wet he was as he wiped the lens with his shirt.

The holo feed came clear once more, showing a thick white mist all around. It was suddenly dark, and the blue sky was gray. Nearby ships lay blanketed in mist, disappearing wraith-like into the distance.

A black wall of water came raging out of the mist, lifting and capsizing all of those ships in an instant. The cameraman cursed again, and ran for a nearby ladder. He looped an arm through the rungs and went back to recording. People screamed and cried in the background as the wave approached.

The cameraman's vessel lurched suddenly, turning so it could face the wave head-on. Now the cameraman was alternating between curses and prayers, rambling nonsensically to himself. The wall of water loomed, blotting out the sky. Then it hit, and the ship tipped up suddenly.

The sky was back, then gone again as the ship rode down the back of the wave. The cameraman screamed. It was an impossibly long way down, and the ship was racing too fast into the trough behind the wave.

The bow hit and dug in. The cameraman lost his grip on the ladder and fell screaming. A tremendous screech of metal drowned out his screams as the ship cracked apart. Black, foaming water and jagged debris swallowed everything in a burst of static.

Back were the trio of WANN reporters.

They looked like Caty felt. The woman's mouth hung open, as if she'd been about to say something, but the footage had left her unable to speak. One of her colleagues broke the silence, "We've just received confirmation, Orbital One has been cut free of its tether in a Confederate surprise attack. If you are anywhere near a major city center, you are advised to get to the nearest fallout shelter immediately."

Caty heard something then, and she sat suddenly straight in her chair. The news reporters droned on about emergency procedures, but she wasn't listening anymore. She muted the holoscreen with a wave of her hand, and suddenly the sound snapped into clearer focus.

It was a siren. Caty recognized the sound from the Alliance's last civil defense drill.

Heart pounding, Caty ran from her living room and out the front door of her home. Her palms were cold and sweating. This couldn't be happening. She reached the front lawn and looked up to the night's sky just in time to see hundreds of bullet-shaped objects falling, wreathed in orange fire. *Missiles.* As she watched they blossomed like fireworks, splitting into *thousands,* of smaller warheads that spiraled and streaked toward the bright urban center of Los Angeles.

Caty stood frozen with terror and morbid fascination, watching the missiles rain down. Bright blue laser beams snapped up from the city below, detonating countless hundreds of missiles before they could hit the ground. The explosions dazzled her eyes, mesmerizing her.

Those premature detonations weren't nuclear blasts, but the remaining missiles were just seconds from impact, and they weren't likely to be so small. An electric jolt of adrenaline spurred her into motion.

Caty ran back inside the house, flying down the stairs to the basement and jumping the last five steps to the ground. Her shoulder slammed painfully into the heavy steel door. She wrenched it open, and musty air gushed out. A light flickered on and she hurried in, slamming the door behind her and turning the handle to lock it. She leaned back against the door, gasping greedy lungfuls of the musty air.

The civil defense sirens droned on in the distance, now muffled by the heavy door. Then, suddenly the sirens were drowned out by a terrifying *roar*. It sounded like an old-fashioned train was barreling down on her. The sound reached a deafening pitch, and then Caty heard wooden beams creaking and snapping overhead. Heavy *thuds* shook the basement as debris crashed and fell. A loud *bang* thundered against the door with such force that the impact felt like a fist between her shoulder blades. Caty jumped away from the door and turned to look at it, her eyes wide and staring, as if she expected a monster to come crashing in at any moment.

A stampede raged in her living room. Dust trickled down from the concrete ceiling in a steady stream. The overhead lights flickered out and came back on, now dimmer than before, and running on battery backups. Caty's legs shook like a newborn calf's and gave out suddenly. She hit the ground with a jolt and sat with her palms pressed to the cold cement floor, listening as debris settled overhead.

After a few minutes, the noise gave way to a ringing silence. Then the air grew uncomfortably warm, and Caty realized that what was left of her home was probably burning. The basement was insulated and air-tight, so she wouldn't suffocate, but given how fast she felt the temperature rising, she might still cook like a lobster in its shell.

Waves of heat poured down from the ceiling. Panic gripped her. Caty stood on shaking legs and walked past row upon row of canned food and bottled water to start up the basement's hydrogen fuel cell. It was at the back of the shelter, right beside the bathroom. Caty flicked a simple mechanical on/off switch, and the fuel cell started up with a quiet *hum* of electricity. That done, she configured a control panel on the wall beside it and activated the basement's climate control system. The thermostat read 90 degrees… 91 degrees…

No wonder she was so hot!

Fumbling with the controls, she set the system to *power cool,* and selected an unlikely target of 65 degrees. A welcome *whoosh* of cool air came rushing out through overhead ducts. Caty breathed a sigh of relief and went to stand under the nearest vent, letting the air wash over her face and dry her sweat.

As she stood there, she mentally took stock of her situation. From what Alexander had explained about the shelter's life support systems, the air was all recycled, not circulating in from outside, so there was no threat of radiation creeping in through the vents. As for the heat exchanger responsible for the cool air, it was heat-sinked through an underground tank of water that supplied the shelter's bathroom, so the system's cooling capacity would likely outlast any firestorms raging overhead. She probably wouldn't want to take a shower until the tank cooled down, but otherwise she'd be fine.

Caty looked around the basement. Food, water, and liquid hydrogen for the generator lined the walls. The supplies would last for a month, but without Alexander to share them, she could stretch that to two. With rationing maybe two and a half. She wouldn't be able to run the generator constantly, but since the main power draw was from the heat exchanger, she could afford to turn the generator off just as soon as the fires died down outside. The lights would stay on for days running on battery backups before she'd have to turn the generator on and charge the batteries. The refrigerator was another matter; it would run the batteries down in an hour or less, so she'd have to turn it off and keep it shut whenever the generator wasn't running.

Two and a half months. Radiation would be down to survivable levels by then. Assuming the basement door wasn't completely blocked with debris, she would be able to get out and go find help. If there was any help to be found…

Caty's mind flashed back to the swarm of missiles raining down over Los Angeles. She saw the city's defenses flashing up, bright blue beams slashing the sky open and turning incoming missiles to molten clouds of debris. She hadn't stuck around to see the remaining warheads get through, but it wasn't hard to imagine what had happened next. That blinding flash of nuclear fire had haunted humanity's collective nightmares for centuries. *That's what this is—* Caty thought with a sudden desperate hope *—a nightmare.* She squeezed her eyelids shut, willing herself to wake up.

But when she opened her eyes once more, she wasn't lying in bed, waking up from a bad dream; she was standing in her basement, alone, and facing months of isolation while waiting for a rescue that might never come.

Nuclear war. How many other cities had been hit? For all she knew the entire planet was one big smoldering cairn, and her two and a half months of emergency supplies were all she would ever get.

Caty's thoughts went to Alexander, and she wondered if he'd already died in the fighting. Her eyes grew hot and blurry. Fat teardrops slid like burning embers down her cheeks.

You left me, Alex. You promised you were coming back. Liar! I told you not to make promises you can't keep. Caty shook her head and sank to the ground, watching her teardrops make a puddle on the concrete. She dragged her finger through it, using her tears to mop the dusty floor.

Dust to dust... she thought, smiling bitterly. *I guess that's all that's left now.*

CHAPTER 10

"Good luck, *Lincoln,* and rest assured that your loved ones are all safe and well." President Ryan Baker saluted the camera and smiled. The red recording light of the holo camera winked off, and the cameraman gave him a thumbs-up before carrying the camera and its attached tripod out of the office.

Fleet Admiral Wilson nodded to him from the far corner of the room. "That should satisfy their curiosity about Earth, sir. It should come as a relief."

"Yes, that's the good thing about lies. They can be a great comfort if you believe them. I'm just not sure they will."

"We couldn't tell them the truth without putting their mission in jeopardy, and their mission is more vital now than ever."

Baker frowned and glanced behind him in time to see the holoscreen behind his chair fade from a pre-recorded view of his office in the presidential palace to a blank screen with a concrete wall behind it. The presidential palace was long gone, a pile of rubble lying hundreds of feet above their heads. Baker turned back to Wilson. "That all depends if the cease fire lasts long enough for them to return."

"The Confederacy is hurting just as much as we are. Maybe

more, and with dozens of cities all around the world reduced to radioactive ash, I don't think anyone would be stupid enough to launch a second strike."

Baker sighed and shook his head. "If we were stupid enough to launch the first, we could be stupid enough to launch the second, and now that the genie is out of the bottle, it's a lot easier to contemplate a nuclear strike than it was before."

"Then we'll need somewhere to go after the dust settles," Wilson replied. "Wonderland sounds like a good fit to me."

Baker blinked twice before he remembered to smile and nod. For a moment he'd forgotten that Admiral Wilson didn't know. The truth about Operation Alice had died with Lewis Station's crew when their lifeboat was taken out by shrapnel. That was probably for the best. The fewer people who knew about Operation Alice, the better.

"We should go. We're late for a meeting with the Joint Chiefs of Staff."

"After you, Mr. President," Wilson said, gesturing to the door.

* * *

"Cutting things a bit fine, aren't you, Commander?" Alexander asked as he sat down in the chair facing his XO.

Korbin shook her head and covered a yawn with one hand. "You're my last interview before we hit the tanks, sir."

"Good. Why don't you give me the rundown."

"Lots of fear and uncertainty over the situation back on Earth. Most people aren't buying the president's reassurances. Not a lot of signs of aggression directed at the Alliance, but plenty against the Confederacy. There's also early signs of depression in at least half of the crew."

Alexander nodded. "What did you think of McAdams?"

"Sad, angry—guilty for not noticing the engine malfunction."

Alexander nodded. She was becoming less and less likely as a suspect. He and Davorian had already looked over McAdams' proposed updates to shipboard systems after she and her engineers finished their shift, and there was nothing amiss this time around.

"She gave me no reason to suspect she knew about the bad code."

"Well, let's hope it was plain oversight on her part and not collusion."

Korbin nodded. "She's young and inexperienced, particularly to be a ship's chief engineer, so oversight makes sense."

"All right, then who was responsible for the faulty code?"

"The engineers were all equally aghast when I interviewed them. One of them admitted to being in charge of that section of the code, but he's adamant that it wasn't his fault."

"So all signs point to Williams."

"I do think he was lying about his involvement."

"But you can't be sure."

"No, not without a confession."

"You're a deception expert."

"It's an art not a science. But speaking of that art, there was one other thing I noticed. You know that all of the meetings in my office are recorded."

Alexander nodded.

"When I was going back over the recordings to see if the surveillance system picked up on anything that I'd missed, I noticed that the ambassador's interview was flagged with multiple counts of possible deception and masking."

"You think *he* sabotaged the ship?"

"No... not exactly. We were talking about Wonderland and the ambassador's role with the mission when the cameras flagged his deceptive behavior." Korbin looked down at a holopad she was holding. "Behaviors flagged were looking to the right—lying and fabricating; scratching his nose while talking—same thing; excessive eye contact—dishonesty or honesty, depending—but given the previous two cues I'd guess the former. There were also plenty of tight-lipped smiles, clenched teeth, crossed arms, hesitation when answering questions... it all agrees. He's hiding something about his role with the mission, Captain."

Alexander snorted. "That covers a lot of ground. He's the president's direct representative, and a *politician,* so I'm sure he has plenty to hide. As for his reasons for being here, I never bought that line about first contact. If aliens built the wormhole we're busy traveling through, we wouldn't be the ones making first contact—they would."

Commander Korbin tilted her head to one side and raised her eyebrows. "Aliens? That's the official reason he's here?"

"He didn't tell you?"

Korbin shook her head.

"Then maybe that's what he was hiding. Admiral Flores discussed the possibility with me on Orbital One before I came aboard. That's supposedly why he's here. To represent our government in case we run into any intelligent lifeforms on the other side of the wormhole."

"Interesting. He said he was about to retire and he requested this assignment so that he could observe and document the trip."

"And you believed that?"

"There's a lot of people back on Earth who would have jumped at the chance, but none of them have the necessary security clearance. It seemed plausible."

Alexander snorted. "More plausible than aliens, anyway."

"Do you want me to speak with the ambassador again?"

Alexander stroked his chin as he thought about it. "There's no time. We have to be in the *G*-tanks in less than an hour. And besides, my guess is Max didn't become plenipotentiary to the Alliance by spilling state secrets right and left. You're not going to get anything out of him besides what he's willing to share. We'll keep an eye on him just in case, and you can schedule another meeting with him when we get to Wonderland. Meanwhile, he can't get into much trouble while he's sleeping in a *G*-tank."

"Yes, sir." Korbin checked her comm band. "We have fifteen minutes left. You ready for your interview?"

Alexander shrugged. "Do we have to?"

"You're the captain of the ship. Our lives are all in your hands more than anyone else's. You need to watch your mental health—especially now, with everything that's happened."

"What about you?"

"Me, sir?"

"You've spent the past day listening to everyone unburden themselves on you. By now you must be ready to explode."

Korbin folded her hands on top of her holopad, fingers steepled and pointed toward him. "I'm trained to deal with the burden, Captain."

"That's defensive body language," Alexander said, nodding to her hands. "You're creating a barrier."

Korbin looked down at her hands and then relaxed her posture. "Your point?"

"You're not the only one who can read people, and I know that you've been worried sick about your kids."

"Everyone's worried about their loved ones, Captain."

"But they all have someone to talk to—you. So who do you

talk to?"

Korbin started to say something but then stopped herself, as if there was nothing she could say.

"Exactly," Alexander said. "You can talk to me, you know."

"All right, then let's interview each other. We'll take turns."

Alexander nodded. "Fair enough."

Those fifteen minutes went by quickly. By the end of the meeting Korbin was crying and Alexander ended up giving her a hug. "Come talk to me any time you need to, Sirena, and don't give up hope. Your kids are in a first-rate government institution. Even assuming the worst, that school will have one of the best-equipped shelters in the city."

Korbin nodded against his shoulder. "Thank you, Alex."

"Don't mention it," he said, smiling as they withdrew. "Go clean yourself up and meet the rest of us on Blue Deck. Doc Crespin must be waiting for us by now."

"You think it's safe? Putting us in a coma for seventy days?"

"I don't think any of this is safe, but what choice do we have?"

"It's strange," Korbin said, brushing a stray lock of brown hair behind one ear. "In all those interviews, no one talked about how dangerous this mission is, about how we might all die or never come back. We're all too busy worrying about the people back home."

Alexander nodded. "Maybe that's a good thing. See you on Blue Deck, Commander."

"See you there, Captain."

CHAPTER 11

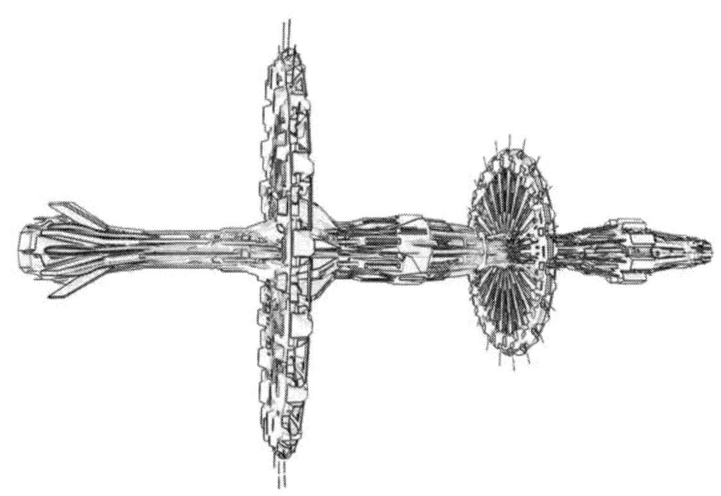

Alexander stood on level nine in a circular chamber, surrounded by all 57 of his surviving crew. Numbered doors ran around the edges of the room, each one leading to a separate G-tank. The tanks had been installed specially for *Operation Alice.* The crew already had experience using them from their mission training, but back then they hadn't known what the tanks were for.

Now Doctor Crespin settled the mystery for them by going over the basic functions of the tanks. The doctor explained that the fluid inside the tanks was set to carefully mimic the density and temperature of their bodies. Their lungs would be flooded with an oxygen-rich perfluorocarbon and breathing handled by a liquid ventilator. There were relief tubes for waste handling, and a nutrient line for food and water—just like the ship's acceleration couches.

Doctor Crespin compared it to being a baby in its mother's womb, the relief tubes and nutrient line made up the umbilical cord, and the tanks were the wombs.

Someone asked how the tanks worked, and Crespin explained that any extreme forces their bodies might be subjected to while traveling through the wormhole would be evenly distributed as a pressure gradient inside the tank. Crespin went into some technical details about how liquids aren't compressible so the water would push back and prevent blood from pooling. It all sounded reasonable enough, and Doctor Crespin assured them it was quite safe and really no different than deep sea diving.

"What about muscle atrophy?" someone asked. Alexander turned to see that the question had come from Lieutenant Ryder of 61st Squadron. He had plenty of muscles to worry about atrophying.

"Hormone regulation and involuntary stimulation will help to maintain the majority of muscle tone and strength, but without active loading, some atrophy is to be expected. Don't worry, the gym will still be waiting for you when you get out." A few of the crew snickered at that. "Any other questions?"

"What if something happens to the ship while we're in the tanks?" Max Carter asked. "No one is going to be awake to keep an eye on things?"

Doctor Crespin shook his head. "If anyone could safely avoid using the tanks, then all of us could."

"But what if there's an emergency?"

"Such as?"

"Anything. Engine failure."

"Then we're going to be locked in the tanks a lot longer than we thought. The system is only set to wake us when it's safe, and that will be when we're almost already through the wormhole."

"How long can our life support last?" McAdams asked.

"The tanks can keep us going for decades, so even in the

worst case, we should still make it to Wonderland."

Alexander frowned. *Worst case being we all lose a few extra decades of our lives?*

"Are there any other questions?"

A chorus of *No, sirs,* and head shakes went around the room.

"All right then. I've sent your tank assignments to your comm bands—and no switching please. I don't care what your lucky number is. I've already pre-configured the tanks to meet each of your individual needs, and if you pick the wrong one you're either going to starve to death or wake up a lot fatter than you remember. Once you find your tank, please strip and store your personal belongings in the locker beside it and then wait for me or one of the nurses to assist you."

Alexander checked his comm band and found that his tank was number 23. He walked up to it, noting as he did so that the saboteur, Lieutenant Williams, was being escorted to his tank by Lieutenants Stone and Ryder. There was no need to make special provisions inside Williams' tank. Between the medically-induced coma and the tank's auto-locking door, there was no way Williams would be able to get out. Alexander wasn't sure he liked the idea that the G-tanks could double as prison cells, but at least he wouldn't be aware of his confinement.

As Alexander stripped out of his pressure suit and uniform, his hand brushed the pocket where he kept Caty's farewell gift to him. He reached in and withdrew the pocket watch, running his thumbs over the engravings and reading them once more. Then he depressed the catch and stared at the photograph of him and Caty on the inside of the cover. He studied her face, burning her features into his mind. If he was going to have any dreams while he was in a coma, he wanted them to be of her.

As an afterthought, Alexander read the time and date on the watch—just in case something went wrong and he ended up waking up after *years* rather than months. The hands of the watch pointed to one and two—*1:10*—and the date read *Mar|9|90*. Alexander marked the date and time on the calendar in his comm band, then he counted 70 days ahead. If everything went according to plan he'd be waking up in the Wonderland System on May 18th, 2790—although, from Earth's perspective more than a year would have passed.

Alexander shut the watch and finished undressing. He wrapped his comm band and pocket watch inside his uniform and pressure suit for padding and then stuffed the bulky bundle into the middle compartment of his locker. He clipped his helmet to the rack above that, and then stowed his gloves and boots at the bottom.

Now completely naked, Alexander stood hugging his shoulders and shivering as he waited for Doctor Crespin to assist him. Peripherally, Alexander noted that Seth Ryder was standing to one side of him, and McAdams to the other. Alexander deliberately kept his eyes glued to the hatch in front of him, but he noticed that Ryder was taking full advantage of the situation to ogle the female members of the crew.

Alexander shook his head, and called out, "Eyes to the fore, people."

Ryder shot him a grin. "We're all adults here, Captain."

"Most of us, anyway," Alexander muttered, sending the CAG a narrow-eyed look.

"What if we don't wake up? You want the last thing you see to be my junk?"

That brief mention caused Alexander to notice said junk. He scowled and looked away.

Seth chuckled. "Didn't think so."

"Oh, I don't know, the view's not so bad from where I'm standing..."

Alexander's eyes darted left to see who was talking, but his ears had already identified her as McAdams. She was facing him, likewise naked, but unashamed of that fact. Of course, as a gener, it wasn't as though she had anything to be ashamed about. She was perfect. Her eyes met his and she smiled at his involuntary scrutiny, as if admonishing him for rejecting her last night.

You should see my wife, he thought.

At least he no longer ran the risk that Seth Ryder's junk would be the last thing he'd ever see.

"Ready, Captain?" Doctor Crespin asked, walking up beside him.

Alexander nodded and gave an involuntary shiver while he waited for the doctor to configure his G-tank. A moment later the hatch slid open and bright lights snapped on inside the tank.

"Would you like any help, sir?"

Alexander shook his head. He'd had plenty of practice with the tanks while training for Operation Alice. "I'll be fine, thank you, Doctor." He walked inside. Out of the corner of his eye he saw Doctor Crespin salute him.

"See you on the other side," the doctor said, and then he triggered the hatch shut. The door slid back into its frame with a *boom* that echoed loudly in the confined space.

Alexander went to the harness in the middle of the tank and quickly strapped himself in. He pricked the needle of his nutrient line into the implant in his wrist, and the sensation of cold fluids entering his bloodstream made him shiver. He then inserted the tracheal tube, gagging once as it slid down his throat, and finally, he inserted the rectal line and strapped on his urinal cup.

The tank detected he was ready and the lights began to dim. Alexander's head lolled with a spreading warmth that turned conscious thought to mush. The coma-inducing drugs were already buzzing through him. A warm liquid swirled in around his toes. He blinked, and suddenly he was floating inside his harness and the liquid was up to his neck. Startled, he realized that he must have drifted off. A green light snapped on beside his ventilator and warm liquid began *whooshing* into his lungs. It was like drowning without drowning. His lungs felt full and heavy, but there were no burning demands for oxygen. The perfluorocarbon in his lungs was an even more effective oxygenator than air.

Alexander shut his eyes and pictured Caty's smiling face. He smiled back, and his mind drifted away on a sea of drugs and warm, enveloping water.

Crespin was right with his analogy. This must be exactly what it felt like to be a baby in its mother's womb. No worries, no nagging physical needs, nothing to do but sleep and dream... Sleep and dream...

* * *

Maximilian Carter awoke to find himself hanging from his harness. All the liquid had already drained from his tank, and his skin was dry. He suffered a momentary panic attack when he saw the tubes trailing from his body.

Then he remembered where he was and why.

Reaching up carefully, Max withdrew his tracheal tube. Then he removed his nutrient line and relief tubes. Finally, he unstrapped from his harness. Free once more, he walked up to the hatch inside the tank and waved the door open. Cold air rushed in, and he shivered, cursing under his breath. He hurried out and opened the locker beside his tank to remove his clothes and his pressure suit.

Once dressed, Max began walking in a circle around the room, checking the other *G*-tanks to make sure that everyone else was still locked inside their tanks and sleeping.

They were all perfectly oblivious. Max smiled.

CHAPTER 12

One Month Later - April 6, 2790
(Earth's Frame of Reference)

Catalina's eyes sprang open. It was dark. Morning? Night? She wasn't sure, but she wasn't sleepy anymore. She checked her comm band. The holo display bathed the room in a cold blue light. It was 11:00 AM.

Skitter skitter skitter.

She sat up, and the lights came on overhead, sensing she was awake. Looking for the source of sound, Caty's eyes fell on a pile of discarded cans of food in the far corner of the room. A pair of cockroaches were busy crawling over them. Caty shivered.

Mystery solved. How did they get in? she wondered. The shelter was meant to be airtight. *They must have already been inside when I locked the door. Now we're all stuck with each other. Just me and my pets. Here roachy roachy…*

Caty smiled wryly. Of all the things she and Alexander had thought to stock the basement with, somehow a garbage can and garbage bags had escaped their list of important survival items.

There was plenty of bug spray to make up for it, but unfortunately, nothing kills a cockroach.

Skitter skitter skitter.

A cockroach the size of a mouse went racing toward the pile of cans and the other two fled for their lives. Caty had a brief vision of cockroaches crawling through the ruins of LA, their antennae dancing over the rubble, whole clouds of them flying across the Earth like a plague of locusts…

She shivered again.

Caty swung her legs over the side of the bed and sat blinking the sleep from her eyes. Her basement bunker was a mess. Dirty clothes lay on the floor in heaps, and the air was filled with the fragrant aroma of rotting garbage. No wonder the roaches were flourishing. They thought she was one of them.

First order of business—check the generator and the Geiger counter. She'd been checking the radiation levels religiously every morning. Technically, it had been safe to leave for weeks already, but safe and healthy were two different things. Caty stumbled through the cluttered shelter, kicking empty cans of food and dirty laundry aside along the way.

Caty read the digital display of the Geiger counter mounted on the wall beside the generator. The sensor was mounted inside a hollow pole and could be extended to take readings above ground. Right now the sensor read 110 CPM and 0.066 mSv/hr. The chart pasted on the wall below the Geiger counter readout marked anything over 100 counts per minute (CPM) as *harmful* and indicated that radiation sickness would take hold at seven or eight hundred mSv, which would require more than 10,000 hours of exposure at current levels. Due to the rate of decay, it would be impossible for her to actually get radiation sickness at this point—getting cancer was still a distinct possibility, but that was what immunological implants and nanobodies were for.

Right now the greater concern was her supply situation. She had already spent a month in her basement, and she had one more month of food and drinking water, but the generator was running low on fuel, and pretty soon she would run out of air if she didn't at least crack open the door.

Besides, she had to be realistic.

With an unknown number of cities lying in ruins and potentially tens or hundreds of millions missing and presumed dead, she couldn't wait for a rescue to come to her. Even if rescue workers were searching LA for survivors, it was doubtful that they'd find *her*. She was just one of millions of other missing faces.

Caty turned from the Geiger counter and went to get dressed. That done, she fetched one of Alexander's old navy rucksacks and began stuffing it full of critical supplies. Knife, flashlight, sleeping bag, first aid kit, compass, portable Geiger counter, matches, cans of food, water…

Water was *heavy.*

She needed two liters per day. With activity maybe more. Water on the surface would probably be contaminated, and LA was surrounded by desert. She could carry around eight liters along with everything else, but even that would be a struggle. That meant she could survive for four days. Hopefully she'd find help or a source of clean drinking water before she became radioactive dust.

Grimacing, Caty finished packing. She added two extra pairs of clothes from the rumpled mess inside the basement wardrobe. Her eyes fell on the Beretta sitting on the nightstand beside her bed. She reached with a trembling hand for the pistol. Her hand closed around cold steel. The weapon had a comforting but alien weight. She saw a holoframe with pictures of her and Alexander on the nightstand and she grabbed that, too. She checked the safety on her Beretta and then zipped it in one of the outer pockets of her rucksack.

All packed. Caty slung the pack over her shoulders and stumbled under the weight. She managed to steady herself by leaning forward, but she was beginning to fear she'd make slow progress with such a heavy burden on her back. Not to mention the straps were going to chafe her shoulders raw.

Caty turned in a slow circle, taking in the state of her shelter. Garbage everywhere. Smooth concrete floors, bare concrete walls. Shelves lined with supplies and a messy bed sitting between two such shelves. It wasn't much, but it had begun to look like home. *Let's not be nostalgic about a bunker,* Caty chided herself. She went to the generator and set the auto-off to 10 minutes.

This was it. She was ready.

When Caty arrived at the door. Her hand paused on the handle, her palm slick with sweat, her entire body trembling with fear. What if she was the only one left?

She turned the handle. The door groaned, and the hinges squealed. A crack of sunlight appeared, blinding in its intensity. She opened the door further and squinted against the glare, her eyes watering from a month of living in a windowless basement. The air was cool, but reeking with smoke. Caty coughed and sneezed at the same time. She blinked her eyes wide and forced herself to look into the light. She saw a nest of wooden beams and other debris lying at the top of the stairs, but she spied a hole big enough to crawl out.

"Hello!" she tried, coughing again.

No answer. Wind whistled down the stairs.

Caty started climbing. Soon she was forced to crawl on her hands and knees because of all the debris. Her pack caught on something and she removed it, dragging it behind her instead. Caty reached the hole in the debris and struggled through. Her back brushed an exposed nail and a stinging pain erupted where it had scratched her. She winced and bit her lip, tears coming to her eyes.

Caty crawled out into daylight, dragging her pack after her. She found herself at the top of the stairs, her head poking out just above a big pile of fire-scorched debris that used to be her house. The sky was clogged with smoke, turning the sun into a hazy, red-orange ball. Everything as far as she could see was a crazy rat's nest of ruins. Fat black ashes fell like snowflakes. The silence was desolate and terrifying. A wind thundered by. Charred debris and ashes rolled like tumbleweed in the street. She couldn't see anyone walking through the ruins. Caty felt a sharp stab of panic, and she swayed dizzily on her feet. She really was the only survivor. This was it. The end of the world.

Then a bird chirped and flitted by overhead. Caty watched it, her eyes wide and mouth agape, as if she'd never seen a bird before in her life.

If birds could still survive out here then so could she.

It took a lot of effort to climb out above the debris, but eventually she found herself standing on the street in front of her home. The streets were strewn with debris, too, but they were easier to negotiate and still mostly intact under all the rubble.

Another bird flew by, chirping out a cheerful song. Caty withdrew the compass from her bag, trying to track its course. No doubt it was looking for the same things she was—water, food, shelter.

The bird was headed northeast.

Caty nodded to herself. *Northeast it is.*

CHAPTER 13

Four Days Later - April 10, 2790
(Earth's Frame of Reference)

Catalina tapped the bottom of her water bottle, trying to knock out the last stubborn drops, but nothing came out. She lowered the bottle from her lips, frowned, and scanned the landscape.

She was far enough from the ruins of LA that she'd begun to encounter skeletal forests of burned and blackened trees rather than mountains of rubble, but she had yet to find a river or lake. At this point she'd settle for a dirty puddle. She'd run out of water more than twelve hours ago, and she'd been rationing herself for the past two days, so she was already dehydrated.

Her thoughts did a lazy dance in her head, going in nonsensical circles.

Caty stumbled out of the trees onto something firm and hard. She blinked bleary, sleep-deprived eyes and stared at the ground under her feet, wondering what it was. Then she recognized it.

A road. Roads lead to civilization.

This was exactly what she needed. Maybe she'd wind up at a fueling station. Or a town sitting outside LA's blast radius.

They have to have water there, right?

Caty stumbled along, forcing one foot in front of the other. A long time passed. She began to see the blacktop as a giant slithering snake. It went on and on without end, and soon she could almost see it slither. A snake. A woman. Cast out of paradise, waiting for Death to find her. The garden of Eden came to mind.

Was this the road to hell? Caty looked at the flanking rows of blackened trees and she recalled all the rubble and ruins where she'd come from—everything dead and gone. The road wasn't leading her to hell. She was already there.

Her eyes began to itch, and Caty coughed weakly. She wondered if it was the smoke that made her eyes itch, or if it was the persistent lump in her throat. Lately, whenever she felt like crying, the tears refused to come; instead her eyes would itch like they were two giant mosquito bites. It was all she could do not to scratch them out of her head.

Alexander had left her. He'd promised to stay with her forever, to save her! Where was he now when she needed him the most? Her thoughts took a dark turn, whispering to her about where he must be, but she refused to accept it. *No,* she shook her head. *He's on his way to some far off world, and it'll be ten years before he comes back!*

He knew. *He ran away on purpose.*

Maybe he hadn't been *assigned* to Operation Alice. Maybe he'd volunteered. *He ran with his tail between his legs and left me here to die! Coward!*

Caty's knees buckled and she hit the asphalt with a numb jolt. Her mouth was so dry… her head so thick. How much longer till she died of thirst? She turned her head back and forth, scanning the trees for some shimmer of water, but all was ash and dust.

Then she saw something. Green, white, red—a sign. A big fat *seven* in a clearing on the side of the road, not far from where she sat.

It was a mirage. It had to be.

Caty sat for long seconds, waiting for the mirage to disappear, but it didn't even shimmer. She blinked. It was real. A Seven Eleven. Not the ruins of one, but a real, in-tact store, and what looked like a fueling station, too.

She tried pushing off the ground, but her pack was too heavy. Shrugging out of the straps, she left it on the roadside and rose on sore, shaking legs. Caty cast a glance behind her to her pack, her lifeline. There was no way she could lift it anymore. Not until she regained her strength. She could come back for it later. What she needed right now was *water.*

Caty stumbled toward the fuel station and convenience store. She wanted to run, but she didn't trust herself not to trip over her own feet.

By the time Caty reached the Seven Eleven and pushed open the doors, she was gasping for air and her heart was pounding in her chest. She hadn't run, but that was the fastest she'd ever walked in her life.

Her eyes flicked over the aisles. The store was dark inside, and it took a moment for her eyes to adjust. Some of the aisles had been scavenged already, but there was still a ton of food, and drinks were everywhere. She spied warm cans of soda, and this time she did run. She snatched a Coca-Cola from the shelf and pulled the tab right off. Her hands shook violently, spilling soda everywhere. Grabbing the can in both hands she managed to steady it and lift it to her lips. She guzzled. Coke streamed around her lips and down her neck, soaking her shirt. It was *wet.* She'd almost forgotten what wet was.

As soon as the can was empty she reached for another and emptied that one, too. She was about to reach for a third when a sharp, stabbing pain erupted in her belly, and exploded upward, rising fast. A loud belch thundered from her lips, and she grimaced.

Leaving the sodas where they were, Caty took an extra moment to search the aisle and find a bottle of water instead. She unscrewed the cap and sat down to drink it.

Another sharp pain erupted, and she belched again. At least there was no one around to hear. She took another sip of water.

"Not very lady like."

Caty froze. Her eyes darted to the source of the sound. A hunched shape sat in a dark corner at the end of the aisle. "Hello?" she tried. Her heart began pounding again. She'd found another survivor! How long had it been since she'd heard another human voice? Maybe she was hallucinating.

When no answer came from the shadows, she began to see the hunched shape as a pile of blankets. She shivered. Thinking about blankets made Caty realize how cold she was. She was wearing a windbreaker, but under that her shirt was soaked with Coca-Cola.

Caty squinted into the darkness, trying to make out something more. "Hello?" she tried again.

Still no answer.

Definitely a hallucination. Caty stripped out of her jacket and then took off her soaked shirt. She was just about to go steal one of the blankets when she saw them *move.*

"You're pretty," the voice from before said.

Caty snatched up her clothes and hugged them to her chest. "Who are you? Why didn't you answer me?"

"Not used to talkin'. Been a while, a long while since anyone's come through here."

Caty nodded uncertainly. "You're the first person I've found since… it's been a while for me, too," she said.

The shadowy bundle of blankets moved again and a blinding light snapped on.

A flashlight. It shone on her face and she flinched away from the light, holding up a hand to shield her eyes.

"I was right. Very pretty."

Caty felt a chill run through her that had nothing to do with the cool air or the fact that she'd removed her jacket and shirt. "I need to get going," she said, pushing off the ground to stand on her aching feet. "I have a long way to go still."

"What's the hurry? It'll be dark soon. You might lose your way. Stay here. Plenty of food and water to share." The shadowy mound moved again. "Besides, we have a responsibility now."

Caty began edging toward the door, still holding the bundle of clothes to her chest. She remembered the Berreta pistol in her bag, and suddenly she regretted leaving her pack on the roadside.

"A responsibility?" she asked, and then cursed herself for asking.

"To humanity. We have to repopulate the species."

Caty nodded. "Oh. Yes, that's true," she said. "Maybe I *should* stay, but I left something outside. Let me just go out and get it first."

"I'll come with you." The shadow kept advancing.

She backed away as fast as she could. Her legs trembled violently, and her heart thumped in her chest. She shook her head. "No, you need to stay here. Guard our supplies."

"I already took care of the bugs. They won't be comin' back."

"Bugs?" Caty's mind spun; she tripped over something, crying out as she fell. *Thud.* A painful jolt went up her spine. Then a rotten smell filled her nostrils, and she gagged. The flashlight skipped down to a big yellow mass at her feet. It took a second for her eyes to recognize the hazmat suit.

"Bug," the shadowy man said, flicking his flashlight up and down the body. Caty glimpsed of a pool of red blood and she gasped.

"You killed him?" she shrieked, hugging her legs up to her chest.

"You takin' their side, woman?"

"No, no," Caty said quickly, trying to avoid provoking the man.

"Don't let your eyes fool you, they ain't human anymore. Space bugs infected 'em all, got 'em to start this war. Damn near killed us all! Hey… you ain't with them, are ya? How do I know *you're* human? Suppose you should convince me."

Caty couldn't even speak. It was all too horrible. This person, whoever he was, had obviously lost his mind. He'd killed one of the rescue workers who'd come for him.

"Nothin' to say? Well. I think I know a way to find out if you're human or not. Come here, girl."

Alarm bells sounded in Caty's head. Something fierce and primal rose up in her. She shook her head and bounced to her feet, her blood buzzing with adrenaline. The shadowy form kept advancing.

"All right," she said, trying to sound agreeable. "Come get me."

"I will," the shadow promised, reaching out for her.

She ran in past groping hands and kneed the man where she imagined his groin should be. The shadow cried out, and she turned and ran for her life. She burst through the doors and ran across the parking lot, back the way she'd come. It was almost perfectly dark now. Too dark to see more than fuzzy outlines of things. She couldn't see her pack, but she took a guess and ran to where she thought it must be. The door chimes were her only warning.

"Fucking bitch!" the shadow roared. "I'll kill you!"

Instinct tickled in the back of her head, and she dove, hitting the ground with a spray of gravel.

Boom!

The sound was deafening. The pellets in the shell went whistling by overhead.

"Where are you, bitch?"

Caty's lungs burned, heaving for air, but she willed them to be still. Rolling onto her back she spotted the shadowy figure scanning the ground with his flashlight. It wouldn't be long before he found her like that.

Boom!

This time he shot one of the filling stations, and suddenly Caty realized the danger she was in. A madman was chasing her, shooting a shotgun in a fuel station.

Chuk-chuk.

He's reloading! Taking advantage of the brief respite, Caty scrambled to her feet and ran. Gravel skittered underfoot.

"What was that? I know you're out there! Just you wait you little bitch!"

Caty sobbed and ran as fast as her tired, aching legs would carry her.

Boom! Then came the roar of an explosion and a sudden flash of heat and light.

"Oh, shit!" the man screamed.

The shockwave hit a second later, an intense blast of hot air that knocked her flat. She hit her chin on the ground, scraping it raw. Caty's ears rang. She blinked and saw that the darkness had been replaced by a flickering orange light.

She rolled onto her back just as it began stinging with a thousand pinprick stabs of pain. Shrapnel.

The gas station was on fire. There was a human torch dancing around screaming and… *laughing.* Caty looked on in horror, unable to tear her eyes away until the figure collapsed and lay still.

This was what humanity had come to. The only human being she'd met in months and he'd tried to kill her.

Caty watched the gas station burn. No need to light a fire tonight. She could lay out her sleeping bag right here and no animals would dare come close, except maybe the more dangerous human kind.

Caty thought about hiding out in the Seven Eleven, but the thought of being in there with that dead rescue worker was too horrible to bear.

She ended up laying her sleeping bag under an elm tree to one side of the blazing fire. The spot she picked was far enough away that she wouldn't catch fire if there were any secondary explosions, but close enough that the light and heat would still be useful.

Caty lay awake, wide-eyed and blinking, watching as tongues of flame danced and noxious smoke clogged the air. She had her Beretta balanced on her belly, firmly clutched in both hands, just in case. Her pack rested under her head, the comforting lump she called a pillow.

Sleep came for her, weighing down her eyelids, making them flutter. Her thoughts became scattered and disjointed. She wondered why the fuel station and the convenience store hadn't burned up in the forest fires that had obviously swept through in the wake of the attacks. She also wondered if there were more survivors. The presence of that rescue worker in a hazmat suit told her that someone was still out there, trying to make order out of the chaos.

That was when she noticed the hover parked in the fuel station. It was nothing but a flaming wreck now. They'd been passing through, trying to fuel up while they continued their aerial search for survivors. Rescue workers had come here, assuming it was a likely place for survivors to hide out. Caty wondered if there were more bodies lurking between the aisles of the Seven Eleven…

Her eyes grew wide, and she shivered. She was never going to fall asleep.

* * *

"Wake up!" Alexander shook her shoulders.

Caty sobbed. "You left me! You left me here to die!"

"I had to go."

"You didn't!" she insisted.

"I go where they send me, remember?"

"I didn't ask you to join the navy!"

Alexander shook his head, his eyes full of sorrow. "You're going to be okay, Caty… wake up…"

"Wake up, ma'am! Wake up!"

"Ma'am?"

Caty blinked. Men in bulky yellow suits loomed over her. One of them was shaking her by the shoulder, a loud voice saying, "Ma'am, wake up please!"

Caty sat up quickly, her heart already pounding in her chest. "Who are you?"

It was a stupid question.

"We're here to help. Are you hurt?"

Caty nodded. "Not bad. What happened? How many cities got hit?"

"Please try to remain calm. We'll explain everything as soon as we can. Do you feel sick? Nauseous?"

Caty shook her head. "Please. I've been alone for a long time. I need to know. How bad is it?"

"We lost eleven cities. The rest of the missiles were intercepted. Reds lost fifteen or more, but it's hard to be sure."

"New York?"

"And Washington, Chicago, Houston, Miami, LA… Most of the Alliance is still fine, though, especially the South."

Caty breathed a sigh of relief. "And the fleet?"

"We lost a lot of ships, and the space elevator, but so did they. There's a cease fire on right now."

"How many ships did we lose?"

"Ma'am, I've answered your questions. Now I need you to cooperate. We need to keep moving. Is there anyone hiding in the store?"

Caty shook her head. "There was. He…" She swallowed thickly.

"We know. One of ours called it in before he died. Come on. We need to get you to a shelter."

A shelter. Survivors. Despite the news that eleven major cities had been turned to radioactive dust, Caty felt so happy that she could dance. She smiled and climbed to her feet, tears streaming down her cheeks. This wasn't the end of the world.

Not yet.

PART TWO: WONDERLAND

"Throw your dreams into space like a kite, and you do not know what it will bring back, a new life, a new friend, a new love, a new country."

—Anaïs Nin

CHAPTER 14

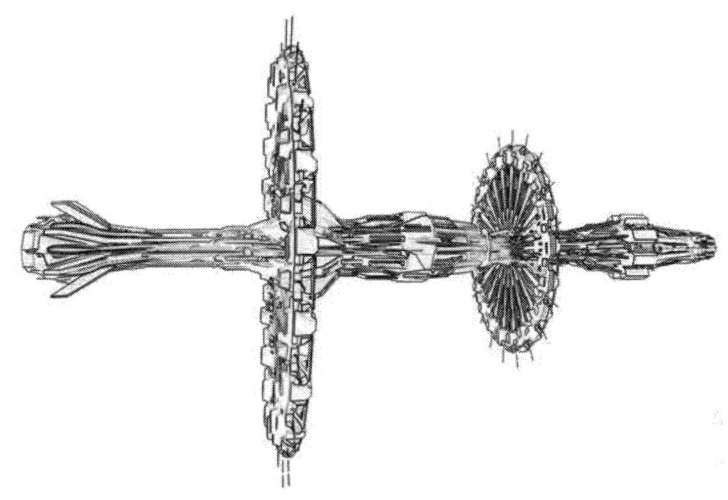

70 Days Later - May 18, 2790
(The Lincoln's Frame of Reference,
Now Separated from Earth by 350 Days)

Alexander's eyelids fluttered open. His head felt like it was stuffed full of cotton. As he became aware of his surroundings, his heart raced, and his palms began to sweat. He felt something choking him. Then he noticed the tube protruding from his mouth and he hurried to pull it out. He gagged as the tube came out, but his stomach was empty so no danger of throwing up. Once free of the invading apparatus, he closed his aching jaw and swallowed. There was a bad taste in his mouth, and his tongue felt swollen, but otherwise he was okay.

Alexander disconnected the remainder of his life support, starting with his nutrient line. He had to force himself to be gentle with the equipment and suppress his urgent need to get out of the G-tank. He could feel the walls closing in, suffocatingly close. To keep the panic at bay, he focused on what lay ahead.

The very fact that he was awake right now meant that they were about to arrive in Wonderland. He'd been half expecting to die in transit and never to wake up again, but instead here he was, about to make history.

When he was done disconnecting his life support, Alexander unstrapped the tank harness and took a few shaky steps toward the door. His knees buckled and he fell. A lifetime of doing push-ups saved his nose, but a sharp stabbing pain in his wrists and knees reminded him that gravity was back. At this point in the trip gravity was generated by deceleration as they headed engines first into the Wonderland system.

Alexander pushed off the deck with a grunt and stumbled toward the hatch. He waved the door open and stepped out of the tank. The air was freezing! Doors slid open to all sides as the rest of the crew came floundering out of their tanks. Alexander turned and opened his locker and removed his bundle of clothes. He worked quickly to separate his uniform from his combat suit, and in the process his comm band and pocket watch clattered to the deck. The watch landed on its end and sprang open.

Cursing, Alexander bent to pick up the delicate gift. As he did so, he checked the date and time. The hands pointed to three and nine—3:45—and the date read *May|18|90.* Alexander tried to remember the date they were supposed to have arrived. Then he recalled marking it on his comm band's calendar before entering his *G*-tank.

Alexander picked up the comm band and strapped it around his wrist. He powered it on and checked the calendar. The dates recorded there confirmed it: they'd entered the tanks exactly 70 days ago, meaning they were on schedule. That was reassuring.

Alexander hurried to get dressed. Once his combat suit was on, he withdrew his helmet from the locker and tucked it under his arm.

"Captain."

Alexander saw Commander Korbin ambling up to him. She was obviously taking it easy, giving her legs time to adjust to walking again.

"Commander. It's good to see you again. Part of me was afraid we weren't going to wake up."

"I'm glad we did. Now all we need to do is find a way home before our supplies run out."

Alexander smiled. "We haven't even technically arrived yet. We still have a planet to explore. Speaking of which, we need to get to the bridge. Who knows what we're going to find on the other side of the wormhole?"

"Well, the Alliance sent probes ahead of us, so we already have some idea."

"Probes that captured only a few minutes' worth of data," he replied. "Anything we discover after those first few minutes is all uncharted territory, assuming of course that we don't suffer the same fate the probes did."

Alexander turned to address the rest of the crew. Doctor Crespin and his nurses were still busy checking the crew's vital signs, so Alexander waited. As soon as the doctor was done, he clapped his hands and called out, "Wonderland awaits! Everyone to your stations!"

The crew filed into the elevators in the central column of the room. Alexander rode up one floor to the bridge with the rest of the bridge crew. They strode out and up to their control stations on the far wall. Alexander stopped in front of his station and regarded his helmet with a sigh. After a momentary hesitation, he slipped it on, and it sealed with an automatic *hiss.* Reaching for the rails on the armrests of his acceleration couch, he lowered himself down. Korbin eased down beside him while the rest of the crew hurried up the access ladders mounted on the walls.

"Systems check!" Alexander said while he strapped in.

"All systems green, sir," McAdams reported from engineering.

"Davorian, how long until we emerge from the wormhole?"

"Approximately... five minutes, sir."

"Good. Keep us posted. Hayes, get ready to send a transmission back through the wormhole. Attach our log data and a status update."

"Yes, sir."

"Willi—" Alexander broke off, remembering Williams' treachery. He struggled to remember the new sensor operator's name...

"It's Lieutenant Vasquez, sir—you promoted her to bridge crew before we left, remember?" Korbin whispered from beside him.

"Right. Williams' reserve. I remember. Just checking if you did." Like McAdams, Vasquez was new to the ship. Otherwise he would have known her name instantly.

Korbin arched an eyebrow at him.

"Vasquez!"

"Sir?" she replied.

"Get a scan of Wonderland ready to send along with Hayes' transmission."

"As long as we're still inside the wormhole, we've got tunnel vision, sir."

"That's better than nothing. We don't know how long the wormhole is going to stay open on the other end, so we might not get another chance."

"Yes, sir."

Alexander watched as the main holoscreen came online, showing a warped view of stars and space from the ship's cameras. Gone was the depthless black void of the Sol System. Instead, he saw faint red wisps of ionized gas running between the stars like gossamer threads.

"Davorian, what was time dilation going through the wormhole?"

"One minute, Captain."

"A minute?"

"I'm still working on it, sir."

"Doesn't the ship track time dilation automatically?"

"The nav system isn't designed to measure time dilation due to changes in the geometry of space-time, sir. Wormhole travel is relatively new to us, but I'm using measurements that were taken along the way to generate a function that expresses how time dilation changed at different points in our trip. Using the integral of that function I can find the average value, which is the average time dilation factor for our entire trip. Then I just have to add average time dilation due to the speed we were traveling."

Alexander frowned. "More calculating, less talking, Davorian."

"Yes, sir."

"You asked..." Korbin chided.

"There's a reason I'm not the *Lincoln's* astrophysicist."

"Bad study habits?"

"Allergies."

"Allergies?"

"As soon as Davorian mentioned *integrals,* my brain started to itch."

Korbin snorted. "Ha ha. We can schedule a session to help you deal with your phobias later, Captain."

"Got it!" Davorian said. "Time dilation from the wormhole was an average of five point triple eight times Earth. Dilation due to our velocity was one point zero double eight. The combined time dilation factor was five point nine six."

"Good work. Now tell me what that equates to in terms of elapsed travel time for us and for Earth."

"Seventy point one days elapsed for us since we entered the tanks while approximately four hundred and twenty days elapsed on Earth."

The bridge grew quiet. Everyone had been expecting that, but somehow it was only really hitting them now. Their loved ones back on Earth had already been waiting more than a year for them to return. Alexander wondered if Caty had moved on already.

"Good work, Davorian. Send that data to Hayes so that he can attach it to our message home. They can check your math on their end once the message arrives."

"Yes, sir. One minute to arrival in the Wonderland System."

"Better hurry up and send that message then. Hayes—did we receive anything from Earth while we were in the tanks?"

"A few pings went back and forth, but nothing more substantial than that."

"Guess the president was serious about comm silence. Well, at least we know someone's still alive and checking on us." Alexander winced as he said that. Not the best idea to remind everyone about the war that had broken out before they left.

"Message sent," Hayes reported.

"Good. Get ready to send a second one. Another snapshot from sensors. Coordinate with Vasquez to send it at the exact instant that we emerge from the wormhole."

"Yes, sir."

"ETA thirty seconds!" Davorian called out.

The countdown appeared at the top of the main viewscreen, and Alexander watched stars and space ripple around them as they approached the end of the wormhole. It looked as if they were trapped inside a glass bottle looking out. The countdown reached 10 seconds and a robotic voice began echoing through the bridge.

"Ten, nine, eight… three, two, one."

A dazzling flash of light blinded Alexander and he called out, "Punch it, Hayes!" Bright spots danced before his eyes in a sea of darkness. He was blind!

A more rational thought occured to him—no matter how bright that burst of light had been, it couldn't have flash-blinded him. There were no physical viewports on the bridge, and holoscreens couldn't generate enough lumens to blind him.

Alexander looked around. All the crew stations were dark. He felt weightless, so the engines were offline, too. But most troubling of all was the ringing silence. Even life support was offline.

The *Lincoln* was completely dead in space.

CHAPTER 15

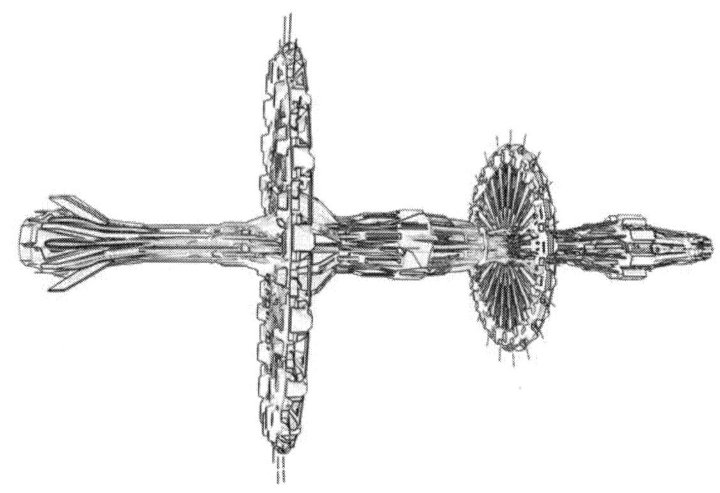

The crew exclaimed about the situation in a confusing babble of voices. A light snapped on, and absolute darkness peeled away to reveal a world of shadows that shifted and danced as that light swept around the room. More lights swelled out of the darkness, and dimly-lit faces appeared.

Helmet lamps. Alexander yelled to be heard above the rising tumult. "Quiet!" Silence fell, and he continued, "McAdams, what the hell just happened?"

"I don't know, sir. Everything is offline, so I can't exactly run a system diagnostic to find out."

"Then give me your best guess."

Davorian answered first. "That flash of light could have been caused by some kind of arcing. Positively-charged particles and negatively-charged ones coming into contact with each other. The outer hull must have built up either a strong positive or negative charge while we were traveling through the wormhole, and when we emerged we came into contact with a cloud of oppositely-charged particles."

"You mean like the ionized hydrogen in a nebula?" Alexander asked, remembering the reddish strands he'd seen between the stars in Wonderland's galaxy. "Wait a minute—are you saying we just got hit by space *lightning?*"

"That's exactly what I'm saying."

"That doesn't make sense," Vasquez said.

"You have a better theory?" Davorian replied.

"Hold on," Alexander said. "Why doesn't it make sense, Vasquez?"

"Because the gas particles inside a nebula are too spread out to cause lightning. They need to be in close contact, brushing up against each other, exchanging electrons."

"So what if this nebula is dense enough to cause that?" Davorian asked.

"A dense nebular cloud in the middle of a star system?"

"Why not?" Davorian asked.

"Because any free-floating clouds of gas would gravitate toward the system's sun and nearby planets, not collapse in on themselves," Vasquez replied.

"Not if the wormhole has a stronger gravitational pull," Davorian insisted.

"What kind of data do we have from the previous probe missions?" Korbin asked.

"A few unlovely tunnel-vision snapshots like the one we took just before we emerged from the wormhole," Vasquez said.

That set off alarm bells in Alexander's head. "Wait a minute—you mean we don't have any real sensor data from the Wonderland side of the wormhole?"

"I thought you knew that, sir?"

Alexander recalled his briefing with Admiral Flores. She'd said the probes all stopped transmitting soon after they arrived, not *before.* Alexander smacked his palms into the armrests of his acceleration couch. "Damn it!"

"What's wrong?" Korbin asked.

Alexander switched to a private comms channel with his XO. "They tricked us, Commander. They sent us out here without even knowing whether we actually could make it through the wormhole alive. They knew that all the probe missions failed before arrival, and they sent us anyway. They didn't even give us the dignity of the truth. This whole mission was one big fat shot in the dark—literally!"

"Well, I knew," McAdams said before Korbin could reply to his rant. "It was part of my briefing on Orbital One."

Alexander blinked and mentally switched back to the bridge's comm channel. "Did everyone here get a different briefing?"

McAdams went on, "Maybe they told me because I'm the only one who can do something about it. Our redundant systems were all upgraded to provide extra protection against electrical surges. The mission planners knew what they were up against, but for some reason, they didn't think to tell everyone."

"And you didn't think to mention this until now."

"I didn't think it was important until now, sir. And I didn't realize that no one else knew. Sorry, sir."

Alexander grunted. "Well that doesn't explain why we're all still sitting in the dark. The backups should have come online by now."

"Some of the circuitry for the automatic switch-over must have been fried, but I should be able to get things running again. All I need to do is get to the engine room and manually switch to the redundant systems."

Alexander activated his helmet lamps and unbuckled his harness. "Then what are we waiting for? Let's go."

"Yes, sir."

"Davorian—"

"I have the conn?"

"You're a mind reader. Korbin, you're with me and McAdams."

"Yes, sir."

Alexander pushed out of his chair and floated back toward the elevators. With power out all over the ship, the elevators weren't working, but that's what the access ladders in the shafts were for. Alexander mentally activated the microjets in his pressure suit and fired a few bursts from his palms to keep himself on course. He reached the elevator doors and grabbed one of guide rails to keep from bouncing away.

Korbin and McAdams reached the guide rail on the other side of the doors and waited while he opened an access panel to expose the manual crank. He worked the crank with one hand while he held onto the rail with his other. Once the doors were open wide enough for them to climb through, they piled in and McAdams opened the access hatch in the floor of the elevator, exposing the fathomless depths of the shaft below them. As they climbed down, Alexander's mind went to the problem at hand—what had disabled the *Lincoln* in the first place?

Space lightning? Alexander didn't buy it. Vasquez was right; it would take a very dense nebula to cause that. Something on the order of a planetary atmosphere. But what else might have happened?

Alien interference? He recalled Admiral Flores telling him that the wormhole probably wasn't naturally-occurring, and Max Carter was assigned to the *Lincoln* in order to handle first contact if the need arose, but Alexander still didn't give the idea of Alien involvement much credence. If there were aliens guarding the exit of the wormhole, then why hadn't they traveled through to visit Earth?

Reassuring as that logic was, his certainty eroded steadily as they crawled down the elevator shaft. Their head lamps cast deep shadows in every doorway on every level, and Alexander's heart pounded, his mind conjuring alien monsters to fill in the blank spaces.

Suddenly all of those shadows vanished. Lights snapped on inside the elevator shaft, and the ship lurched back into motion, accelerating at a full *G*.

The ladder rungs ripped free of Alexander's hands and he fell head first toward the bottom of the elevator shaft. McAdams and Korbin went tumbling down ahead of him, both screaming. The acceleration stopped just as suddenly as it began, but the damage was already done. The bottom of the elevator shaft came rushing toward them at more than 10 meters per second.

Smack!

All the shadows came rushing back.

CHAPTER 16

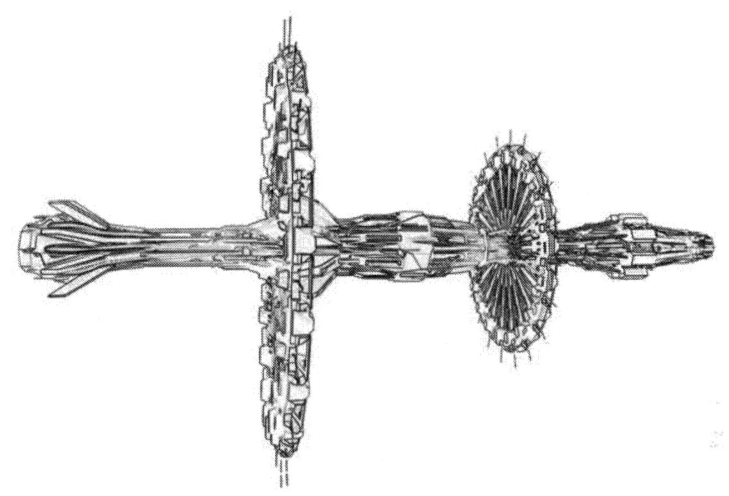

Alexander woke up lying in the ship's infirmary. A nurse came in, followed by Doctor Crespin. The nurse checked his vital signs, and Doctor Crespin came to stand beside his bed.

"How are you feeling, Captain?"

Alexander struggled to remember what had happened to bring him to the infirmary. Then he recalled hitting the bottom of the elevator shaft, and he winced. "I'm okay, I think."

"You took a nasty fall."

Alexander tried to sit up, but Crespin placed a hand on his chest to stop him. "Easy. Let me help." He reached out and adjusted something below the cot, and the top half of it began to rise, lifting him into a sitting position.

"How's that?" Crespin asked.

"Fine. How long was I out? And where are McAdams and Korbin?"

"We're still monitoring them, but there were no serious injuries. And to answer your question, you've been unconscious for about an hour."

"That sounds like a pretty bad concussion to me."

"We're going to keep you here under observation while we make the approach to Wonderland."

"We're on approach already? What did I miss? And how the hell did this happen? There are fail-safes to prevent the engines from coming online suddenly after a power failure."

"Easy, Captain. From what I understand, the power surge fried the safeties."

"But not the engines? Great. I'll have to congratulate the engineers who built this ship when we get back to Earth. They built more surge protection into the engines than they did into the emergency cut-outs that might stop them from turning us all into pancakes."

"Bad luck, Captain. Fortunately, Davorian was able to kill thrust manually."

"What about the wormhole? Did it collapse? And did we confirm the source of the power surge?"

"I don't know, but you should be resting. I can check into all of that for you."

"No, where's my comm band? If you need to keep me here, at least let me stay in touch with my crew."

Crespin hesitated, but then he nodded and ordered the nurse to bring Alexander his personal belongings. A moment later the nurse returned and passed a bundle of clothes to the doctor. Crespin found the comm band and handed it to him. Alexander put it on and made a call to Davorian.

"It's good to hear from you, sir."

"Report, Lieutenant."

"We are three days out from Wonderland at a steady one G of deceleration. Repair crews are busy getting our systems back online, but the critical ones came back by themselves."

"What caused the power surge?"

"Well, it wasn't lightning. We ran into a belt of intense radiation around the exit of the wormhole. The crew is calling it the David Davorian Belt. If we'd known the belt existed we could have shut down the ship's systems ahead of time and cruised safely through."

"We'll keep that in mind for next time. What about the wormhole? Did it collapse?"

"Not yet, sir."

Alexander blinked. "We'd better send Earth an update before it does."

"I don't think the wormhole is going to collapse, sir."

"Really?" Alexander tried not to get his hopes up. "What makes you say that?"

"For one thing, we were able to see straight through to the galaxy on this end while we were still inside the wormhole. That means it was already open; we didn't have to force it open. The radiation belt explains the failed probe missions. I'm not sure how scientists came up with the collapsing gateway theory that you mentioned in your mission brief, but I think we've effectively disproved it."

"So we don't need anyone to rescue us."

"No, sir."

"That's *really* good news, Lieutenant. I hope you're right."

"So do I, sir."

"Has Hayes sent a mission update back through the wormhole?"

"Not yet."

"What's he waiting for?"

"Are you sure you want to send an update?"

"Why wouldn't I?"

"We already know that our probe data fell into enemy

hands. Whatever we send now could be intercepted or leaked to the enemy as well."

"Encrypt the transmission and keep it short on details. All the Alliance really needs to know at this point is that we made it here safely, the wormhole is open, not shut, and we're on our way to Wonderland to assess the planet's habitability. Oh, and tell them about the David Davorian Belt and how to avoid radiation damage for future missions."

"Yes, sir."

"Good. Let me know if there are any other interesting developments."

"Yes, sir."

Alexander ended the call and settled back against his cot.

Doctor Crespin had stuck around to eavesdrop. "Sounds like good news, Captain," he said.

"The best." Alexander couldn't help grinning. He was going to see Caty again! Maybe in just a few short months—from his perspective anyway. From hers, two and a half years would have passed. That wasn't an insignificant amount of time, but it wasn't a whole decade either. Now he regretted giving her permission to move on without him. What if she'd already moved on?

"You may as well get some rest, Captain," Doctor Crespin said on his way out.

"I'm not tired."

"Maybe not, but your body needs time to recover."

Alexander sighed. "Yes, Doc."

"I'll have one of the nurses bring you your dinner."

* * *

387 Days Ago - April 11, 2790
(Earth's Frame of Reference)

The passenger compartment was full of dirty, shell-shocked faces. Caty had been expecting to see sick and injured people, but the ones rescued were all like her—more or less intact. People eyed her with unblinking stares, and she eyed them back. She clutched her pack of survival gear to her chest like a teddy bear—her shield against the world.

From the air the devastation was immense. Caty looked out the window and felt ill. There were mountains of debris and rubble in all directions. LA was a wasteland all the way out to the smoke-clouded horizon, and there wasn't a single shred of anything green.

Caty shuddered and looked away. The pilot came on the intercom and told them they were going back to the shelter now to drop them off and re-fuel before continuing their search. Relieved sighs and exclamations bounced from one passenger to another. Then someone came back into the passenger compartment to ask if any of them were natural-borns and to raise their hands if they were.

The rescue worker said something about radiation sickness being more likely if they were natural-born. Caty scanned the dirty faces around her, her gaze flicking from one person to the next. They all had colorful eyes and hair—but that didn't mean much, hair and eye color could be changed with retroactive treatments. Caty had opted for those treatments herself; she'd been born with brown eyes and hair, but had later changed her eyes to blue and hair to blond. More telling (and impossible to change after birth without surgery) were the passengers' exaggerated feminine and masculine features. Skin tones ranged the gamut, but all of them were stunningly beautiful, and that could only mean one thing: they were all geners. Besides her, no other natural-borns had been rescued. Maybe that was just an unfortunate side effect of the fact that geners had the money to afford shelters in their homes and so-called degenerates typically didn't, but Caty wasn't too sure.

"Ma'am?" someone asked close beside her ear.

Caty flinched and turned to see who it was.

It was the rescue worker. "Are you a natural-born?" he asked.

She nodded without thinking.

The man smiled and went back into the cockpit. Then the pilot announced that they would be arriving at the shelter in Irvine soon. *Irvine...* Caty thought, trying to picture it on a map.

Smack in the middle between the blast craters in LA and San Diego.

Twenty minutes later as the van hovered down, Caty saw a vast field of tents and camp fires. *So much for* shelter. *More like a refugee camp.* Still, it was better than nothing.

The van touched down with a muffled thump and she rose to her feet. She was eager to get out of the cramped passenger compartment. Caty dragged her pack over to the doors at the back of the van. She was first in line. No one else seemed to be in a hurry to get up.

The doors slid open, and a rescue worker came up behind her. "Head to the circus tent for processing," he said, pointing dead ahead.

It was hard to miss the big red and white pinstriped tent. "I guess it's too much to ask for someone to hold my hand," Caty said.

"I have to get back out there," the worker replied.

Caty nodded and started down the ramp, dragging her pack behind her as she went. Everywhere she looked dirty, bleak faces turned to stare at her. None of them were wearing hazmat suits, but at this distance the fallout wouldn't be too dangerous.

She was relieved to see that all of the people in the immediate area seemed to be natural-borns even though everyone in the van had been a gener.

The discrimination was just in her head, then.

Caty looked behind her to thank the worker, but he was already climbing back inside the hover. The ramp retracted under the van and the doors slid shut. A few short seconds later the van hovered up, generating a wicked wind that whipped dust into her face and forced her eyes shut. Then the wind died down, and she opened her eyes to see the hover roaring away into the distance, already a dwindling speck against the slate gray sky.

Something felt wrong about that. Caty turned back to the camp with a frown, feeling suddenly alone and vulnerable. She caught some of the refugees glaring up at the hover van as it left, and her bad feeling grew stronger. Suddenly she realized what was wrong. The van had left *her* here, but all the geners were going somewhere else. *Somewhere nicer, maybe?*

So much for all the implants and retroactive treatments to make her like them. Natural-born still meant *degenerate* to them. Caty frowned. Hefting her pack off the ground, she slung it over her shoulders and walked up to the nearest person in the camp—a man with a scraggly brown beard and an unruly mop of hair to match. He was handsome in a rugged way, but not nearly enough to be a gener.

"Hello, I'm Catalina de Leon," she said.

The man tore his gaze from the sky to regard her. "Dahveed," he said with a strong accent. "*¿Hablas espanol?*"

She nodded. "I speak Spanish, but it's better not to up North. Raises too many eyebrows."

David snorted. "True that. You can get away with it I suppose."

Caty cocked her head. "Get away with what?"

"Speaking English. Pretending to be a gener. You're pretty enough to fool them."

"Well, I'm not trying to fool anyone."

David's brow wrinkled. "You *should* try to fool them. You might live longer that way."

Ice trickled through Caty's veins. "Live longer? What do you mean?"

"You don't know?"

"I just arrived."

Another snort. *"Supongo que yo debo orientarte entonces. Mira—aqui, somos sus perros."*

"How's that?"

"You're really going to stick with English?" David sighed and shook his head. "They make us go out, no suits, no protection. They use us like dogs to find other survivors and bring them in."

"But the ones who rescued me were—"

"Geners rescuing geners. They must have thought you were one of them, and only realized their mistake later. Like I said, you can pass for one, but me?" David shook his head. "I was picked up by a rusty old street bus. The driver was a Mexican. All Latinos on that crew. We find ours and they find theirs, but there's always a guard with us to make sure we pick up any geners we find. No one's really looking for us."

"Then why are there so many people here?" Caty jerked her chin to the field of tents.

"They need to conscript rescue workers somehow. The more of us they rescue, the more of them they can find, but as soon as we stop finding geners you can bet we're going to fall through the cracks and straight into hell."

"It can't be that bad."

"No? Go talk to the warden."

"The warden?"

"That's what we call *el jefe aqui*. Go tell him you don't want to join the crews. Then go get your rations for tomorrow. You'll get a liter of dirty water and a bag of saltine crackers. Go back tomorrow night and tell him you changed your mind. You'll get four liters of clean water and enough food to keep you from dreaming about it all night. Either you join the search or you join the search. Only children get a full ration if they don't go."

"What about the sick and injured?"

"Don't have any. We gather them up and call in the hovers to get them, but who knows if they actually rescue the natural-borns. Anyway, point is, this is a work camp, and they only rescue us because they don't want to risk their own lives out there looking for each other."

Caty's jaw dropped a few centimeters. "No suits?"

"No."

"What about the radiation?"

"It's bad, but no one's going anywhere close to the epicenters yet, so you'll be okay—at least for the next ten years while the cancer grows. Suppose cancer later is still better than starving to death now."

Caty blew out a breath. "I guess I'd better go volunteer then."

David nodded. *"Deberias."*

"See you."

Ten minutes later, Caty was standing in front of Warden Theodore. She didn't bother asking him to check if conditions were as bad as David had indicated. Despite David's obvious resentment toward geners, he had no reason to lie to her.

After promising to join the search effort, she was given two cans of corn, three cans of beans, a can-opener, a spoon, and a four-liter jug of water. They were about to give her a pack and bedroll, too, but she explained that she already had hers, so all they did was assign her a tent number. They told her to follow the white numbers spray-painted on the ground until she found 5097, and then report for duty tomorrow morning with the bell. Five o'clock sharp.

Caty made her way up the rows of tents until she found hers. A teenage girl with black hair tied up in a bun sat outside the tent beside a dying fire, scraping beans out of a pot with an old rusty spoon.

"Hi," Caty said.

The girl looked up, then back down into her pot.

"I'm Catalina, but you can call me Caty," she said.

"Rosa," the girl replied.

"Pretty name. Fifty ninety-seven is your tent?"

Rosa nodded.

"Me, too. Guess we'll be getting to know each other better then. I just arrived."

No answer.

"You here all alone?"

Rosa got up from her tree stump stool and breezed by. *"Voy a dormir."*

Caty frowned. The sun hadn't even set yet. Wasn't it too early to go to bed? Rosa climbed inside the tent and zipped it up after her. Caty sat down on the tree stump and regarded the empty pot. It wasn't clean, but something told her that was too much to ask for. Her stomach grumbled. She hadn't eaten yet. Picking up the pot, Caty shrugged out of her pack and found a can of beans she could heat up. The can-opener didn't work very well, but she managed to get the can open and pour the beans into the pot. Then she stoked glowing orange embers into the pale gray sky until the fire was radiating enough heat to make her cold beans hot—lukewarm actually, but she was too hungry to care.

She drank a few cups of water with the meal and soon she needed to use a bathroom, but she hadn't seen any facilities, and it was already too dark to walk around and look for one, so she waited until it was fully dark and found a patch of grass between her tent and the neighbor's. She'd grown used to using grass and bushes for a bathroom since leaving her shelter, but usually not with thousands of potential spectators nearby.

That night Caty slept beside the glowing coals of the fire, out under the stars. She lay awake listening to people cough inside their tents. There was too much smoke in the air from all the forest fires. Caty's throat itched, too, but she muffled her own coughs, not wanting to draw attention to herself. Every now and then she heard someone walking between the tents, the gravel crunching underfoot, and she remembered the shadowy man at the Seven Eleven.

Caty cringed. Best to keep quiet.

"You're pretty," the dead man's words echoed inside her head, making her skin crawl. She'd never even seen his face, so it was easy to imagine a monster rather than a man.

That had been her wake-up call. Now she knew better than to trust other survivors.

Unfortunately the rescue workers had confiscated her Berreta. It was probably better they didn't let refugees enter the camp armed, but Caty felt naked without it. She was beginning to wish she *had* pretended to be a gener—or dead. It might have been better if they'd left her at the Seven Eleven.

Someone screamed nearby.

There came a piercing silence, as if the entire camp had woken up and stopped coughing so that they could listen. Caty's heart thundered in her chest. She lay frozen on the ground, wanting to get up and run for her life, but too scared to move.

They can't see me in the dark. They'll think I'm a log.

Caty squeezed her eyes tightly shut, willing the danger to pass. *I'm a log, I'm a log, I'm a log...*

The coughs came once more, and Caty didn't hear any more screams. Maybe she'd imagined it.

The next morning, after the bell went off, news spread about the woman who'd been found dead in her tent. Caty found David in the line to board the buses, and she asked him about it.

He just shrugged. "The ones who don't join the crews have to survive somehow. When they get hungry enough, they steal. If you see them, they'll kill you not to get caught. Someone tries to steal your food, you let them. Pretend to be asleep, look the other way."

Caty's eyes grew round and she nodded. "What about security?"

"What security? There are ten thousand refugees and only fifty guards. There's only ten of them on patrol at night. That's one for every thousand people, or one for every five hundred tents."

"There must be something we can do. What if we organize our own night watch?"

"Tried it. Not allowed."

"What? Why not?"

"We need to keep up our strength for the searches, and the warden doesn't want any vigilantes in his camp. Curfew has us in bed by nine and up at five."

"Then we should leave. We don't have to stay here, do we? They can't force us to stay."

"No, not yet anyway, but where would we go?"

Caty shrugged. "Somewhere, anywhere!"

David smirked. "And eat what? Drink what? Do what? Like

it or not, they have us all here as willing slaves until we can find some way to fend for ourselves. Right now the only job for any of us is here, searching for survivors."

A thought occurred to Caty. "What about the military?"

"The military?"

"Aren't they accepting recruits still?"

"You want to trade one certain death for another? The entire fleet was destroyed. If this cease fire ends, you'll be the first one to die. At least down here you might last for a few more years."

Caty felt her whole body grow cold. "The *entire* fleet?"

David nodded. "Both sides are defenseless. Why do you think they called a cease fire? They don't have any guns left. You go ahead and sign up. I'm not even sure they'll know what to do with you. At this point they might strap you to a missile and get you to be the guidance system."

Caty blinked a tear. David frowned and looked away. That was when it really hit her. Alexander was *dead.*

A few seconds later, David turned back to her and opened his arms awkwardly. "*Ven aqui.*"

She didn't argue. He enfolded her in a strong hug. He didn't smell very good, but then again neither did she.

The line started moving to board the buses, and they shuffled along together. He held her, whispering reassurances and apologies. They sat down together on the bus. Caty sniffled, feeling foolish and embarrassed. Then the bus jolted into motion, and David gave her a haunted look. "I lost someone, too. *Ella era mi todo.*"

"Your wife?" Caty asked.

"My everything," David said again, this time in English.

Caty nodded and looked out the window, watching blackened, fire-scorched trees blur by. "Alexander was mine," she whispered.

CHAPTER 17

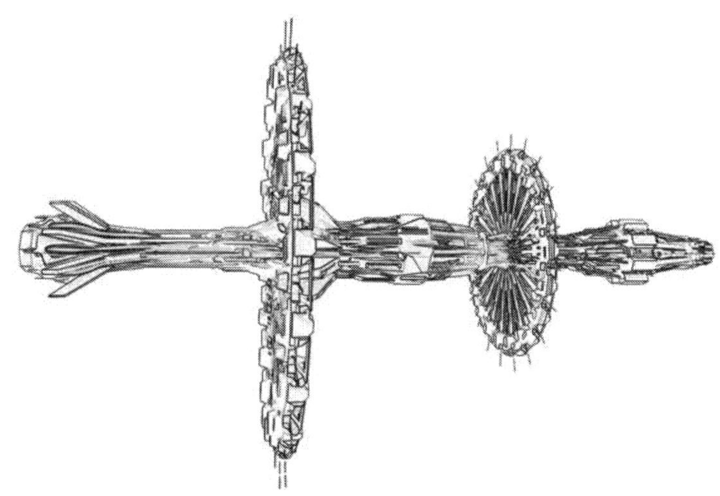

Max Carter sat in his quarters watching the approach to Wonderland under normal gravity. After passing through the so-called *David Davorian Belts,* the mission was back on track.

Max set the viewport in his room to show the view from the *Lincoln's* bow cameras and then magnified and enhanced Wonderland for ease of study. A mottled blue and white ball appeared, floating in a glittering sea of stars. They were still three days out, but with magnification the planet now looked close enough that he could reach out and touch it.

Beautiful. Amazing what technology can do, he thought.

Max considered everything that lay ahead for him and the crew of the *Lincoln.* So far *his* mission was going according to plan, and the crew of the *Lincoln* was none the wiser. He had detected some suspicion from Commander Korbin during a routine interview before everyone had entered the G-tanks, but Korbin didn't really have anything to go on.

Suspicion and proof are two very different things.

Max smiled. *Catch me if you can.*

* * *

May 22, 2790
(The Lincoln's Frame of Reference)

After three days of forced rest, Doctor Crespin reluctantly discharged Alexander from the infirmary so that he could watch the *Lincoln's* final approach to Wonderland from his seat on the bridge.

The planet swelled before them, looking startlingly like Earth. The day side of the planet lay dead ahead, with the terminator line on the far left side of the planet, making Wonderland look egg-shaped rather than spherical. The day side shone a familiar blue with white patches and swirls. Somewhere near the center of the planet, mottled reds and purples peeked out through the white.

Someone whistled.

"She's a real exotic beauty," Lieutenant Stone said, identifying himself as the whistler.

"Vasquez, what are sensors telling us so far?" Alexander asked.

"Land temperatures on the surface range from twenty degrees Celsius on the day side to five degrees on the night side. There's ice at the poles and—"

"Ice?" Alexander interrupted. "Then you've confirmed that the blue we're seeing is liquid water?"

"Yes, sir."

A cheer went up from the crew. Water wasn't all that rare, but liquid surface water was a big requirement for human habitability.

"What about those colorful smears? Are they what I think

they are?" Alexander asked, pointing to the mottled red and purple areas.

"Possibly plants," Vasquez replied.

"Damn straight!" Lieutenant Cardinal replied from gunnery.

Alexander smiled. As the mission's botanist, Cardinal had a vested interest in finding alien plants on Wonderland.

"Could also be rock formations," Stone replied. "If they're plants, why aren't they green? Don't they need chlorophyll for photosynthesis?"

"Assuming alien plants derive energy from photosynthesis in the first place, they don't need to absorb the same wavelengths as plants on Earth," Cardinal replied. "The surface of Earth gets mostly green light, but that's the color that our plants reflect *away* from them. Evolution doesn't always yield the most efficient design. I'll bet you a month's wages those colorful regions are plants."

"You're on," Stone replied.

Alexander smiled. "As long as we're betting, I'll bet that the atmosphere is breathable, and that we'll find plants *and* animals."

"Well, if we do find animals, the first thing I'm going to do is slap one of them on a grill and see if it tastes like chicken," Stone said.

Laughter rippled across the bridge. Alexander joined in, but Korbin shot him a dark look, and he wiped the smile off his face.

"Our first encounter with alien life and you want to cook it?" she demanded.

"Why not?" Stone replied.

"All right, you do that, and when you die from some alien parasite, we'll just chalk it up to karma being a bitch."

Alexander cleared his throat. "He was joking, Korbin."

She sent him a thin smile. "Who says I wasn't?"

Alexander snorted. "Davorian, how long till we enter orbit?"

"Ten to fifteen minutes, sir, depending whether it's a high or low orbit."

"Make it a low one so we can do our first pass around the planet in less time."

"Aye-aye, sir."

"Vasquez, start scanning for the best place to land our shuttles."

"Already on it, Captain."

"Good."

Alexander settled back to watch as Wonderland grew steadily larger on the MHD. It was a beautiful planet—mottled red and purple landmass, bright turquoise oceans, and familiar white swirls of cloud. It looked startlingly like home, except for the odd colors and the greater percentage of surface water.

Once the *Lincoln* established a low orbit, Davorian killed thrust to the engines, and let Wonderland's gravity do all the work. Without active thrust, the sensation of gravity disappeared, replaced by the zero-G free-fall of orbit.

It took over ninety minutes to orbit the planet once. During that time, Vasquez identified the primary landmass as the one they'd seen on their approach. There were also a number of islands, but everyone agreed that they'd learn more by setting down on the planet's Pangaea-like super continent.

"Time to go pack our things, everyone," Alexander said. "We're all going down to the surface together—except for Davorian and Hayes."

"Except for me, sir?" Davorian sounded crestfallen.

"We're not going to see Wonderland?" Hayes added, putting in his own objection.

"Davorian, your specialty is astrophysics and astronomy, so you're better off staying up here to see if you can find some indication of where we are in relation to Earth and the rest of the universe. And Hayes—we need someone manning the comms in case Earth tries to contact us. But besides that, we need at least two qualified bridge crew to take shifts up here on the bridge. Davorian, you have seniority, so I'm leaving you in charge."

"Yes, sir," Davorian said.

"We'll be in touch. As for the rest of you, let's go." Buckles clattered as everyone unfastened their harnesses. Alexander lingered an extra moment to send Davorian a private comms. "Keep an eye on Hayes."

There was a brief pause, and then Davorian replied, "What should I be looking for?"

"Acts of sabotage. When you leave him alone on bridge, I don't want him manning anything besides the comms. Zero access to everything else. Make sure you shut down all of the ship's stations and keep them locked whenever you're not there. If there's some kind of emergency while he has the deck, all he needs to do is wake you up, and you can deal with it. Worst case, you give him your lock codes, and he can react while he's waiting for you to get there, but that's only in case of a dire emergency."

"That's… somewhat unconventional. What excuse am I going to give Hayes for locking him out?"

"We have one act of sabotage that's still unaccounted for—the bad engine code. Until we know for sure who's responsible, you're the only one I can trust. Tell him that. It's true anyway."

"What makes you so sure you can trust me?"

"Because you were the one who stopped that bad code from leaving us derelict in space. If you were the one responsible, you could have just let it execute and then covered your tracks after the fact."

"Good point."

"Keep an eye on things up here, and keep me posted."

"Aye, Captain. Any chance I'm going to get to see Wonderland?"

"No promises, but I may be able to trade places with you at some point."

Davorian sighed. "I guess that will have to do."

"It will."

"Captain, are you coming?" Korbin asked.

Alexander saw her floating free of her acceleration couch and angling her feet to push off from the seat so she could float toward the elevators without the need to fire the maneuvering jets in the soles of her boots.

Switching from comms to external speakers, Alexander said, "I'll be right there. Hold the elevator for me."

"Aye-aye," she said, and pushed off from her couch.

Alexander commed the rest of the crew on an open channel to let them know who would be joining the landing party, and who would not. Besides the bridge crew, he ordered Max Carter, Doctor Crespin, two of his nurses, and five of the ship's seven surviving Rapier pilots to meet them in the shuttle bay. That done, he unbuckled his own seat restraints and maneuvered himself to push off from his seat.

Once he made it to the elevator, navigating the rest of the ship was easier. The bridge deck was one of the few places where the ceiling was high enough and the walls far enough apart that he could end up stranded, floating in mid-air too far from the nearest handrail to physically guide himself through the ship.

Even with handrails in easy reach, navigating the ship in zero-G was a slow, awkward business. Getting to his quarters took five minutes, which was five minutes longer than it should have taken, and packing his things took forever. Pulling things out of his locker resulted in them flying all around the room, and he spent a long time just catching up with his underwear.

When he was finally done, Alexander spent another five minutes dragging himself back down the corridors by the handrails to get to the nearest elevator. He didn't encounter anyone else along the way, which meant they were all either faster or slower than him at packing their things. Inside the elevator Alexander selected the deck marked *Shuttle Bay One (SB1)*, which was one deck down from the officers' quarters.

The elevator jerked into motion, and he held on tight to the handrails to avoid hitting his head on the ceiling. A few seconds later, the elevator stopped, and it began spinning on its axis, pulling him against the padded sides. Alexander grimaced. Davorian had already spun up the ring decks. That was going to make getting to them slightly more complicated.

He used the handrail to drag himself around the rim of the elevator until his back was pressing against the doors. A moment later, pressure sensors detected he was ready, and the elevator opened. Alexander flew out of the spinning elevator and landed against the padded inner rim of a spinning hub. *Thud.*

After taking a moment to recover, he crawled along the curvature of the hub until he reached an open hatch. It was a *drop tube* that ran perpendicular to the elevator, going all the way from the central column of the ship to one of the outer rings, like the spoke of a wheel. Alexander maneuvered himself until his feet were dangling over the padded edge of the tube.

Taking a second to steel himself for the fall, he shoved off and landed on the counter-weighted elevator platform waiting inside. The impact overcame the platform's inertia and it began to drop at a lazy pace toward the distant bottom of the tube where the shuttle bay was located. As he fell, the tug of artificially-generated gravity grew progressively stronger until sensors judged the time had come to engage braking pads.

The elevator was un-powered while descending, using his weight and the physics of circular motion to pull him down to the spinning ring deck. The ship's ring decks provided redundant living space for the crew to enjoy the effects of gravity while cruising on long voyages through space, but they were also ideal for launching shuttles, drones, fighters, and even missiles on trajectories that would carry them away from the *Lincoln's* flight path and avoid deadly collisions.

Alexander felt the elevator stop, and the doors opened, allowing him to walk out onto the subtly-curving deck at a comfortable one-half of standard gravity. Everyone else was already there and busy loading cargo crates onto loading platforms. The platforms were demarcated with safety rails and glowing black and yellow-striped boxes painted on the floor with the words *Caution* and *Loading Zone* blinking around them in red.

Each of those loading platforms rested above an airlock leading to one of the shuttles docked on the outer rim of the ring deck. As he watched, the crew summoned a pair of loading platforms back from depositing their cargo inside waiting shuttles. Both platforms rose slowly until their safety rails came into view.

Alexander looked away and crossed over to Lieutenant Vasquez. The curvature of the deck made it feel like he was always walking uphill. At least under half of standard gravity, that wasn't such a chore—even with the heavy pack on his shoulders. Vasquez had her helmet off, revealing short dark hair and a dark bronze skin. She was already snapping orders at the burly Rapier pilots, telling them what supplies to fetch and load onto the shuttles. Vasquez was Williams' replacement as the *Lin-*

coln's quartermaster, as well as its meteorologist and sensors operator, but she didn't have much experience yet, so Alexander felt he had to check up on her to make sure they didn't leave anything important behind.

"Vasquez."

"Sir?" she replied.

"Do you have the cargo manifests ready for me to review?"

"Uh... they're up here, sir," she said, tapping her head. "Sorry, I haven't had time to write them down yet. I can do that now if you like."

"I like. Dictate to your pad. I'll listen."

"All right—sir," Vasquez added hastily as she unslung her pack and withdrew a holopad. She began dictating, "Two shuttles, carrying one rover each. Twenty solar panels, and two fuel cell generators. A month's supply of fuel for the fuel cells. A month's supply of dry rations and drinking water. Spare pressure suits. Lab equipment—each of the bridge crew is responsible for making sure all the equipment they need is loaded. Fourteen inflatable habitation modules—one for each of the bridge crew, one for Max—I mean, Mr. Carter, two more between the infirmary and sleeping quarters for the medical staff, a shared module for the Rapier pilots, one more module for a mess hall and storage, another module for quarantine, and a final one to be used as a spare. Am I forgetting anything?"

Alexander frowned. "You're asking me?"

"Sorry, no, sir. That's it."

"All right. I need you to—"

A new voice interrupted them, calling out across the loading bay, "What about weapons?"

Alexander turned to see Lieutenant Stone walking up to them. "What kind of weapons?"

"All kinds, sir," Stone said, stopping in front of them. "We don't know what we're going to run into down there."

"What do you suggest?"

"Sniper rifles with thermal and night vision scopes. Automatic rifles. Handguns. Grenades. Land mines. Cheetahs."

"Land mines? *Cheetahs?* What do we need assault mechs for?"

"They're faster than rovers over uneven terrain, and unlike the rovers, they're armed, so they'll make good escort vehicles. Not to mention their sensors will save us a lot of trouble watching our perimeter at night."

"The rovers are armored, and we can guard our perimeter with those sniper rifles you mentioned. Cheetahs will be overkill, not to mention heavy as hell. We'll need to take an extra shuttle for each of them."

"Is that a problem, sir?"

"There are only six shuttles. If we take four, there won't be enough left for the *Lincoln's* crew if they need to abandon ship."

"Aye, but if they need to abandon ship, then we're all screwed anyway. Besides, sir, when we meet T-rex's hairy cousin on the surface, you'll be glad we brought the Cheetahs."

Alexander snorted. "All right, fine." Turning to Vasquez, he said, "You get all that? We're taking four shuttles, two Cheetahs, and all that other stuff Stone mentioned."

"Yes, sir."

"I'll help her," Stone replied.

"Good. While you're at it, have your men check people's packs, and all of the cargo before it's loaded."

Stone's brow furrowed. "Check how, sir? Like a customs check?"

Alexander nodded. "Exactly like that. After the bomb scare with Lieutenant Williams, we can't be too careful."

"Right. Understood, sir," Stone saluted and about-faced.

"Packs on the ground people!" he called out as he went. "Daddy wants to know if you packed your toothbrushes."

"You think it's going to be dangerous down there, sir?" Vasquez asked.

Alexander shrugged. "I don't know, but it's probably best to be careful."

"Aye, sir—" Vasquez nodded. "—it probably is."

CHAPTER 18

Alexander listened to the shuttle rattle and shake. Wonderland's atmosphere roared against the hull as they made atmospheric entry. He stared out the palladium glass cockpit canopy, watching as Wonderland came swirling out of a cottony white carpet of clouds. Vibrant purples and reds snapped into sharper focus.

Lieutenant Cardinal gasped. "Those are plants. They've got to be!" he said.

Alexander was inclined to agree. Even at this altitude those mottled streaks of color didn't look like rock formations. "Looks like you're going to lose that bet, Stone."

The ground raced up fast, and Lieutenant Stone leveled out to decrease their angle of descent. "Altitude is 2500 meters and dropping," he said.

They entered the clouds and everything went white. Raindrops pelted the cockpit canopy.

"Rain..." Vasquez whispered, her voice full of wonder, as if she were seeing it for the first time.

"Captain, I've got something on sensors," Stone said.

Alexander glanced left to the sensor display to see what it

was. Then the comms crackled.

"Shuttle One, this is Two. Are you getting this?"

"I see it," Stone replied. The sensors display showed multiple unidentified contacts dead ahead and about 500 meters down. "Let's take a look." Without warning, he dove sharply and burst out of the clouds. Leveling out again, they saw the dusty purple horizon crowded with hundreds of black dots.

Range to the unidentified blips dropped swiftly, and Alexander's heart raced. He saw more of them out his side window, silhouetted in the rosy light of the sinking sun. Turning back to the fore, Alexander watched as those dots swelled and details began to emerge. They were spherical and black, but otherwise featureless.

"I'm going to slow down so we can get a good look," Ryder said. "Brace for braking thrust."

Alexander slammed into his harness. He gritted his teeth and waited for the sensation of having his eyeballs sucked from their sockets to pass. Braking forces were called *eyeballs out* for a reason.

The sensation eased, and the unidentified black spheres began whipping by all around them. They were semi-translucent and hollow. Papery fins flanked the spheres, and long, delicate tentacles trailed from their lower halves. They looked like giant floating jellyfish. Alexander saw the sun shining through one of them, illuminating venous patterns in its… *skin,* he decided.

"What *are* they?" Cardinal asked.

The comms lit up with exclamations from the other shuttle pilots, and Alexander grinned.

"They're *alive,* that's what they are."

* * *

The shuttles flew on for another hour, chasing the sun so night wouldn't fall before they had a chance to see the planet with their own eyes. Lieutenant Stone flew them low over an alien jungle of purple and crimson-leafed trees and towering black mushrooms. Maybe they weren't mushrooms, but that was what they looked like to Alexander.

They landed on the distant shore of the continent just as the sun was setting over a bright turquoise ocean, splashing the sky and clouds with familiar reds and golds.

Now standing in the airlock, they were all in a hurry to disembark, but no one more than Lieutenant Cardinal. He'd spent an hour salivating over all the different species of alien plants, and he was just about to get his first hands-on look at some of them.

"No one takes off their helmets," Alexander reminded them. Doctor Crespin had warned them about the dangers of breathing the air before they left the *Lincoln,* but Alexander didn't want anyone to get caught up in the excitement and forget. "I don't care what your suit says about how breathable the air is. Until Doc Crespin clears the air as safe, it's not breathable. Understood?"

Heads bobbed.

A green light came on above the outer airlock doors, indicating that pressure had equalized. Stone waved the outer doors open and in streamed dazzling beams of sunlight. In the distance Alexander could hear the ocean crashing on the shore. The crew jumped out one after another, sand *skrishing* as they landed. Two out of three fell on their hands and knees. Only Stone was able to jump out without falling over.

They'd all lost a lot of muscle from the past seventy days floating in the G-tanks. Alexander decided to climb down using the guide rails for support. Once he was standing on the sand, he saw Lieutenant Korbin and McAdams come striding over from Shuttle Two.

"Did you see that?" McAdams called out as they drew near.

"See what?"

"Those balloon creatures," Korbin said.

Alexander nodded. "Our first major discovery."

"They're incredible!" McAdams said, smiling. "They were actually *floating!* They must be filled with some kind of gas that's either lighter or hotter than air. I wonder if all avian life on Wonderland flies by the same mechanism? What do you think they eat? Imagine what happens to them in a storm. Either the storms here are incredibly mild, or they are tougher than they look. We've *got* to catch one of them!"

Alexander smiled. McAdams was talking a mile a minute. "That's what you're here for," he said.

"How long are we staying?"

"As long as it takes to determine whether or not the planet is habitable. A week or two I'd guess."

"That's it?" McAdams asked, her smile collapsing.

"It's obvious that Wonderland is habitable," Korbin said. "The atmosphere is a breathable mix of oxygen and nitrogen, just like Earth's. We shouldn't need more time than that."

Alexander looked around. To one side, a shadowy jungle of red and purple trees soared. A few gargantuan black mush-rooms towered over them. There was already a group of people headed toward the jungle, spear-headed by Lieutenant Cardinal. Alexander frowned and mentally activated his comms to send a message to the whole landing party at once.

"Listen up, everyone. This is a strange planet. We don't know what's dangerous and what isn't. For now, no one goes more than 50 meters from the landing site."

Acknowledgments streamed in, and Alexander nodded to

McAdams and Korbin. "I'm going to go dip my feet in the water," he said, and started off toward the ocean. The clearing where they'd landed was full of scraggly bone-white shrubs pricking up through the sand. Opposite the jungle, the ocean sparkled invitingly beneath the fiery sunset. Waves thundered and crashed on the shore below the clearing.

Alexander reached the top of a sand dune and all but fell down the other side. The beach dropped steeply into the ocean. That meant there'd be a strong current. Maybe he wouldn't dip his feet in the water after all. On his way down, Alexander watched the sand, looking for sea creatures. On Earth he would expect to find holes and the scuttling crabs that had dug them, or maybe even jelly fish and seaweed that had washed up on the shore, but he didn't see anything here.

Alexander stopped a few feet from the smooth, wet sand and looked out across the turquoise ocean. Waves curled and crashed right in front of him. He imagined the salty spray coming off the water.

The sun was dimmer now, lying just above the horizon. The sky glowed a pale red, and the clouds looked like they'd been soaked in blood.

As the sun sank below the watery line of the horizon and that crimson stain seeped away, Alexander shook his head and swallowed past a painful lump in his throat. This wasn't just the end of another day on Wonderland—it was the end of an entire species.

Humanity.

He hadn't spent much time dwelling on the worst-case scenario. He'd tried to stay optimistic, and he wanted to believe President Baker had been telling the truth when he'd said, *Your loved ones are all safe and well,* but Alexander knew a lie when he heard one. The question wasn't whether or not anyone had died back on Earth—but who, and how many.

"Goodbye, Caty," Alexander whispered.

Commander Korbin walked up beside him, her feet *skrishing* through the sparkling lavender sand. She laid a hand on his shoulder.

"They're not gone, Captain," she said, her voice trembling with stubborn conviction.

Alexander regarded her with eyebrows raised.

"Call it a hunch, call it faith, but they're still alive."

"I hope you're right, Commander." His thoughts went back to Caty, and he tried to imagine her smiling face to make Korbin's optimism seem more real. "I hope you're right," he said again.

Somehow they'd reversed roles, with Korbin the one clinging to hope while he gave into despair. Korbin had two sons back on Earth, wards of the state being raised by a first-class institution in New York City. New York was a high priority target for enemy missiles—maybe the highest—followed by LA, where Caty was. They'd picked LA because it had a vibrant immigrant community. Plenty of people still spoke *Español* there. It had seemed like a great way to transition to life in the northern states at the time, but now Alexander wished they'd chosen some sleepy town in the middle of nowhere instead.

He forced his thoughts back into the moment. They had a planet to explore. He looked away from the fading light and up at the dark, brooding jungle beyond the clearing where they'd landed their shuttles. "We'd better get back and help the crew set up the hab modules."

Korbin nodded.

Alexander slung his arm through hers to help her up the beach. Not that she needed his help. If anything, he needed hers. They both stumbled equally as they went. Near the top of the beach, where lavender sand met ivory-colored shrubbery, they found Junior Lieutenant McAdams watching the sunset, her cheeks wet with tears behind her helmet.

"Hello, McAdams," Alexander said.

"Sir," she replied.

McAdams' parents had spent their life savings on her so that she could be born a gener. As an adult she'd returned the favor, signing up for the navy against their wishes in order to save them. That was before the nukes had begun flying up North. Alexander remembered McAdams confessing her fears to him at the memorial service—*'I killed them,'* she'd said, and the sad part was, she probably had. But by that reasoning, Alexander had gotten Caty killed, too. He shuddered and pushed those thoughts away, forcing a smile for McAdams' benefit.

"They could still be alive, Lieutenant. Regardless, we're going to have plenty of time to grieve for the planet we lost. Right now we need to focus on the one that's under our feet."

Something ugly flickered through McAdams' eyes, but then she sniffed and nodded. "Yes, sir." With that, she about-faced and trudged back up to the landing site.

Alexander frowned, watching her go. He had a feeling he'd just put his foot in it.

"Onwards and upwards, Captain," Commander Korbin said, nodding as they continued up the hilly shore.

"Excelsior," Alexander replied.

"I'm sorry?"

"That's what it means—onwards and upwards."

"Onwards to a brighter future, and upwards to the stars..." Korbin replied.

Alexander smiled. There was just enough optimism in that sentiment to dull the hollow ache in his chest.

"Excelsior..." he whispered.

CHAPTER 19

By the time Alexander and Korbin reached the landing site, the stars were already pricking out overhead. Both of Wonderland's moons were out—one of them a large, angry red eye, the other a silver crescent that was more reminiscent of Earth's moon.

Alexander activated his comms and said, "Gather round, everyone!" He waited while people stopped what they were doing and turned to face him, their head lamps sweeping his way. A group of headlamps came bobbing in from the direction of the jungle—*Cardinal, et al.*

Speaking to Korbin, Alexander said, "Get me a head count." He studied the landing site while he waited. The shuttles' landing lights were on, casting a muted golden glow across the sandy shrub-infested ground. The jungle appeared as a black, featureless wall towering over everything. Night was falling fast. The stars grew sharper and more numerous in the sky with every passing second.

It reminded Alexander of going camping back on Earth when he was a kid. He remembered his family telling scary stories around the camp fire while he watched wide-eyed as the firelight made shadows dance in the trees. Back then the night had been alive with unseen terrors. The mind of a child could be a scary place. When he'd grown up, he'd realized that the only really scary predator on Earth was man, but being here on Wonderland brought all his childish fears rushing back. There could be anything out there.

Even T-rex's hairy cousin.

Alexander pictured a giant teddy bear, and a silly grin sprang to his lips.

"Sixteen. All present and accounted for, sir," Korbin announced.

"Good," he replied, nodding. He dialed up the volume on his helmet's external speakers rather than use the comms. If he was being honest, that was just because he wanted to make some noise. Maybe he would scare off whatever was lurking in the jungle. "It's time for us to set up camp, but first we're going to go back to our shuttles for dinner. Leave whatever samples you've collected outside. That goes double for you, Cardinal."

People began muttering their objections, and Cardinal started to say, "But—"

"This entire mission needs to be conducted with strict quarantine protocols. The airlocks in the shuttles and our habs have been equipped to flash cook anything that hitches a ride on our suits, but that doesn't mean we should push our luck. There could be any number of deadly pathogens in the air, let alone any samples we collect. This planet does appear to be habitable, but that doesn't make it safe. Go eat something, and I suggest you all take a caffeine tablet. It's going to be a long night, and I don't want anyone fainting from exhaustion."

Helmets bobbed and *aye-aye, sirs,* echoed around the circle as people headed back to their shuttles. Alexander used his finely-honed sense of intuition to locate his, finding the one with *Shut-*

tle One written on the side in bold white letters.

Korbin followed him, even though it wasn't her shuttle, and McAdams joined them while they were waiting at the airlock. "Mind if I eat with you, Captain?" she asked.

Alexander smiled and nodded. "Sure." Maybe he hadn't offended her as badly as he thought.

Cardinal and Stone joined them a moment later, followed by Vasquez. "You won't believe what we found!" Cardinal said, his face full of wonder behind his helmet.

"What did you find?" Alexander asked.

"The plants *move*. They all *move!*"

McAdams arched an eyebrow. "Move how? Reflex or voluntary movement? Are you sure you were looking at plants?"

Cardinal gave her a look of strained patience. "Yes, to the plant question, and if you're asking whether the movement was self-directed by the plant, I guess that would depend on whether or not it has a brain. My bet is that it does, but probably a very rudimentary one. I tried tests involving movement, light, and water. The plants I tested reacted to shadows caused by movement, turned toward the light, and gave no reaction to the water."

Alexander frowned. "So plants on Wonderland don't need water?"

"More likely the ones I tested weren't thirsty. They must have an abundance of rain on a planet like this."

"So you're saying the jungle could sneak up on us while we're eating."

"No, of course not—well... I don't think so. Just the branches and fronds move. And they're not dangerous, just curious."

Alexander looked to Lieutenant Stone. "What do you think?" He was in charge of mission security, and his expression was guarded, not awed.

"I think I'm glad we brought the Cheetahs. It might not be safe to explore the jungle on foot—especially not if we have to hack our way through. Who knows how those *curious* plants will respond if we start chopping off their limbs."

"Is violence your first response to everything?" Korbin demanded. "We're not going to hack our way through a *living* jungle."

"Why not, ma'am? They're just plants."

"Plants that *move,*" McAdams said. "That makes them more like animals than plants."

Stone shrugged. "Plants, animals… We eat 'em both, so what's the big deal?"

"All right, enough bickering," Alexander said. "We're not going to be eating any alien life forms, and we should probably wait until we've studied this new environment before we start hacking it to pieces."

"Yes, sir," Stone replied while climbing up into the shuttle airlock.

Once they were all standing in the airlock, they activated the radiation shields on their helmets, and their visors polarized, effectively blinding them. Lieutenant Stone gave the airlock a verbal command to pressurize, and a warning siren sounded briefly; then a deep, resonating *hum* filled the air as the flash-cooker sterilized their suits. Another tone sounded, this one pleasant and musical to let them know it was safe to deactivate their radiation shields. They did so, and the airlock's inner doors swished open.

In the shuttle's cargo hold, Lieutenant Stone found a food crate and began passing out ration packs and bottles of water. They all removed their helmets and sat on the floor to eat.

Alexander picked up a meat-colored protein stick and sniffed it suspiciously. It smelled like old socks. He was beginning to agree with Lieutenant Stone about checking to see if the native fauna tasted like chicken.

McAdams sat down beside him and handed him a caffeine pill. He nodded his thanks and set his ration pack aside to swallow the pill with a swig of water.

"What do you think we're going to find down here? Anyone have any predictions?" Korbin asked.

"Well I predicted we'd find plants, and we did," Cardinal said. "You owe me a month's wages," he added, looking at Lieutenant Stone.

The geologist grunted, but gave no reply.

"I think we're going to find plenty of animals, too," McAdams said. "We already found avian life on our way down. Those jungles are probably teeming with all kinds of amazing creatures."

Vasquez spoke up, "In terms of climate, I suspect the tides will be either more frequent or more pronounced thanks to Wonderland's two moons. The climate is pretty mild, but there are signs of water damage on the trunks of some of the older trees, so we might find hurricanes or tsunamis here."

"Tsunamis are usually caused by earthquakes," Stone said. "I guess we might have to call them something else here… Wonderquakes?"

"Sounds like a breakfast cereal," Alexander replied.

"Let's just call them tremors. Anyway, if there's seismic activity, that means plate tectonics, which in turn means volcanic activity, island formation, mountains, sea floor trenches, and so on. We might find a lot of the same geological features as Earth."

"Sounds like you have some theories to work on already," Alexander said as he took a cautious bite of a protein stick. Thankfully it tasted better than it smelled.

"If there's water damage on the trees, I think it's safe to say we need to find a new camp site," Korbin said. "We don't want a tsunami or a flood to come crashing over us while we're sleeping."

"Good point," Alexander said. "We'll tell the other shuttle captains as soon as we're done eating." He took another bite of his rations. A veggie stick this time. It tasted like spinach-flavored cardboard.

His comm crackled, and Alexander heard Seth Ryder's voice. He was the pilot of Shuttle Two. "Captain… there's something happening out here."

"Out where? You're supposed to be in your shuttle eating."

"We finished already, sir."

"Where are you?"

"On the beach. Listen, sir…"

All he heard was static. "I don't hear anything, Ryder."

"Exactly, no waves, because the water isn't here anymore."

"The tide's probably going out. Vasquez was just talking about how two moons could mean stronger tides."

"Maybe," Ryder said. "But this ain't like any tide I've ever seen. The water's runnin' away from us faster than we can chase it."

Alexander saw Vasquez suddenly sit up straight. "How long has it been doing that?" she asked over the same comm channel.

"About ten, twenty seconds," Ryder replied.

"You need to get out of there *now!*"

"What?"

"Run! Get back to your shuttle and take off ASAP."

"Yes, ma'am… Ryder out."

"What's going on Vasquez?"

She bounced to her feet and ran toward the cockpit. "Tell the other shuttles to take off!"

Stone hurried after her, already on the comms telling the

other shuttles to lift off. They all crowded into the cockpit and took their seats. Alexander's mind raced, trying to come up with an explanation for the way Vasquez and Stone were behaving.

"What's going on?" McAdams asked.

Lieutenant Stone was too busy cold-starting the shuttle's engines to reply.

"There's a tsunami coming," Vasquez replied, her brown eyes wide.

CHAPTER 20

"A tsunami?" Alexander asked. "How do you know?"

"Sometimes the water runs out before a tsunami hits. That's what Ryder was seeing."

"You sure it's not just the tide?" Alexander asked.

"No tide is that fast, not even with two moons. We've got a minute or two before that wave hits. Stone, you need to hurry."

"I'm going as fast as I can!" he snapped.

Alexander looked out the side window and saw Seth Ryder and Max Carter come racing up the beach. They piled into Shuttle Two's airlock, and the doors slid shut behind them.

"They're not going to make it..." Vasquez warned, her voice a whisper.

"Oh, shit..." Stone said.

Alexander saw what had made him swear. A black wall of water was racing toward them, shimmering in the moonlight, and already curling at the top.

"Come on, Stone! Take off!" Vasquez screamed.

"I'm working on it!"

"We're not going to make it either," Korbin said.

Alexander blinked, and in that time the water had swept up

and blotted out the sky. Tsunami's were *fast.*

Suddenly the shuttle lurched and hovered straight up. Spray sprinkled the canopy and windows. Two of the other three shuttles rose beside them.

"Hang on!" Stone said. He pulled up and ignited the thrusters at full burn. The acceleration pinned them to their chairs. Then the wave crashed and went surging up the beach. Water splashed over them, washing the windows clean. Alexander imagined the water weighing them down and sucking them under, but a split second later they were through and racing toward the stars. Stone leveled out and looped back around to look for Shuttle Two, but it was nowhere in sight.

Stone keyed the comms. "Report in," he said.

Shuttles Three and Four checked in, but Two was dead silent. No one said anything. Stone and the other shuttles swept their landing lights over the surging black water, but nothing came bobbing up to the surface. Shuttle Two was gone. By now the water was rolling them along the ground, slamming them into tree trunks and cracking them open on rocks.

Alexander watched the trees bending. The smaller ones got sucked under, while the tallest ones weathered the assault just as they probably had a thousand times before. More water damage to add to their trunks.

"Fuck!" Stone said. "Why didn't he stay in his shuttle?"

"What are the odds..." Korbin whispered. "We were just talking about earthquakes and tsunamis, and then one hits us."

"If they had time to strap in, they might still survive, even if they're trapped under the water," Alexander said. "Shuttles are armored and air-tight."

"I don't know," Stone replied. "They're going to take one hell of a beating."

"We can't leave until we know for sure," Alexander said.

"How long can we hover before we run out of fuel?" Vasquez asked.

"A while, but we should save our fuel."

"We're not going to be able to effect a rescue until the water subsides anyway," Vasquez added.

Alexander rounded on her. "You want to leave them here?"

"For now. Tsunamis aren't just one wave. They're a series of waves, and it could be hours, even days, before the water subsides. We can't do anything for them right now."

"She's right," Stone said. "We need to find higher ground and start setting up camp. We'll come back and look for them as soon as we can."

Alexander ground his teeth. "All right. Let's go."

* * *

"Over there," Stone pointed to the elevation map on the shuttle's main holo display. The map was compiled from orbital imagery taken by the *Lincoln*. It showed a line of cliffs running along the coast.

"Elevation?" Alexander asked.

"Around a hundred meters."

"How big was that tsunami?"

"About twenty meters. It would take one hell of a wave to reach us up there," Stone replied.

"All right. Set us down."

The landing was smooth. Nothing much to see out the viewports until the shuttle hovered down close enough to the ground that its landing lights peeled away the shadows. Alexander saw they were setting down in a field of red grass. A field of blood. It was a painful reminder of the crewmates they'd left behind. For all anyone knew Max and Ryder were already dead, but they could also be using debris as a life raft while the receding floodwaters took them out to sea.

Alexander listened as Stone checked in with the other two shuttle pilots. A minute later the other shuttles landed around theirs. As the noisy roar of engines faded to silence, everyone unbuckled and made their way to the cargo hold. No one said a word.

Stone sealed the door to the cockpit and opened the inner doors of the rear airlock so they could begin loading it with cargo crates. It was hard, sweaty work. Once the airlock was full they all piled in with the cargo and shut the inner doors. Then Stone cycled the outer doors open. After a few moments, a green light went on above the outer doors and they swished open. Then Cardinal and Stone climbed down while Alexander, McAdams, and Korbin passed crates to them.

They had to repeat the process three times to completely unload the shuttle. Next came the job of unpacking the hab modules and inflating them. The shuttles had landed in a semicircular formation with the open end facing the cliffs and the closed end toward the jungle. Just in case.

Alexander eyed the jungle, imagining the plants in there moving restlessly, their branches writhing like tentacles—or snakes. He shivered.

He hated snakes.

Commander Korbin walked up to him. "They'll be okay, sir."

Alexander frowned. She'd noticed him gazing distractedly into the jungle and assumed he was wrestling with some kind of survivor's guilt. Now he felt doubly guilty for worrying about more trivial things instead. "I hope you're right," he said, glancing her way with a tight smile.

He turned back to the camp and watched as McAdams tried

to move a fuel cell generator five times her size. It was on wheels, but in the knee-high grass those wheels were digging in.

There came a heavy *clanking* and *thudding* sound and Alexander saw a jungle-colored Cheetah assault mech come stomping up to them. The cockpit was lit up with the predominantly blue glow of holoscreens. Lieutenant Stone grinned down on them. The mechanized biped reached out and under the generator with the wide flat fingers of its hands held straight like the tongs of a forklift.

"Where do you want it?" Stone asked over the Cheetah's external speakers as he picked up the generator.

"Over there," McAdams replied. She pointed to a half-assembled hab module and Stone stomped up to it, making the ground shake with every step.

"Come on, we better make ourselves useful," Alexander said. "The sooner we get everything set up, the sooner we can go back and look for Ryder and Max." He hurried over to a stack of cargo crates where Vasquez was struggling to unpack another hab module all by herself. Korbin followed him there.

It took almost four hours of hard, sweaty work to get all the hab modules assembled. When they were done, they had was a cluster of white, dome-shaped tents, otherwise known as habitation modules, illuminated from within and puffed up with air. The air regulators and electrical generators were hooked up and running. All of the remaining supplies were stacked high inside the habs, still packed inside their crates.

Sweat trickled down Alexander's back, causing a maddening itch. He longed to peel out of his suit and breathe air that wasn't perfumed with his own BO, but first they had to sterilize the habs. Doctor Crespin stood with McAdams beside one of the air regulators, discussing what conditions alien microbes and hitchhiking insects were least likely to survive.

"We're on an alien planet," Crespin said, "so speculating about what may or may not kill alien organisms is a waste of effort. All we can do is limit the risk."

"Agreed," McAdams replied.

Alexander left them to it. He noticed the rest of the crew was at a loose end, standing around waiting, so he ordered them back to the shuttles to get some sleep. He didn't see Lieutenant Stone anywhere, but after asking a few crew members about his whereabouts, Vasquez told him where to look.

"He's out in a Cheetah watching the perimeter."

"Thanks. Go get some sleep, Vasquez."

"Yes, sir."

Alexander walked past the shuttles, feeling nervous as he left the comforting glow of their landing lights. The red grass turned black with the night. He used his suit's sensors to look for Stone's comm beacon, and his HUD promptly highlighted a large shadow standing halfway between the shuttles and the trees.

"Lieutenant Stone," Alexander said, making comms contact as he approached.

"Hey there, Captain."

"You see anything interesting out there?"

"Maybe."

"Maybe?"

"I thought I saw something moving on infrared, but it was only there for a second."

"Well, apparently the trees move, so I wouldn't get too worried."

"I don't think it was a tree."

"Why not?"

"The air is down to four degrees. Ground is close to that—black and purple on infrared. The jungle traps heat, so it's one big wall of blue at around ten degrees. Any warm-blooded animal would run a lot hotter than that, making it stand out in green, yellow, or red. Whatever I saw was in that spectrum, and it was *big.*"

"How big?"

"Hairy T-rex big."

Alexander smiled. "You have an active imagination, Stone. Might be your conscience persecuting you for threatening to fire up your grill and start sampling the native cuisine."

"Might be."

Alexander's smile faded. Stone usually had a good sense of humor. Whatever he'd seen had scared him. "Why didn't you report what you saw?"

"I was about to, sir. You found me first."

"Well, we already know that Wonderland is full of life, so it's no surprise you saw something. Doesn't mean it's dangerous to us. Just keep an eye out and make sure nothing gets too close. But if it does, don't shoot unless it's making threatening moves, understood?"

"Yes, sir."

"I was going to ask you to take one of the shuttles with me and go look for Max and Ryder, but I guess we need you here. Anyone else who can go with me?"

"There's Fernandez with Shuttle Four. I sent him back there to get some sleep a few hours ago. By now he should be more rested than anyone."

Alexander nodded. "Sounds good." He lingered a moment longer, eyeing the dark wall of trees, looking for signs of movement.

Nothing.

He took comfort in that as he walked back to the protective circle of shuttles.

CHAPTER 21

Seth Ryder sat in the cockpit of Shuttle Two, watching as black alien waters raged by, separated by a thin glass barrier. Even with the shuttle's landing lights activated, visibility was zero. Seth glared at the shuttle's other occupant.

"What?" Max asked sharply.

"It was your idea to leave the shuttle."

"You didn't have to follow me."

"Actually I did. As part of the mission's security team, I had to accompany you."

"So you're saying I'm the reason we're in this mess."

Seth shrugged. "If the shitprint matches the shoe..."

"Funny. Rather than laying blame, we should be thinking of a way out of this."

"Okay, sure, let's do that. We're trapped under an unknown quantity of water, pinned down by debris. We could go cycle the airlock and swim for the surface, but debris will probably kill us on the way up, or the current will sweep us under something heavy like it did with our shuttle. Even if we survive and manage to climb one of the trees, I wonder how alien vegetation that *moves* will react to climbers. Maybe they'll squeeze the life out of us like a boa." Seth shook his head. "No, we need to stay here. Wait until the water recedes, then we can climb out the airlock onto dry land. We'll make our way back to the landing site and wait. They'll be back to look for us as soon as the water subsides."

Max nodded. "Fine."

Something *thunked* off the cockpit canopy, and they both turned to look.

"How strong is that glass?" Max asked.

"Strong as it gets. That's palladium glass. It would take one hell of an impact to break it."

Thunk.

"Well, Wonderland is busy doing a stress test for us."

BANG!

Seth sat up straight. "What the shit?"

"Everything's about shit with you, isn't it?"

"When I'm up to my neck in it, you bet." Seth walked up to the canopy and ran a hand along it, looking for imperfections that his eyes couldn't see, but it was all smooth…

A siren sounded and a warning flashed up on the shuttle's MHD. There was a hull breach just aft of the cockpit, and… *in* the cockpit, too.

"What's going on?" Max asked.

"Quiet!"

Seth listened. All he could hear was the sound of his own breathing, but then he heard something else… a sharp hissing noise.

"We've sprung a leak," Seth said, scanning the ceiling to find the leak. He didn't see anything. Then he lowered his eyes and spotted a fine stream of mist in a corner beside the hatch.

"We need to go," Max said.

Seth snorted. "Sure, and then we'll be the ones springing

leaks. No, we can patch this. It won't take me long. Why don't you make yourself useful and go check the cargo bay to see how bad the other leak is."

"There's *another* leak?"

"The patch kit can handle it. Just check it for me, would you?"

Max mumbled something under his breath as Seth went to get the patch kit from the cockpit's emergency locker. Max waved the hatch open, and in came a rushing stream of water. Seth cursed as the water filled up the front half of the cockpit and covered his toes.

"I'm out of here," Max said. "You can take your chances and stay, but I'm not going to wait until we're both pressed against the ceiling, fighting over the last bubble of air!"

Max snatched his helmet from the back of his chair and strode through the open hatch.

Seth scowled after him. "Get back here!"

No answer.

Walking over to the hatch, Seth grabbed the guide rail to steady himself amidst the slick river of water still pouring into the cockpit. He took one look at the cargo bay and immediately realized why Max wasn't listening. There were no less than a dozen high-pressure jets of water streaming from the walls and ceiling. The entire ship would be flooded in less than an hour at this rate.

But if they'd sprung that many leaks from debris hitting their shuttle, what would happen to an unarmored human in a pressure suit?

Better to stay put. Even if the shuttle flooded, they each had a few hours of air in their suits and spare oxygen tanks in the cockpit. Besides, the rear compartments could flood as much as they liked. The cockpit was separated by a bulkhead, and there was only one small leak there. "Max, get back here! The cockpit is still safe. We'll seal ourselves in and wait it out."

"You're crazy!" Max called back from the rear airlock. "I'm not going to sit here and wait around to die!"

The inner airlock doors breezed open, and Max walked in. Seth wracked his brain trying to come up with a way to convince him to stay, but with water rushing past his ankles and stealing his remaining air, he didn't have much time.

"Are you coming, or not?" Max asked from the open airlock.

Seth shook his head. "Good luck." He shut the hatch and set to work patching the leak in the cockpit.

It didn't work.

The patch was designed for space, where the positive pressure inside the shuttle would hold the patch against the hull until it stuck. With the shuttle underwater and greater pressure outside the hull pressing in against the patch, it refused to stick.

Seth tried holding it in place with his hand. That only half worked. Water still squirted out around the patch. He sat down to get better leverage, and noted with dismay that he was sitting in a puddle of water. Fortunately his pressure suit kept him dry—for now, anyway. He cast about for his helmet and found it high and dry where he'd left it, hanging from the back of the pilot's chair. Sooner or later he was going to have to don that helmet and start using oxygen tanks. Hopefully the water would run back out to sea before he ran out of air.

Seth sat for a while, listening to debris *thunking* against the hull and water *hissing* in. He felt like the legendary Dutch boy with his finger in the dyke. Glancing over his shoulder to the cockpit hatch, he thought about Max and wondered if the ambassador would fare any better.

Maybe he should have gone with him. *No,* he decided, shaking his head. If he ran out of air, he could always follow Max and swim for the surface, but this way there was a chance he wouldn't need to leave the safety of the shuttle. A rescue might come before the shuttle filled with water.

This way he had options.

Seth's arm began cramping, and he shifted positions to bring his other arm into play. He laid his head back against the hull and fatigue fell over him like a warm blanket. His eyelids felt heavy. He squinted and blinked rapidly, trying to keep his eyes open. If he fell asleep now, he'd drown. Not to mention he wouldn't be able to hold the patch, and he'd run out of air a lot faster.

He could only hope the water subsided and a rescue came for him soon…

* * *

159 Days Ago - November 29, 2790
(Earth's Frame of Reference)

It's thanksgiving today, Alex, but there's no turkey and no thanks to give. What do I have to be thankful for?

You're not here.

It's been almost a year already. That short? It feels longer. I know when you left you said you could be gone for ten years, but you were counting on me staying busy, building a life for us here while I waited for you to return. Instead I'm left picking up the pieces after World War III.

I'm still living here in the rescue workers' camp, but there's rumors that we might be leaving soon. I keep trying to imagine where we'll go, and whether or not it will be any better. Then I try to imagine you there with me.

People look at me funny every time I talk about you. They're laughing at me, Alex. They all think you're dead. You need to come back and prove that I'm not crazy.

Oh, I do have some good news! I finally lost those five pounds I always said I would. Actually I lost fifteen, but who's counting? There is some bad news, though. My hair is falling out. I'm not sure if it's because we ran out of vitamin pills or because I only get to shower once a month. My head itches a lot, so it could be the shower thing. You should see your blushing bride now—hands callused, bruises and scars from digging through debris to find survivors. I've personally found and rescued over a hundred people already. At least that makes some of this worth it, but it's not worth quite so much when you think about what you're saving them for.

The camp is full of every kind of crime you can imagine, and a lot of crimes you can't. Tents are thin, so we hear it all. Most people here have a partner. The women all fight over the biggest, scariest men to keep them safe, but sometimes I wonder if the price they pay is worth it—more than a few have been raped or murdered by their bedfellows. I don't know how my tent-mate, Rosa, got by before I came here. She was all alone. I keep trying to talk to her, but she's all locked up inside behind those haunted brown eyes. I keep thinking maybe she went through something like that. The camps are not a good place for a young girl—a girl of any age, really.

A few people tried things with me, but that's what my shiv is for—and David. He managed to move his tent next to mine. I know you wouldn't like him, because he tried to kiss me. I don't like that either, but please try to understand, Alex. He really thinks you're dead, and he's the only friend I have. I need *a friend. He's been looking after me.*

A couple nights ago there was someone outside my tent, trying to get in. David got out and I heard some kind of fight. The next day he showed up at the buses with bruised knuckles. He told me the sound I heard was a raccoon and he hurt his hand with the crews, but you and I know better.

I'm not trying to make you feel guilty for leaving me here. Or maybe I am, a little, but I'm not angry with you anymore. Mostly I'm just sad. You promised to send me a message every day. I kept my end of the bargain. I even went back and filled in the gaps as best I could. What about you? I haven't heard a thing Alex. I just need to know if you're alive. I need a reason to keep holding on.

Please message me soon. I love you. I can't wait to see you and prove everyone wrong. You are alive. I know you are.

All my love,
Caty

Caty put her pen and paper down. Her tears splashed on the page, making the ink run. She cursed under her breath and dabbed the page with her shirt. The damage was done, but at least her words were still legible. Caty folded the letter carefully, opened her rucksack, and tucked her latest journal entry in with the rest. The compartment was bursting with folded papers—over a hundred of them. Paper was hard to come by, but she'd managed to get it from the warden by trading him some of her rations. She would have recorded the messages on her comm band, but it was long ago out of power and there was no way to recharge it here.

Caty sighed. Someone scratched on the tent. It was the closest thing they had to a knock.

"Come in," she said.

The zipper *zzzed* and the flap flopped open. David's head popped through. His shaggy brown hair and beard made him look like a young Santa Claus.

"*Hola bella,*" he said, grinning at her with yellow teeth.

Caty smiled back. "I'm not beautiful," she replied. "Not anymore." She wiped away a tear with the back of one hand.

"*¿Que paso?*" he asked, his smile fading to a look of concern.

She shook her head. "Nothing."

David crawled inside the tent and regarded her with a frown. "You were writing to him again, weren't you?"

"Yes."

"Caty..."

"We're not doing this right now."

"You have to stop. You're torturing yourself."

"Stop what? Believing that he could be alive? Or being sad that he's not here with me?"

"Both. When every day is a struggle just to survive, you have to focus on the living, not the dead."

Caty felt a hot flash of anger toward him. She glared and pursed her lips.

"I know it's tough, but you have to be *fuerte.*"

"I'm tired of being strong!" Fresh tears sprang to Caty's eyes. She swiped them away, flinging them against the sides of the tent. "It's not fair! He served his time! They should have sent someone else."

"Catalina..."

"He *should* be here!"

"But he is not."

Caty shook her head. Her lower lip trembled with fury.

"Ven aqui," David said, and pulled her into a hug. *"Esta bien. Esta bien.* Shhh. I'm here."

Caty's entire body trembled as she sobbed and gritted her teeth. She wanted to push David away, to lash out at him and tell him to leave her alone!

But she didn't.

"Tengo una buena noticia," he said.

"There's no such thing as good news anymore."

"No? We're leaving."

Caty pulled away sharply. "Leaving? Where to?"

David grinned and shrugged. "We haven't found more survivors for a while now, so they're disbanding the camp."

"But..." She'd been raging against life in the camp for so long, but now that she was finally going somewhere else, she wasn't sure she wanted to go. "Where? How?" They were all still refugees in need of water, food, and shelter.

"The government's building new communities for us all over the country. We just have to pick one and go there."

"We?"

"You thought I was going to leave you alone? *No, mi chiquita. Ni loco.* Not a chance."

In spite of the ulterior motive Caty felt sure was lurking somewhere behind David's Santa beard, she smiled and relief coursed through her.

"So what are the options?"

"The warden posted them on the news board. Come see."

David led her out by the hand, all but dragging her to the bulletin board where memos had been posted to keep them all in the loop with important news. The evening air was chilly for California, but the birds were out and chirping, and the sky was a cheerful shade of blue. It was tempting to believe that this really was good news and things were about to get better.

They reached the news board, but they had to push through a crowd to get close enough to read. David was a big guy, so no trouble there. Most people were scared of him. Only Caty knew that he was a big teddy bear.

Standing on the muddy ground in front of the cork board, under the eaves of a tin roof, Caty read the latest memo. It summarized exactly what David had said about the government building new communities for the refugees. Below that was a list of ten cities where those communities were being built.

Caty scanned the list briefly before spying one city that appealed due to the weather and the familiar mix of Northern and Southern culture. "What about Sacramento?" she asked, turning to David with a smile. She was so unused to smiling that it hurt her face.

David grinned back at her, his brown eyes dancing. "I was thinking the same thing, *mi chiquita.*"

CHAPTER 22

May 23, 2790
(Wonderland's Frame of Reference)

Alexander covered a yawn with one hand and shook his head, trying to shake off his exhaustion the way he might shake off a bug. Last night he'd spent hours scanning the raging black water for bobbing heads, but all he'd managed to do was to waste precious fuel. This morning, after only two hours of rest, and a handful of caffeine pills for breakfast, Alexander was back at it. He couldn't sleep while he knew that two of his crew were missing—well, one crew member and one pleni-po-pain-in-the-ass politician.

"How's it look?" he asked Lieutenant Stone.

"Water seems to be back out where it should be. Lots of debris on the beach. The jungle's a mess. No sign of Shuttle Two."

"Maybe they were dragged out to sea?" Commander Korbin suggested.

Alexander frowned. "Maybe."

All three shuttles were up and searching. They'd left Petty Officer Suarez back at the hab complex in a Cheetah to watch the perimeter while Dr. Crespin and McAdams checked air samples for airborne pathogens. Everyone else was in the shuttles. They'd brought one of the Cheetahs and a rover, but looking at the ruined state of the jungle, they weren't likely to get very far anyway. Thick black mushroom stalks and splintered tree trunks lay glistening wet on the beach, overturned mushroom caps the size of boulders lay gills up and drying in the sun. Severed fronds and branches covered in red and purple leaves were scattered everywhere like seaweed.

"That's our original landing site, there," Stone said. "I'm going to take us down for a closer look,"

Alexander stared at the ground. What had once been a wide beach was now a thin, dirty strip of land strewn with vegetation. Alexander scanned the area, looking for the missing shuttle or the telltale flash of reflective white pressure suit fabric. He imagined Max or Ryder waving their arms and doing jumping jacks to get his attention, but nothing down there was moving. In the distance Alexander saw black tree trunks rising like obelisks against the dusty blue-gray horizon. All the branches and leaves had been stripped from the bottoms of the trees, but up higher they were still alive with vibrant reds and purples.

Stone circled the landing site, all the while shaking his head. "We're looking for a pair of needles in a tree stack."

"I doubt they would have made their way back here," Cardinal put in from the back of the cockpit. "Their shuttle was probably rolled along the beach until it fetched up against the trees. Assuming they managed to get out, they wouldn't even know how to find our landing site without the Shuttle's nav system to guide them, and if I were them, I'd stick as close to the shuttle as possible, because it will be easier for us to detect—not to mention it's the only place that's sure to be safe."

"You're assuming the shuttle survived," Korbin replied.

Alexander considered that. "Even if it didn't, Cardinal's right, it would have been rolled toward the jungle. If they were forced to abandon it, we might find them clinging to one of those trees. Stone—"

"Already on it," he said, banking and flying inland.

Alexander watched the ground sweep by in a blur of red foliage, black dirt, and lavender sand.

"I've got a ping on sensors!"

"Where?" Alexander scanned the sensor display, his heart pounding with anticipation.

Stone pointed to the blip on sensors. "It's faint, but stands out from the jungle."

Alexander squinted out the canopy as they approached. Then he caught a glint of something shiny. "There!" he pointed.

"On it," Stone replied.

A tiny white speck appeared standing on top of a pile of vegetation and waving a shiny square of metal at them.

"We got one!" Stone said. The comms crackled with similar exclamations from the other shuttle pilots.

"Just one?" Korbin asked. "Where's the other?"

"Maybe he's inside?" Cardinal suggested.

"Why isn't he contacting us on the comms?" Alexander asked.

Stone shrugged. "Don't know. Maybe his suit's damaged. How are we going to get him up here? There's nowhere to land."

Alexander was already rising from his chair. "That's what we have EVA tethers for. Hover over him and I'll throw down a line."

"I'll help," Cardinal said.

"Likewise," Korbin added.

A minute later the three of them were standing in the airlock with the outer doors open and a tether dangling over the side of the shuttle.

Korbin was down on her hands and knees, peering over the edge. "He's got it!" she called out as the tether pulled taut.

Alexander activated the winch and began reeling him in. The motor groaned and turned with agonizing slowness. It wasn't designed to fight against gravity.

"Help me reel him in!" Alexander said, grabbing the line with both hands. Korbin and Cardinal took up positions in front of him and added their strength to his. After a few seconds they were all gasping for air, and Alexander's arms were shaking, but they were making progress.

"It has… to be… Ryder," Cardinal said between gasps for air. "Someone needs to tell him to lay off the 'roids."

Alexander grunted his agreement.

Stone's voice came to them over the comms, "You got him yet?"

"Almost," Alexander gritted out.

A pair of white-gloved hands appeared and grabbed the edge of the airlock. Before anyone could help, Ryder's face appeared as he pulled himself up.

All three of them rushed forward to lend a hand. As soon as he was inside, Alexander waved the outer doors shut and cycled the airlock.

"Are you okay?" Korbin asked Ryder.

Alexander saw him bobbing his head and tapping the side of his helmet to indicate his comms weren't working.

"Helmet got wet!" Ryder said, his voice muffled. As soon as the inner airlock doors slid open, he removed his helmet and took a deep breath.

"Never thought I'd be so happy to see such an ugly face," Cardinal said, removing his own helmet and pulling Ryder into a backslapping hug.

"Where's Max?" Korbin asked.

Ryder shook his head. "I don't know. We sprang a leak and he left. I tried to stop him..."

Alexander scowled. *Typical. Just like a bureaucrat to go making more work for everyone.* He sighed and pressed his lips into a grim line. "We'll find him."

* * *

After an hour of aerial searching they still hadn't found Max, and they were running low on discretionary fuel.

"We'll have to land and continue searching on foot," Stone said.

Alexander nodded. "Do it." He bit into a ration bar and took a swig of water from his flask to wash it down.

"What if there's another tremor?" Korbin asked. "We could *all* get caught this time."

"Odds of that are slim," Cardinal said. "The jungle was overgrown when we first saw it. How long do you think it took to bounce back after the last tsunami hit? This is probably the worst disaster the area has seen in a hundred years."

"And we arrived just in time to see it. That's some kind of luck," Stone said.

"The worst," Ryder croaked from the back of the shuttle.

Alexander glanced back to see how he was doing. He looked pale despite the half a dozen ration bars he'd eaten, and his eyes were red from sleep deprivation, but otherwise he was no worse for the wear. "We need to get Ryder back to Doc Crespin for examination."

Stone nodded as he landed on the beach. "We'll send him back with one of the other shuttles."

Their shuttle touched down with a subtle jolt. Buckles

clacked and clattered as everyone rose from their seats and filed out the hatch to the rear airlock.

A minute later they were standing on a dirty beach amidst a field of shredded plants. A black tree branch with drooping red leaves was coiling and uncoiling like a snake.

Lieutenant Cardinal walked over to it and went down on his haunches to examine the severed limb. Alexander turned to see Stone speaking with Lieutenant Fernandez from Shuttle Three. Fernandez looked as exhausted as Alexander felt. They'd both stayed up late last night searching for Ryder and Max.

Stone indicated Ryder, and Fernandez nodded. He would take Ryder back for a check-up—probably also so that he could get some sleep.

"Captain, you need take a look at this," Korbin said over the comms.

Checking his suit's sensors for her comm beacon, he found her standing further down the beach, beside a giant black boulder. He jogged to catch up with her.

"What is it?" Alexander asked.

Korbin pointed to the boulder. That was when Alexander noticed it rising and falling.

It was *breathing.*

He flinched and jumped back. "What the hell is that?"

"I think it's some kind of whale."

Alexander walked around it, noting the creature's collection of fins, and its smooth, shiny skin. It was at least fifty feet long. "Stone," he said over the comms. "Need you here. Bring your rifle."

Korbin shot him an acid look. "You're going to *shoot* it?"

Alexander stopped in front of the creature's vast, gaping mouth. Its teeth were like daggers, six inches long, and there were hundreds of them. *So you're a predator,* Alexander thought.

Just like us. The whale's fat pink tongue lolled from its mouth.

To find a creature this big on an alien world was an amazing discovery. It looked remarkably similar to whales on Earth, but Alexander was fairly sure that was only because he didn't know enough to tell the difference.

"Where's McAdams when you need her…" he muttered.

"You called me, Captain?" Stone said, jogging up beside him. "Whoa! Hello there," he said, aiming his rifle at one massive red eye.

"Leave her alone," Korbin hissed. "Can't you see she's hurt?"

"How do you know it's a she?" Stone asked, frowning.

"How do you know it isn't?" Korbin replied.

"He, she, it… whatever the gender, this thing's no danger to us on land," Alexander said. "We should get McAdams back here to examine it."

"The whale could be dead by then. We need to find some way to save her," Korbin said.

Alexander pursed his lips. "I don't see how we can… it must weigh thousands of pounds."

"Use the rover! We'll make a harness."

"It won't get enough traction in the sand," Stone said. "Besides, we can't drive under water and pull it in after us."

"Well, we have to do something!"

"We could put it out of its misery," Alexander replied.

"Captain's right," Stone added.

Korbin glared at them. "If that were you, would you want to be put out of *your* misery?"

"That's different," Alexander said.

"How? Because we value human life more than animal life?"

"To be blunt, yes, and speaking of which, we'd better stop getting side-tracked. We're supposed to be looking for Max."

"Suddenly you're a fan. I thought you didn't like him."

"I don't have to like him to save his life. Let's go."

"Glad to hear that, Captain."

Alexander spared a final glance at the whale before turning to Stone. "Go hop in the Cheetah. You have point."

"Aye-aye, sir," Stone replied.

Alexander mentally opened his comms and sent a message to the rest of the crew. "Everyone in the rover."

CHAPTER 23

Alexander drove; Korbin sat beside him, and the rest of the crew filled the back seats. The rover jumped and skipped along at 10 kilometers an hour as he negotiated fallen trees, exposed rocks, and piles of vegetation. The going was so rough that it made Alexander feel sick. The sheer density of debris was almost too much for the eight-wheeled rover.

Up ahead Lieutenant Stone made much better progress in his Cheetah, stepping over glistening black logs or reaching down to pick them up and move them out of the way.

"Anything yet?" Alexander asked over the comms.

"No, sir," Stone replied.

They were both using their sensor suites to the max, looking for footprints, metallic objects, movement. Sensors flagged movement constantly as surviving plants and trees writhed around them, slapping the sides of both the rover and the assault mech. Alexander watched as a giant branch of purple flowers swept down and smacked the windshield. Smaller branches danced over the glass like feelers while the flowers opened up to reveal big yellow circles with black dots in the center. *Eyes?* he wondered.

The branch got caught under the wheels and sucked under. Alexander grimaced as he heard wood snapping and leaves rustling as the rover turned them to mulch.

"We need to get out of the rover," Korbin said. "We're doing too much damage here. What if those trees can feel? Don't you think they've suffered enough?"

"I agree," Cardinal said. "We came to explore, not demolish."

"Are you crazy?" Alexander said. "What if the plants are carnivorous and they eat us?"

"Even if they are, they won't smell us through our suits, and we do have weapons. We're not exactly defenseless," Korbin replied.

Alexander shook his head. "They can't smell us in here, either, so what do they want with our rover?"

"Maybe they're just curious."

"Or maybe on Wonderland you don't eat the salad, the salad eats you," Alexander replied.

The comms crackled. "Hold up! I've got something..."

"What is it, Stone?" Alexander hauled back on the throttle. Tree branches swept in from all sides, groping the rover and blocking all the windows. Fronds and branches writhed over the glass like snakes, making rustling noises that they heard clearly through both the rover and their helmets. Alexander nodded to Korbin and pointed to the aggressive move from the jungle. *See?* he mouthed to her.

She pressed her lips flat and looked away.

"Looks like... footprints," Stone said. "Yep, definitely footprints."

Alexander's heart pounded in his chest. "Human? Is it Max?"

"No... I don't think so. Too big, wrong shape... four toes."

Alexander sighed. "Let's keep looking then."

"Sure, but what if we run into this thing?"

"You're in a Cheetah and we're in a rover. So what if we run into it?"

"Well, let's just hope it doesn't step on us."

Alexander blinked. "That big?"

"Maybe bigger."

"Follow those footprints."

"Follow them, sir?"

"Something that big is bound to be hungry. Max is about the right size for a snack. I bet that thing can find him a whole lot faster than we can."

"Aye, I suppose it's better than hunting around aimlessly."

They endured a half an hour of groping plants before Stone suddenly stopped in front of them. Alexander slammed on the brakes. Seat belts locked, heads whipped forward.

"Shit," Alexander muttered. Keying the comms he said, "You almost caused the first traffic accident on Wonderland, Lieutenant! What's going on?"

"The jungle's too dense up ahead for us to get through. I think we've come to the end of the damage caused by the tsunami."

"Where do the footprints lead?"

"Back the other way. Looks like our friendly giant turned around here, but he wasn't happy about it. There's a trampled area and some freshly-busted foliage. I think he tried to force his way in."

"Did he?"

"No gaps big enough to suggest that, and his footprints reappear again going back the way he came."

"Why was he so desperate to get into the jungle?"

"Chasing smaller prey would be my guess, sir. And there's

something else. I've got a reading on sensors that could be Max."

"What? Why didn't you say so sooner?" Alexander scanned his sensor display, but there was nothing flagged. "Where? I don't see anything." The Cheetah's sensors were much more powerful than the rover's, so that wasn't too surprising.

"About one klick in. Something metallic—small but dense."

"It could just be a ferrous rock."

"It could be, yes."

"So what are our options?"

"We go out on foot and check the coordinates," Stone said.

"And if the jungle eats us?" Alexander asked.

"We shouldn't all go. Just one or two of us at a time," Stone replied.

"I'm going," Korbin said.

Alexander shot her a look. "Hold on. No one's going anywhere yet."

"Based on the size of the anomaly, we could be looking at Max's helmet," Stone said, "and if we find that, we'll probably find out what happened to him."

Alexander's eyes narrowed to slits. "That, or a we'll find a useless hunk of rock. Have you tried contacting him?"

"I've been broadcasting an automatic message since we set out. If he has a working comm system, he should have picked up our signal and replied by now."

Alexander sighed and looked to Korbin. "You can't go."

"Why not? My purpose with the mission is to replace you if the need arises. Other than that all I do is manage the crew's emotional well-being."

"Because I'm going, and as you pointed out, you're my replacement if something happens to me."

Korbin opened her mouth to object, but Alexander raised a palm to silence her. "No arguments. Any other volunteers?" he asked, turning to the rest of the crew.

"I'll go," Cardinal said. "I know plants."

"Not these ones."

"Which is why I need to take samples."

"All right." Alexander keyed the comms. "Stone—"

"Sir?"

"Grab your rifle and dismount. You're coming with us."

"Aye-aye, Captain."

* * *

The rover's airlock hissed and squealed as it matched pressure with the air outside. Alexander waited, his eyes on the status light above the outer door. His right hand fell to his waist and he drew the high-powered laser pistol he'd strapped there. Projectile weapons were typically longer-ranged and more efficient at killing while in atmosphere, but when it came to fighting plants, the heat generated by a laser bolt would be much more useful. Bullets would probably just tickle a giant tree, but a searing bolt of light would set the whole thing on fire. If any trees tried to eat him he'd turn them into matchsticks.

The light above the door glowed green and a tone issued from the airlock just before the doors slid open. Hot, humid air swept in, and Alexander's faceplate fogged up. He wiped it on his sleeve before following Cardinal out. Rather than carry a weapon of his own, the botanist had a large sample container open and at the ready, along with an entire pack full of matching containers just waiting to be filled.

Alexander jumped down onto a pile of shredded, waterlogged black wood. He spied a spiky purple ball not far from where they stood and wondered if it was alive. It didn't move.

"Stone?" Alexander commed.

"Coming... sir..." Stone replied, sounding distracted.

Alexander gazed up to watch the tree canopy. Black branches and wide red leaves all but blotted out the dusty purple sky. What spaces they left were filled by fat black mushroom caps that rose high above the canopy. Between all of the foliage, sunlight streamed down in thin white beams, revealing clouds of rising vapor and something else... what looked like soap bubbles rising with the vapor. He saw one or two of the closer ones suddenly contract, distorting into an elliptical shape before making a spurt of movement. He was reminded of the balloon-shaped birds they'd seen on their way down. Were these the miniature versions?

"Wow..." Cardinal said. "No shortage of wonder on Wonderland."

Leaves rustled in the breeze, the sound transmitted by his helmet's external audio pickups. He turned to look and saw tree branches snaking down to greet them. The leaves weren't rustling in a breeze, he realized, they were rustling with the trees' movement.

"We've got incoming!" Alexander said, aiming his pistol at the nearest group of branches.

"Hold your fire, Captain," Stone said. "They already got to me. The trees are not hostile. Repeat, not hostile. Can't promise they'll still be friendly after you shoot them, though."

Alexander cringed as the nearest branch swooped down and slithered over him, feeling him up from head to toe. Then it withdrew and seemed to regard him with giant purple flowers with yellow and black centers. Now he was sure those flowers were some kind of eyes. Alexander stared back. The tree branch remained where it was, flower-eyes still watching, smaller branches writhing like worms while the larger ones undulated slowly.

"These trees sure the hell are creepy," Alexander said.

"Literally creepy," Cardinal said.

Stone walked up beside them, covered in blood.

Alexander flinched. "Medic!"

Stone shook his head. "It's just tree sap," he explained, reaching out to wipe a blotch of matching crimson gunk off Alexander's suit.

"Actually…" Cardinal said, wiping more of the same off his own suit and studying it in his hands. "Since these trees move, the sap might actually be the trees' blood. I'd need to study both the sap and one of the tree branches to know for sure."

Alexander's brow furrowed. "So they're bleeding all over us? Are they dying or something?"

"Maybe."

"Well, take some samples and let's get moving," Alexander said.

"Yes, sir."

Turning to Stone, Alexander asked, "You have a fix on the sensor anomaly?"

"I've got a bearing on my direction finder," he said, hefting the handheld device. "Two hundred and fifty five degrees."

"Compasses work here?" Alexander asked while another branch surreptitiously wiped more sap on him.

"Yes, sir."

"And they still point north?" Cardinal asked, walking up to them with two sample containers full of vegetation.

"Magnetic north, yes. Compasses always point to magnetic north."

"Right. I must have plants on the brain," Cardinal said.

Alexander nodded to Stone. "Well, so long as we have a heading, we shouldn't get lost. Lead the way."

"Yes, sir."

"And keep an eye out for anything that might be dangerous."

"I'll just watch everything then," Stone said.

"Exactly."

They walked past Stone's Cheetah, standing sentinel at the line of debris that marked the end of the devastation caused by the tsunami. Here the debris was thicker than ever. They climbed over half-dead trees and branches that writhed and slithered as they were stepped on. All three of them hesitated when they reached the dense wall of red and purple foliage. The jungle looked impossibly dark. There could be anything in there, and if the trees suddenly decided to become hostile, no amount of laser fire would be enough to save them.

"I don't like this," Alexander breathed, panting over the comms as he balanced on top of a piece of driftwood the size of the rover.

"We could turn back," Stone said. "No one will blame us for leaving him. If we had contact with Earth I bet they'd order us not to go any further."

Alexander frowned and took two steps closer. The jungle reacted to his approach by reaching out with leafy branches and feeling him up once more. This time they didn't leave a sticky trail of sap, and they withdrew after just a moment. Alexander took that as good sign.

Shrugging, he turned to regard Lieutenants Stone and Cardinal. "I was never very good at following orders. That's why they made me captain. Let's go."

"Yes, sir."

They walked in, gently pushing tree branches aside. Once they were below the canopy, daylight vanished. The darkness was suffocating, but not absolute. Some of the ground cover radiated its own light—glowing blue ferns and fuzzy yellow growths sprouted from tree trunks. Clusters of crystalline rock glittered on the ground in all the colors of the rainbow, pulsing out beams of shifting light.

The soap bubbles they'd seen earlier floated everywhere, glinting in the shadows.

"This deserves a hologram," Stone said while stepping through a curtain of glowing purple vines. "Where's Max when you need him? Wasn't he supposed to be documenting this trip?"

Alexander watched the vines react to Stone's intrusion. Hair-like tendrils stood on end, feeling him, while the length of the vines furled and unfurled restlessly.

"What kind of evolutionary purpose is there for plants that move?" Alexander wondered.

Cardinal crouched down beside one of the blue-glowing ferns, but it shied away from him, turning out the lights and furling up its leaves. "Protection maybe?" he suggested. "Movement could also be justified and reinforced by active food and nutrient gathering, a result of plants vying with each other for limited space. Reproduction is another possibility. Maybe that sap isn't their blood, but rather some kind of reproductive fluid?"

"Way too much information, Cardinal," Alexander said, regarding a sticky red stain on his uniform with a wrinkled nose.

"Agreed," Stone put in. "Let's get to that sensor anomaly and get out of here before we start growing baby trees."

The comms crackled with Korbin's voice. "How's everything in there?"

"Nothing hostile so far," Alexander said. "Jungle is pretty dense, and a little too much on the touchy feely side, but no problems yet. Our heading is 255 degrees. We have one klick to cover before we get to the anomaly. At the rate we're going, we should stumble on it in about half an hour."

"That long?"

Alexander grunted as he climbed over a wall of tree roots as tall as he was. "Maybe longer. We'll be in touch."

It actually took forty minutes before Stone held up his hand and called a halt. He was staring as his direction finder and shaking his head.

"What is it?" Alexander asked.

"Whatever we saw on the sensors has to be around here somewhere," Stone replied, turning in a slow circle and searching the ground cover.

"I don't see anything," Cardinal said.

Alexander didn't either, but it wasn't easy to see through all the phosphorescent ferns. "Let's sweep the area. Push aside the ground cover wherever it's obscuring the ground."

"Roger," Stone said.

"What's that?" Cardinal said, pointing up to a hanging curtain of crimson vines. They were rolling down to the ground like a roller shade. As the vines unfurled, Alexander saw a familiar flash of reflective white fabric—fabric that had been designed to stand out against the black of space.

Cardinal gasped. "Is that…"

"Come on," Alexander said, already running toward the vines. By now they could see arms and legs, and Max's wavy blond hair.

"Where's his helmet?" Cardinal asked, crouching down beside him to check for a pulse. "He's alive," Cardinal said a second later. Max's eyes were shut, and his face was pale, but otherwise he appeared fine.

Stone called it in. "We've found Max. He's alive, but he lost his helmet somewhere. That must be what we picked up on sensors."

"Is he hurt?" Korbin replied.

"As far as we can tell he's fine," Cardinal replied. "He's just unconscious."

"Then he's not fine," Korbin said.

Alexander commed back, "You'll have a chance to examine him soon. If I didn't know better, I'd think you have a crush on him."

"I cherish life in all its forms, Captain. I don't need a vested interest to care about my fellow man."

"Fair enough."

"How are you going to carry him back?"

"There's three of us. We'll figure something out."

"Let me know if you need anything, sir."

"Will do." Alexander glanced up at the vines. They were busy furling back up into the trees.

"What do you think they were doing with him?" Stone asked.

"And why did they drop him here when we arrived?" Cardinal put in. "You think they realized he's one of us?"

"Let's not get carried away," Alexander said. "Get over here and grab his legs."

Before Cardinal could move to follow that order, Max's eyes flew open. He sat bolt upright and screamed at the top of his lungs.

CHAPTER 24

"**M**ax!"

Max went on screaming as if he hadn't heard, his eyes glassy and unseeing.

"Max!" Alexander slapped him. "It's us! What's wrong? Are you hurt?"

The diplomat shut his mouth and turned to look at his aggressor. It took an extra moment for his eyes to focus. "Captain?"

"You're safe now. Are you hurt?"

"We need to get out of here!"

"Why?"

Instead of answering, Max looked around wildly. His blue eyes were big and black in the dim light of the jungle.

"What are you afraid of?" Stone asked.

"I… you didn't see it? It was chasing me."

Alexander nodded. "We saw the footprints. Don't worry, it didn't follow you in here."

"That's because the jungle kept it out. They drew blood, and it killed one of them."

Alexander remembered the sticky red *sap* the trees had been wiping off on them, and suddenly he realized what it was. That had been the creature's blood.

"They who...?" Cardinal asked.

"The trees! That monster turned one of them to splinters!"

"What did it look like?"

"A dinosaur is the closest thing I can compare it to, but it wasn't reptilian. It had black fur all over its body."

Alexander traded looks with Stone.

"Like a hairy T-Rex?" Stone asked.

"You saw it?" Max asked.

"Just a lucky guess."

"We need to go," Max insisted. "Before it comes back."

"How did you get caught up in those vines?" Cardinal asked.

Max shook his head. "What vines?"

"You were rolled up in a bundle of vines when we found you. They dropped you on the ground when we arrived."

Max frowned. "I fell asleep on the ground..." He looked up, his eyes darting between the trees. "You don't think they were going to eat me, do you?"

Cardinal shook his head. "If what you said about them defending you is true, they might have been trying to protect you."

"Can you walk?" Alexander asked.

"I think so," Max said.

"Good, then let's get out of here. You have enough samples, Cardinal?"

"No, but I'm out of sample containers, so it'll have to do for now."

"You still have my rocks, right?" Stone asked.

"Yes, I still have your *rocks,* but maybe you should carry them."

"Sure. I'll just put my rifle down so I can do that. If we run into Mr. T. you can pat him on the head and tickle his tummy."

"Never mind," Cardinal muttered.

"Move out," Alexander said. "Stone you're back on point. I'll take the rear." Mentally activating the comms, Alexander said, "Korbin, Max is ambulatory. He woke up. We're on our way back."

Korbin breathed a sigh of relief. "That's good to hear."

"Any sweet nothings you want me to whisper to him for you?"

"Ha ha."

Alexander smiled. "Just checking."

* * *

By the time they reached the shuttles, the sun was high in the sky and so hot that they could feel its heat radiating through the rover's hull.

"So this is what it feels like to be in an oven," Alexander muttered. Up ahead they saw Stone's Cheetah taking long strides toward the shuttles, kicking up sand and bits of sodden vegetation.

The comms crackled and Stone said, "Captain, there are more of those footprints up ahead."

"Leading to the shuttles?" Alexander asked. He studied the gleaming hulls in the distance, but none of them appeared damaged.

"Around them. Headed for the ocean. Should we check it out?"

Alexander's first impulse was to say no, but they were safe in the rover. Besides, it would be better to find out what these creatures were like now, rather than wait for them to come sniffing around the hab complex.

"Go for it. We'll follow you."

They didn't have to go very far. The footprints converged on a large pile of red, black, and white vegetation. As they approached, Alexander began to doubt it was vegetation. A frown wrinkled his brow and he keyed the comms once more. "What is that, Stone?"

"Not sure. Magnifying…" A burst of static came over the comms as Stone made a noise of disgust. "That's the beached whale we saw."

Korbin leaned forward in her seat, her eyes wide. "Poor thing."

It was a grisly sight—black whale skin clinging to jutting white bones. Bloody red meat and pink whale fat were scattered all over the beach.

Alexander found the sight curious. That whale had been so similar to an Earth whale that it could have washed up on a beach on Earth and no one would have batted an eye, and now with its innards exposed, that was no less true. Besides the balloon creatures and moving trees, life on Wonderland seemed a lot like life on Earth. Was that a coincidence? Animals with red blood and white bones, and trees with leaves and trunks. Evolution had somehow picked a similar path twice. *Very curious.*

"Any sign of the predators that ate the whale?" Alexander asked.

"No, sir," Stone replied.

"Then let's pack it in. We need to get Max back to Doctor Crespin for a thorough examination."

"How's he doing?"

"I'm fine," Max replied from the back of the shuttle.

"All the same," Alexander said. He made a wide circle around the whale carcass and opened the shuttle's loading bay as he approached. The doors parted, the ramp dropped, and Alexander drove straight up.

The rover and Lieutenant Stone's Cheetah were now both thoroughly contaminated, and there was no airlock big enough to sterilize either, so they couldn't take off their helmets yet. The airlocks back at the hab complex would sterilize them all—except for Max. Thanks to his exposure to the elements, he was about to enjoy an extended stay in the quarantine module.

The flight back to the habs was short. Alexander saw the white domes gleaming on the horizon long before they arrived.

After they landed, Korbin passed Max a spare helmet inside the shuttle airlock on their way out; then they went from the shuttle's airlock to a field of red grass, to the quarantine module of the hab complex.

Doctor Crespin greeted them all on the other side of the airlock. "Welcome back," he said, his voice transmitted by external speakers in his helmet. They'd called ahead, so he knew to expect them. "How are you feeling, Max?"

"Never better."

"Tired?"

"Actually no. I had a good sleep."

"Well, that's good to hear. Please follow me—all of you, and do keep your helmets on for now—although if our findings continue to hold true, we may be able to take them off soon."

"How's that, Doctor?" Alexander asked.

"It would be better if I showed you."

The quarantine module was the same size as all the others—about a thousand square feet, but this module seemed smaller for all the equipment that had been crammed into it—not the least of which were four stretcher beds. Alexander spied Seth Ryder lying on one of them, sitting up and watching them as they approached. Lieutenant McAdams stood beside him. Both of them still had their pressure suits and helmets on in order to keep them safe from all the potentially dangerous samples in quarantine.

"While you were gone, I've been studying the atmosphere with McAdams as you requested, Captain. The composition of elements in the air is definitely breathable, but I suppose you already know that from Max."

Alexander nodded.

"The air is also *safe* to breathe as far as we can tell. We've only collected samples around the habs, but we didn't identify any airborne pathogens, and I've been using Ryder here to do a few controlled tests for allergens. Again, at least as far as he's concerned, we didn't find anything worrying, but we won't know for sure until we test a sizable group of people. He is apparently a good test subject, though. How did you put it, Mr. Ryder?"

"Just lookin' at a flower back on Earth makes me sneeze. My nose is a snot farm in the spring."

"Lovely," Korbin said.

Crespin smiled behind his helmet. "Yes. Here comes the really interesting part." He reached over to a table beside him and picked a vial of dirt from a case of matching vials. He held it up to the light so that everyone could see. "We had some extra time, so we got to studying soil samples. We were particularly interested in finding strains of bacteria that might be harmful to humans, since that would be a significant obstacle to the planet's habitability. "So far, we've identified fifty-two different strains of bacteria, and twelve viruses found living inside of them. The viruses are completely inert to us because what passes for DNA and RNA on Wonderland is literally worlds apart from our own genetic code. For them to mess with our cells using their genetic instructions would be like trying to force a square peg into a round hole."

Alexander nodded. "That's a relief."

"As for the bacteria, there's a much more interesting story

there..."

"How so?"

Alexander noticed that McAdams was fidgeting, looking like a pot of boiling water ready to explode.

"Why don't we turn down the lights?" she suggested.

Crespin nodded. "Yes, let's do that," he said, and made a gesture to the hab module's optical sensor.

The lights faded to black, leaving them in darkness, but for a weak radiance bleeding through the hab canvas overhead.

"Wait for it..." Crespin said.

"Wait for what?" Alexander asked.

A split second later the vial with the soil sample began glowing blue. Alexander remembered the glowing plants in the jungle. Maybe that effect had been caused by bacteria.

"Incredible..." Cardinal breathed.

"Bio-luminescent bacteria," Alexander guessed.

"Yes, and their photosynthetic counterparts."

"Photosynthetic?" Alexander felt his eyebrows floating up. "Like plants?"

"Exactly," Crespin said. "One type of bacteria produces light, while another type feeds on the light that they produce."

"Wouldn't that make them parasites?" Cardinal asked.

"It would, but the photosynthetic bacteria also produce things that the bio-luminescent ones need. They're symbionts. Without one, the other can't exist. *Lights,*" Crespin said, issuing a verbal command this time. The hab's illumination returned to normal and the vial stopped glowing.

"So what does that mean for us?" Alexander asked.

"It wouldn't mean much, except that there's no sunlight inside our bodies, so the photosynthetic bacteria can't survive there without their bio-luminescent counterparts, and after extensive testing, I've confirmed that the bio-luminescent bacteria can't live inside of us. The environment in our bodies is completely toxic to them."

"So you're saying we don't have anything to worry about."

"Well, no. We have only studied a very small number of bacteria so far. I'm saying that we don't have to worry about *these* bacteria. We'd need to spend years testing samples here with a team of hundreds or maybe even thousands to be sure that none of Wonderland's microorganisms are infectious to us."

Alexander felt himself growing impatient. "So you really haven't established anything yet."

Doctor Crespin drew himself up, seeming to take umbrage at that. "We've found bio-luminescent bacteria living in symbiosis with photosynthetic ones. I thought you might find that interesting."

Alexander sighed. *Scientists.* "It is interesting, but it's not the green light for colonization that we're looking for."

Crespin nodded to Max. "If you want a green light, all we need to do is study him. One day's exposure to the elements without a helmet is going to give us more insight than a year's worth of tests. It's a lucky thing that happened. We never could have authorized intentionally exposing someone to Wonderland, but now we don't have to."

"I'm not sure if I should feel honored or insulted," Max said.

"Definitely honored," Crespin replied. "If you die, you will have saved the lives of thousands of colonists by preventing them from coming here—or at least by preventing them from exposing themselves to Wonderland the way you have. And if you live, you'll be responsible for making colonization a possibility much sooner than would have otherwise been the case. Either way you'll be a hero."

"A dead hero."

"Better than a live failure," Alexander said.

"I'm the president's direct representative! Hardly a failure."

"Yes, of course," Crespin said, his tone indulgent.

"Keep us informed, Doctor," Alexander said. "Do you need to perform any tests on the rest of us?"

Crespin shook his head. "No. Not unless someone else was exposed to the elements?"

They all shook their heads.

"Then you're free to go."

Alexander nodded. "Let me know if there are any more developments."

"Of course."

Alexander nodded to the rest of the crew. "Let's go get some food and rest. We've earned it."

"Actually," Cardinal began, "I'd like to stay here and begin studying my samples. Given McAdams and Doctor Crespin's findings I have some interesting leads to follow."

"Suit yourself. Stone?"

He shook his head. "I can study rocks later. They'll still be waiting for me after a meal and a hot shower."

Alexander walked to the nearest hab module entrance and joined Stone and Korbin in the airlock for yet another decontamination cycle.

Stone shot him a look. His furrowed brow showed clearly through his visor. "We need to talk, Captain."

"I'm listening." Alexander said, as he activated the radiation shield on his helmet. His visor polarized, blinding him.

Korbin gave a verbal command to initiate decontamination, and a warning siren sounded. A second later, the airlock began *humming* like a giant microwave.

Stone had to raise his voice to be heard above the noise. "There's something strange going on here," he said.

"More than one something," Korbin added.

Stone glanced her way. "No, I mean…"

A musical tone sounded and Alexander deactivated his radiation shield. His visor became transparent once more, and he saw the light above the airlock doors turn green. The inner doors slid open, admitting them to the adjacent mess and recreation module. As soon as he was on the other side of the airlock, Alexander twisted his helmet to break the seal and breathed his first breath of fresh air in more than twelve hours of search and rescue operations.

Korbin walked by him, already twisting off her helmet, but Stone stuck around.

Alexander ran his fingers through sweaty hair, enthusiastically scratching at itches that had been taunting him for hours. Stone removed his own helmet and scratched, too, but his hair was shaved so close that it looked like a shadow on his scalp, so Alexander wasn't sure what was making him itch. Alexander nodded to the nearest couch. "Let's sit. My feet are killing me after that hike through the jungle."

Stone nodded.

Once seated, Alexander asked, "What's on your mind?"

"Wonderland. Have you noticed how many coincidences are piling up?"

"I've noticed a few—why?"

"A few? We all predicted breathable air. Vasquez predicted tsunamis and then one of them hit us. I joked that we might run into a hairy T-rex when I was trying to convince you to take the Cheetahs, and Max confirmed that's what was chasing him… do I need to go on?"

Alexander shook his head. "What are you trying to say, Stone? That Wonderland is haunted?"

"No… maybe. I don't know. All I know is that every time we predict something here, it has a way of happening."

"Let's not get superstitious. Statistically, coincidences have to occur eventually, even a chain of them, and in retrospect those coincidences tend to look more ordered than they are. Our brains are good at recognizing patterns, but that doesn't mean there's any meaning to them. There's no possible mechanism for a relationship of cause and effect between our predictions and what we actually find on Wonderland."

"Logically, I have to agree, but the evidence is mounting. Come on. Try it. Predict something. If it happens, we'll know that something strange is going on here."

"Or we'll know that we made a reasonable prediction based on the available evidence."

"So make an *unreasonable* prediction."

"All right, fine. I predict that the trees are going to start talking to us."

"That's good, but I think Cardinal already believes that—especially now that he's found plants that *move.* Try something more specific."

"Okay, they're going to tell us to go home before we destroy their planet the way we did ours."

Stone smiled. "Good. That'll do."

Alexander suddenly looked up to the ceiling, then all around him, as if tracking a fly.

"What is it?"

Alexander cocked his head and put a hand to his ear. "Do you hear that?"

Stone's brow dropped and his eyes narrowed. "No."

"It sounds like... leaves rustling in the wind... I think they're saying something! It's not very clear..."

"Very funny."

"Hold on, I have it—*Humans go home.* That's it. They want us to leave. We'd better start packing our bags. Sound the alert,

Lieutenant."

"All right, I'm out of here," Stone said, rising from his couch.

Alexander feigned surprise. "You didn't hear them?"

Stone leveled a finger at him. "Joke all you want, but if that actually happens, don't come crying to me."

"If that actually happens, I'll never eat another salad again."

"You hate salad."

Alexander grinned. "So it won't be hard to live up to."

"Yeah..." Stone turned to leave. "Goodnight, sir."

Alexander watched him go, his smile fading to a frown. As ridiculous as it sounded, Stone had put his finger on something that had been bothering Alexander for days. So far Wonderland had met all of their expectations, and at this point, talking trees wouldn't surprise him one bit.

That night, as Alexander lay in his hab module, drifting off to sleep with his mind caught in a hallucinogenic state somewhere between awake and dreaming, he thought he heard leaves rustling. The rustling became indistinct whispering, and he dreamed of giant, kilometer-high trees waving their branches in a deliberate dance, as if trying to communicate with him through sign language.

Alexander's mind flashed back to a memory from the jungle—black branches writhing like snakes, larger ones undulating like waves. Under the influence of dream-logic, the patterns all made perfect sense, and he understood what the trees were trying to say, but they weren't saying *humans go home.*

They were saying *welcome home.*

Alexander awoke the next morning with a deep frown and a furrowed brow. He tried to focus on his dreams, to remember them clearly, but they slipped away like sand running through his fingers. All he could remember clearly was the trees had been talking to him.

Alexander smiled as reason intruded on that fantasy. It was just a dream, and he'd had that dream as a direct consequence of his conversation with Lieutenant Stone.

Just another coincidence, he insisted to himself.

CHAPTER 25

30 Days Ago, April 8, 2791
(Earth's Frame of Reference)

"**M**r. President—"

Ryan Baker looked up from the intelligence brief he was reading, his eyebrows beetling. His secretary stood in the doorway to his office, looking nervous. She brushed violet-colored hair out of her face, and shifted her weight from one foot to the other.

"What is it, Miss Cathaway?"

"I have Admiral Wilson waiting to see you, sir. Shall I let him in?"

"Yes, of course, and Cathaway—"

"Sir?"

"We are not to be disturbed."

"Of course, I'll see to it that no one intrudes."

Ryan rose to his feet and waited for Fleet Admiral Wilson to come in. He didn't have to wait long.

"Admiral Wilson," Ryan said, smiling.

"Mr. President," Wilson replied, striding in and stopping in front of Ryan's desk. The admiral snapped to attention for a quick salute. Ryan returned it with a lopsided version of his own.

Despite the on-going state of emergency and the lack of sleep and downtime that had entailed, Wilson still somehow looked rested and at ease. His black navy uniform was neatly pressed, and his white hair still cropped short. In Wilson's case white hair wasn't a sign of age—which had been frozen for him at around 30—but of distinction. The same went for the fine lines around his mouth and eyes. Both features were considered fashionable for Wilson's rank and position.

Ryan looked a lot younger than Wilson with his comparatively smooth skin and straight brown hair. He could always change that with a visit to a gene parlor—assuming the rest of the Alliance didn't get nuked before he had a chance—but he didn't believe in maintaining appearances for anyone other than himself. Young and virile was the only look he spent any time reinforcing.

Ryan indicated the sitting room in his office. "Let's make ourselves comfortable. We have a lot to discuss."

"After you, sir," Wilson said.

Ryan led the way, passing between two couches on his way to the bar. "Would you like a drink?"

"No, thank you. I try not to drink while on duty, but don't let me stop you, sir."

"Well..." Ryan hesitated with a bottle of Scotch half-tipped toward his glass. "Don't mind if I do. Makes the bad news more palatable."

Wilson nodded. "I imagine it does."

Ryan poured two thumbs of Scotch before going to sit in a chair facing the admiral. "You first. How's our standoff at the Looking Glass progressing?"

"The Confederates have upped the ante somewhat. They now have a second carrier, and two more destroyers. That's a total of ten capital-ships."

"What about us?"

"We're recalling ships from the colonies as fast as we can, but so far we only have fourteen. We have five more en route and another six we could call on if we had to, but that would leave the colonies completely defenseless."

Baker took a sip of Scotch and shook his head. "Do we have any idea of the relative strengths of the two fleets right now?"

"To the best of our knowledge we're at two to one in our favor—a sneak attack notwithstanding."

"And if they do sneak attack us?"

"They might put themselves on an even footing before we could respond."

"So, unless we fire the first shot, we're actually looking at a one-to-one strength ratio. We may as well flip a coin to see who wins! That's not acceptable, Admiral."

Wilson sighed. "With all due respect, sir, unless you authorize me to utilize our own first strike potential, there's not a lot we can do."

Ryan shook his head. "The Confederates still have plenty of missiles here on Earth, and so do we. If we destroy the last dregs of their fleet, we'll be backing them into a corner, and they may feel they have no choice but to bring on Armageddon."

"You really think they'd do that after there's already so much devastation on both sides?"

"I don't know. It's hard to comprehend the mind of the Confederate ant. They don't think like we do. What alternatives do we have?"

"We could get some distance between us and them. That would reduce the danger of a first strike."

Ryan frowned. "And abandon the Looking Glass?"

"Under the circumstances, what makes the Looking Glass so important? We're fighting for our lives here, and we're risking all of our assets to defend a gateway to a planet that may or may not even be habitable."

Ryan set his tumbler down and steepled his hands beneath his chin, contemplating how much he should tell the admiral. The fewer people who knew the better, but it would be nice to be able to share his burden with someone. Particularly someone who would understand the importance of what they were doing.

"First of all, I'm sure you know that our unwillingness to share the Looking Glass with the Confederacy is what sparked this war, so there is the principle of the matter to consider. Giving up the Looking Glass now would be tantamount to saying that all of those millions of people died for nothing."

Admiral Wilson nodded. "I understand that, sir, but we can't repair one error in judgment with another."

"Perhaps not, but we *can* give meaning to an otherwise senseless war. What if I told you that if Operation Alice is successful, we will be able to wipe out the entire Confederate Fleet, bankrupt their economy, and ultimately defeat them once and for all?"

"Then I would say it was worth it."

Ryan smiled. "Suppose I also told you that we could do all of that without firing a single shot."

Wilson's lips parted, his expression frozen halfway between surprise and disbelief. "Then I would say there's something you're not telling me, and Operation Alice is a lot more important than it appears to be."

Ryan nodded gravely. "There's a lot of things I'm not telling you, and as for Operation Alice being more important than it appears—it's actually the most important mission in the history of the Alliance. But—" Ryan raised a finger to point out the all-important caveat. "—if we give the Confederacy access to the Looking Glass now, the mission will be forfeit."

Wilson blinked and swallowed visibly. "Maybe you'd better fill me in, sir."

Ryan picked up his tumbler for another sip of Scotch. "That's why you're here, Admiral," he said, lowering the glass from his lips. He tipped it toward Wilson. "Maybe now you'd like to have that drink?"

"Perhaps, yes… Vodka. Neat."

"Coming right up."

CHAPTER 26

Catalina awoke to the sound of an alarm screeching at her. The alarm was inside her head, a phantom sound that disappeared as soon as she woke up. It was more reliable to set a mental alarm via her parietlar implant than it was to set a physical alarm via her government issue comm band.

Caty sat up. "Lights," she said, whispering to the home's control system.

The lights rose gradually to full brightness, and Caty rolled out of bed. She shuffled to the home's only bathroom, and found the door already shut and a warm bar of light creeping out along the floor.

She knocked lightly. "David?"

"¿Si?"

"Are you almost done?"

"Casi, casi. Puedes prepararnos un cafe mientras."

Caty sighed, annoyed by his constant use of Spanish. She turned and went to the kitchen to prepare a pot of coffee like he'd suggested.

Coffee was one of the few things the government didn't ration, but that was because all of the plantations were in the

South, and the Confederacy hadn't nuked anything below Texas.

Scarcity, crime, poverty, and misery in general were all on the rise in the North, and if trends continued, soon the North and South would be on a par with each other. *All that trouble to immigrate up here, and soon we'll be flocking back down south,* she thought.

Caty set a pot of water to boil. They didn't have a real coffee maker yet. Too expensive. She glanced down the hall to see that the bathroom light was still on, and this time she sighed audibly.

Sharing a bathroom was difficult, but everything else was made easier by having David living with her. They'd pretended to be a couple in front of the government workers in charge of assigning homes to refugees so they could get a two bedroom bungalow instead of a one-bedroom. The extra bedroom provided for couples was there in case they chose to get pregnant—something the government was actually encouraging now—but that was far from the real reason they wanted a two bedroom house. The government loan on a two bedroom place was easier to pay than two separate, slightly smaller loans. Not to mention Caty slept better knowing that David was in the room next to hers.

The interviewer's suspicions about their marital status turned to sympathies when she learned that their previous spouses had been officers in the fleet. Officially both of their spouses were MIA—*Missing in Action,* and had been for more than a year. To the government that meant they were dead, but Caty knew better. Alexander's mission had been top secret, so his official status wouldn't be accurate. Besides that, he'd left at least a week before the fighting had started, so she was sure he'd escaped.

Caty had a friend in Sacramento, Lieutenant Tatiana Muros. Tatiana was quietly looking into Alexander's MIA status for her.

So far no news, but Caty was hopeful that might change now that the Alliance was getting more organized.

The pot on the stove began whistling and Caty took it off the hotplate. She heaped instant coffee into two cups and began pouring in boiling water. As she was pouring the milk and spooning out sugar, she heard the door to the bathroom open and footsteps approaching. David dialed up the lights to full brightness as he approached, and she turned to him with his cup of coffee.

He smiled and kissed her on the cheek. "*Gracias, cariño.*"

"I'm not your honey," she said, arching an eyebrow at him.

He grinned and took a sip of coffee. "But you are sweet like honey," he said.

"Mmmm, smooth-talker." Caty sat down at the kitchen table, regarding David over the rim of her coffee mug as he poured cereal for himself. He was already dressed in his work uniform—jeans and an old t-shirt. He'd had an easy time adapting to life after the attacks. Before the attacks he'd been a handyman and carpenter. Now he was working with a large contractor to help build more homes and infrastructure for the refugees.

Caty hadn't been so lucky. Before all hell had broken loose, she'd been finishing her doctoral thesis in fine arts while working as a museum curator. Under the current circumstances, appreciating art was the last thing on anyone's minds. Not to mention that the Alliance's greatest art collections had all been incinerated along with its largest cities.

Now the best job Caty could find with her skills was cleaning house for rich geners in Sacramento. That meant spending two hours on a bus every morning to earn a paltry thousand sols per month. She had to be thankful, though. Unemployment was around thirty five percent in her neighborhood. People were tripping over each other to get jobs like hers, and the only reason she'd gotten her job at all was because her employers, the Waltons, had an extensive private collection of art, and Caty had managed to impress them with her knowledge of that collection.

Caty smirked around another sip of coffee. *It's a bold new world out there. Now you have to study for eight years just so you can go scrub toilets for a living.*

"What are you thinking about?" David asked, sitting down with his coffee and bowl of cereal. "Something funny?"

Caty shook her head. "Something sad."

"You were smiling."

Caty shrugged and wiped the smirk off her face. She pretended to study the bottom of her coffee mug.

"Was it Alex?"

"No." Caty didn't look up. She didn't feel like talking—especially about Alex. David was sure he was dead, and she was never going to accept that. Not until she had some kind of proof.

"Has your contact found anything yet?"

Caty got up from the table. "Not yet." She put her mug in the sink.

David paused for a spoonful of cereal. "Maybe there is nothing to find," he said.

"I'm going to take a shower," she said.

When she was done, he was waiting for her at the front door with a puppy dog look in his eyes.

"I thought you would have left already," she said as she put on her shoes.

"And leave you to walk to the bus alone?" He shook his head. "Something could happen to you."

As soon as she was done putting on her shoes, he lifted her chin, forcing her to look up at him. "I'm sorry, Caty."

"For what?"

"For not being more understanding. I miss my wife, too."

Caty shook her head. "I know, but this is different. Alexander really could be alive. He—"

"I know. Top secret mission. I get it. You have hope, and I don't." His face fell dramatically and the light left his eyes. "Maybe that's why I am not more sensitive. Maybe I am jealous."

Caty felt a pang of guilt and she rubbed his arm. "I'm sorry, too."

They stood there for a long moment, whole sentences hanging in the air unspoken between them. "We're going to be late for work," she eventually said.

He nodded, and they went out the door together. David walked her to her bus to make sure she got on safely. Everyone in the North was supposed to be well-adjusted and non-violent thanks to their endocrine implants, but crime was still rising steadily. There was a standing nationwide order for all natural-borns with behavioral implants to go get them adjusted, but Caty had a feeling people were reluctant to dial back their primal instincts when they couldn't be sure that their neighbors were doing the same.

"See you tonight," David said, waving to her as she climbed on her bus.

Caty nodded and waved back. "See you."

Three hours later she was busy dusting an explicit Kama Sutra-inspired Koons sculpture in the Waltons' master suite when her comm band rang with an incoming call.

"Hello?" she answered.

"Caty? It's Muros."

"Tatiana?" Caty's heart became a drumbeat in her chest. "You heard something?" There was a notable pause on the other end. "Taty? Are you there?"

"I'm here. Your husband's ship was the *Lincoln,* right?"

"Yes, why?" *Thud-thud. Thud-thud...*

"Maybe you'd like to meet with me for lunch today?"

"I'm working."

"I could come to you."

"If you know something, just tell me. I've waited long enough. I *need* to know, Taty. Is he okay?"

Caty heard the other woman sigh. "The *Lincoln* is listed as a confirmed casualty in our records. I don't know why your husband's status is still MIA, but the crew went down with the ship. They didn't have a chance to deploy lifeboats or escape pods."

"That's impossible! They would have updated Alexander's status."

"Maybe, but everything is a mess right now, so a lot of things can slip through the cracks. Checking personnel records is a low priority. I'm really sorry, Caty. If there's anything I can do, you just let me know, okay?"

Caty's eyes blurred with tears. "No, thank you. Goodbye."

"Bye, Caty... Take care."

Caty ended the comm call on her end and walked over to sit at the foot of the Waltons' bed. She sat staring at her hands as her tears rained into them, slipping between her fingers.

"Caty? Are you all right?"

Caty looked up to see Mrs. Walton standing in the doorway, an uncomfortable look on her face. "I'm fine," Caty said.

Mrs. Walton frowned and stared at her pointedly. "Clearly you're not fine. Otherwise you would be doing your job rather than wrinkling a thousand sol bedspread with your posterior."

Caty stood up quickly and wiped her eyes. "I'm sorry... I just heard news about my husband."

"Captain Alexander?"

"He's..." She couldn't bring herself to say it. So many

months of holding onto hope and for what? She had written literally *hundreds* of letters to him. Letters he was never going to read.

Mrs. Walton's disapproving frown gave way to another look of discomfort. "Oh... I see. You can take a personal day if you like, Caty. I'm sure you can catch up on all the housework tomorrow."

Caty wiped her tears again and managed a broken smile. "Yes. Thank you, Mrs. Walton."

The subsequent hours both dragged and raced, passing in a dimension where time had been replaced by a terrifying void. The bus ride was shorter than usual—no traffic at this time of day. Caty walked alone from the bus stop to her home, scarcely noticing the hungry, desperate faces peering at her from curtainless windows and barren doorsteps as she passed by.

She went straight to bed and slept a haunted sleep until she woke with a knock at her door.

"Caty?" It was David. The door cracked open. "Are you asleep?"

She didn't reply, hoping he would leave.

"You weren't at the bus stop. Did something happen?"

"No. Nothing. I'm fine."

The light from the open door increased. More footsteps. *"Obvio que no estas bien, mi chiquita."*

"Go away!" she sobbed.

The bed sank with his weight, and she buried her face in the pillows. She felt a hand on her shoulder.

"It's okay," he said. "Whatever it is, we'll get through it. You lost your job?"

She shook her head.

"Then what?"

Suddenly she was furious with him. What right did he have

to intrude on her like this? What was he even doing sharing a house with her? He should just go! Caty burst from the covers, her eyes flashing, her heart pounding. "He's dead. Are you hap py now? Alexander is dead!"

David's lips parted and his brown eyes grew wide. It took him a moment to recover from her outburst. "How do you know?"

Caty looked away. Hot tears welled in her eyes once more. "They called."

David said nothing, seemingly frozen in place.

A tear fell from Caty's eye lashes and ran down her cheek. David snapped out of it and pulled her into a strong embrace. She sobbed anew while he whispered in her ear, telling her everything was going to be okay.

He was wrong. Alexander wasn't coming back to save her. The world was never going to go back to the way it had been before. Nothing was going to be okay ever again. She soaked David's shirt with her tears, and he rocked her back and forth, stroking her head for what seemed like hours.

Eventually the cold fury of grief gave way to the warmth of that embrace, and Caty began to notice David's hands running lightly beneath her shirt, up and down her back, making her skin tingle.

A part of her that had been denied for more than two years came roaring to life, making her blood sing in her veins. Pent-up grief became red hot desire, and everything else ceased to matter. Why hold back any longer? The words *till death do us part* came to mind, and suddenly she turned her head from David's shirt to face him.

She pulled his lips down to hers and drank him in. He smelled like sweat and tasted like beer, but somehow that was better than perfume and mint. He was real. He was alive.

With every desperate touch and gasping kiss, she realized that this was something they'd both wanted for a long time. Caty surrendered to the moment, fumbling with the buttons on his shirt while he ripped her blouse open and stripped her naked. He spent a moment admiring her before she pulled him down on top of her.

A few minutes later, she lay gasping on the bed beside him. The heat of the moment was gone, leaving her cold and shivering. Suddenly she felt smothered under an impossible weight of grief and… guilt. She bit her lower lip and rocked her head from side to side on her pillow. *What have I done?*

David lay on his side, staring at her, his hands running lightly over her naked chest. Her skin glistened with sweat in the dim light pouring in from the hallway. David's eyes glinted at her, diamond pinpricks of light adrift in a sea of darkness.

"He would want you to be happy, Caty."

Shock coursed through her. Was she that easy to read?

"I know, because that is what I would want, if I was him."

Caty nodded. Alexander *would* have wanted her to be happy, but this still felt wrong. It felt like she'd betrayed him. She hadn't even waited a day between hearing that he was dead and moving on with another man!

Ice crept inside her soul, making her shiver. What kind of wife jumped into bed with another man as soon as she heard that her husband was dead? A painful lump rose in Caty's throat, and David began showering her with kisses. David stroked her cheek, wiping away a fresh tear.

"It's okay. You're safe. I'm here, and I'm not going to leave you. Not even death can take me, *mi chiquita.* It already tried. I will make you whole again."

Caty nodded once more even though she knew those were all lies. It wasn't okay; she wasn't safe; and David could try all he wanted, but he would never be able to fill the hole that Alexander had left in her heart.

"I think... I need to be alone," she said, not looking at him.

David's expression darkened. "Alone? *Despues de lo que hicimos?*"

"I'm sorry. I just... it's been a long day."

He looked angry, ready to object, but all he said was "*Entiendo,*" and then he rolled out of bed and walked away, not even stopping to put on his clothes.

Caty watched him leave, thinking that he really didn't understand. He'd already grieved for his wife. He'd given up hope a long time ago. He didn't have hundreds of unread letters written to a ghost. She hugged a pillow to her heart, and half-prayed, half-whispered her apologies to Alexander.

She wasn't sure if some part of him still lived on and was listening, but it made her feel better. She vowed never to do it again. David would have to understand. She couldn't be with him. Maybe she would move out. The Waltons might be willing to take her as a live-in. It would be nice not to have to spend four hours on a bus every day.

Thinking about that made her feel better. *I'm sorry, Alex,* she whispered to her pillow for the hundredth time. *I'm so sorry...*

CHAPTER 27

11th Day On Wonderland - June 2, 2790
(Wonderland's Frame of Reference)

Alexander stood in his hab module, staring out a transparent square in the side of the dome. Rain streaked down, beading on his window and roaring against the hab canvas. Outside, floodlights lit up the perimeter of the compound, illuminating driving swaths of rain. As Alexander watched, the night's sky flashed with a dazzling fork of lightning that left a fading purple bruise on the clouds. A split second later there came a deafening *bang!* followed by a throaty roar from the alien sky.

Outside, the wind whistled and intermittently punched the hab canvas, making the normally smooth white dome ripple and undulate like a living thing. Alexander hoped it would hold.

There was something particularly frightening about weathering a storm on an alien world, even more so considering they were weathering it in a bunch of glorified tents.

Alexander's comm band trilled at him, and he answered, "Captain speaking."

"Sir, it's Korbin. You asked me to check in with our department heads for an update. I've finished compiling a summary of their findings. Would you like me to send it to your inbox or deliver the report in person?"

Another fork of lightning bruised the sky, followed by a noisy clap of thunder. "In person. I don't know about you, but I could use the company."

"I'll be right there," Korbin replied.

"See you." Alexander signed off, and a gust of wind hit the window in front of his face. Cold canvas touched the tip of his nose, making him flinch.

Alexander went to wait for Korbin in his sitting room. The electro-magnetically sealed flap at the entrance of his hab opened a moment later, and she walked in.

"Captain," she said, saluting him.

"Take a seat, Commander."

She sat down opposite him on an inflatable couch that matched the inflatable armchair where he sat. Thunder rumbled, and Korbin's eyes drifted to the ceiling as it billowed above their heads.

"Quite a storm," she said.

Alexander nodded, waiting for her report.

Korbin's eyes returned from the ceiling, and she began, "All good news so far. Wonderland is looking more and more habitable by the day."

"How's Max doing?"

"No signs of any active infection. Toxicology scans also came back clean."

Alex's eyebrows floated up. "That *is* good news."

Korbin nodded. "Doctor Crespin finished analyzing the rest of the soil and air samples, and there's still no sign of a human-compatible strain of bacteria or virus. Crespin wants to continue testing, but even he admits that it's unlikely we'll find anything pathogenic at this point."

"How confident is he about that?"

"Ninety-nine percent."

"So apart from potentially hostile flora and fauna, we're ninety-nine percent sure that Wonderland is habitable for humans."

A booming peal of thunder punctuated that statement, and Korbin nodded.

"What about agriculture? What's Cardinal have to say?"

"He's already got corn, wheat, rice, and potatoes growing. It takes some work to prepare the soil, but otherwise it looks like we won't have any trouble. So far our plants don't appear to be compatible with Wonderland's microbial life any more than we are, and the crops Cardinal has growing outside the lab haven't attracted any insects yet, so there's a good chance that we'll be able to grow food even more easily here than we do on Earth."

"So what's stopping us from leaving in the morning?"

Korbin shrugged. "The consensus among the crew is that everyone would like to stay for at least another week, but I don't think we really need more time to call Wonderland habitable."

Alexander tried to keep his excitement in check. They could be back home in another seventy days—give or take a few weeks of transit to and from the wormhole on either end. "They have tomorrow to consolidate their findings and pack their samples, and then we're out of here."

"Yes, sir. I'll be sure to let them know." Thunder boomed louder than ever, and this time both of them looked up at the ceiling.

Alexander's comm band beeped at him, and he absently brought it up to his mouth to answer. "Captain speaking."

"Sir, it's Ryder. I've got movement on infrared, out at the tree line. Six signatures."

"Trees or animals?"

"Animals, sir. Big ones."

"What are they doing?"

"They appear to be headed for the hab complex."

"Why would they come here?"

"Maybe they saw the floodlights?"

"We've had our lights on since day one, and they haven't bothered us before. Who's out there with you?"

"No one. Lieutenant Stone just left to change out with Fernandez."

"Bad timing. All right, see if you can scare them off, but don't engage unless they attack you first."

"Yes, sir. What if they breach the perimeter?"

"Then let them have it, precision fire only. We don't want to risk hitting the habs."

"Roger."

Alexander listened as high caliber rounds roared over the comm band's speakers. "Seems to be driving them off… wait, no… they're comin' my way now. Shit!"

"Ryder, how close are they?"

More weapons fire. "Close!" This time Alexander picked out the deep vibrating *hum* of laser fire. "They're not spookin'!"

"Shoot them!"

The sound of weapons' fire intensified, followed by Ryder cursing. Then came an eardrum-bursting roar, followed by static.

"Ryder!"

No answer.

"Ryder, come in!"

The comm call ended automatically, and the words *connection lost* appeared hovering in the air above his comm band.

Korbin shot him a wide-eyed look, her mouth agape.

Alexander bounced to his feet. "Change of plans. We're leaving *right now.* Evacuate the crew to the shuttles."

"What about our research?"

"It will be worthless if we don't live to tell about it. Spread the word and get everyone out as quickly as possible."

"We should at least backup our data to the *Lincoln*."

"I'll leave you in charge of that, but don't stick around to wait for the backup to finish."

"I won't. What are you going to do?"

"I'm going to take the rover out and try to draw them away." Alexander took off at a run. Behind him he heard Korbin giving the order to evacuate. He tried to tell himself that it was just a precaution and nothing was going to happen, but if those beasts had taken out a Cheetah assault mech, how much easier would it be to trample a few tents?

CHAPTER 28

Alexander ran across the grassy field to the rover, his heart pounding as rain pelted his pressure suit. Lightning flashed and thunder boomed as he raced up the ramp to the rover's rear airlock.

Seconds later, as he dropped into the driver's seat and belted in, his comm band trilled with yet another incoming call. Alexander routed the call through the rover's comm system.

"Hello?"

"Captain, it's Fernandez. I'm on my way to the perimeter now. Tracking six targets. Permission to engage."

"Permission granted."

"Engaging…"

Alexander heard lasers humming and crackling over the comms. He brought the rest of the rover's systems online and activated the vehicle's headlights. Dead ahead he saw the hab complex, a cluster of white domes. To one side, he saw a group of people running out to the nearest shuttle. Then he checked sensors and saw the incoming animals. They were very close to the habs. As he watched, Fernandez's Cheetah cut two of them down. The remaining four switched directions, heading straight for Fernandez. They were almost on top of him, and moving fast.

Alexander hit the accelerator, and the rover lurched into motion. "Fernandez, you need to get out of there!"

"Aye! I'm runnin'."

"I'll see if I can distract them for you," Alexander said. He began honking the rover's horn and flashing its lights to draw attention to himself. Pretty soon two of the blips on sensors broke off and started chasing him. Alexander drove toward them, hoping to get a visual. He squinted through the driving rain, watching the twin cones of light beaming out from the rover's headlights. Nothing yet, but visibility was cut significantly by the rain.

Then one of the two burst into view. It was big all right—black fur wet and glistening. It ran on its hind legs, balanced with its tail, and held its shorter forelegs in the air, just like a T-rex. Alexander blinked, shocked by the similarities. The beast was almost identical except for the fur. It ran right by him and body-checked the rover as it passed.

Alexander heard a *crunch* as the metal hull gave way. Cursing under his breath, Alexander turned the wheel, circling back around to chase the creature. He was just in time to see the other one go barreling through the hab complex, snapping its jaws on white canvas and air as it tried to kill a big, hollow white dome. The creature trampled the entire complex in seconds, dragging several of the domes along with its momentum before tripping over the swaddling canvas and collapsing in a thrashing heap.

Alexander watched helplessly as the monster shredded white canvas with its claws and teeth. Twin crimson beams shot by the rover and the other dino collapsed right in front of him, hitting the dirt with a ground-shaking *thud.* Alexander couldn't stop in time, and the rover rolled up and over the furry beast. He went careening down the other side of it, headed straight for what was left of the hab complex. Alexander slammed on the brakes and stopped just before a staccato burst of laser fire sliced through the billowing pile of canvas to hit the last dino.

"That's it. We got 'em all," Fernandez reported.

Alexander sighed. "Go check on Ryder. I'll get the crew together and we'll see what we can salvage here."

"Yes, sir."

Alexander dialed Korbin's comm and sat listening to it ring. By the fifth ring he was starting to worry. What if she'd still been inside the habs when that dino tore through them?

Then he noticed a strange golden light blooming in the rumpled pile of white canvas. It took him a moment to recognize that light for what it was—

Fire.

Fernandez had used lasers to kill the dinos, and the heat had set the canvas ablaze. Korbin might still be in there! Alexander placed a distress call on an open channel. Stone answered from Shuttle One.

"What's wrong, Captain?"

"Is Korbin with you?"

"No, I thought she was with you?"

Alexander's eyes flared. "She told you that?"

"No, but—"

"Never mind. The habs are on fire and I think she's still inside."

There was a brief pause on Stone's end, followed by, "We're on our way."

Alexander hurriedly unbuckled his restraints and bolted from the driver's seat, racing toward the rear airlock. *I'm coming, Sirena,* he thought.

But by the time he reached the habs, the entire complex was one big blazing inferno, and there was nothing left to do but watch it burn.

The rest of the crew came up beside him. Stone skidded to a stop and made a strangled sound over his suit's speakers before screaming, "Shit!" and kicking the dirt with his boot.

The crew looked on in despair, watching their mission go up in the smoke of Korbin's funeral pyre.

"Max is missing, too," Stone said.

"What?" Alexander blinked.

"I just did a head count and Doc Crespin told me Max stayed with Korbin to help her with the backups."

Alexander shook his head. After all the time they spent rescuing him, Max had ended up dead anyway. "This planet really is haunted. It's time to get the hell away and go home."

"What's that?" Doctor Crepsin asked, coming up beside them. Alexander saw that he was pointing to a pair of shadows silhouetted to one side of the inferno.

"It's them!" McAdams shouted.

They all ran to assist. Max stumbled along, half dragging, half carrying Korbin.

"Hello," Korbin said weakly over her helmet speakers.

"Why didn't you answer me on the comms?" Alexander demanded. "We thought you were dead!"

"You tried to contact me?" she asked, sounding confused.

"She took a blow to the head when those monsters brought everything crashing down," Max explained. "She just came to a few minutes ago."

"We need to get her to one of the shuttles so I can examine her," Crespin said. "Can she walk?"

Max shook his head. "I think she twisted her ankle. It might be broken. Not sure."

"It's definitely broken," Crepsin said, pointing to the odd way it was bent. "Stone, would you help Maximilian to carry her, please?"

Alexander looked on with a frown. "What about you, Max?"

"What *about* me?" he grunted while handing Korbin over to Crespin and Stone.

"Why didn't you comm us for help?"

"Or answer *my* call," Stone put in.

"Too busy saving Korbin's skin. Besides what was I going to say? I'm under a heap of burning canvas, come find me! All that would do is get the rest of you into the same mess as us."

"Hmmm. Well, I guess you're safe now," Stone said.

"What about the mission data?" Cardinal asked as the group began shuffling toward the nearest shuttle.

Max shook his head. "We couldn't finish the backups in time. I had to drag Korbin away."

"So we lost everything…" Cardinal said.

"We can take new samples in the morning," Alexander replied. "And as for the data, when was the last offsite backup?"

"Three days ago."

"Good enough. We'll rebuild from that as best we can. Add your observations from those three days to fill in what's missing. It's still enough to call this mission a success and go home."

"We're going home?" McAdams chimed in. "I thought we were going to stay another week?"

"No, you all *wanted* to stay another week, but we were going to leave soon anyway, and now we really don't have a choice. We don't have any more habs to deploy and all of our equipment is busy melting to slag."

"We could work from the shuttles. Use whatever equipment we have as spares on the *Lincoln,*" Cardinal suggested.

"And wait for more dinos to come find us?" Alexander shook his head.

"I don't understand why they came here at all," McAdams

said. "It's not like they could have smelled us through the storm and the habs."

"Ryder suggested we might have attracted them with our floodlights. And speaking of Ryder, Fernandez should have reported in by now..." Alexander mentally placed a call.

Fernandez answered a moment later, "I've got Ryder, Captain. He's unconscious."

Alexander scowled. "Seems like everyone's getting hit on the head tonight. All right, hang tight. I'll bring over a medical team in the rover."

"Yes, sir."

"Doc, we have another head injury!" Alexander called out over his helmet speakers.

"Take Ensign Perez and Rios! I've got my hands full."

The two nurses fell out of the group and joined Alexander on his way back to the rover. By the time they reached Ryder, he was already awake and lying outside of his broken mech. The Cheetah looked like it had been put through a trash compactor.

"How's he doing?" Alexander asked, suddenly worried.

"I'm fine," Ryder snapped, pushing away the nurses and stumbling to his feet.

"Sit down, Mr. Ryder," Ensign Rios said. "You were unconscious. You're *not* fine."

Ryder snorted, but allowed them to examine him this time. "What happened, Captain?"

"They trashed our camp, but Fernandez put them all down before anyone got eaten. We lost the mission data, though."

"Shit."

"We'll rebuild it from backups."

"So now what?"

"Now we get the hell away from this rock and go home."

"You think there's a home to go back to?"

Alexander frowned, and looked back out at the flaming ruins of the hab complex. It still looked like a funeral pyre, but fortunately no one had actually died. The same couldn't be said for all the fires that must have raged across the Earth in their absence. "I guess we're about to find out," he said.

CHAPTER 29

Twenty Minutes Earlier…

Max watched Korbin racing from one terminal to another with a screwdriver, opening casings and yanking out data drives.

"I thought we were going to do a backup?"

"This is faster," she replied, yanking out another drive. That did it for the ones in the quarantine module. "Let's go!"

"I'm under quarantine," he reminded her.

"Just put your helmet on. You're your own quarantine module like that."

Max nodded and slipped his helmet over his head. It sealed around his collar with a squeal of pressurizing air.

They raced into the airlock between quarantine and the rest of the complex. Korbin grumbled about being forced to wait for the decontamination cycle.

Max smiled. He knew why she was so anxious to save the data. He was anxious for the same reason. This was her chance, and she wasn't likely to get another one.

Once the light above the airlock doors turned green and they slid open, Korbin raced out through the mess hall like she was on fire. The next hab module they entered was Cardinal's greenhouse. His terminal was full of data on how to grow plants on Wonderland. Critical information for a future colony.

Max watched as Korbin hurried to extract yet another data drive. She slipped it into an outer pocket in her suit, glancing his way as she did so.

Did she think he would try to stop her? He wanted nothing more than to help, but it wasn't as though he could *tell* her that. Or could he?

Korbin ran from the greenhouse to Stone's geological lab. She already had enough data, but the more the better. Stone's terminal would have detailed info on Wonderland's wealth of natural resources. Max followed Korbin there and watched as she removed yet another drive and tucked it into her pocket. Again, she glanced at him. "Aren't you going to help?"

"How are you going to explain stealing those?" Max asked, nodding to her pocket.

"Excuse me?"

"You need time to copy all that data, which means you're going to need to come up with a good excuse to hang onto those drives."

"I don't know what you're talking about, but we don't have time for this."

"Exactly. Tell them you tried to backup the data, but there wasn't enough time. Rig this place to blow, and no one will ever be the wiser. We'll say those monsters must have tripped over a case of grenades. They'll be here soon. I stole one of their eggs."

"You stole a..."

Max shrugged. "I lost it in the jungle while I was running from them, but they obviously don't know that. They tracked us this far, so I doubt they'll stop until they've turned this place upside down."

Korbin gave him a dark look. "You've put this entire mission in jeopardy!"

"What do you care? You have the data; you've got what you need."

Korbin's brow furrowed and she shook her head.

Being subtle wasn't working with her. "You have what you need for the Confederacy. All that's missing is the nav data from the *Lincoln,* and I can help you get that, too."

Korbin's hand drifted to another zippered pocket on her hip, and Max began to worry that she had a weapon concealed there.

He held up his hands in a placating gesture. "Wait. I'm on your side."

"I'm not so sure about that anymore."

Could he have been wrong? No. His intel was rock solid. Max smiled. "You were the one who sabotaged the engine code. The Confederacy gave you orders to ax the mission, but it didn't work. You're not an engineer, and Davorian obviously knows his stuff, so he shut down the bad code before anything happened."

"I'm not a spy."

"Yes, you are."

"I have two kids back on Earth—in the Alliance. Why would I risk their futures by betraying my own country?"

"You've visited your kids exactly once a year for the past five years."

"I'm a Commander. I barely get shore leave. Besides, it's easier for them not to see me too often."

Max shook his head. "No, you've been reconditioned to put group interests ahead of your own. That goes for putting group interests ahead of your childrens' interests, too. What do two lives matter when compared with the greater good of billions?

At this point, those kids are just another part of your cover. No one would suspect a mother of two of being a traitor, but you are. Your sabotage didn't work, so you figured you could help your side by sharing the mission data. Well, here's your chance. Steal the data and say it was destroyed."

Thunder boomed ominously.

"At the risk of repeating myself, I'm not a spy."

"You were undercover in the Confederacy for three years. They captured you, and you escaped. Pretty lucky for you, but I think they *let* you go."

Korbin's eyes hardened and she unzipped her pocket. "Sounds like you have everything figured out." She withdrew a small pistol, confirming his suspicions about that pocket. He held up his hands again. "I'm sorry, Max, but this is bigger than either of us. There's a greater good at stake."

"I agree, so let's trade—my life for the *Lincoln's* nav data."

Korbin snorted. "You can't deliver that."

"And what if I could?"

"I can't take the risk."

"I can show it to you."

"How?"

"Don't shoot." Max slowly raised his comm band and mentally summoned one of the nav charts from the device's memory. The chart sprang to life, projected in the air between them. It showed the *Lincoln's* path through the Looking Glass.

"How did you get that?"

"How do you think the Confederacy got the nav data from our probe missions?"

"That was you?"

"I had help, but yes. You're not the only Confederate sympathizer in the Alliance. It's hard to badmouth a Utopian society that actually *works.* We're stuck in the past, still thinking that socialism is the devil, and maybe it was back in the twentieth century, but that's because self-interest is hard-wired into us. Ants are communists, and they make it work. There's a reason they call us ants. Our brains have been re-wired to think more like them. We know how to put group interests ahead of our own."

"They reconditioned you, too?"

Max nodded. An animal roar interrupted them, sounding distant and near at the same time. He looked out the nearest window, half-expecting to see a giant eye peering in. Instead he saw the headlights of the rover. "We don't have much time," he said.

Thud. Thud. Thud-thud-thud…

"Something's coming!" Korbin screamed.

The floor heaved under their feet and the ceiling came crashing down. Rock samples went flying. Canvas framing poles clattered and fell in a tangled mess, some of them clunking off Max's helmet. Hab canvas swaddled them, and Korbin cried out, either in surprise or pain. The lights were gone, and the darkness smothered. Max felt himself being dragged along, then he heard another alien roar, followed by a ground-shaking *boom* as the beast fell, tripping over what was left of the complex.

Max listened to the sound of his breathing reverberating inside his helmet; then came more roaring sounds as the monster began thrashing, trying to get back up. They needed to find a way out before it accidentally killed them. He activated his headlamp and sent a private comms to Korbin. "You okay?"

"I'm… fine," she managed.

He looked around, casting twisted shadows in all directions. She was lying beside him under a pile of fist-sized rock samples. Max slipped out from under a bird's nest of bent framing poles and looked around for an exit. The complex hadn't completely collapsed, but there was no way they'd be able to make it to one of the external airlocks. They were going to have to cut a way out, but with what?

Max waited a second longer, wishing for an exit to appear. There came another roar, and a giant billowing slit opened up right in front of him. "Let's go!" He said, lunging for the opening before it disappeared. He reminded himself to think positive.

Max heard Korbin cursing over their private comms channel, and he turned to see her collapsed and struggling to regain her footing. Her ankle wasn't cooperating. He grabbed her by the wrist and yanked her to her feet. "Come on!"

Her leg buckled once more. "I think it's broken!"

Max grimaced. "Lean on me." They hobbled away with the hab complex twisting and bucking around them as their attacker continued thrashing on the ground. The tear in the hab canvas billowed wide, and they stumbled out. Max risked a look over his shoulder. The complex looked like a collapsed circus tent, but it was still more or less intact. The crew would find the missing drives as soon as they went back to assess and repair the damage. He stopped hobbling, a frown creasing his brow.

"The captain's trying to reach me," Korbin said. "I'm going to tell him where we are."

"Don't answer yet. We need to go back in!"

"What? Why?"

"They're going to figure out what we did! The habs are collapsed, not destroyed." Max watched the thrashing monster. Hab canvas flapped and billowed. Max wondered how they were going to get back in with that dino in there. Then a pair of blood-red laser beams lanced out of the darkness, converging on the fallen beast. It screamed and lay still.

Problem solved.

"It's too late," Korbin said. "We'll find another way to get the data."

Max wasn't ready to give up yet. He wished for a solution to present itself. Abruptly a bright golden glow appeared in the center of the ruined hab complex, illuminating the white canvas from within. That radiance grew steadily, and he smiled.

"It's on fire…" Korbin said.

Max nodded. It made sense. Someone shot a pair of high-powered lasers into a pile of combustible material. He couldn't have planned a better solution. Yet another coincidence on Wonderland—or maybe this time it was Fate.

Turning to Korbin, Max said, "You'd better give me the drives. I'll hang onto them for now."

He saw her eyes narrow suspiciously behind her helmet. "Why would I do that?"

"Because you need an excuse for why you didn't answer the captain's call. We'll say you were unconscious. No one's going to doubt that you could have bumped your head, but while they're examining you, they might discover the drives in your pocket. No one will bother examining me. I'm not hurt."

"Fine." Korbin unzipped her pocket and passed him all four of the thumb-sized drives. "Now what?"

Max's comm began beeping with a call from Lieutenant Stone. He ignored it. He'd say he was too busy fleeing from the blaze. "Now, we go announce our return from the dead and tell everyone the bad news about the mission data."

"What if they find something in the wreckage?"

"They won't. Trust me." *Not if Maximilian Carter has anything to do with it,* he thought.

CHAPTER 30

Present Day, May 18, 2791
(Earth's Frame of Reference)

Catalina paused in mid-sweep of the grand ballroom-sized foyer of the Waltons' home to wipe the sweat from her brow. The Waltons' sweeper bot sat neglected to one side of the room beneath an antique chair. The bot had broken down twice this week, and this time the failure was permanent until spare parts could be found.

Unfortunately for Caty, whose job it now was to sweep every nook and cranny of the twenty-seven thousand square foot home, manufacturing sweeper bot parts was a low priority. Every spare scrap of metal was spoken for with government contracts, and every 3D printer and automated factory in the western hemisphere had been commandeered (somewhat illegally) to produce components for new starships. War had never been a bigger business, and the Alliance's cherished free market was starting to look dangerously like a command economy.

Caty stretched her aching arms, and her comm band trilled with an incoming call, giving her a welcome excuse not to go back to sweeping just yet. The caller ID said the call was from Lieutenant Muros from NAS Lemcroft. Caty's jaw went slack and her eyes drifted out of focus. The last time she'd heard from Muros was when she'd found out that Alexander's ship had gone down with all hands on board.

"Hello?" Caty said. Her hands felt cold, her entire body stiff.

"Caty, are you sitting down?"

"No."

"I'll give you a moment."

Caty eyed the antique chair in the corner of the room. What if it broke? She imagined sweeping floors for the next twenty years, and decided not to risk it. "I'm sitting," she lied. "What is it?" Her heart played a staccato in her chest.

"I made a mistake, Caty. There were two ships called the *Lincoln*—a destroyer class, and a battleship class. The battleship was the one that we lost, but the destroyer is still listed as *active.* I looked a little deeper, and your husband's name shows up on the roster of the destroyer, but not the battleship. He could still be alive."

Caty shook her head, hot tears sizzling down her cheeks.

"Caty?"

"How could you make a mistake like that!" she burst out.

"I..."

"Do you have any idea what you've done?"

"I'm very sorry. I really—"

Caty ended the comm call there and stood glaring at her comm band. *Stupid woman.* Some distant recess of her mind whispered to her that maybe the lieutenant wasn't the only one she was mad at, but she wasn't ready to listen yet.

Six hours later she was walking back from the bus with David, listening to the sound their feet made in the hard-packed mud. After the night they'd spent together a week ago, Caty had explained that she still needed time to get over Alexander. David had accepted that, but not happily. Now that she knew Alexander might still be alive, she would need more time than ever. Closure had come and gone, leaving a trail of guilt and a gaping hole in her chest.

Caty's comm band rang. It was probably Mrs. Walton. The band went on ringing, and David glanced at her, his bushy eyebrows lifting. Feeling suddenly annoyed at him, she answered the comm just to avoid a conversation about why she wasn't answering it. This time she didn't even bother to read the caller ID before answering. "Hello?"

"Caty, don't hang up."

Muros. The name burned like acid in her brain. "Why not?"

"You don't have to forgive me."

"I know."

"Well, there's a message here on file from Alex, addressed to you. The date stamp is from over a year ago. Do you want me to send it to you?"

Caty gaped at her comm, unable to believe what she was hearing. A message.

"Caty?"

"Was that message before or after the fighting concluded in orbit?"

"Ummm… after."

"So he *is* alive." Caty pretended not to notice the cold look of betrayal on David's face.

"That's looking more likely, yes."

"Send it. Thank you, Muros. This doesn't make up for anything…"

"No, I know."

"But thanks."

"You're welcome."

The comm call ended from the other end and Caty was left sharing an awkward silence with David as they walked the last block to their home.

"He is alive."

No Spanish this time. Caty couldn't decide if that was a good thing or not. "Yes."

"When did you find out?" he asked, turning to look at her. His eyes were like stones.

"Today."

He nodded, looking away again. "Then you were not lying about needing time."

"No. I wasn't. I felt like I cheated on him with you. Now that he might be alive, I feel more like that than ever. Being with you was a mistake, David. I'm sorry."

David stopped suddenly and grabbed her roughly by the arm. His eyes were wide and flashing, his breathing fast and shallow. She could smell the alcohol on his breath, and for the first time it really hit her that he always smelled like alcohol. *"Te equivocaste?"* He all but spat the words at her.

"David. I'm a married woman."

"You're with *me* now! He left you here! *¡Yo te cuido, yo te acompaño!"*

She shook her head. "I've never led you on, David."

"No, ¡solo te acostaste conmigo como una cualquiera!"

Caty blinked. Was he really calling her a whore? How dare he! She jerked her arm out of his grasp. "You knew my situation from the start. I never led you on. You took advantage of my grief when I thought Alexander was dead. If anything this is *your* fault."

David's jaw clenched, and all of the light left his eyes.

Slap!

Her cheek exploded with fire, and David shook a finger in

her face. *"¡El culpable eres tu!"*

He stalked away, leaving her stunned and trembling with a mixture of fear and rage. She stood there frozen, watching until David walked around the block and out of sight. He'd *hit* her... she couldn't believe it—the man who'd been her guardian for more than a year had just assaulted her.

It was only a slap. He's been drinking. His feelings are hurt.

No. She shook her head. She wasn't going to make excuses for him. Wrong was wrong. The adrenaline left and the pain in her cheek intensified. Caty felt light-headed and nauseous. She sat in the grass beside the footpath with her head between her knees.

After a while, she recovered enough to wonder about the message that had caused the fight. She checked her inbox on her comm band and found a message from Muros with Alex's message attached in a video format. She opened the file for playback and immediately saw Alexander's face projected in the air above her wrist. Her heart leapt into her throat, creating a painful lump to compete with the fire burning in her cheek.

He smiled briefly. She smiled back, imagining he was really there to see it. She reached out with one hand to touch him, but it passed straight through the hologram and out the other side, causing a fuzz of static to wash through his features.

"Caty, by now you know more about what's happened than I do. I hope to God you're somewhere safe. As for me, I'm okay. The *Lincoln* is well on her way to her destination, but there's a lot they didn't tell us about this mission. I don't think I can say much without this message getting edited all to hell before it reaches you, but due to reasons I can't discuss, I'm not going to be able to keep contact with you. I'll still record messages every day that I can, but you probably won't get them for a long time. It's going to be years before we see each other, Caty—at best. I'll wait for you, just as I promised, but if you can't…"

She saw him swallow visibly, and her entire body went cold once more.

"Above all, I want you to be happy. Whatever that means, I won't hold it against you, okay? Keep yourself safe. I love you, Caty. *Te amo.*"

Somehow, he'd known. He'd *known* she would cheat, and that made her infidelity twice as bad. Was it some intrinsic part of her? A flaw too deeply-woven for her to deny?

Alex's message ended there, and he faded out of sight, leaving her feeling more miserable and alone than she ever had in her life. He'd just given her permission to be with David, but she didn't want to be with him.

I just want you, Alex! Caty fell forward with her face in her hands and sobbed. *I just want you.*

* * *

June 3, 2790
(Wonderland's Frame of Reference)

Alexander stood at the bottom of Shuttle One's ramp, surveying the damage to the hab complex by the light of day. There was nothing left but a mountain of char-blackened canvas clinging to equally blackened framing poles. It was like the carcass of some giant alien monster. The real alien monster lay somewhere in the center of those ruins.

A stiff breeze blew, stirring big papery flakes of canvas to life and driving them like snow. Overhead, through the swirling ashes, the sky was a pale ice blue. It was a chilly morning for Wonderland, just under twenty degrees—not that Alexander could feel the weather through his suit.

"There's nothing left…" Korbin said beside him, sounding

forlorn.

Alexander sighed. "How's your ankle?" he asked, nodding to the bulge in her pressure suit where the cast was hiding. Doctor Crespin had managed to fashion crutches for her out of spare framing poles.

"Better."

"You're lucky Max pulled you out. Whatever he was hiding, I guess we can rule out collusion with the enemy. If he was with the Reds, why would he save you?"

"He wouldn't."

"So Williams must have been the one who sabotaged our engines. What I don't get, though, is why he didn't just confess to it. He already confessed to planting a bomb."

Korbin shrugged. "Why would he admit to it? He's already in enough trouble without adding to the charges against him."

"True." Alexander nodded and looked away, back to the ruined hab complex. "Well, there haven't been any other acts of sabotage since we caught Williams, so I guess that must be it. Fleet investigators will have to handle the case when we get back. Speaking of which, we need to pack it in. I'm going to go contact Davorian and have him set up a flight plan for us to rendezvous with the *Lincoln*. Meanwhile, I need you to supervise the crew while they collect their samples. Just make sure they don't wander too far. At this point safety is our main concern. Even without further research we're all witness to the fact that Wonderland is habitable."

"I'll keep an eye on them, sir."

"Good. And Korbin?"

She regarded him with eyebrows raised behind her helmet's faceplate.

"Cheer up. We're going home. You're going to see your kids again very soon."

Korbin flashed half a smile. "And you your wife, sir."

He half-smiled back and nodded.

Neither one of them voiced their fears about what they would find on Earth when they returned, but Alexander still clung to stubborn hope. Caty was alive. She had to be.

CHAPTER 31

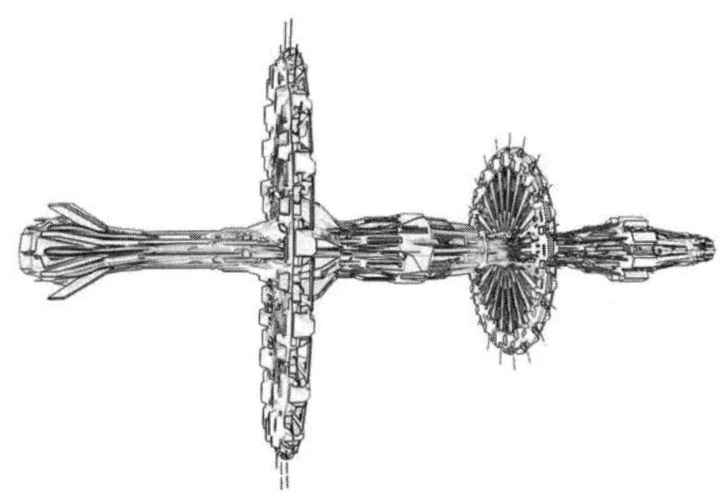

Three Days Later - June 6, 2790
(The Lincoln's Frame of Reference)

Alexander watched their final approach to the Looking Glass on the main holo display. It still looked like a clear glass marble to him. It was hard to imagine that bubble of distorted space-time was a tunnel from one galaxy to another.

Davorian had spent his time in orbit well. He'd studied the stars to identify familiar galaxies and their distances from Wonderland in order to triangulate Wonderland's position in relation to Earth's. All of his stargazing had paid off, because he was now positive that Wonderland was situated inside the local group at just over three million light years from Earth. More specifically, Davorian had determined that Wonderland was located inside the distal arm of the spiral galaxy M33, otherwise known as the *Triangulum Galaxy.*

"ETA five minutes until we enter the wormhole," Davorian

announced from the helm.

"Keep me posted," Alexander said. Turning to his XO, he added, "Looks like our mission was a success, Commander."

Korbin nodded without looking away from the forward display.

"How's Max doing?" he asked.

"He's still in med bay under quarantine, but Doctor Crespin and McAdams can't find anything wrong with him. We should probably release him. If you're worried, we can keep him in a pressure suit until he gets to his G-tank. The tank will act as an effective quarantine unit."

"I think that would be the safest course of action. If viruses on Earth sometimes take weeks to incubate, then the same could be true for Wonderland, and we may not know we're dealing with a harmful pathogen until it's too late."

Korbin nodded once more. "That's what McAdams said."

"Well, she's a smart girl."

Korbin arched an eyebrow at him.

"What?" he said.

"Just rumors, Captain."

Alexander felt a frown crease his brow. "What rumors?"

Korbin switched to a private comms channel so that the rest of the crew wouldn't overhear. "Before we entered the G-tanks, McAdams left the memorial service saying she was going to go find a bunkmate for the night. At that point you were the only one who'd left the officer's mess without a partner. We all just assumed…"

"That the captain was sleeping with his junior officer, and breaking his marriage vows while he's at it."

Korbin shrugged. "You wouldn't be the first to give into temptation in absentia. What happens in space stays in space, Captain."

"Well, I didn't. McAdams came to my quarters, drunk. She tried something, but I turned her down, and that's more than I should be telling you. Next time you hear the crew gossiping about their captain, I hope you'll have the sense to put those rumors to rest before they travel."

"Yes, sir," Korbin replied.

Alexander blew out a breath and shook his head. He hadn't meant to be so defensive, but it wasn't just about the inappropriateness of the crew talking about him behind his back. It was about the sanctity of his marriage, and the fact that everyone just assumed allowances should be made for infidelity due to the nature of their circumstances.

What happens in space, stays in space.

Those words echoed through Alexander's mind with mocking clarity.

What if Caty felt the same way about their situation?

Now that he knew they were going home, and much sooner than anticipated, he wished he hadn't given his wife permission to move on. He'd been a fool. What if she took his advice? He could only hope she hadn't gotten his message.

Thinking about messages reminded him what they had to do next. "Hayes—"

"Sir?"

"Get ready to send a transmission through the wormhole with our reconstructed mission data, along with my report."

"Is that wise, sir? We don't know who's waiting to receive our message on the other end."

"We have to risk it. If something happens to the *Lincoln* while we're all asleep, and we don't make it back, then all of this will have been for nothing. Use the best encryption algorithms you can and punch it."

"Yes, sir."

* * *

May 22, 2791
(Earth's Frame of Reference)

Caty didn't even turn to look when she heard the front door open. She sat at the kitchen table, warming her hands around a cup of hot tea and chewing her lower lip as she thought about the impossible predicament she was in. Peripherally, she saw David walk in. His stride faltered when he saw her sitting there.

"Hola bella," he said.

She didn't reply. She didn't feel beautiful, and besides, she wasn't talking to him.

He pulled out the chair in front of her and reached for one of her hands.

"Mi amor, perdóname."

Forgive me. She wasn't even thinking about him slapping her, but this was probably the thousandth time he'd apologized for it over the past four days. There hadn't been any further incidents, but her trust in him was still thin and brittle as ice.

She risked glaring at him, and saw his brown eyes big and sad and full of hope—hope that this time she really would forgive him.

Forgiving and forgetting are two different things, she thought.

On the other hand, could she really afford to be so strict with him now? They both had bigger issues to deal with. Part of her was bursting with joy, but the other part…

Afraid. She was afraid of how he would react. What if he lashed out again? She could smell the alcohol on his breath. He wasn't drunk, but he wasn't sober either.

"Háblame," he implored. *"Por favor.* I'll even talk to you in English. Just don't ignore me."

Her lip twitched and she looked down into her tea cup. She began circling the rim of the cup with her index finger. "There's something I need to tell you." Looking up, she found his eyebrows raised, and his head tilted with one ear angled toward her. He wrapped both hands around hers, trapping them between the tea cup and him.

"Anything, my love. Tell me. I will listen."

Caty wanted to object to the way he kept addressing her in a romantic way, but she contained herself. David might not be the prince that Alexander was, but he was here, and he was trying to make amends. Maybe that also meant that he deserved a second chance. She took a deep breath and let it out in a shaky sigh. She could work her way up to it some more, but she didn't want to draw this out. Sometimes it was easier just to deal with things head-on.

"I'm pregnant," she said.

David flinched, his head jerking back as if she'd punched him. His hands recoiled from hers.

"*¿Como? ¡Es imposible! Tienes...*"

"I'm three weeks late. I got a blood test. It's positive. Then I got another one to be sure. It's positive, too."

David's eyes narrowed suddenly. "You tricked me?"

Caty's jaw dropped and hot rage came boiling into her chest, puffing it up with air. "I *tricked* you?"

"You have an implant. Everyone does. You're supposed to be sterile until it's disabled. So you must have disabled it without telling me. Then you seduced me..." He began nodding as if it all made perfect sense. "All you wanted from me was a baby. You *used* me."

Caty shook her head, incredulous. "No." *Unbelievable!* She began rising from the table. "Never mind. I'll figure this out on my own."

"Wait." He grabbed her wrist, turning it white.

She eyed his hand. "Let me go."

"If you didn't plan this, then how did it happen?"

"I don't know! Implants fail. Sometimes they move out of position or they just don't work. They're not a hundred percent effective."

His grip loosened and some of the suspicion left his gaze. She jerked her wrist out of his grasp and turned away, shaking her head.

He stepped in front of her, blocking her way. She felt cornered. Her heart began to pound…

"I'm sorry for the way I reacted. Give me another chance."

Caty frowned and crossed her arms over her chest, regarding him with thinly pressed lips. She thought she'd just given him a second chance. *Now he wants a third. Three strikes, you're out.*

He went on, "I'm still processing. This is… good news," he said, as if trying to convince himself. "Yes." Now he smiled, fully convinced. "Very good news. I promise I will do everything I can to be the best father, and… more than just a father, if that's what you want."

"I don't know what I want yet, but you *are* the father, so you'd better be a good one."

"I will. The best." David grinned.

"Good. You can start by not drinking anymore."

David blinked, shocked. Then his lips curved up in one corner. "If I don't drink, I'll die of thirst. I have to hydrate myself."

"I agree, but water is better than alcohol for that. No more alcohol, David. I'm serious."

His wry expression vanished, and he blew out a sudden breath. "I need to relax somehow! You never see me drunk do you?"

"I don't know. Maybe you just hide it well."

He shook his head. "One or two drinks a day, that's it."

"Every day. And how do I know that one or two doesn't turn into three or four? Listen, you want to make this work, you want me to forgive you, you're going to have to show me you're serious."

David hesitated, eyes narrowed, teeth grinding… at last, he nodded. "Okay. For you, *mi amor.*"

"Good, but alcoholics don't just quit because they want to."

"I'm not an—"

She held up a hand to stop him. "Whether or not you are one, you're going to go get yourself adjusted. Tell them you slapped me, and that you have problems with alcohol. You're in the North, not the South. All it takes is a few minutes in a gene parlor and you'll be cured."

"You want to turn me into a puppy dog who will sit and roll over when he's told? How am I supposed to protect you if you take away all of my strength?"

"You slapped me. I had a bruise on my cheek for *two* days. Mrs. Walton asked me about it, and I had to lie and say I was robbed so that the police wouldn't come for you. Does that sound like *protecting* me?" David swallowed visibly, but said nothing. "You've been coming home smelling like beer for weeks… months now that I think about it, and that's the last thing you need with your impulse control problems."

"I…"

"Don't do it for me. Do it for yourself, and for your baby."

"I will go tomorrow. *Te prometo.*"

"Good. I want to see the adjustment report. If we feel like they over-adjusted something, we'll go back and fix it."

David began nodding. Before she knew it, he wrapped her up in a big bear hug, picking her up off the ground and spinning her in a circle. "*Te amo,* Caty!"

He *loved* her. Did she love him? Did it matter? They were going to have a baby together, and for that baby's sake, she had to do her best to make things work. "*Yo tambien te amo,* David," she said, but it came out sounding like a question.

He put her down and withdrew to an arm's length to look her in the eye. "*¿Me amas?*"

He obviously didn't hear the question mark. She hesitated. "I *care* about you," she said, trying to backtrack from love.

"What about Alex?" David asked, again choosing not to read between the lines.

"He sent me a message over a year ago, telling me to move on. To be happy. I just got it—the day that you slapped me."

David's eyebrows floated up. "He told you to move on?" David shook his head. "Then he never loved you."

Caty recoiled from him, shoving him away. "How *dare* you!"

David took a deep breath and held up his hands in surrender. "I'm sorry. What I meant was… I can't imagine ever letting you go. I don't know how he could do that if he still loves you. Maybe he has also moved on, and that is why he told you to do the same."

Caty's jaw dropped. *That* hadn't occurred to her, but maybe it should have. He was a captain on a ship with plenty of women, and over the past ten years he'd spent far more time with them than he had with her. Maybe he'd been cheating on her for years already and she hadn't even known? She remembered the engraved pocket watch she'd given him before he left, and then she remembered that he hadn't thought to get her a parting gift. Suddenly, that looked more like neglect and emotional distancing than simple forgetfulness.

"I am sorry, Caty. I didn't mean to upset you."

She shook her head. "It doesn't matter. He's gone. What we

had is in the past. It's time to focus on what lies ahead. Even if he comes back, it's too late. Too much time has passed, and I'm having a baby with you, not him.

David nodded, stepping in close to her. "You have made me a very happy man."

Caty searched his eyes, trying to gauge the truth of those words. The love she saw shining in his gaze warmed her heart and melted some of the ice between them. She relaxed her posture and smiled. "Get yourself adjusted, David. We have a whole life ahead of us, and I need you to be the best possible version of yourself if we're going to make it work."

"I will, and it *will* work." He leaned in for a kiss. Caty resisted the urge to turn away, reminding herself that she had to make an effort, too. The scent and taste of him filled her nostrils, and she relaxed still further. He wrapped his arms around her, and suddenly the whole world felt right. For a brief, blissful moment, forgetting didn't seem so hard.

She forgot all about David's outburst, and all about Alex. This time instead of feeling guilty, she felt justified. She knew she was doing the right thing. They hadn't planned to get pregnant, but by some miracle her implant had failed, and maybe that was a sign—something telling her to move on.

David withdrew, leaving her in a dreamy bubble of hope. Suddenly, her world looked bright, as if from now on everything was only going to get better, not worse.

Onwards and upwards, she thought.

CHAPTER 32

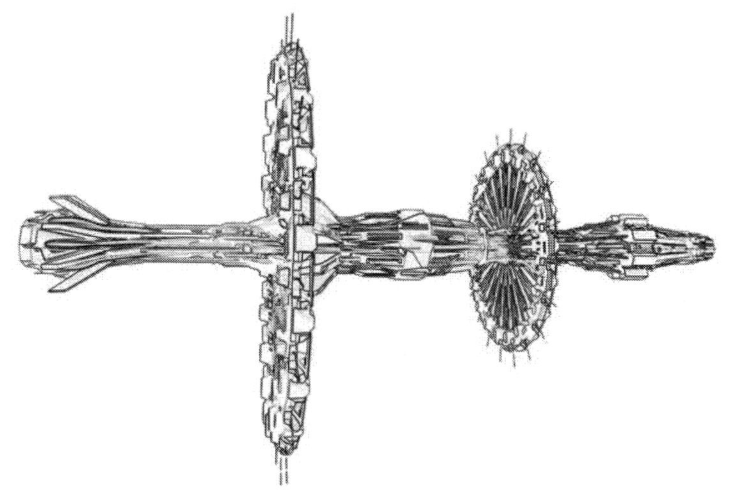

June 6, 2790
(The Lincoln's Frame of Reference)

"I'll take him from here, Doctor," Korbin said.

Doctor Crespin looked uncertain. "I should be the one to escort him to the G-tanks. He is my responsibility."

"You have enough to do as it is. The crew's safety is just as much my responsibility as it is yours. I'll make sure he doesn't take off his helmet or otherwise compromise the integrity of this ship."

Crespin scratched at the stubble on his face. Obviously he needed to give himself another round of depilatory treatments before he entered the tanks. "Okay."

Korbin flashed a smile at Max. "Let's go."

They marched away, out the doors from the med center and down the corridor to the nearest elevator. The *Lincoln* was still under one G of acceleration, so gravity was functioning normally throughout the central column, but soon, once everyone was safely ensconced in the G-tanks, the ship would go from one G to ten and continue that way for almost three weeks while it accelerated up to half the speed of light.

As they reached the elevator doors, Korbin glanced around to make sure they were alone together, and then she sent Max a private comms—text only, which she composed mentally via her cerebral implant.

The captain sent the mission data through the wormhole ahead of us in case something happens to the ship on the way home. Should we do the same?

Max glanced her way before replying. *I'll make it happen.*

How?

I have a way to stay awake and get out of the G-tanks while everyone else is asleep.

Korbin blinked, shocked. *How?* she asked again.

Too complicated to get into right now. Just trust me. I can do it.

You'll be crushed like a bug.

There's a half an hour window between entering the G-tanks and accelerating up to speed. That's long enough. How do you think I got the nav data?

She had to admit that did answer a nagging question. *Okay, but this is different than simply stealing data. Even if you find a way to use the* Lincoln's *comms to send the data, the Alliance will pick up any transmission you send.*

I'll use Confederacy encryption algorithms.

Then they'll know there's a traitor on board.

Max shook his head. *But they won't know who, and we already have Williams to pin it on.*

He's in the brig.

I'll plant a hacked comm band with a backdoor into the Lincoln's *systems in his personal effects. People will wonder how he smuggled that into the brig, but most will just take it at face value.*

And if they don't?

Then one of us needs to take the fall. I'm too valuable to compromise myself, so it will have to be you.

Korbin considered that with a frown. Her reconditioning told her to leave self-interest out of her decision-making, and when relying on unbiased logic, comparing her value to the value of a spy who was the president's direct representative, there was no contest.

Agreed, she texted back. *I'll take the fall if it comes to it.*

You have the perfect excuse. You were captured and reconditioned.

Yes.

Korbin hit the call button for the elevator. They waited a few moments for it to arrive. When it did, the doors parted to reveal Captain de Leon.

"Korbin—I thought you would be waiting at the G-tanks by now."

She shook her head. "I came to check on Max first."

Alexander appeared to notice Max for the first time. "Oh, so did I," he said. "I guess we can go up together, then."

Korbin smiled. "I guess so, sir."

Alexander held the doors open for them as they walked in, and Max traded a look with her behind Alexander's back.

Leave everything to me, he texted.

She gave no reply, afraid that Alexander would somehow overhear their very thoughts, but of course that was impossible.

"Something on your mind, Korbin?" Alexander asked, turning to her with eyebrows raised.

She jumped, afraid that he somehow *had* read her mind.

"No, sir, why do you ask?"

"You're unusually quiet."

She shook her head and smiled. "Just thinking about my

kids back home."

"I'm sure they're fine. We need to be positive, Commander."

She nodded. "Yes, sir."

* * *

Alexander stood in front of *G*-tank number 23 once more, stripping out of his pressure suit and uniform to stow them in the locker beside the tank. As he rolled up his uniform, he noticed the heavy weight in the inside pocket of the jacket. That had to be the pocket watch his wife had given him.

He unrolled the uniform and withdrew the watch. He studied the engravings, running his thumb over them as he read. He smiled and depressed the clasp at the top of the watch, popping it open. Inside he saw the photograph of him and Caty. Then his eyes drifted down to study the time. The hands pointed to eleven and one—*11:05,* and the date read *JUN|6|90.*

Less than three weeks had passed since they'd emerged from the *G*-tanks. Not bad considering they'd been afraid they might end up stuck in the Wonderland system for *years.*

"See you on the other side, Captain," McAdams said from the tank beside his as Doctor Crespin opened the hatch for her.

He nodded to his engineer, pretending not to notice her nakedness, and making sure to keep his eyes on her face. "See you in seventy days, Lieutenant." She walked inside, giving him a nice view of her rear. He looked away with a frown, chastising himself for allowing his gaze to linger. *You're a married man.*

"All ready over here, Captain?" Doctor Crespin asked.

Alexander nodded and noticed the doctor's gaze sliding down to the pocket watch in his hand. "I didn't have you pegged for an antique collector," Crespin said.

"A memento from my wife," Alexander explained.

"So you can count the seconds you're apart," he said, nodding. "Sounds like an appropriate gift from a loving wife."

"It was. I just hope it still is."

Crespin nodded absently as he configured the tank, as if he understood what Alexander meant by that. "All set." The tank doors slid open, and lights snapped on inside the small chamber. "If there are no unforeseen emergencies, you'll be waking up in seventy days—from our frame of reference that will be August 15th, 2790. Of course, from Earth's frame of reference it will be about two years later than that. You know—even if we don't end up colonizing Wonderland, I bet we could use the Looking Glass to sell one-way tickets to the future."

Alexander smiled. "But who would buy them?"

Crespin shrugged, and Seth Ryder chimed in from the tank beside Alexander's. "If we're lucky, the entire Confederacy will. Maybe we can work a deal where we take turns ruling Earth. Their government schedules a trip to the future, and when they come back it's their turn."

Alexander sent Ryder a bland smile. "I doubt that will fly. More likely we'll end up nuking each other until everyone is lining up to buy tickets to a future where Earth might be habitable again."

"Yeah..." Ryder said, and looked away.

Alexander grimaced. Not the best comment to make under the circumstances. He was going to have to get his implants adjusted for impulsivity.

"Captain," Crespin gestured for him to enter the tank. "By your leave, sir."

Alexander finished stowing his belongings in the locker and nodded to the doctor before entering the tank. He walked straight up to the harness and life support in the center of the chamber and began separating his life support lines. The door of the tank slid shut with an echoing *boom.* Alexander glanced at the now-shut door and shivered. He looked up at the glaring overhead lights inside the tank, then all around at the gleaming walls, and he felt trapped. The tank could easily double for a coffin if something happened in transit.

Best not to think about that.

Alexander went to the harness in the middle of the tank and quickly strapped himself in. He began attaching umbilicals. He connected the nutrient line to the implant in his wrist, slid the tracheal tube down his throat—gagging as it went down—strapped on his urinal cup, and finally, inserted the rectal tube.

Now trailing no less than four different tubes, Alexander hurried to strap himself into the harness. Soon after that, the tank detected he was ready, and warm water began streaming in around his feet. Alexander felt himself growing drowsy. His nutrient line must already be delivering the coma-inducing drugs.

The tank filled up quickly, and Alexander began to float. Then a tone sounded, and a green light went on beside the valve in his tracheal tube. It opened up and the ventilator began pumping an oxygen-rich perfluorocarbon into his lungs, replacing all of the air. Now he stopped floating and the water began rising over him. He listened to the ventilator *whooshing* and *swishing* as it pumped the perfluorocarbon in and out of his lungs, the rhythmic sound was lulling him to sleep.

The lights inside the tank grew gradually dimmer, and Alexander's head lolled. He felt his eyes closing, and the warmth consumed him.

He dreamed he was suntanning beside a pool with Caty.

Hello, Darling, she whispered in his ear.

He turned lazily to look. She looked like Caty—her hair like luminous strands of gold in the sun, her blue eyes bright and shimmering like the Caribbean Sea... but her face was too narrow, nose too long, and cheekbones too high for this woman to be his wife. Her breasts didn't fit either. This was McAdams, not Caty.

An objection bubbled up inside his throat, but no words came out. She leaned down and kissed him. He was paralyzed, unable to resist, and a guilty part of him accepted that excuse. Her tongue slid past his lips and into his mouth, then all the way down his throat, gagging him with its alien presence. He opened his eyes to see that she was a hideous alien with lumpy blue-green skin, bleached white hair, and reptilian eyes. He recoiled from her and his eyes snapped open.

He was back inside the tank, dim lights slowly rising in brightness. The water was gone, his skin itchy but dry. He could still feel that tongue inside his throat, and it *hurt,* as if the dream had been real.

Then he saw the ventilator and remembered where he was. Alexander hurried to withdraw the ventilator, gagging and wincing as it came back up his throat. The damn thing had hurt him somehow. As life sparked back into his nerves, he felt the unwelcome pressure of the urinal cup and the invading presence of the rectal tube.

Feeling violated, he hurried to disconnect himself from life support. His face began to itch, and he reached up to scratch his cheek. He was immediately shocked to feel a thick, bushy beard growing there—the hair still damp and clinging to his skin. He recalled that he'd forgotten to get an extra round of depilatory treatments from Doctor Crespin. Too many months had passed since receiving those treatments back on Earth.

Alexander unhooked his harness and shambled up to the door on stiff and shaking legs. He waved the door open and stumbled out into the circular room beyond.

The lights were too bright, making his eyes burn and water

after spending so long in darkness. The air felt much colder outside the heated tank. Soon his teeth were chattering, and his entire body trembling.

Fumbling with the control panel beside his locker, Alexander opened it and withdrew his belongings. All around him he heard tanks swishing open and people stumbling out, making exclamations about the cold and their various states of confusion and physical discomfort.

Alexander's throat still felt raw from the tracheal tube. Maybe he'd inserted it incorrectly? He might have scratched himself, but after this long, that should have healed. He hoped there wasn't a raging infection in his throat—though by now his implants should have detected that and deployed nanobodies to fight whatever bacteria had taken hold. Hopefully the pain didn't speak to a failure in his immunological implant. He'd have to go see Crespin later to see what was up.

Alexander hurried to don his uniform and then his pressure suit and boots. As he strapped on his comm band, he noticed that there were twelve new message alerts flashing on the comm band's small screen.

Alexander made a note to check on that ASAP. Finally, he withdrew his pocket watch. Curious, he depressed the clasp to check the date and time. Still ticking. He smiled at the photo of him and Caty. Then he checked the time. The big hand pointed to the one, and the small hand to the five. 1:25. *PM or AM?* He wondered. Not that it mattered much on a starship. Then he noticed the date.

JUN|7|90

Alexander frowned. The seventh of June? They'd entered the tanks on the *sixth.* Exactly one day had passed—not the seventy days that should have.

"Davorian!" Alexander called out, already consulting his

comm band to see what the alerts were about, and to double check the date.

"Sir?" Davorian asked, sounding out of breath.

Alexander turned to him and his eyes grew wide, shocked to see the other man's curly black beard and the bushy mop of hair on his head. Apparently Alexander wasn't the only one who'd forgotten to get depilatory treatments.

"We've been awoken early," Alexander said. "Something's gone wrong. We need to get to the bridge *now*."

Davorian shook his head, looking confused. "Sir, it's been seventy days…"

"No it hasn't. Look at my watch!" Alexander angled his palm so that Davorian could see the pocket watch.

The other man peered at it for a moment, then shook his head. "It's wrong. Check your comm band."

Alexander did. The date was August 15th 2790. He blinked and narrowed his eyes. "My watch stopped?"

"It's mechanical. Ten *G*s must have been too much for all the moving parts."

"It worked fine the first time," Alexander said through a frown, watching the second hand move around the clock with perfect regularity. "And it's still ticking."

"Regardless, the correct amount of time *has* passed. My comm band shows the same date as yours. Besides, if only a day had passed, how would we have grown such long hair and beards?"

Davorian had a point there. "Then what are all these alerts about?" he asked, more of himself than the ship's helmsman. Alexander mentally summoned a screen from his comm band and made selections in the air to check the latest message.

It was a comm recording from Fleet Admiral Wilson of the Alliance, routed to Alexander's comm band via the *Lincoln's* comms. The admiral's face appeared hovering in the air above Alexander's wrist. Short-cropped white hair emphasized his seniority and rank, but also reminded Alexander of the alien version of McAdams from his dream. Bumpy green skin. Long, slithering tongue… He shivered again and pushed the image from his head.

Wilson's blue eyes flashed and the fine lines around his mouth and eyes looked pinched with fury. "What in the hell is going on aboard your ship, Captain? You want to explain to me why we received a message with Confederate encryption? We have the best analysts working to crack that code, but so far we've confirmed that the message was sent via the *Lincoln's* comm system. Best case, you have a spy on board and you need to find that person—*fast.* Worst case, you and your entire ship has gone rogue. I'll be waiting to hear from you as soon as you wake up. Wilson *out.*"

Alexander stood there, swaying on his feet, stunned speechless.

"I don't understand…" Davorian said, shaking his head. "We were all in the tanks. The last message we sent before we locked the bridge was the mission data, but that was sent with Alliance encryption."

Alexander shook his head. "Obviously that wasn't the only message we sent. Williams must have been telling the truth about not sabotaging the engine code. We've had a spy in our midsts all this time."

"What if this was Williams, too? What if there was a deeper motive behind his sabotage?"

Alexander gave Davorian a hard look. "He's been in the brig ever since we entered the G-tanks for the first time. How the hell would he gain access to the *Lincoln's* comms?"

"Maybe we should ask him that, sir."

Alexander nodded and they stalked over to where Williams was being manually awoken from his tank. Doctor Crespin stood at the control panel, configuring the wake cycle. Lieutenants Stone and Fernandez stood waiting to escort Williams to the brig once he emerged. Alexander walked by them all, straight up to Williams' locker. He waved it open and looked inside. Not seeing anything, he began tossing items out onto the deck—uniform, pressure suit, boots...

The boots *thunked* on the deck and then something clattered out along the metal floor grating.

"Hello there," Davorian said, bending to retrieve a comm band that Williams shouldn't have had in his possession. "I think we have our spy."

"Spy?" Stone asked, taking sudden interest in what they were doing. "Who's a spy?"

Alexander took the comm band from Davorian and checked through the message logs. Nothing there. Then he checked the unit's deleted logs, and there it was—one very large data burst sent on an open channel with an *unknown* encryption. "Williams is a spy," Alexander said, nodding to himself and turning to shake the comm band in Stone's face. "How did he get a comm unit?"

Stone paled and shook his head. "I swear we checked him, Captain. He didn't have that on him."

"Did you check his boots?"

"Everything! We scanned him thoroughly when he left the brig and again before he entered the tank. He was clean."

"Well you obviously missed something," Alexander growled. "I don't know what he sent, but it was one hell of a big message, so it could be anything—or *everything*. We have to assume that our mission has been compromised. Everything we know about the Looking Glass and Wonderland, the Confederates now know, too. I only hope that this doesn't result in another war." Doctor Crespin stared open-mouthed at the offending comm band, distracted from configuring the *G*-tank. "Wake Williams up," Alexander snapped.

Crepsin nodded. "Yes, sir."

Alexander handed the comm band to Lieutenant Stone. "Make sure he doesn't have any other restricted items in his possession. Check his cell on the brig. Do a cavity search. The works. Then get to work interrogating him. We need to know what he sent in that message. Do whatever it takes."

"Understood, sir."

Alexander felt the weight of those words pressing on his conscience—*do whatever it takes.* That was a vague order, but at the same time perfectly clear. Williams' comfort, well-being, privacy, and even his sanity were all forfeit now. Under the circumstances, if it came to it, even killing him would be a legal means to an end. There were too many other lives at stake, and this was war.

Alexander pushed through the crowd of assembled crew. He heard urgent whispers rustling through the room as he went. "Everyone to your stations! We are now at condition yellow."

The crowd dispersed and flowed in a steady stream toward the elevators. On his way there, Alexander bumped into his XO.

"How did he get his hands on that comm unit?" Korbin asked.

Alexander shook his head. "I have no idea, but at the moment I'm more concerned about what he said than how he said it."

Korbin nodded. "Right."

Alexander regarded her with a frown. "Maybe we need to be interrogating Max, too."

"Why Max?"

Alexander shrugged. "Maybe Williams had outside help. You said yourself that Max was hiding something."

"He saved my life."

"Exactly. Maybe he did that to put our suspicions to rest."

Korbin appeared to consider that. "He's been under quarantine since Wonderland. When would he have had a chance to visit the brig? He was confined to Blue Deck, with more than fifty decks between him and Williams."

Alexander pressed his lips into a thin line. "Where is Max?" He looked around for the diplomat and found him only now emerging from his tank, already dressed and wearing a helmet. Quarantine protocols dictated that he had to take his pressure suit and helmet with him into the tank and put them on before he left. As a further measure of security, Max's tank had been configured to flash cook the outside of his suit before he emerged from the tank. Alexander watched him being escorted away by Doctor Crespin and a pair of nurses.

"Looks like he's going back into quarantine," Korbin said.

The elevators came back down after taking the first half of the crew to their various stations. Alexander felt the press of the crowd shuffling toward the elevators and he crowded into one of them with the rest of his bridge crew. Someone selected the bridge deck from the control panel, and the doors slid shut to carry them up.

Alexander hated to admit it, but Max wasn't a good fit for a Confederate spy. He didn't like the man, but Max simply wouldn't have had the opportunity to do anything without someone noticing that he'd broken quarantine.

"We'll check the surveillance tapes," Alexander said, more to himself than Korbin. "If Williams had outside help, we'll catch that person visiting him, or possibly even planting the comm unit in his belongings before we entered the tanks."

Korbin nodded. “That’s a good idea, sir.”

CHAPTER 33

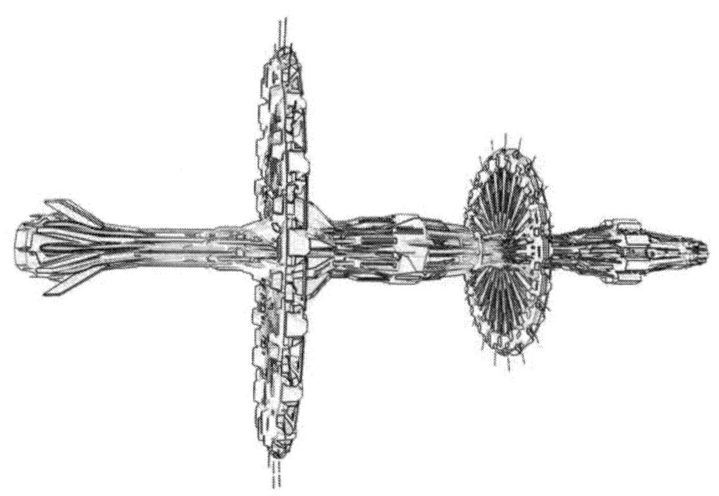

It was anything but a *good idea* for Alexander to check the surveillance tapes, Korbin realized as she sat down beside him on the bridge, waiting for all hell to break loose. The ship's surveillance tapes would reveal Max waking up from the tanks after everyone else had passed into a comatose state. Alexander would likely also see Max planting the hacked comm band in Williams' things. And what about the data drives she'd stolen? Would Alexander follow Max's every move and somehow uncover those, too? At that point she would be implicated as well. Only she could have recovered those drives from the hab complex before it got trashed and burned to a crisp.

Peripherally, Korbin noted Alexander scowling and taking angry stabs at the holographic keys projected from his control station.

"Something wrong, Captain?"

He shook his head. "The surveillance data is missing. The last recordings are all dated to before we entered the *G*-tanks for the *first* time. We don't have a single recording since then—Stone!"

"Sir?" Stone asked, half turning from his station.

"Are you, or are you not in charge of security on this ship?"

"I am, sir…"

"Then can you please explain to me why we don't have a single frame of surveillance for the past one hundred and fifty nine days?"

"That's impossible. I checked and backed up the logs before we entered the tanks."

"Well check again, because there's nothing there."

Silence reigned for a long, breathless moment while Lieutenant Stone double-checked things from his control station. "Shit, they're gone," he said. "Backups, too."

"Then someone deleted them, and there's no way that could have been Williams."

"Only a few people have that kind of access," Stone replied. "We're talking about one of the bridge crew, or someone else with stolen access—though I don't know when they would have ever had a chance to get down here, or even to CIC, without one of us noticing. It would have to be someone who's authorized to be there and who wouldn't have to explain what they're doing in a restricted area."

Alexander let out a growl. "All right, Davorian you are above suspicion, and I'll be sure to explain why I think so when the time comes. As for the rest of us, I'm going to submit us all into custody, including myself, as soon as we come into docking range of the nearest Alliance vessel. I'm sure the interrogations won't be pleasant, but we're out of options at this point. We might be granted a measure of mercy if we go willingly. Hayes—get me Admiral Wilson on the comms. It's time to reply to his accusations with what we know on our end."

"Yes, sir."

"Ahh... hold up, Captain," Davorian said from the helm.

"What is it?" Alexander snapped.

"The nav data appears to also have been erased."

"What?" Alexander cursed viciously, and Korbin cringed. "What about the backups?"

"Also wiped."

Another stream of curses blistered out.

Korbin didn't know how Max had managed to break into all of those systems, but he'd definitely gone too far. If he had been more subtle about things they might have gotten away with pinning it all on Williams. Now the truth was bound to come out. With her history, having been captured by the Confederates, fleet investigators would zero in on her in no time. If Alexander had known about her brief imprisonment in Confederate territory, he probably would have turned her in himself. At this point, all that she would accomplish by waiting to confess was to buy time for herself, but if she turned herself in, fleet investigators would pick through her brain until they found memories and thoughts to incriminate Max, too, and in the end they'd execute her anyway. There was really only one way out. For the greater good.

Korbin unbuckled from her couch and stood up. The ship's current state of zero-G cruising made it easy. Alexander regarded her with a furrowed brow. Then she pushed off the couch and drew the combat knife from her utility belt. No live-fire weapons were permitted on the bridge, but knives were necessary in case someone needed to cut their way out of their safety harness.

Alexander craned his neck to watch her float away. Then he appeared to notice the silvery glint of the blade in her hand. His eyes flew wide and he lunged against his restraints.

Korbin regarded him with a small, pitying smile before turning to address the rest of the crew. Raising her voice, she said, "Long live the Confederacy!" and then she plunged the knife under her sternum, straight into her heart. The searing heat took her breath away and sent her body into spasms. She was dimly aware of people screaming at each other. Then Alexander appeared floating beside her, his expression frozen somewhere between horror and fury.

"Why?" was all he asked.

Korbin struggled to move her lips. She was about to lose consciousness, and there would be no coming-to after that. "They're n-ot the enemy," she belched out with a painful gasp. "We are."

"Sirena!" he screamed at her, but she was gazing up at the main holo display and the warped pattern of stars around the mouth of the wormhole. The black of space grew, snuffing out the stars and flowing toward her like a living thing until it was rapping with greedy knuckles on the shuttered, starlit windows in her eyes. With a final, shuddering sigh she let the darkness in, and out went the light.

PART THREE: THE LAST WAR

"Patriots always talk of dying for their country but never of killing for their country."

—Bertrand Russell

CHAPTER 34

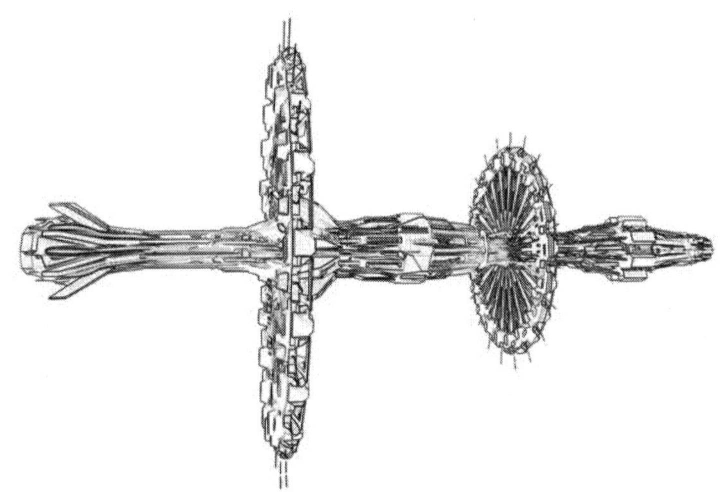

They conducted clean-up under full gravity. Davorian gradually ramped up thrust to avoid splashing the floating globules and balls of Korbin's blood. Even so, the ship's cleaning bots took more than an hour to scrub the deck clean, and Alexander could still see the faded stain of her passing. They'd bagged her body and sent it to the morgue without ceremony.

She was a spy, a traitor, so no tears would be seen to be shed, but that didn't stop Alexander's eyes from burning with the threat of them.

He couldn't understand it. She'd been his right-hand for more than five years! How could she turn on him—on all of them—so easily? Her last words had been clear enough—*They're not the enemy. We are*—but that sentiment still didn't connect to reason in his brain. She had two children back on Earth! He'd met them! She'd betrayed them equally in all of this.

The shocks had kept coming after her act of hari-kiri. The logs weren't the only thing missing from the *Lincoln.* While everyone was still reeling from her suicide, Doctor Crespin had reported that all the mission samples were missing from quarantine storage on Blue Deck. Either Korbin had stolen and hidden them, a tactic that was unlikely to yield lasting results—or she'd jettisoned them from the nearest airlock before everyone had entered the G-tanks.

Alexander had Stone and the ship's master-at-arms investigating, but his gut told him that the samples were floating in vacuum somewhere on the Wonderland side of the Looking Glass. As for the rest of Korbin's actions—the long-term consequences had yet to be fully measured or felt, but leaking the *Lincoln's* mission data to the Confederates could easily precipitate another war once the Confederacy realized just how important Wonderland was.

The flesh around Alexander's eyes tightened with simmering rage, and he saw the star field narrow to a paper-thin slit. The bridge was silent, everyone going about their tasks with a minimum of interaction and a maximum of introspection.

Hayes broke that silence with an update from the comms station. "Captain, I've updated Admiral Wilson with recent developments. We're still a few light minutes apart, but he's summoned you for a private meeting. Would you like to take it here, via your HUD, or in a more private setting?"

Alexander considered that. He could feel Korbin's ghost haunting him from the empty couch beside his. It would be nice to have an excuse to get off the bridge for a while.

"I'll take the meeting in my quarters, Lieutenant. Davorian, you have the conn. Don't hesitate to interrupt me if there are any further developments."

"Yes, sir."

"And Stone—"

"Captain?"

"That goes double for you. We need to know ASAP what else Korbin got up to."

"Aye-aye, sir."

Alexander unbuckled and crawled sideways out of his acceleration couch. A cleaning bot whirred by, still scrubbing at stubborn stains. He stepped over it with a grimace, and waved the elevator open as he approached. On his way up, he focused on taking slow, deep breaths to calm himself. The Confederates had gone too far this time.

As he reached his quarters and breezed through the door, the lights snapped on automatically, bringing the sitting room, wet bar, bed, bathroom, and the adjoining wall of his office into focus. A simulated viewport in the sitting room showed a warped view of stars. A hologram of him and Caty hovered above his nightstand. Alexander's gaze lingered on Caty's face as he passed from the living room to his office. He waved open the door and strode straight up to his chair, flopping into it with a sigh.

Half-raising his comm band to his lips, he said, "Call Lieutenant Hayes."

The call went through and Hayes answered, "Ready captain?"

"Ready as I'll ever be."

The holocam on Alexander's desk came to life and a red recording light winked on. The lights in the room dimmed, and the holocam began recording his expression to grant Admiral Wilson a delayed visual response. Given the two-minute comm latency between the *Lincoln* and Wilson's flagship, they would have to take turns speaking, so Alexander settled in to listen to a monologue that was almost sure to be a stern lecture on shipboard security.

Wilson appeared after just a few seconds, his white hair

glowing blue in the light of a tactical map projected in the foreground.

"Captain de Leon, I've just finished reviewing your report. I'm glad the spy chose to reveal herself, because now you and your ship can join the defensive formation around the Looking Glass without suspicion of your loyalties. That said, I'm also deeply concerned. Your mission has been compromised so thoroughly that we may as well have conducted it jointly with the Confederacy. Had we known that, we could have allowed Confederate access to the wormhole from the start and avoided this entire war.

"Sirena Korbin will go down in history for having single-handedly taken all the significance out of that war. We're talking about hundreds of millions of people who effectively died for nothing. If she hadn't killed herself, she would have gone through a very public trial and execution. But she must have known that, hence her decision to accelerate the process.

"I'm not sure how you missed noticing a spy in your midst, particularly you, Alexander. She was your executive officer. Then there's the matter of Lieutenant Williams to discuss, but for now, all of that is the least of our concerns. If there was any negligence on your part or from your fellow officers, I'm sure fleet investigators will uncover it when all of this is over—assuming you don't die in the fighting.

"The message that was leaked from your ship with Confederate encryption arrived six months ago. It was received and provoked an immediate response from the Confederacy. They went into round-the-clock production of a colony fleet capable of claiming Wonderland for their own. Needless to say, the Alliance has matched their efforts. We're in a race for our lives right now—quite literally.

After reviewing the data you sent us, the problem has become abundantly clear to both sides. The David Davorian Radiation Belts, provide a tremendous advantage to whoever gets warships through the wormhole first. They'll find easy picking when enemy ships come through after them with their reactors offline to prevent radiation damage to powered systems.

"Hopefully, given your firsthand experience, you'll be able to give us some additional insight that will help us to overcome that problem. Over."

Alexander blinked. He hadn't thought about that. But if all it took was to get warships on the other end of the Looking Glass to prevent the other side from doing so, then why hadn't the Alliance already sent theirs? That was the first thing he asked.

Wilson replied four minutes later. "The President has ordered us to hold position and defend the Looking Glass at all costs so that we can escort our colony fleet. The fleet will be going to Wonderland with the president and his ministers, as well as all of the Alliance's best and brightest citizens. Thanks to those radiation belts, Wonderland is much more defensible than Earth. So much so, that the Alliance has decided to move its seat of government to Wonderland.

"By now you should understand why we're holding our ground here. The Confederates are here, too, but right now we're sitting just out of effective laser range with each other. Should they attempt to close the gap, we'll open fire. Likewise, I'm sure they'll fire on us if we try to get any closer.

"It's a stand-off for the time being, and our Intel suggests the Reds are also waiting for their colony fleet to arrive before they make a move.

At the moment we outgun them, but that isn't expected to last, which is why you'll be joining our defensive screen immediately. If they try to wrest control of the wormhole from us, even one extra ship could make the difference. We have supply ships waiting to re-arm and re-fuel the *Lincoln* as soon as she arrives. Over."

Alexander gaped at the hologram of Admiral Wilson and slowly shook his head. As a captain in the fleet, his brain should have been greedily absorbing tactical and strategic information, but it sounded like all of those decisions had already been made, so all that was left to consider were the personal ramifications.

Wilson had said that Korbin's treachery meant *hundreds of millions* had died, and that meant that Caty was almost certainly dead.

A painful lump rose in Alexander's throat and he worked some moisture into his mouth so that he could speak. "Admiral, under the circumstances, I think it would be best for you to pass along any personal messages that might be waiting for myself and my crew from loved ones back home. It might help to remind all of us what's at stake here. Over."

Almost four minutes later, Wilson reacted to that request with a grim frown. "There are messages waiting, but not many. Channels of communication were cut soon after the fighting broke out on Earth, but I've anticipated your request and located all of the crew's surviving family members. I'm not sure what will be better for morale at this point—the desire for revenge or, in a few cases, the comfort of knowing that there's still something left to fight for. I'll send what messages there are and let you share them at your discretion, Captain. Should any of you choose to correspond with living family members, you will be allowed to do so.

"Since you've chosen not to respond to our current tactical situation, I will assume that you have no further input to provide, which means that this conversation has reached its end. I'm sending an updated flight plan to your helmsman along with a tactical map of currently-known ship positions. I encourage you to consult that map with your crew and see what we're up against.

"Something else—you'll need to choose a new executive officer. Ordinarily I'd leave that to you, but you're short-handed as it is with Williams riding in the brig, and there's a ready candidate that you probably haven't considered. As a favor to the president, he has requested that you promote Maximilian Carter to the position. Carter was once a Commander himself, so he is the perfect choice, and yes, before you ask, Baker is already here with the fleet, but keep that to yourself. Given our positions relative to the enemy it should be all but impossible for them to intercept this conversation, so they will remain safely unaware of Baker's location until it's too late. Were they to locate him now, they might realize we're going to re-locate the seat of government away from Earth.

"One last thing, Captain—don't forget to shave. I can hardly see you through that beard. Over and out."

Alexander frowned. He could read between the lines. They were *abandoning* Earth, and along with it, everyone who was still living there. It almost didn't matter if Caty was still alive. She wouldn't be for long.

CHAPTER 35

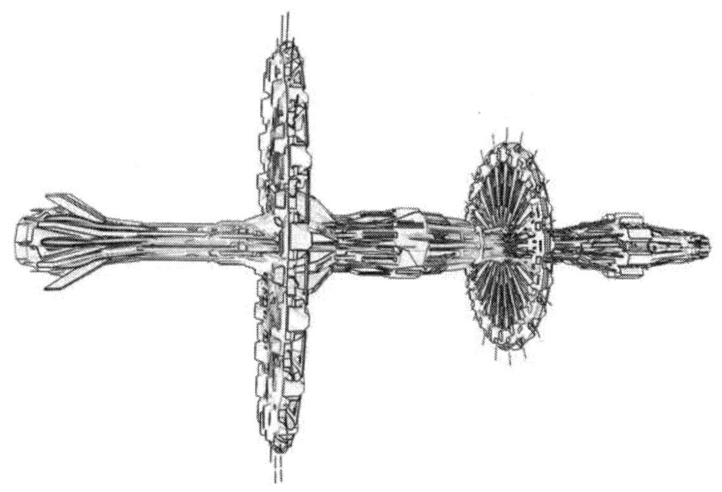

After his virtual meeting with Admiral Wilson, Alexander remained seated in his office, anxiously checking and rechecking his inbox for the private messages that Wilson had promised to send. After waiting for almost twenty minutes, he was in a bad mood. He was about to contact Hayes to remind the admiral, when his comm band chimed with a message alert. It was from the *Liberty*, Admiral Wilson's flagship. Alexander opened the message and saw all of the attached video recordings. There was one archive for each member of the crew, but some archives were much bigger than others. Alexander hurriedly scanned through the list for an archive that bore his name.

7. ENS Beseler, Sara
8. LT Cardinal, Guillermo
9. LCDR Crespin, Diego
10. LT Davorian, David
11. CAPT De Leon, Alexander

Alexander stopped there. He tapped on his name and scanned the list of files in the archive. Inside was a folder that bore Caty's name. He opened that one, too, and his gaze immediately settled on the dossier file. He opened it and was greeted by a heart-wrenching hologram of his wife's head and shoulders. Blond hair, pale skin, blue eyes, gaunt cheeks, lips cracked, dark circles under her eyes... She wasn't smiling, and she didn't look well, but she wasn't scarred beyond recognition with radiation burns either. How old was that image? He hoped she was doing better now, and that nothing had happened to her since it was taken. To the left of the hologram was a list of known details about her.

Personal Data:
Name: Catalina Abigail
Surname: Castillo de Leon
Date/Place of Birth: 2 April, 2761
Guadalajara, Mexico
Current Residence: Sacramento, California
Status: ALIVE

Alexander's eyes hovered over the last line, his eyes blurring with tears, his heart instantly pounding. A smile sprang unbidden to his lips, and he shook his head. This data wasn't old. It was current. His eyes skipped down and read the date stamp at the bottom of the file. *Last updated April 10, 2792.* Alexander's brain buzzed, trying to process that. It had been updated two years into the future? Then he remembered time dilation.

Grinning now, Alexander closed the dossier and scanned the contents of the archive. The remaining files were all video recordings, six of them. They were dated two years prior, one for each of the days between when he'd left and when—he assumed—the fighting had broken out on Earth.

He opened the first message and watched. It was heart-wrenching to see her holding back tears and speaking hopefully about his return. She injected little updates from her life, her studies, and her job as a museum curator. He wondered how life had changed for her since the war. Given her current address was in Sacramento, Alexander had to assume that LA had been wiped out. Subsequent messages were much of the same, alternating between the sad and the mundane, but Alexander could have sat there listening to his wife make small talk for hours.

Her last message was more urgent. Rumors had reached Earth about the fighting in space. She hoped he was okay and that he'd made it away before he could be dragged into the conflict. By the end of the message she was sobbing and begging for him to be okay.

Alexander swallowed past a hard knot in his throat and let out a deep sigh. He wiped his eyes and thought about how he should reply. Two years had passed since she'd last heard from him. What could he say now?

He considered sending her a message right away. If it were sent directly, it would take about ten minutes to arrive on Earth, but there was no telling how long it would take to be parsed through Navy censors before they relayed it to her on Earth. Alexander sat absently stroking his beard as he considered the matter. Feeling that long mop of facial hair reminded him that he needed to shave. He wouldn't want Caty to have to struggle to recognize him.

After a long encounter with an electric razor and a quick shower, Alexander was back at his desk—now shaved, his hair cropped short. Feeling more himself, he decided to pass along the other message archives via Lieutenant Hayes, along with instructions to temporarily downgrade the *Lincoln's* readiness from *condition yellow* to *condition green.* It would be nearly a day before they left the wormhole and joined Alliance forces on the other side, so they could afford to take some time off.

Additionally, he gave instructions for his crew to take some personal time and compose replies to their loved ones wherever possible. A large number of the crew would have *Status: DECEASED or Missing and Presumed Dead* in their loved ones' dossiers, so replies wouldn't be possible, but Alexander felt that the crew had a right to know. They'd waited long enough.

Hayes responded to those orders with a date and time update from Earth along with the tactical maps and updated orders and flight path for the *Lincoln*. Alexander checked the date.

August 4, 2792.

Just over five months had passed for the *Lincoln* and her crew since leaving Earth, but time dilation due to wormhole geometry and their cruising speed meant that those five months had become more than twenty-nine back on Earth. Alexander winced. *Almost two and a half years.*

He wondered what that meant for him and Caty. He had no way of knowing what had happened in the past two years. Had she moved on? Was she still grieving for him, having given him up for dead? How was she making ends meet?

He had so many questions, but he would have to wait for her reply before he could answer any of them. The good news was that she was alive, and in spite of everything else that had happened, that had him smiling from ear to ear as he recorded his message.

CHAPTER 36

August 5, 2792
(Shared Frame of Reference)

Catalina awoke to the sound of her comm band trilling with an incoming call. She mumbled a command to turn on the lamp beside her. Blinking the sleep from her eyes, the first thing she did was check to see if Dorian was okay in his crib. Seeing that he was still fast asleep, she relaxed somewhat. On the other side of the bed David groaned and rolled over, mumbling something in Spanish about turning the light off. Her comm band trilled again, and Caty answered it with a whisper before the noise could wake Dorian.

"Hello?"

"Caty. It's Muros. Sorry to call you so late, but I thought you'd want me to wake you."

Caty blinked. *Muros?* Where did she know a *Muros* from… then it came to her: *NAS Lemcroft.* Lieutenant Muros was her contact there. She hadn't heard from Muros in more than a year. If the lieutenant was contacting her again now, it had to be something to do with Alex. Caty glanced at David, suddenly nervous.

"What's going on?" she asked, still whispering.

"I have a message here from Alex. Do you want me to send it to you?"

A message from Alex. He was *alive?* It took a moment for that to filter through to her sleep-clogged brain. She'd moved on. She couldn't keep doing this to herself. But there was this other part of her that *needed* to hear from him, to see his face and hear his voice. That part of her made her heart pound and her palms sweat.

"Yes... Thank you, Muros."

"You're welcome. If you want to reply, just let me know."

"Reply?"

"To Alexander. I'm sorry I guess I wasn't clear. He's within comms range. This message was sent two hours ago."

Caty blinked, her eyes widening slowly. He really *was* back. "I'll let you know," she said, unable to think clearly. This was a dream. It had to be.

"Roger that. Take care, Caty."

"Bye," she whispered. She sat on the end of the bed for a long moment, watching her comm band, waiting for the blinking red light of a message alert to appear. She didn't know what to think. Her mind raced. What would this mean for her and David? She couldn't get back together with Alex, even if he landed on Earth tomorrow. She had a son with David—baby Dorian. He was about to turn five months.

But hearing news from Alexander stirred to life feelings she'd thought were safely buried. She still *loved* him, but did he still love her? Had he moved on, too? Even if he hadn't, Alexander wouldn't want her now that she'd been with another man and had a son by him. Who could forgive that? Alexander *had* given her permission to move on, but she doubted that he'd meant for her to move on temporarily and then get back together with him when he returned.

"He's back."

Caty jumped and turned to look at David. He was sitting up in bed, his eyes darkly shadowed in the low light of the room. His expression spoke volumes. He was angry. Maybe he had a right to be, but he needed to understand—this was not easy for her. Alexander had been... he'd been the love of her life. Not that she could tell David that. He'd lose it.

"Are you going to reply to him?"

Caty flashed a sad smile and shook her head. *And say what?* She wondered. Just then, her comm band chimed with an incoming message. It was from Alexander.

"Entonces?" David insisted, nodding to her comm band.

She shook her head. "I haven't even watched his message yet. How am I supposed to know if I should reply?"

"Como vas a saber..." he muttered, repeating her question like it was the most ridiculous thing she could have asked. David climbed out of bed and began pacing the room. Caty watched him with a frown. An acid rush of adrenaline began buzzing in her veins. Fight or flight.

He stopped beside her and brought his face down to hers, a sarcastic smile on his face. His brown eyes flashed mere inches from her nose. She could feel the angry heat in his gaze. He was just about to boil over. Self-preservation kicked in and she looked away, not wishing to challenge him. He had a temper. She wasn't stupid. It was best to let him cool down before they discussed anything.

"Let's not deal with this tonight," she said, turning away to put her comm band back on the night stand.

He caught her by the arm, his grip painfully tight.

"Let me go," she said, her own temper rising to pour some

heat into her words.

"You're *mine,*" he said through gritted teeth.

That did it. "I'm yours because I choose to be. I'm not your property. Maybe I *should* reply."

He flinched as if she'd slapped him. She saw his face contort with disgust, and a sick feeling crawled into the pit of her stomach. She'd seen him this way before.

In the time it took for her to blink, a loud *slap* rang in her ears, followed by an explosion of pain in her cheek. She tried counting to ten in her head, taking deep breaths, but it was too late. He'd awoken *her* temper now. How *dare* he slap her! Making things worse, Dorian was right with them in the room. Caty's eyes darted to his crib, suddenly afraid for her son. If David even so much as breathed on him… She glared at David with all the hate she could muster. He stepped back, his lips twisting derisively, his head bobbing as if she deserved what she'd got.

No amount of behavioral adjustment had ever seemed to work with David. This wasn't the first time, and it wouldn't be the last. What he needed was for someone to stand up to him. To fight back. She stood straight up, her entire body shaking with rage, and she took a long step toward him. She tried to put coherent thoughts together to say something that would hurt him badly enough. All she could think of was, "You're *right* to be jealous. Alexander is a thousand times the man you'll ever be!"

David froze, a monument of rage. Then he screamed and came at her with a closed fist. The next thing she knew, she was lying on the bed, staring up at the ceiling through one eye, her other one shut in darkness, and feeling like it had been knocked out with a hammer. David went on screaming, but she wasn't listening. She was too shocked. Too angry and hurt for words to express. What she did hear were baby Dorian's cries. Their fighting had woken him up.

"*¡Callate!*" David screamed at their son.

Dorian screamed louder, and Caty felt another white hot flash of fury. She sat up, watching David through her good eye to make sure his attention didn't linger on Dorian for long. David looked away from the crib, shaking his head. He began pacing around the room, muttering to himself in Spanish. Caty watched him carefully, quietly, this time knowing better than to speak.

Tears leaked in warm rivers down her cheeks. Her swollen eye felt like it was the size of a watermelon. Her head throbbed like there was a miniature drummer in there, pounding away.

Caty went to Dorian's crib and picked him up, shushing him and whispering sweetly that everything was fine. That she was fine. Dorian calmed down, believing the lies despite the tears that dripped onto his face. She rocked Dorian gently in her arms until he fell asleep once more, all the while keeping an eye on David; he avoided her gaze, still pacing. Caty laid Dorian back in his crib and then went over to her bed and lay down, too. She felt dizzy and sick, staring up at the blurry ceiling. Thinking actually hurt. She rocked her head from side to side. Then she felt his hands on her again…

But this time his fists were open, and his were hands gentle—shaking. It was like being caressed by a snake. She shivered and cringed, but said nothing. She didn't want to anger him again. He said something to her in Spanish, but she couldn't understand him. She realized that was because he was sobbing. He was apologizing profusely, stroking her stinging cheek, fingertips tracing lines around her swollen eye.

He said something about *hielo*—ice—and his weight abruptly left the bed.

In his absence, Caty's first thought was to run, to take Dorian and get as far away from David as she could. But right on the heels of that thought was cold, unfeeling reality. Where would she go? And how? She hadn't worked for six months. She didn't have a job waiting for her with the Waltons anymore, and getting a job that would pay enough for her to cover daycare and other childcare costs was simply impossible. She'd be lucky to pay for her own living expenses, let alone those of raising a child. There was government help, but too little of it, and there were simply too many mouths to feed. Now, in the midst of yet another arms race, the Alliance was even less charitable than usual, and if she decided to risk it and appeal for government aid, there was always the chance that they'd take Dorian away from her and give him to some rich gener family who *could* provide for him.

That was actually a very likely outcome.

She could always run back to the South and take Dorian to her family, but then he'd grow up in a bad neighborhood where half of the kids end up dropping out of school and joining the local gangs for a living. Given that as an alternative, it would actually be better for Dorian to end up with a couple of rich geners.

Her heart would never bear it. Losing him would destroy her. Dorian was all she had left.

David returned with a bag full of ice and applied it gently to her eye, barely touching her with it, but she winced and almost screamed from the pain. Fury boiled once more, but she clamped down on it, forcing herself not to react.

The last thing she wanted from David now was for him to try to make amends—or to hammer her with another blow. This act was getting tired. It was the same thing every time. He saw someone looking at her and blamed her for being too provocative, or he would feel she was being distant and cold, so he went out and got drunk. If he used her roughly when he came home, well it was just because he *loved* her so much. What were a few slaps between lovers? That was just part of the foreplay.

Caty cracked a bitter, self-deprecating smile. She was tired of asking him to get adjusted and tired of scanning line after line of adjustment reports that gave her hope where there was none. David was a broken, broken man, and no amount of tampering with his DNA or hormones was going to fix that.

Caty felt herself growing cold inside, shutting down and blocking him out. She pushed his hands away and sat up. "I need to be alone," she said.

"Caty, please… I am so, so sorry… Don't do this. Focus on the good things. I'm human! I make mistakes."

She took a deep breath. "We all make mistakes," she said, thinking that hers was meeting him. Her gaze slipped sideways to her comm band as her thoughts went back to Alex—her way out.

"You are thinking about him." She heard a bitter edge in David's voice. "I get it. You want me to leave you alone so you can answer him. Well, I'm not going anywhere. We will watch the message together and we will reply to it together."

Caty turned to him, incredulous that he could go from apologetic to jealous and demanding in a matter of seconds. He had no right. None. But from the crazy look in his eyes, she knew that if she said no he would fly into another fit of rage, and this time maybe he wouldn't stop. Maybe he'd feel justified for hitting her, the unfaithful slut.

Self-preservation won out in the end. She nodded and wordlessly reached for the comm band. They watched the message together. Caty through one eye, David through two. Her heart almost broke when she saw Alexander's face. He was so happy, so excited—talking about how he couldn't believe that she was alive, how he couldn't wait to see her again. Then his smile vanished and he became hesitant.

"I don't know anything about your life right now... what you've been through... I don't even know if I have any right to contact you anymore. I know I told you to move on. Believe me there have been many many days and nights that I've regretted that, and you should know that I haven't moved on, but if you did, and you're happy, then..." His brown eyes were bright and shimmering with tears, and his lips trembled ever so slightly, but he managed to smile again. "All I've ever wanted is for you to be happy, so that's all that matters.

"I wish I could say I'll see you soon, but I don't know that yet. They want us to join the fleet to defend Alliance space, and my guess is that it could be another six months before we actually come home, but there's also a good chance that things go bad. Really bad. Caty you need to—" The message jerked and suddenly Alex's head appeared in a different position than it had been a second ago. "—be safe."

That blip brought a frown to her lips and made her swollen eye throb and sting as the skin around it tightened. Something had been cut from his message. He'd been trying to warn her, but he'd been censored. Reading between the lines made her think he was telling her to go find the nearest bomb shelter and check herself in—not that it was even possible with the kind of money they had to live on.

Alexander went on, "I hope to hear from you soon, Caty." He held up the pocket watch she'd given him, dangling by its chain and swinging like a pendulum. "Your love *is* my truth. It always has been. I love you." He looked like he wanted to say more, but he stopped himself with a smile, and the message ended there.

Now what?

Caty's thoughts ran in confusing circles, bringing her back to her situation. Trapped. Alone. Praying every night to a God she didn't believe in for some way out. And now that Alexander had contacted her... she felt this crazy, optimistic hope that maybe this was the answer to her prayers. It was a miracle Alexander was even alive, let alone that he'd come home so soon. Maybe he wouldn't care that she'd moved on. Maybe once he learned about her situation he would understand, and he'd accept and love Dorian like his own son. Maybe...

But he wouldn't be back for another *six months,* and he'd admitted that he might not even survive what was coming. With that much uncertainty hanging over them, Caty knew she couldn't afford to hold out hope for Alexander, and that meant she couldn't afford to leave David. All she could do was try to make things work, try not to provoke the beast sitting on the bed beside her, and focus on her son. Dorian was all that mattered now.

"What are you going to tell him?" David asked, breaking the silence that had grown between them in the wake of Alexander's message..

Caty shrugged, feeling defeated. "What else? I have you and Dorian now. I couldn't wait around for him forever."

David nodded and sighed. She could almost feel the devil slither out of him with that breath, sated for the moment. "We can send him a message in the morning. Lie down," he said.

Caty shook her head. "I'm okay," she said. She did her best not to look at David. He sat there, looking guilty and miserable—a little boy staring at his feet. He looked up briefly to try another apology, but she stopped him.

"We don't need to talk about it. Tomorrow you'll go get adjusted again. I'll do my best not to make you jealous, and you'll have better self-control next time. It won't happen again."

He nodded, eyes back on his feet.

Caty swallowed past a painful lump and held back bitter tears. Here she was—one eye swollen shut, cheek red in the shape of his palm, and *she* was the one reassuring *him*.

"I'm going to tell him not to contact me again," she said. The words caught in her throat as she said them, and a deep ache began radiating in her chest, but she knew it was the right decision. Alexander was a sore spot between them. Getting closure once and for all might just be enough to get David to calm down and stop being so jealous.

Now that she thought about it, his jealousy and insecurity was at the root of all of their fights. Take that away, and maybe he'd finally become the man she'd always hoped he could be. Maybe they could make things work for Dorian's sake.

What other choice did she have?

CHAPTER 37

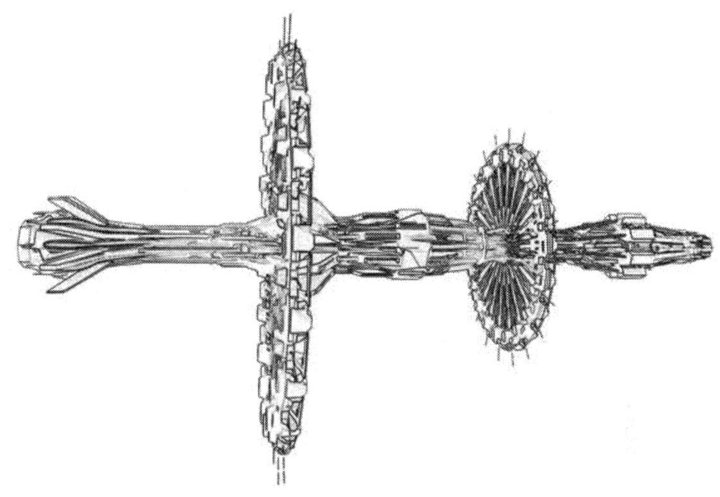

Alexander woke up to the sound of his comm band chiming. He blinked the sleep from his eyes to see his comm band mere inches from his nose. He'd fallen asleep like that, with his arm tucked under his pillow, keeping the comm band where he could see it. Seeing the new message light blinking, Alexander sat up straight and hurriedly checked his messages. Sure enough, there was one from Caty. Alexander's pulse quickened. Suddenly he was out of breath.

Grinning, he opened the message and held the comm band upright to watch as her hologram played out above his bed.

His grin vanished the instant that he saw her. She looked almost the same as the hologram in her dossier, except that she was wearing an eye patch and her hair was tied up in a bun. Sitting in her lap was a small baby boy. Sitting beside her was a man he didn't recognize, with brown eyes, unruly brown hair, and stubble to match. He was Latin, good-looking.

"Hello, Alex," Caty said, her tone flat. She wasn't smiling. "I don't know how to tell you this, so I'm just going to say it. I've moved on, just like you told me to."

Alexander blinked, his eyes widening in horror. *No.*

"This is Dorian," she said, picking up one pudgy baby hand to wave at the camera. "And David," she said, identifying the Latin man beside her without looking at him. That man reacted by wrapping an arm around her shoulders and leaning his head against hers in a proprietary way.

David. He could be President fucking Baker for all Alexander cared. All that mattered was that he had his arm around Caty's shoulders, and his head was leaning against hers.

"We're a family," she said. "I wish I had better news for you. I wish..." This time she glanced at the man beside her before looking back to the camera with a frown. "I wish I didn't have to hurt you like this. I'm sorry, Alex." She bit her bottom lip and he saw tears welling in the eye without the patch. She shook her head. "This is goodbye. It would be better for both of us if you didn't contact me again. I wish you all the best. All I want is for you to be happy, too. Keep safe. I..." She glanced sideways once more as if... as if she were asking for his permission? But fucking David didn't react to that. He just went on smiling like an idiot.

Alexander frowned and shook his head. Caty gave the camera a bitter smile. One tear went streaking down. Baby Dorian began to cry. "That's all I can say. Goodbye, Alex."

Alexander sat in utter shock, his heart aching, his mind spinning. He shook his head and stood up from his bed. Anger, loss, betrayal, and confusion waged a bloody war in his brain. He got dressed in his uniform and stormed out of his quarters, his heart pounding an angry rhythm in his chest. He was in a big hurry with nowhere to go. He couldn't run from what he'd just seen and heard. The echoes of Caty's words haunted his every step.

His stride faltered as he passed the other officers' quarters. He almost stopped to knock on Korbin's door, but then he remembered she was gone—a traitor—and now there was a supercilious impostor sleeping in her bed. After Admiral Wilson's *recommendation* to make Max the *Lincoln's* new XO as a favor to the president, Alexander had done exactly that—not that he'd had a choice in the matter.

Alexander scowled and kept going. As he reached McAdams' room, he stopped and turned. He rapped his knuckles on the door rather than using the intercom to announce himself. His brain was so thick and fuzzy with grief that he couldn't think straight. What was he doing going to McAdams? She wasn't Korbin's replacement as the ship's counselor.

The door *swished* open and there she stood, dressed in a flowing black night gown, her blue eyes red and puffy from crying, her blond hair loose and flowing over her shoulders. In that moment she looked a whole lot like Caty. He'd been a fool to wait for his wife.

"Captain?" McAdams asked, sounding nasal, her voice weak.

He took a quick step forward, grabbed her face in his hands and kissed her. She stumbled back a step and then returned the kiss, biting his lip and running her hands greedily over his shaven head. The door swished shut behind them, and he pulled the drawstring of her gown, dropping it around her ankles. She was naked underneath, her perfect body curving against his, nipples firmly aroused.

He pressed himself against her, and she began undressing him, fumbling with the buttons of his uniform, then his belt. In no time at all, she had him naked, too.

She grabbed him below his waist, her hands shaking, and he

ran a hand between her legs, slipping his fingers into her. Their bodies shivered, but from heat not the cold. They ran into the bottom of her bed and collapsed into it. She slid down to him and he slipped into her. She gasped and wrapped her legs tight around his waist, trapping him there. Their tongues danced inside each other's mouths as their hearts beat against one another's like drums. Their bodies rocked to the beat, and for a few short minutes, ecstasy wiped away the pain.

CHAPTER 38

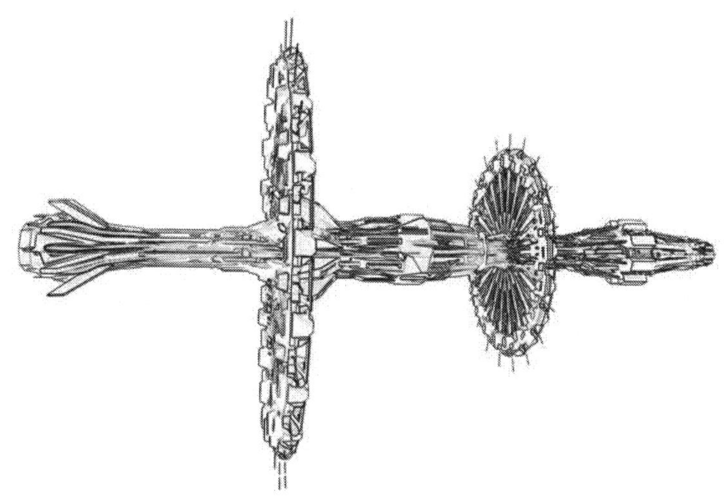

Six Months Later - February 18, 2793

Alexander sat on the bridge, his gaze tracking the approach of the Confederacy's colony fleet. The Alliance's colony fleet was still stuck back on Earth, only now getting ready to launch. They were running almost a week behind the Confederacy. That meant the Confederacy was poised to travel through the wormhole first, but in order to do so they had to get through the more than twenty Alliance warships blockading the entrance. Currently the relative strength of Alliance to Confederate forces was sitting at 1 to 1.1 in favor of the Confederacy, and that ratio was expected to tip even further in their favor once their colony fleet arrived with its bevy of escorting destroyers and carriers. Negotiations and posturing were ongoing between both sides, but it wasn't looking good. Last Alexander had heard, the Confederacy had issued an ultimatum: let them through the wormhole, or else.

The Confederacy seemed determined to press their advantage in order to be the first ones through the wormhole, no doubt so that they could be the ones to blockade it from the other side.

"Davorian, what's the ETA until the Confederate colony fleet arrives?"

"Two hours, sir."

"Vasquez—any changes in the Confederate formation?"

"Not yet, sir," she replied from sensors.

Alexander nodded. "Keep me posted."

Beside him, Commander Max *"plenty-potent"* Carter sat up straighter in his couch. "We need to make contact with the enemy fleet. It's time to negotiate."

Alexander gave his XO a frown. "That's not our job, Commander."

Max met that frown with a grim smile, his blue eyes dancing behind his helmet visor. "Actually, it is. I'm still plenipotentiary to the Alliance, Captain."

Alexander felt his frown deepening. He switched to a private channel with his XO. "You and I both know the president is with the fleet. He can negotiate directly. He doesn't need you as a middle man."

"If he negotiates directly, he'll be changing the stakes by admitting that he's with the fleet. The Confederacy may wish to open fire just for the chance to kill Baker, and even if they don't place that much value on him per se, the very fact that he's standing by, ready to travel to Wonderland is a problem. The Confederacy might deduce that we're abandoning Earth."

"You're telling me the president has authorized you to speak on his behalf in these negotiations. Why am I only hearing about this now?"

"Go ahead and ask Admiral Wilson. He'll confirm my orders."

Alexander held Carter's gaze for a few seconds longer before turning away and mentally switching from private comms back to his helmet's external speakers. "Hayes!"

"Sir?"

"Get me Admiral Wilson on the comms."

"Yes, sir."

The admiral's face appeared, dead ahead on the main holo display. He was strapped into an acceleration couch, a glowing blue tactical map projected in front of him. Wilson's hands flew over holographic controls, making gestures to manipulate the map. He didn't even appear to notice that Alexander was watching him.

"Admiral Wilson," Alexander prompted.

The admiral looked up with a scowl. "Captain, what are you doing contacting me? We have literally hours left on the clock to Armageddon. You should be in the middle of negotiations with the enemy."

Alexander blinked. "Just confirming that Commander Carter has been authorized to conduct those negotiations, sir."

"He's authorized. Now let him do his job! We'll be watching how things play out. Make sure your weapons are all hot and ready. Things could go bad in a matter of seconds, and we need to be able to react."

"Yes, sir." The visual vanished and back was a glittering field of stars.

Alexander sighed and shook his head. "Hayes—"

"Already on it, sir... contact established with the enemy flagship. Transmitting..."

A visual of the Confederate admiral appeared, transmitted directly from the bridge of their flagship, the *Liaoning—whatever that means,* Alexander thought. The admiral wore a white pressure suit and matching helmet. Hayes zoomed in on the man's face to help them get a read on his body language. His name and rank appeared above the display: *Admiral Zhang.*

"Admiral Zhang," Carter began.

"Ambassador," Zhang replied, nodding. "I did not realize you were with the fleet."

"I have been appointed to handle negotiations from here on out."

"Of course, but what is there to negotiate? You already have our terms. Allow us through the wormhole and we will not open fire."

"Yes… there is a problem with that."

"Admiral Wilson was kind enough to explain his concerns to me already. I will tell you the same thing I told him. If you are afraid we will try to stop you from traveling through the wormhole after us, then send your fleet with ours. We will arrive at the same time, with roughly the same firepower. If either side chooses to betray the other, the consequences will be the same as they ever have been. I believe you call this *mutually assured destruction."*

Alexander found himself looking from Carter to Admiral Zhang and back again, as if his head was mounted on a swivel.

"The problem with that, Admiral, is that if we don't travel through in perfect tandem there will still be the question of whoever arrives first having the drop on late comers, and how do we know you won't simply push your ships harder to get through first? We'll all be asleep."

Alexander nodded as he listened to that. All signs pointed to a drop down fight before anyone even entered the Looking Glass, but if a fight broke out now with the strength ratios being what they were, the Confederacy would win.

"I have already discussed all of this with Admiral Wilson. I could ask you the same question. What guarantee do we have that you won't try to beat *us* to Wonderland? The answer is there are no guarantees, so we must either settle this now, or agree to trust one another. I'm sure we can all agree that no one wants another nuclear war on Earth."

"Yes, we can agree on that, and in the spirit of continuing peaceful relations, I've been authorized to agree to your demands."

Admiral Zhang appeared taken aback by that. Alexander watched his eyes widen fractionally, and then narrow to oriental slits once more. "That is very wise of the Alliance," he said, each word slow and deliberate, spoken with a wary precision.

"There is a catch."

"Ah, yes." Zhang nodded. "I am listening."

"We will follow you in, just outside of effective laser range."

"Without your colony fleet?"

"Yes."

"We will all be asleep. How can we be sure you won't try to sneak attack us?"

"With what? Autopilot and pre-programmed firing solutions?"

"Yes."

"That goes both ways, Admiral. As you said, we will have to trust one another."

"I suppose we will. Why don't you go through the wormhole first?"

Alexander had been wondering the same thing. If the tactical advantage went to the first one through the wormhole thanks to the radiation belts on the other side, then why wasn't the Alliance taking that advantage for themselves?

"We have to wait for our colony fleet in order to escort them. President Baker is allowing you to go first as a token of our good will. And as for the situation on the other side of the wormhole, there are ways to manage that risk. Our terms are that we will allow you to go through first if you agree to go straight to Wonderland. If our probes detect you are waiting for us on the other side of the radiation belts, we will turn around and head straight back to Earth with our fleet. You will be able to keep Wonderland for yourselves, but we will have Earth."

"We will follow you back."

"I'm sure you would, and there would be open war again. Since none of us want that, I think we can all agree to these terms. As for Wonderland itself, my government is insisting that we divide the planet's primary landmass straight down the middle. Since none of us know which part of the continent is more valuable, we'll agree to roll the dice and let you pick which side of the continent to settle."

Admiral Zhang nodded. "These seem to be fair terms. I will relay them to my government. Please wait while I confer with the Chancellor."

"Of course."

The display faded from Admiral Zhang's face to show the Confederate flag—golden stars in a hammer and sickle pattern on a red background.

Alexander turned to Carter. "We fought a nuclear war to defend our sole rights to the Looking Glass, and now we're just going to give it up?"

Carter gave him a grim look. "What choice do we have? Their fleet is stronger than ours, and thanks to Korbin's treachery, the Confederacy knows exactly what's at stake. They don't even need to wait to send their own probes. It's her fault that the war we fought was meaningless. Fighting another meaningless war now won't change that."

Alexander looked away. Carter was right, but he still

couldn't believe or accept that Korbin was at fault. The Confederacy had gotten to her somehow and brainwashed her. That was the only explanation.

He had to admit he was relieved by the turn that negotiations were taking. It didn't look like either side was eager to start another nuclear war, so Caty would have a chance at happiness with her baby and David. Alexander's lips curved into a shadow of a smile. The dull ache in his chest told him he still hadn't moved on, but given enough time he would.

Alexander's thoughts trailed off as he noticed the Confederate flag fade away and Admiral Zhang's face reappear on-screen.

"We have decided to accept your terms, Ambassador Carter. We request that you withdraw your fleet from the entrance of the wormhole to a distance of one light second and maintain that distance between our two fleets for the duration of the trip through the wormhole."

"Agreed. We will begin withdrawing immediately," Carter replied.

"I shall await confirmation of that. Good day, Ambassador."

The holo display faded back to the starry blackness of space, and Alexander breathed a deep sigh. So that was it. Disaster averted. The Looking Glass was functioning like a valve to let off steam and take some of the pressure off Earth. There was a new frontier and a new frontline, with plenty of new territory and resources to fight over. Alexander wondered if colonists had realized what they were signing up for when they decided to go to Wonderland. Did they know that they were trading one war zone for another?

"Lieutenant Hayes, please contact Admiral Wilson," Carter said.

"Yes, sir."

The admiral's face appeared on the main holo display and

Alexander listened while Carter relayed the terms of their treaty with the Confederacy.

"Good work, Ambassador," Admiral Wilson said once Carter had finished speaking. "It's time to see if the Confederacy lives up to their end of the bargain. Captain, stand by to receive your new flight plan."

"Yes, sir." The holo display faded back to stars and space as the connection ended. "Davorian, prepare to set new course and heading."

"Flight plan received. Heading set. Accelerating to one *G*."

Alexander felt himself growing gradually heavier until his body resumed its normal weight. He hoped they weren't playing into the Confederacy's hands by letting them through the wormhole first.

"What's wrong, Captain?" Carter asked.

Alexander shook his head. "Nothing."

I hope.

CHAPTER 39

One Week Earlier - February 11, 2793

"Why not?" Caty demanded. "It's a chance for a new life away from all of this!" she gestured helplessly to their surroundings.

"You think things will be better there?" David demanded. "You're wrong."

"There will be plenty of jobs. The Alliance promised free land, free housing, everything we need to start a new life on Wonderland. And at least there we'll be away from the constant fear of war."

David sneered. "That's what they want you to believe. The Confederacy is going, too. New planet, same problems."

"But more space, so less pressure and competition. It will take a long time for those problems to catch up. Look at the colonies—when war broke out on Earth, they didn't automatically start fighting each other, and for the most part they remained unscathed. Think about it, David!"

He looked away, out the living room window at the dusty patch of dirt they called a yard.

Sensing his indecision, she went on, "And think about Dorian. What kind of future does he have to look forward to here? Even if there isn't another war, there aren't enough resources to go around, and competition's too fierce. Either you're rich or you're poor. There's nothing left in between."

David shook his head. "I can't," he said quietly.

Caty's eyebrows shot up. "Why not?"

"Soy ilegal."

She blinked, convinced she hadn't heard him correctly. "What?"

"I'm illegal, Caty. I can't go anywhere."

She shook her head. "You're *illegal?"* She gaped at him, still refusing to believe it. "What about your wife? She joined the Navy to buy your citizenship."

"I was never married."

Caty felt her blood run cold. "You lied to me."

He turned to her with a miserable expression. "I didn't know you back then. I was afraid you would tell someone and get me deported."

"What about later on? We've been together for *years.* We have a son together. How did you even get your name on the birth certificate? How have you done anything at all? Do you even have a job? All those adjustment reports… no wonder you never got any better! They were all fake! Is your name even David?"

"It's Angel."

Caty gaped at him, speechless.

David held up his hands to placate her. "Let me explain."

"Explain what? Everything you've ever told me is a lie!"

He shook his head. *"Mi amor, por favor dejame explicar."*

"I'm not *your love.* Not anymore. And there's nothing left to explain. You've finally gone too far." Caty smirked at him, suddenly seeing David for the pathetic excuse of a man that he was. She didn't need him anymore. For what? To beat her and abuse her? The Alliance had offered her a way out and she was going to take it. "I'm leaving, and I'm taking Dorian with me."

David's eyes flashed. "You can't do that. Dorian is my son just as much as he is yours."

"Actually, Dorian's father is registered as David Porras, but since you're not David, good luck trying to claim your rights. You don't have any."

David gritted his teeth, but said nothing. She started toward the bedroom to go pack her bags.

By now she should have known better to turn her back on him. One minute she was walking, her steps buoyed with adrenaline and righteous anger, and the next she was crashing to the ground with strong hands wrapped tight around her throat.

They landed on the carpeted floor and she struggled, punching and kicking him, trying to throw him off, but her blows didn't even faze him. His eyes were wild; his lips parted in an ugly grimace; a gob of spittle glistened in the corner of his mouth.

She gasped, trying desperately to suck in a breath, but his grip was too tight, his hands too strong. Her lungs began to burn, and her blows became weaker and more frenzied.

Her vision narrowed to a dark tunnel and she knew she was close to blacking out. She also knew that she couldn't afford to black out. David might kill her if she did, but even if he didn't, he would take Dorian and she would never see him again.

Imagining her son alone with that monster gave her new strength. She tried to knee him in the groin, but he had her legs pinned to either side of his and she couldn't reach.

She shook her head from side to side and bit her tongue until she tasted blood, forcing her mind to stay alert. That was when she saw it. They'd landed beside one of the end tables in the living room. Sitting on top of that table was a dirty plate with knife and fork. She made a desperate grab for the knife, but her hand found the fork instead.

Good enough.

She lashed out with all of her remaining strength, hoping her aim would be good enough. The fork sank deep into David's neck. Blood spurted and he screamed.

He rolled off her, and she gasped, sucking in a deep breath. Spots danced before her eyes, and she shook her head, trying to clear it. She knew she didn't have much time. Hacking coughs racked her body, sapping her strength. David screamed curses at her in Spanish.

She leapt up and grabbed the very next thing she could find, a heavy potted plant sitting on the end table. She whirled around to find David on his knees, struggling to pull the fork from his neck. He saw her a split second before she reached him.

Too late.

She smashed it over his head. His eyes rolled up and he collapsed, the fork still protruding from his neck and blood bubbling out onto the carpet.

Worried he'd be up again soon, Caty ran to the bedroom. Dorian was awake and crying. She skidded to a stop in front of his crib and leaned down to pick him up. He dropped his stuffed animal, and screamed even louder, but there was no time to worry about that. Caty ran back through the house, leaping over David's unconscious body, not even stopping for her shoes.

She ran out the front door and into the street. The gravel road bit through her socks, and the wintry air sliced through her thin blouse, making her shiver. Dorian cried even louder.

She turned to look over her shoulder and make sure that David wasn't chasing her. No sign of him yet. *Good—*

Smack! Caty bounced off something solid. Dorian cried out with the impact, and Caty blinked, stunned. She found herself face to face with a vaguely familiar married couple. They were walking back from the bus stop outside the neighborhood.

"Are you okay?" the woman asked, her brow pinched with concern. Her husband winced and rubbed his belly—the *something solid* Caty had run into.

"I..." Caty looked from one to the other, not sure what to say, where to start... Just thinking about it was overwhelming. She burst into tears.

"Oh no, don't cry—Eduardo, *debemos llevarla a la casa.*"

Eduardo nodded.

They took her back to their house, gave her a warm cup of tea, and coaxed her story out of her. Soon after that they called the police. Half an hour later they arrived at Caty's house, but David was already gone. The bloodstains and the fork he left behind confirmed her story.

The police took her to the station to get her statement. As soon as she was done, she told them that she wanted to join the fleet headed for Wonderland, and they called *NAS Lemcroft* to relay her request. They assured her that she and Dorian would be welcome to join the last group of colonists, but they would have to hurry.

Hours later, Caty sat on a couch in the police captain's office, waiting for him to take her home so she could go pack her things. Dorian was exhausted from crying and had settled for chewing on a soother the police captain had found for him. His bright baby eyes were wide and staring.

Caty bounced him on her knee and rubbed his back. "We're going to be okay, Dorian."

He made a babbling sound that sounded agreeable to her. She smiled and pulled him close for a hug. "Yes, there's nothing to worry about anymore. We're going far away."

Dorian sounded like he wanted to cry again, but she shushed him and patted his back. "There's nothing to be afraid of."

She really believed that. She'd read the brochures. Warm, tropical jungles. Sparkling blue oceans, empty, unsettled land as far as the horizon... nothing dangerous and nothing harmful, just one big, natural paradise. Best of all, they'd be leaving Earth and all of its problems far behind, including and especially David.

He'd eluded police custody so far, but it didn't matter. Even if they didn't catch him for years, he would never be able to follow her and Dorian to Wonderland. They would be safe. Making it on her own still scared her, but Dorian was older now, and the Alliance had promised ample benefits for colonists on Wonderland.

Dorian started fussing again, and she began bouncing him on her knee once more.

"Shhh. It's okay. We're okay. We're going to be okay," she amended, this time more to reassure herself than Dorian.

* * *

"Davorian, set course and cruising speed. Forward thrust three *Gs*," Alexander ordered.

"Aye-aye, setting course."

Alexander felt himself growing progressively heavier. It became hard to speak, hard to breathe, hard to move, but his mind remained free to interact with his control console and to think about recent developments.

The Confederate fleet had preceded them into the wormhole, and they were now more than a light second away. The

Alliance was determined to catch up and hold to that distance rather than let them get any further ahead. Alliance colonists would end up trailing behind them by nearly a week, but that was better for their safety.

Alexander wondered why the Alliance fleet wasn't hanging back, too. The fact that they insisted on keeping no more than 300,000 klicks between them and the enemy told him that there was still a chance the two fleets might clash. One light second was well out of effective laser range, but it was still well within missile range, and it wouldn't take much time for Alliance missiles to catch up with the Confederate fleet.

Alexander gritted his teeth through what seemed like hours of high-*G* exposure. His lungs and muscles began to ache, and his heart labored with the strain. It felt like he had an elephant sitting on his chest.

Soon they passed through the mouth of the Looking Glass and Alexander watched the starfield curve up and warp around them like the inside of a fish bowl. Suddenly the elephant got up, and Alexander could breathe again.

"Range and cruising speed attained," Davorian announced.

"Finally…" Carter muttered.

Alexander rolled his shoulders, feeling suddenly light as a feather. "Stay sharp everyone." He turned his attention from the main holo display to the tactical map hovering between his and Carter's control stations. The map showed a wireframe model of the wormhole curving around them in a funnel shape. Racing down the center of that funnel was a cluster of red dots—almost thirty Confederate warships, and easily twice as many colony ships—followed by a smaller cluster of friendly green dots. Being a destroyer-class, the *Lincoln* was best suited to intercepting enemy missiles and drones, so it was leading the charge down the gullet of the wormhole with a group of six other destroyers.

This time literally hours did pass with no detectable change between the two fleets. Both sides seemed content with the standoff. Alexander tried to cover a yawn, but his hand hit glass, and he remembered he was wearing a helmet. He shook his head and blinked the glaze from his eyes. He needed to keep his head in the game.

"Captain, I'm detecting a change in the enemy fleet. They're accelerating, sir. Five *G*s. Wait… ten, no twelve."

"Confirm that, Vasquez. Take your time."

"Confirmed," she said a moment later. "They're holding steady at twelve *G*s."

"They must've hit the *G*-tanks already. Someone's in a hurry."

"Captain, I have orders coming in from Admiral Wilson," Hayes reported from the comms. "We're to set the autopilot to match speed and heading with the Confederate fleet and configure the auto-fire controls to launch our missiles in the event that sensors detect incoming weapons fire from the enemy fleet."

"Acknowledged—Cardinal, Davorian, set the autos. Everyone else lock your stations and stand by. Hayes, alert the rest of the crew. Wonderland, here we come. *Again.*"

Silence answered that quip. A few crew members groaned, others grumbled. Alexander knew just how they felt. This wasn't exactly the homecoming they'd expected.

Over the next few minutes all stations reported ready and Alexander gave the order for them to leave the bridge and head down to the *G*-tanks.

This time as Alexander stripped and placed his pressure suit and clothes in the locker beside his *G*-tank, he didn't take pains to avoid looking at McAdams, he admired her openly, and she regarded him back with a sly smile. Doctor Crespin came and configured McAdams' tank. It swished open, and Alexander watched her turn and give him a parting salute before crossing the threshold.

On the other side of him, Alexander heard Seth Ryder make a lewd comment about the look McAdams had given him. He ignored it. Crespin came by to configure his tank. A few seconds later, it swished open, too, and in he went.

Alexander hooked himself up to life support in a fraction of the time it usually took. As the water rose past his lips and his liquid ventilator whirred to life, his mind drifted away on a lullaby of drugs into the random nonsense of dreams.

He dreamed about him and McAdams back on Wonderland, but this time as colonists of the new world. Somehow, they already had a baby together, a girl. In his dream she was already walking and talking, playing outside in a fenced garden, teasing the plants to life. Next door Alexander saw a familiar face peering over the fence.

It was Caty.

"You left me," she said, her blue eyes sad and accusing.

He shook his head, his mouth agape. What was she doing there? "You moved on," he explained.

"You *told* me to move on." Caty's gaze slid away, and Alexander followed it to where McAdams was busy trying to make peace between their daughter and an angry red-leafed sapling. "You told me to move on so you could be with *her*," Caty said.

Alexander shook his head, feeling sick to his stomach. "No, that's not true."

"Yes, it is." Caty turned away, disappearing from sight.

An angry klaxon burst through the air and the sky flashed with a strange crimson light. Alexander's head snapped up, and he saw missiles streaking through the sky, thousands of fighters buzzing and roaring, trying to intercept. The war had followed them to Wonderland.

"No!" he screamed, his gaze darting to McAdams and their baby girl once more. They were still playing with the plants, oblivious to the danger all around them. A flaming piece of debris fell screaming from the sky and engulfed them both in an angry flare of light.

Alexander's eyes snapped open and the klaxons sounded suddenly louder and clearer than they had in his dream. Red lights flashed, shimmering off the wet, glistening sides of his G-tank. He felt his throat burning with the invading pressure of the tracheal tube. Doctor Crespin had checked him out after the last time and said it was a mild irritation—nothing to worry about.

Alexander fought through mental sludge to understand what was happening. The color-coded lights made a faster connection in his brain than the more ambiguous klaxons—*someone sounded general quarters.*

An electric jolt of adrenaline spurred him to action and he hurried to disconnect himself from life support.

Something had gone badly wrong.

CHAPTER 40

Catalina sat strapped into an acceleration couch on the floor of a large passenger cabin with row upon row of seats, though she wasn't sure they could be called *seats* when everyone was lying down on the deck.

She lifted her head and studied the orderly row of shiny white helmets at her feet. It was unnerving to see so many people in the cabin with her, yet hear none of the noise. Their helmets were near-perfect insulators, making the cabin so quiet that Caty could actually hear her heart beating.

Looking left, she saw baby Dorian, wearing a miniature version of the colonists' standard-issue white pressure suits. He was strapped into a baby seat that looked a lot like a front-facing car seat to her. Caty studied his face through the glass visor of his helmet. He was blowing spit bubbles as he stared up at the live holo recording from the ship's bow cameras projected on the ceiling above them.

Looking away, she joined her son in admiring the view. She couldn't blame him for drooling.

Earth appeared directly above them, curving away with vast, sparkling blue oceans and thick blankets of cloud. She couldn't see even a single dot of land, just endless reams of ocean. Caty imagined this was what Wonderland must look like—an earth-type planet with only one major landmass and one all-encompassing ocean.

It was exciting to finally be here. She'd spent the past week training at NAS Key West, where she'd learned how to negotiate a ship in zero-*G* using either handrails or micro maneuvering jets. They'd also taught her how to don a pressure suit and control the basic functions of both her suit and Dorian's by giving mental commands. Then she'd learned how to use an acceleration couch and a *G*-tank.

But after barely a cursory introduction to all of that, she'd been whisked away to the Alliance's new Anchor Station off the shore of Curaçao and filed into the next available climber car headed for orbit. Then she and Dorian had spent the next two days in that climber car, riding up to Freedom Station at the top end of the elevator, followed by a further six hours waiting aboard the station to board their colony ship.

Theirs was the last ship to join a fleet of more than fifty waiting in geosynchronous orbit over Earth. Now Caty could see at least a dozen matching colony ships in the distance, all of them gleaming specks of silver against the black of space. From this distance they seemed tiny, but she knew better. She'd seen hers up close from Freedom Station's viewports. The ships were massive, five hundred meter-long spears with detachable shuttles clinging to them like barnacles.

Caty was amazed by how much the Alliance had managed to do in such a short time. The first space elevator had taken over a decade to build, but this one had gone up in a year. Granted they'd fished the old elevator ribbon out of the ocean, and Freedom Station was actually a decommissioned Alliance battleship rather than a brand-new station, but one year was not a lot of time to do anything, let alone carry a 100,000 kilometer-long elevator ribbon back into space, section by section. Then there was the matter of mass-producing spaceship components and sending them up the elevator to assemble the colony fleet.

No wonder there hadn't been enough government aid for the war refugees.

Dorian began making noises like he was about to start crying. She had his comms set to the same channel as hers so she could use them like a baby monitor. "Num num!" he said, smacking his lips.

He was hungry. She didn't have to wonder why. They hadn't eaten or drunk real food for days. Instead, they were fed and hydrated with an intravenous nutrient solution, but that did nothing to stop their stomachs from feeling achingly empty. Mission trainers had warned them that first-time space travelers would go through some initial discomfort during the switch from solid to liquid food. Personally, Caty found the self-inserting relief tubes that snaked up from their seats to be much more uncomfortable than the IV, but Dorian was probably pleased with his perpetually dry diaper.

Caty counted the silvery specks of distant starships to pass the time while waiting for the captain of the ship to announce that they were leaving orbit. She found there were twenty specks, and her brow furrowed. She could have sworn there'd only been twelve a moment ago. Maybe the fleet was repositioning itself and more of it was coming into view. That had to be it, Caty thought.

Caty watched a pinprick of fire ignite and engulf one of those specks. She frowned, squinting at the sight. *The ship's thrusters,* she decided. Finally! They were moving out!

Then the fire faded, and gone was the silver speck.

Caty blinked. Was she seeing things? It had to be some mistake, a trick of the light. Suddenly another ship erupted in an orange ball of flame, and promptly winked out of existence. Caty's heart pounded.

She tried switching to the crew's comm channel so she could get some information, and her helmet was instantly flooded with a confusing babble of voices, dozens of passengers all asking the same questions at once.

The sound cut off abruptly, and a stern male voice interrupted, "Please remain calm and stay seated. Hostilities have erupted between Alliance and Confederate forces, but our point defenses should be more than sufficient to shoot down any missiles that come our way."

A flurry of questions, pleas, and demands erupted in the wake of that statement, but no further explanations followed. Caty had the feeling that the crew had more important things to do right now than mollify the colonists.

Another flare of light punctuated that thought and underlined the seriousness of the situation. They were in a *colony* ship in the middle of a war zone, and they weren't equipped for war. Caty looked at Dorian; he was still smacking his lips, chewing on air, blissfully oblivious.

Turning back to the view, Caty's eyes drifted out of focus. Blood roared in her veins, adrenaline sparking through her body, urging her to do *something,* but there was literally nothing she could do. It wasn't as though she could pilot the ship to safety or bail out with a parachute. The passenger cabins were all aboard the ship's detachable shuttles, so technically they could abandon ship if their shuttle pilot deemed it necessary.

Caty saw a glittering cloud of debris emerge from the starfield, heading straight for them. One by one, each twinkling speck erupted in brief burst of flame and then vanished. A shadow fell over them, and their view of Earth was blotted out by a dark, bristling gray beast—an Alliance battleship. Caty watched, wide-eyed as it flew by, missiles streaking from its bow in a steady stream.

That glittering cloud of debris grew nearer and nearer until it came into sharper focus, and she saw it for what it really was—a wave of enemy missiles. Missiles went on exploding, intercepted by unseen means. She remembered reading somewhere that lasers were invisible in space, and she decided that the battleship must be shooting the missiles down.

Caty stared at the underside of that giant ship, trying to identify individual gun emplacements. Then the surviving missiles streaked in. A dazzling burst of light blinded her, and she winced away from the sudden glare. The deck lurched and the ship shuddered under them. Next came a deafening *roar*. Suddenly zero-G was gone and they were being pressed *hard* against the backs of their couches. Dorian screamed, and Caty gritted her teeth, fighting the urge to do the same. Worried for her son, she managed to turn her head despite the impossible weight of it. She saw Dorian's face scrunched up in terror, his eyes streaming with tears, and she struggled to speak over their shared comms channel, telling him that everything was going to be all right.

Turning back to the view, she saw that they were headed straight for Earth. Lights flickered inside the passenger cabin, dimming to a soothing blue glow, and then the speakers inside Caty's helmet crackled with a new voice.

"This is your shuttle captain speaking. We lost the colony ship and four shuttles. Ours is damaged, but not too badly. I'm taking us down for an emergency landing. Please familiarize yourselves with the nearest exits and the life vests under your seats, and remain seated and strapped in at all times. Thank you."

Caty's eyes widened. Her heart pounded erratically in her chest. *We lost the colony ship. We're in a damaged shuttle, heading back to Earth for an emergency landing.*

Earth grew larger and closer with every second. The view she'd thought to be so breathtaking before was now terrifying. She imagined the gleaming ocean swallowing her and Dorian whole, dragging them down into its black and briny depths. Caty shook her head to clear the image away, reminding herself that the shuttles came equipped for water landings.

The heavy hand of acceleration didn't let up, nor did Dorian's cries. He was terrified. She couldn't blame him. She was terrified, too. Caty tried to reach under her seat for her life vest, but her arms were pinned to her couch and too heavy to move. Biting back tears, she cursed her stupidity. What had she been thinking? They never should have left Earth. Wonderland had seemed like an easy out from all of their problems, but she should have known better.

Humanity couldn't run from itself.

CHAPTER 41

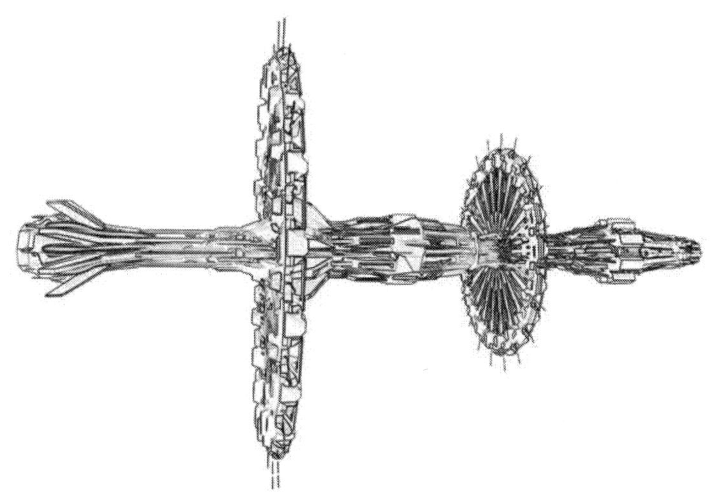

Alexander dropped into his acceleration couch and strapped in. Relief tubes snaked out, but he didn't even blink at the intrusion.

"Hayes, Vasquez, report! What's going on out there?" Alexander demanded, even as he summoned a tactical map from his control station.

Vasquez was first to reach her control station. "Our fleet is on its way out of the wormhole, headed back to Earth. The Confederates appear to be following us out, but they're a lot further in than we are."

Alexander's brow furrowed. He already knew from the date and time on his comm band that they'd been awakened from the *G*-tanks early.

"What about the enemy fleet? Did they open fire? Did we?"

"Our missiles are still locked and loaded in the launch tubes," Cardinal reported.

"I've got nothing on our scopes," Vasquez added. "The Confederacy is still holding fire."

"Then what's the general quarters alarm about?"

"Looks like it was sounded automatically by the ship's threat detection system," Hayes said from the comms.

"So where's the threat?" Alexander asked, feeling exasperated.

"What the... Captain, more than half of the Confederate fleet is missing!" Vasquez reported.

"What? Check the sensor logs. I want to know what took them out."

"Yes, sir."

"Incoming message from Admiral Wilson," Hayes announced.

"On screen," Alexander replied.

Wilson didn't look well. His cheeks were pale and gaunt, his eyes wide and feverish. "Admiral, I was just about to contact you," Alexander said. "It looks like the fleet encountered some type of emergency and the autopilots turned us around."

"Don't repeat to me what I already know. Listen up, Captain. I'm dealing with the Confederate Admiral right now. He's beyond reason, and accusing us of tricking his fleet into a suicide mission."

Alexander shook his head. "A suicide mission?"

"Confederate ships were ripped apart by tidal forces inside the wormhole. They were lucky to escape with the few ships that they did. The only reason *we* escaped unscathed is because we were trailing far behind them. They think we knew that the wormhole was no longer traversable and we tricked them into going through first."

"That doesn't make any sense. We just returned from a successful trip through the wormhole. If something's changed since then, we were equally unaware of it."

"Tell that to Admiral Zhang."

"What do you need us to do?"

"I'm handing the negotiations to Carter. Maybe he can talk some sense into those ant-brained communists. Failing that, we're going to press the advantage that nature's just given us, and blow them all straight to hell."

Alexander nodded. "Yes, sir."

"I'm transferring you now, keep me posted."

"I'll do my best to avoid another war, Admiral," Carter replied.

Admiral Wilson disappeared, and Admiral Zhang took his place. Alexander was taken aback at the enemy admiral's appearance. His nose streamed with blood behind his helmet, and his face was blistered and red with a profusion of broken blood vessels.

"Admiral Zhang," Carter began. "It's a pleasure to—"

"Do not speak," Zhang rasped. "You will listen. I am told I do not have long to live, so I do not have time for lies. My fleet was all but destroyed by the wormhole. We were not even a third of the way to the center when this happened."

Carter shook his head. "The wormhole must have collapsed since we last traveled through it, but I can assure you we had no knowledge of the danger."

"Lies!" Zhang coughed up a bit of bloody spittle that stuck to the inside of his helmet and blurred their view of his face. "You knew. That is why you allowed us to go first. That is also why you stopped accelerating long before you reached cruising speed. Otherwise, why not remain at your negotiated range of one light second? When our fleet began to be ripped apart, yours was more than five *million* kilometers away. That is over *fifteen* light seconds. We are only now beginning to catch up with you."

Alexander blinked, confused by what he was hearing. He

switched to a private comms channel with Lieutenant Davorian and ordered him to double check those facts. If true, it would go a long way toward proving what Admiral Zhang was saying.

Beside him, Carter shook his head and sighed. "Admiral, we negotiated one light second as a minimum range, not a maximum. We needed to wait for our colony fleet to catch up to us."

"You think we are fools."

"I didn't say that."

"You did not have to, but perhaps you were equally unaware of your government's treachery. I encourage you to contact Earth. When you do, you will learn that your colony fleet is *armed,* and firing on what few ships we have left in orbit. Perhaps you will not believe me, but *we* did not fire the first shots. We were ambushed. There is a reason your colony fleet did not launch with ours. They were just another part of the ruse. Congratulations. I believe the writing is on the wall, but you will not kill this old fox without a fight."

The connection ended abruptly, and Zhang's face disappeared. It took Alexander several seconds to recover, but Carter was much faster on the uptake.

"Contact Admiral Wilson! We're about to come under fire."

Alexander worked some moisture into his mouth so he could speak. "Hold on. They're still a long way off," Alexander replied, studying the tactical map and the range between the two fleets. "Let's not be in a rush to start another war.

Carter glared at him.

"Who's the Captain of this ship?" Alexander made a show of glancing down at the rank insignia on his pressure suit. "Oh, I guess that's me."

"Admiral Wilson was very clear that I should inform him as soon as I concluded my negotiations."

"And you will, but not yet." Turning away from his XO, Alexander said, "Davorian, what do our logs show?"

"It's true, Captain. We were holding back the whole time at zero thrust. They put us in the *G*-tanks for the hell of it. Admiral Wilson must have known that the wormhole had collapsed."

"So how did the Confederacy miss seeing that?"

"It's not immediately obvious from sensors, sir," Vasquez said.

"Hayes, what about Earth? Can you confirm that the fighting has already started there?"

"We're ten light minutes away, sir."

"I can wait."

"Well, I can't," Carter said.

Alexander shot him a look of strained patience.

"I'm going to save you some trouble, Captain. Admiral Zhang is a hundred percent correct. The fighting *has* already started; our colony ships *are* armed—heavily armed, in fact—and we *did* fire the first shots."

"You want to explain to me how you know all of that?"

"That's need to know, Captain. Ask Admiral Wilson, and he'll confirm everything. Right now, we have a war to fight. You heard Admiral Zhang. He's determined to get his pound of flesh. It's our job to make sure that for every pound he gets, we extract two."

"I thought you were supposed to be a diplomat. You're talking like a blood-thirsty warrior."

"We have the enemy badly outnumbered on all fronts, and we have a chance to defeat them once and for all. If we win now, this will be the last war humanity ever has to fight. That's the kind of peace I'm brokering, Captain—the kind that puts you out of a job."

Alexander considered that. He might have to change his opinion of Carter now. "Hayes, get the admiral on the comms.

We have a war to end."

CHAPTER 42

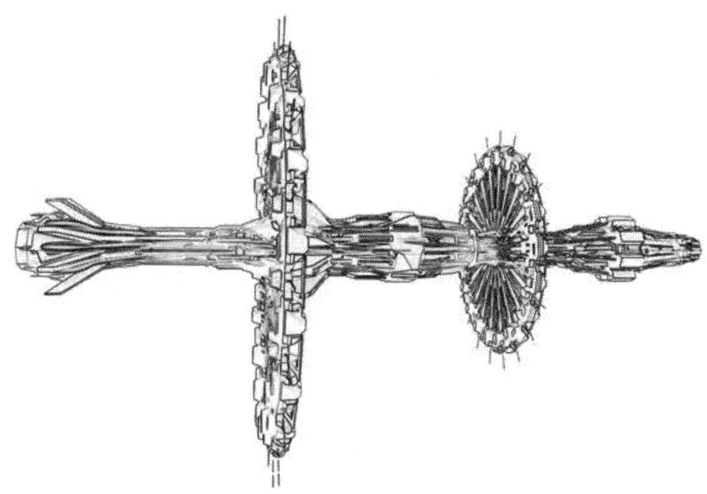

"Target data coming in from the *Liberty*," Hayes announced from the comms.

"Received, setting targets," Cardinal replied from gunnery.

Alexander watched the tactical map hovering between his and Carter's couches. The enemy was getting closer by the second, racing out of the wormhole at more than 1,000 kilometers per second, meanwhile the Alliance fleet was holding steady, blocking the mouth of the wormhole. Range between the two fleets was just under a million kilometers. That meant roughly fifteen minutes until they physically reached one another, but just five minutes before they reached optimum torpedo range.

Alexander looked up and watched as two red boxes appeared on the main holo display, each one drawn around a specific gray speck. Those were the *Lincoln's* targets.

"What are we looking at?" Alexander asked, already checking his tactical map for an answer. Ice formed in his gut as he read the ship classes. They were both Warsaw-class transports.

"They're colony ships, sir."

Alexander shook his head. "Why aren't we focusing on their warships?"

"I don't know. We could ask for clarification."

"You don't need clarification, Captain," Carter said. "Look at their formation. Their warships are flying in the transports' wake. They're using their own colonists as a shield."

Alexander pressed his lips into a firm line. "They're hoping we won't have the guts to kill innocent people."

"Exactly."

Alexander ground his teeth, desperately trying to think of a way around it. Those ships were loaded with innocent civilians whose only crime was to dream of a better life on a new world, somewhere far from all of Earth's problems. There would be nothing but families and happily married couples on board. Young children with their whole lives ahead of them…

"Captain?" Cardinal prompted. "Four minutes until we reach firing range."

"You have your orders," Carter intoned.

"Is there any way we can fire around them?" Alexander asked, ignoring his XO.

"We could launch missiles with very slight angles of deflection so they spread out in a cone around the targets. Once they pull alongside the colony ships, the laser-armed fragments will have line of sight on any warships hiding in their wake. But given the speed the enemy is traveling, and how close they are to those colony ships, we're looking at a very short window of attack.

"The good news is our missiles will be at point-blank range, well within ELR, and those colony ships don't just shield the enemy from us; they'll also shield our missiles from interception."

"You're assuming the Confederacy won't launch drones and

fighters to intercept," Carter said.

Alexander fixed him with a dark look. "Then our missiles will re-direct their fire until the fighter screen has been eliminated. We'll keep up our strategy until we punch a hole and hit our intended targets."

"It's inefficient. We'll be throwing away all of the missile fragments with live warheads. There's no way they'll be able to go around the colony ships, but if we shoot through them, there's even a chance that stray debris will damage whatever ships are traveling behind."

"You can't win a war if you become the evil that you're fighting against. The only way to win a war like that is to defeat yourself, so unless you are advocating that we surrender, I suggest we find a way to save as many innocent lives as we can—even if that way is *inefficient.*"

Carter held his gaze for a number of seconds, his gaze unblinking behind his helmet. "You better clear your strategy with the admiral first. There's fifteen colony ships left out there, and we're only targeting two, so I'm sure we're not the only ones with orders to fire on civilians."

"Hayes, get me the *Liberty* on the comms, and make it quick. Clock's ticking."

"Yes, sir."

A few seconds later, Admiral Wilson's face appeared. He didn't look happy to see them. "What is it, De Leon?"

Alexander explained his strategy to avoid hitting the colony ships, and the Admiral's expression darkened. "What do you think this is? The fifth annual war games? Do you think they cared about how many civilians they killed when they nuked LA, New York, or Chicago?"

"We nuked them, too."

"Exactly, so get your shit together. A few thousand colonists are *nothing* in the grand scheme of this war, and they're probably all already dead from radiation and high-G exposure anyway. You want to turn chicken shit on me, you better tell me now so I can put Carter in command.

"Remember, they chose to hide behind their colony ships. We didn't make them do that. They're forcing our hands, and on their heads be it. Make no mistake, if you pussyfoot around, you're going to put the lives of our people in jeopardy, and I *will* have your ass court-martialed and deported back to whatever shithole you crawled out of. Do we understand each other, Captain?"

"Yes, sir."

"Good." Wilson's expression softened somewhat and he sighed. "I can sympathize with what you are trying to do, and I know why, believe me, but there'll be time to fix our consciences later."

Alexander nodded, but said nothing.

"Keep your eyes on the clock. Not long now and it'll all be over. We're making history today."

Another nod. Alexander swallowed past the growing lump in his throat and forced a triumphant smile. The admiral signed off and the screen went back to displaying the blood-red squares of their targets. It was easy to desensitize himself at this point, even to separate himself from his actions and pretend like he didn't have a choice, but he *did* have a choice.

He could disobey a direct order, be court-martialed and deported, and lose every personal victory he'd ever made over the past ten years. It would all be for *nothing,* and he would be back where he'd started, but this time without Caty. Alexander swallowed painfully once more. At least he would know that he'd done the right thing.

Out of the corner of his eye Alexander saw Carter shaking

his head.

"I don't like to say I told you so, Captain, but... there you have it. The admiral is right."

Alexander resisted the urge to turn and punch Carter. He reminded himself that he'd never make it through Carter's faceplate anyway.

"One minute to firing, Captain," Cardinal said. "I assume we're going to follow orders?" There was a pitiable amount of hope in that question.

Alexander wanted nothing more than to give Cardinal an answer that they could all live with and to hell with the consequences, but the truth was war had been forcing good people to do unspeakable things since the dawn of time.

It was kill or be killed, and he had a greater responsibility to protect his crew and fellow officers of the fleet than he did to safeguard the lives of enemy civilians. If they allowed enemy warships to get into effective laser range, the Confederacy would get their pound of flesh and then some.

"Ten seconds, Captain... It's now or never."

Alexander shook his head. Maybe he would go get his memories wiped after this was all over.

"Five seconds..."

"We have our orders," Alexander croaked. "Open fire, Lieutenant."

CHAPTER 43

Catalina listened to the shuttle rattle and shake like it was about to fly apart at any second. The main holo display showed gauzy curtains of clouds sweeping by, parting to reveal a broad blue canvas of water below. The height was dizzying. The angle of descent terrifying. Air roared like a living thing against the shuttle's hull, so loud that Caty could hear it even through her helmet. Beside her, Dorian had cried himself into a snotty mess. His face was flushed and streaked with tears. Between his helmet and her safety harness she felt utterly cut off from her son. Desperate to comfort him, she grabbed one of his flailing hands and squeezed, hoping that touch would convey reassurance and not fear.

The speakers inside her helmet crackled and back was the captain's voice, sounding tense. "We lost our thrusters, so we're coasting in. Unfortunately that means we're going to end up landing in enemy waters, just a few kilometers off the coast of Indonesia. I've already alerted the Alliance with our projected landing coordinates, so we should be rescued promptly."

Caty tried to reach the life vest under her couch once more. This time she managed to get at it. She turned and placed it over

Dorian's head, pulling the drawstrings tight around his neck to make sure it wouldn't come off. He stopped crying and looked at her, his pudgy face slack and eyes wide with shock. She smiled reassuringly and then tried to grab the vest under his seat for herself. No such luck. She couldn't reach it, at least not while she was strapped in.

The ocean was getting bigger and bluer, ripples appearing in the canvas. She realized with a start that the water would be teeming with sharks. Even if they survived the landing, they might not survive what came next.

Caty forced herself not to think about it. She reached over and grabbed Dorian's tiny, black-gloved hand. He wrapped it around her thumb and held on tight.

The shuttle leveled out and ocean rushed by, too close, yet still dizzyingly far below. Flaps deployed, intensifying the roar of air against their hull. The murky white line of the horizon turned golden as the sun came sparkling in, kissing the waves with diamonds.

The sun was rising in the East.

Water blurred by, faster and faster, nearer and nearer until it was so close, Caty felt like she could reach out and touch it. As they came eye level with the horizon, Caty thought she saw a glimmer of green peeking through the white haze.

"Brace for landing!" the captain announced.

Suddenly the shuttle deployed air brakes and extended flaps to full. Air roared against those surfaces with renewed fury, shaking the shuttle like a leaf.

Caty gritted her teeth and squeezed her eyes shut.

The shuttle jerked suddenly, and then they were free, flying… she opened her eyes wide just in time to see them touch down again.

Slap! The shuttle hit the water and she slammed into her

safety harness. Water roared against the hull with deafening fury as the shuttle skipped along the waves like a giant speedboat. They slid onward for at least a hundred meters; then the braking forces eased and her harness stopped digging into her shoulders.

Caty blinked.

They were *alive.*

Her gaze fell on Dorian and her maternal instinct took over. She had to get him to safety. Nothing else mattered.

Someone came on the comms directing people to proceed to the nearest exits in an orderly fashion. She undid her harness in a rush. Her relief tubes withdrew and disconnected automatically. She disconnected the nutrient line herself and reached over to repeat the process for Dorian. Then she picked him up out of his couch and stood on shaking legs.

The cabin was already crowded with colonists pushing and shoving each other in their frenzy to escape. Someone stumbled into her from behind, and she whirled around with an angry look. The person who'd shoved her made no attempt to apologize. He could have made her drop Dorian! Scowling, she turned and started down the row of seats.

One of the officers who'd been with them in the cabin shouted over the comms for people to *please remain calm,* but no one listened. Caty's eyes darted around the cabin, searching for the nearest exit. She spied the strips of emergency lighting and followed them to an exit two rows behind her.

"All right, Dorian. Hang on," she said, steeling herself before plunging into a seething crowd of elbows and knees. She held Dorian close, shielding him with her arms. Exits sprang open, letting blinding streams of light in. Caty saw the deep blue sea come lapping up and foaming into the cabin. The exit she was aiming for lay directly over the wing, so there was no inflatable evacuation slide waiting to double as a life raft.

The colonists shuffled and shoved their way to the exit, pushing Caty along like flotsam in a river. A few people appeared to notice the baby in her arms and kept their elbows to themselves.

Then she reached the exit. Seeing water gushing over the wing in a slippery stream, she hesitated, but someone pushed her out. She tripped, screaming as she fell. She managed not to drop Dorian or land with her weight on top of him by landing on her elbows instead. A sharp spike of pain was her reward.

Someone helped her up and asked her over his external speakers if she and her baby were okay. She nodded mutely, having forgotten how to activate her own helmet speakers.

The wing was just as slippery as it looked. Caty took cautious steps, letting the stranger help her along to the tip of the wing, away from the press of the crowd. She watched people jumping into the water and sliding down the flaps with frantic splashes. The man holding her arm shook his head.

"Don't try it," he said. "You don't have a vest." Caty blinked. She'd forgotten to get the vest under Dorian's couch! Turning to the man in horror, she watched him take the vest off his own shoulders and place it over hers. Then he pulled the tabs and it inflated with a sudden puff of air. He reached over and did the same for Dorian.

She'd even forgotten to inflate Dorian's vest. How could she be so careless?

The stranger flashed her a sympathetic smile from behind his helmet. That was when she noticed the rank insignia on his pressure suit—a silver eagle. He was a captain, just like Alexander. This had to be the shuttle captain.

"Now we can go. You ready for a swim? I can take your baby if you need help."

She shook her head and clutched Dorian tighter.

"All right, but you better swim fast. If we don't hurry, I'm afraid there won't be any room left for us on board that raft," he said, jerking a thumb over his shoulder.

Caty followed his gesture to a bright yellow raft busy cruising out from the rearmost exit of the shuttle. Bobbing yellow life vests and shiny white helmets clogged the water all around it. She nodded and the captain jumped off the wing with a splash. He looked back to see if she had followed and then called up to her with muffled, water-logged speakers. "Come on!"

Trying not to think about sharks, she jumped in with Dorian. They bobbed straight up, and she kicked furiously, holding Dorian out in front of her. A big swell hit them and she watched the water run over her faceplate in a blurry stream. At least she didn't have to worry about her or Dorian swallowing water. The air intakes in their suits were self-sealing.

Caty saw the captain swimming for the raft and she kicked after him, determined not to lose sight of him in a sea of matching white helmets. They joined the greedy press of people around the raft, and the captain called out to one of his officers waiting on board. That officer raised a flare gun and fired it to get everyone's attention before calling out in a megaphone voice, "Make way for the captain!"

Caty was surprised people actually listened.

They reached the raft and a pair of officers with the gleaming silver bars of lieutenants reached down to help their captain up into the raft. Colonists crowded into the empty space he left, arms grasping for safety.

Somehow the captain and his crew managed to reach past them to her. She held Dorian high and they took him first. Then they grabbed her outstretched hands and pulled her up, too. Caty mouthed her thanks, and the captain nodded, passing her baby back to her. Dorian had grown so tired of crying that he was actually quiet. Caty saw that the raft was already packed full. No more room, but colonists were still struggling to pull themselves up the sides. The megaphone voice returned.

"Everyone to the next available raft! We are already at capacity. Make way!"

People screamed and cried out objections, their speakers burbling in the water, but the raft left without them, pushed along with ever-increasing speed by some unseen motor.

Caty watched the receding mass of people, arms clawing after them, furious to be abandoned. She shook her head, just as shocked as they must have been.

"Time is critical," someone whispered beside her. She saw that it was one of the lieutenants who had helped the captain up. The blank stare she gave him prompted further explanation.

"This is Confederate territory, and you can bet they saw our shuttle coming down. We need to get to shore and find some place to hide before they come for us or we're going to become hostages and bargaining chips."

Caty's heart thudded in her chest, and her palms began to sweat. It took a few seconds to recover enough from her shock to remember how to activate her own helmet speakers. "Bargaining chips?" she asked.

He nodded gravely. "We're about to win the war, but that doesn't mean we're all suddenly going to be friends. Imagine how many Confederate officers will be able to negotiate leniency for war crimes when they're holding an Alliance baby hostage."

Caty felt her whole body grow cold despite the sweaty heat already bleeding through her suit from the Indonesian air. Her knees shook, and she collapsed on the floor of the raft, hugging Dorian close.

The officer speaking with her went down on his haunches in front of her and fixed her with a determined stare. "We're not going to let that happen, okay? You just hang in there." He patted his thigh, and Caty noticed the black triangle of a sidearm strapped to his hip.

She nodded and swallowed thickly. He flashed a tight smile and turned away, leaving her to bathe in the cold sweat of her fears. She'd been so worried about surviving the landing and the sharks that she'd completely forgotten they were landing in *enemy* waters. The lieutenant was right. With the Confederacy about to lose a hundred-year war, Alliance hostages and prisoners would be more valuable than ever.

CHAPTER 44

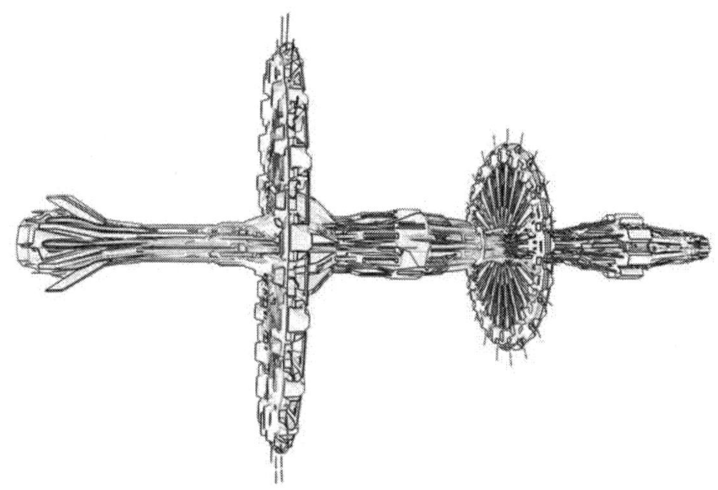

"61st Squadron is away," Lieutenant Stone reported.

Alexander nodded. "Good. Tell them to hold position at five thousand klicks and keep an eye out for enemy missiles."

"Aye, Captain."

"Our torpedoes are splitting. One minute to impact, ten seconds to ELR," Cardinal said from gunnery.

Alexander watched on the tactical as a broad wave of green dots steadily advanced on all fifteen surviving Confederate colony ships. The enemy hadn't deployed a screen of fighters or drones, and so far they had yet to visibly open fire, so those colony ships were completely defenseless. Alexander shook his head, wondering if they were dealing with a ghost fleet. Maybe Admiral Wilson was right and everyone was already dead.

"ELR reached, firing!"

Alexander looked up, watching on the main holo display as simulated lasers lanced out from laser-armed missile shards. A thousand hair-thin blue lines appeared in staccato bursts of light, all vectoring in on just fifteen targets. Then the warhead-carrying missiles impacted, tearing up the black of space with the fiery reds and golds of computer-generated explosions.

As the fabricated light faded, Alexander exhaled slowly, letting out a breath he hadn't realized he'd been holding. *What's another thirty thousand victims in a war of millions?* he thought bitterly.

"Captain! We've got incoming," Vasquez announced from sensors.

Alexander's eyes fell on the tactical map. He saw nothing but a confusing mass of red dots. "Get me vectors!" he snapped.

"Calculating!"

A second later, thin red lines with velocities marked appeared on the tactical grid, showing where individual enemy missiles were headed. There were thousands of them, all busy splitting apart into thousands more.

"Those missiles weren't there a second ago," Carter mused.

Alexander noted how far away the incoming ordnance was from the Confederate warships that had to have launched them, and he shook his head. "They were hiding behind the transports, so close we couldn't even detect them. They were *hoping* we would try to shoot around the colony ships. If we had, those missiles would have gone on undetected until the last possible second. We could have lost our entire fleet."

"Good thing the admiral didn't listen to you," Carter replied.

"They were counting on our humanity to get us killed," he said, suddenly furious with the Confederates and war in general. "Cardinal, launch the next salvo, and Stone, alert 61st Squadron to target those missiles. We don't want anything getting through."

"Yes, sir."

"Enemy fleet is launching fighters!" Vasquez reported. "Three minutes before enemy missiles reach ELR with us," she added, reminding them all how close they still were to a deadly engagement.

"Let's make sure they don't get there," Alexander said, watching as a second salvo of missiles went streaming out from the Alliance formation. A vast wave of Alliance fighters and drones sat glittering on the horizon, each glinting speck enhanced by the *Lincoln's* combat computer until it was bright enough to challenge the stars.

Vasquez spoke again, "Our drones will reach ELR to intercept in five, four, three, two, one."

The drones opened fire, and the ship's combat computer painted invisible lasers an icy blue. Laser-armed enemy missiles answered Alliance blues with crimson reds.

The entire exchange lasted only a fraction of a second. Fiery explosions pockmarked the void, and Alexander glanced at the tactical just in time to see their entire line of drones vanish along with a comparative number of enemy missiles fragments. The remaining missiles sailed on. Alliance fighters opened fire first, cutting enemy ordnance down by half. Then they fired back, stitching space with red laser beams and wiping out hundreds of fighters in an eye-blink.

"61st taking fire!" Stone announced. "We're down by four."

Alexander winced, wondering who had died this time.

The remainder of the enemy missiles went with them, and then the Confederate fleet launched another salvo. Alliance missiles raced past Alliance fighters, leading the charge against the enemy. Soon both waves of missiles split into thousands of smaller shards and the laser-armed fragments opened fire on each other.

Missiles obliterated missiles with random fury, cutting each other's numbers by half and then sailing on to tangle with fighter screens once more. Alexander watched another chunk of their fighter screen evaporate.

"Down two more!" Stone announced. "One pilot left," he said, his tone dark with fury.

Alexander swallowed past a lump in his throat. The enemy's missiles disappeared again, but part of the Alliance salvo got through. He looked up to watch the simulated explosions of three different Confederate capital ships. The light faded, and he checked the tactical. Ten more to go.

"ELR with enemy fleet in three minutes."

"We're going to take casualties if they get to laser range with us," Cardinal warned. "There's no time for another salvo of missiles."

"Then use the hypervelocity cannons," Alexander ordered.

"They'll adjust their headings and evade," Cardinal said.

"So we track shoot! We might score a lucky hit. It's better than waiting for them to hit us. Open fire!"

"Yes, sir."

Alexander watched on the main holo display as bright golden streams of hypervelocity rounds raced out into space, tracking the tiny gray specks of enemy warships.

"They're returning fire!" Vasquez announced.

"Davorian! Evasive maneuvers!"

"Setting thrust vectors. Five Gs maximum. Brace for maneuvering thrust!"

Suddenly Alexander was pinned to his couch, immobilized as the ship executed a series of random maneuvers that would throw off enemy gunners' aim. Stars pinwheeled and zagged in bright silver blurs while hypervelocity rounds went on stuttering out into the void in shimmering waves of computer-simulated light. Enemy rounds came racing back, impossibly fast, and far too close for comfort. Cannon fire streamed by on all sides.

"Taking fire!" McAdams gritted out between bursts of acceleration.

Damage alerts sounded. Then came a tooth-rattling screech of metal shearing and of high caliber shells digging into their armor.

Another alarm blared, this one more distinctive. Every spacer knew that alarm from their drills. The subsequent shriek of air hissing out confirmed it.

"Hull breach! Losing pressure," McAdams said.

Alexander's ears popped and he heard his suit auto-pressurize. His eyes darted around the bridge, trying to find the source of the breach. Switching from external speakers to comms, he ordered, "Seal it up!"

"Repair drones deployed," McAdams replied.

Alexander heard more shells hitting their armor. He winced with every muffled *crunch* of an impact.

BANG!

The main holo display vanished and a gaping hole appeared. A burst of red mist appeared where Davorian was sitting, and Alexander felt himself yanked roughly against his harness as a violent wind ripped by him. The vacuum sucked the debris and Davorian's body out in an instant, along with all of the remaining air on the bridge, leaving nothing but a glaring hole full of stars, and a ragged scar on the deck where their helmsman used to sit.

CHAPTER 45

Catalina saw her raft run aground on the shore of a jungle-infested island. A sea-salt smelling breeze ran through her sweat-matted hair, cooling her momentarily. She'd taken off her and Dorian's helmets soon after making it to the raft. No need to hang on to those anymore.

"Everybody out!" the captain roared as the raft came to a stop. "Move it! We need to get under cover A-*SAP*."

The colonists clambered out, splashing noisily in the shallow water as they tripped and stumbled their way up the beach.

"Let me help you," someone said.

It was the lieutenant she'd been speaking to earlier. Caty nodded and allowed him to lead her to the front of the raft.

He jumped down first and reached up for her to pass Dorian down. She withdrew sharply, as if the lieutenant had threatened to snatch Dorian away from her.

The man smiled and waited patiently, and Caty realized she'd overreacted. It would be safer to pass Dorian down than try to climb out of the raft with him in her arms.

She passed her baby down and then crawled over the side of the raft. As soon as she was standing on the beach, the officer handed Dorian back to her.

"Let's go! Let's go!" the captain shouted down to them from further up the shore. Caty noticed that she and the lieutenant were the last ones out. Everyone else was already fleeing for the jungle.

Caty ran up the beach, kicking sand and trying desperately not to trip. She reached the end of the beach and barreled into a dense green wall of ground cover and trees. Forcing her way through with a crying baby, she caught up to the rest of the colonists. They stood still and frozen near the edge of a clearing, speaking in urgent whispers. Someone scowled and hissed at her to keep her baby quiet. Dorian wasn't the only small child making too much noise, but she got the hint. She did her best to shush Dorian, bouncing him and cooing softly in his ear. That calmed him somewhat, and she looked out at the clearing.

It was some type of farm. Based on the amount of water she saw shimmering in the sun between the bright green tufts of crops, she guessed that it was a rice farm. A trio of workers were out in the field, their conical rice hats shining in the sun.

Caty tried not to give in to despair. The workers hadn't seen them yet. They could go back and walk farther down the beach, look for a more remote area to hide. She heard the jungle rustling behind her and turned to see the captain joining them. One of his officers greeted him and quickly explained the situation. She overheard them arguing about it.

"We *can't* go back," the captain snapped. "There's two confederate destroyers sailing down the coast as we speak. If we go back to the beach now, they'll see us."

"That was fast. What about the other rafts?"

The captain shook his head. "We can't afford to worry about them right now. If they're smart, they'll head for another part of the beach and spread out. Do those rice farmers look armed?"

"No."

"Then that gives us the advantage. Get Guitierrez and let's go. Leave the colonists here until we've cleared the area."

"You want them to watch?"

"They can look away if they have to. Move up."

Caty heard someone shouting in the distance, and she spun around to see one of the workers in the field pointing at them. The others looked up and froze. The captain and his officers made their way to the edge of the clearing, their weapons drawn. Caty followed, driven by the horror of what they were about to do.

"Does anybody speak English?" she called out as loudly as she could. "We need help!"

The captain rounded on her and grabbed her firmly by her arm. "Are you crazy?"

"Someone had to warn them," she said.

"And now *they're* going to warn the nearest platoon of soldiers. Nice work."

"Ahh, Captain..." one of the officers said.

"What?"

Caty saw what—the farmers were approaching, not running away in fear. Maybe they hadn't heard her clearly enough to realize she was speaking English, not Mandarin or Indonesian.

One of them called out in heavily-accented English. "Hello?"

"Shit..." the captain growled. "Let me handle this. Everyone get back under cover!"

Caty refused to budge. The captain stepped out of the jungle with his weapon raised and aimed at the nearest farmer's chest. "Don't move," he ordered.

The Indonesian farmer stopped, his eyes widening. The other two advancing behind him also froze and traded glances with each other.

"Who are you?" the nearest farmer asked in accented english.

"We're Alliance colonists. We crash-landed off the shore. Your people are looking for us. If you take us somewhere safe, I promise no harm will come to you or any of your friends. If you don't, I'm going to shoot you now. Nod if you understand me."

The man nodded once. "You do not have to threaten us. We will shelter you, but you must agree to come quickly, before it is too late."

"We're *enemies.* How am I supposed to believe that?" the captain demanded.

"We are not enemies. Our governments are enemies."

The captain stood there staring at the farmer for a long moment, clearly unsure about what he should do. Caty feared for the farmers' lives and covered Dorian's eyes.

"And if I shoot the three of you here?"

"Your weapon is not silenced. The sound will carry. People will come looking for us, and no one will agree to shelter you after identifying yourselves as hostile. You will trade an uncertain fate for a certain one."

The captain's shoulders slumped, defeated by that logic. "Lead the way."

The farmer nodded once. "We must be quick," he said. He and the other two with him turned in unison and ran, splashing through the field.

"Let's go," the captain called out in an urgent whisper before running after the rice farmers.

Caty followed, trying desperately not to trip in the waterlogged rice field. Here they were placing their lives in the enemy's hands, hoping for mercy. Maybe those farmers really didn't see them as the enemy—*maybe*—but she couldn't help remembering all of those news reports about Confederate people being ant-minded, cold, intensely logical, and self-sacrificing to the extreme.

They were perfect communists, hard-wired from birth to always put the greater good ahead of individual needs. So the question was, did sheltering Alliance colonists somehow serve the greater good?

Caty shook her head, trying not to worry about it.

They ran through the clearing and crashed into another stretch of untamed jungle. Caty felt her arms burning pitilessly from carrying Dorian's weight for so long, but she gritted her teeth and forced herself to focus on something else. Eying the dark shadows between the trees, she imagined enemy soldiers lurking there, the bright red dots of their laser sights landing on the colonists one by one.

But that didn't happen. Instead they came to another clearing, this one much smaller than the one with the paddy field. A well-worn footpath led straight to a short, squat concrete building with a rusted metal door.

Is that a bunker? She wondered. *What are rice farmers doing with a fallout shelter out here in the middle of nowhere?*

Maybe it wasn't a shelter.

Maybe it was a Confederate military base.

Caty felt her heart rate spike with dread. She imagined that rusty door bursting open and hundreds of enemy soldiers boiling out.

It's a trap!

CHAPTER 46

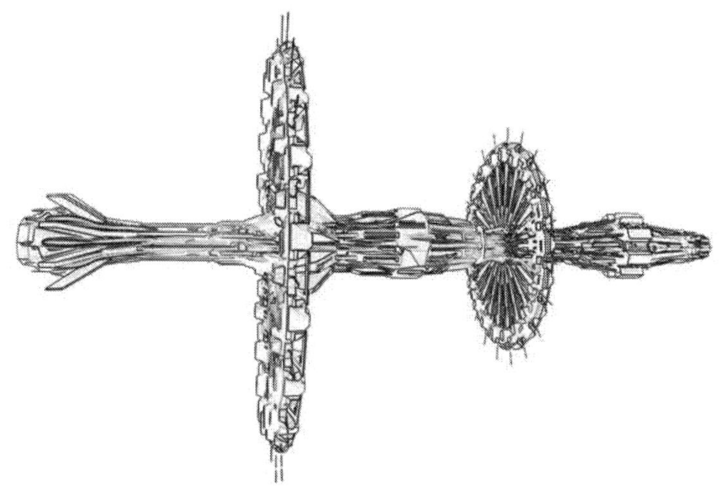

"I'm transferring the nav to my station," Alexander said, glancing at the ragged gash in the deck where Davorian had been sitting a moment ago. Alexander mentally activated the nav functions, and a flurry of control panels crowded the heads-up display inside his helmet, giving him access to the ship's thrusters, maneuvering jets, and a three-dimensional grid for course plotting.

He focused on the grid to enlarge it, and a miniature representation of the *Lincoln* cruised along a jagged yellow vector that zagged back and forth randomly. A second line, this one green, showed the ship's average heading. A sensor overlay highlighted incoming hypervelocity rounds as over-sized golden streaks, moving so fast compared to the *Lincoln* that they were almost impossible to evade. The only advantage the *Lincoln* had was that those rounds took more than ten seconds to reach them, and the payloads weren't nearly large enough to destroy the ship unless a solid stream of them hit.

"Captain, the admiral is ordering us to withdraw," Hayes said. "We're getting too far ahead of the fleet."

Alexander zoomed out the nav map and saw that the *Lincoln* was leading the Alliance formation. No wonder they were taking fire. "Coming about," he said, setting a waypoint behind the rest of the fleet and calculating a new random evasive pattern to reach it—minimum acceleration three G's, maximum seven. "Brace for—"

He didn't even get a chance to finish that warning before the engines and maneuvering jets fired simultaneously at seven g's. Alexander felt that force slam him into the sides of his couch, grinding the cartilage in his ear against his skull with the sheer weight of his now seventy-pound head. A few seconds later, the acceleration eased, and Alexander gulped down a desperate lungful of air.

"Incoming transmission from the enemy fleet!" Hayes announced. "They're surrendering!"

Shock coursed through him. Alexander was about to reply, but another burst of acceleration cut him off. He sent a mental command to pause the evasive flight pattern, hoping the enemy's surrender wasn't a trick.

Hayes spoke again before Alexander could ask for details. "The *Liberty* is requesting to link their comms with ours and join the negotiations."

Alexander nodded and glanced at the main holo display. The repair drones had patched the hole, but the holo display was still damaged. "Patch them through to Carter's station."

"Yes, sir."

Alexander watched as a visual materialized in front of Carter's couch. The screen was divided down the middle—on the right Admiral Wilson of the Alliance, on the left, Admiral Zhang.

Zhang looked even worse than when they'd last seen him. Dried blood crusted his lips and chin where it had run down from his nose. His eyes were bloodshot and glassy, his expression pained, his skin waxy and pale despite the purpling mass of broken blood vessels in his cheeks.

"We will agree to negate thrust and allow Alliance shuttles to board us as soon as we leave the wormhole," Zhang rasped. "We will leave at a steady one gravity of acceleration, and you need not fear that we will betray you. I and my entire crew are going below decks to receive emergency treatment for our injuries."

Admiral Wilson's gaze became intense and suspicious. "How am I supposed to believe that?"

"You can believe whatever you like."

"If we turn around and give you our backs, we'll be reducing our available offensive capabilities, and if we let you leave the wormhole first, you'll have a chance to get to Earth ahead of us. Not to mention you'll pass in and out of effective laser range, and if we don't fire on you, we'll be giving you the chance for a deadly first strike."

"You have us outnumbered. If we open fire, you will retaliate and obliterate us."

"You sacrificed your own colonists for a chance to destroy our fleet, how am I supposed to believe that this is any different?"

"Yes, we did not think you could be so heartless. We were wrong."

"Likewise. Their blood is on *your* hands, Zhang."

Carter cleared his throat. "Admirals, if I may interrupt, the only way to broker a surrender here is for both sides to trust each other."

Admiral Wilson's gaze remained narrowed and sharp.

"Yes… Zhang, you said earlier that you don't have long to live. I assume you're not the only one."

"Without medical attention I will die soon, as will many of my crew."

"That means you don't have much to lose—not that you ants ever think about self-preservation. Why surrender?"

"Because it is over. We have lost. Reports from Earth tell us this same thing. There is no point to continue the fighting. We are now thirty seconds to ELR. You must make a decision soon. If you accept our surrender, you may add our fleet to your own. A small risk for a great reward."

"Ten warships," Wilson clarified.

"Yes," Zhang replied, "and us as your prisoners."

A chime sounded quietly inside Alexander's helmet, drawing his attention away from the negotiations to a text message on his HUD. The message was from Lieutenant Cardinal, and it was marked urgent.

Heads up, Captain. I've just been ordered to fire on the enemy fleet with all guns, half a second before ELR.

"I accept the terms of your surrender," Wilson said.

Alexander blinked, horrified at the lie.

"Good. With your permission, I must now see to my injuries."

"Permission granted, Zhang. Goodbye."

Zhang's visual disappeared, but Admiral Wilson kept the comms open. "The war is finally over," Carter said.

Admiral Wilson regarded him with a small smile. "Not yet, Ambassador."

Alexander gaped at the admiral. "You're planning to fire on a surrendered enemy. That's against military law, Admiral. They're noncombatants now."

Wilson cocked his head. "Military law? Out here I *am* the

law, and I'm calling the shots Captain."

Alexander looked away from the hologram to address his crew. "Cardinal! Belay those orders. You will *not* fire on the enemy."

"Captain, if you disobey that order, you and your entire crew will be tried for treason."

Alexander set his jaw. "Maybe. Maybe not—Hayes mute that channel."

"Aye, Captain."

Carter turned to him, eyes wide and looking shocked.

"Hayes, send an update to the rest of our fleet. Let them know that we're disobeying orders, and why. Suggest they do the same."

"Too late..." Carter whispered, pointing to a tactical map he'd brought up from his station. Bright red laser beams lanced out and drew pinpricks of fire from the enemy formation.

Alexander shook his head, stunned that no one else had disobeyed Wilson's order. "Hayes, unmute the comms. I want to hear what Wilson has to say for himself."

"Aye-aye..."

"Admiral—"

"Let me stop you before you make things any worse for yourself, Captain."

"You lied!" Alexander snapped.

"Of course, I lied. I'm sure they lied, too. We were just better at it."

Alexander shook his head. "They didn't need to die."

"Are you a hunter, Captain?"

"No."

"Then perhaps you wouldn't understand. If you're going to shoot a bear, you better shoot to kill, and if you wound one, you better hope you get a second shot. The only thing worse than turning your back on an enemy is turning your back on a wounded enemy."

"They were already defeated. We could have gained ten warships!"

"We also could have lost ten."

"You never planned to accept their surrender, so why even bother involving us in the negotiations?"

"Because bringing Carter into things made it look like we were willing to negotiate. Meanwhile, we were busy aiming our guns. There is a reason I'm an admiral and you're a captain, *Captain.* War is no place for ethics, and you are an ethical man. Unfortunately, our enemies have no regard for what's noble or right, only what is expedient and logical. From the start we have been forced to behave in exactly the same way as them and do things which seem terrible to us in order to achieve our ends.

"They bred themselves for war, so it came naturally for them, but we had to learn our killer instincts. It was nature versus nurture and nurture won. There's a lesson in that."

Alexander ground his teeth, but said nothing. This entire engagement left a bad taste in his mouth.

"I'm going to do you a favor, Captain. You've served your country well, so rather than focus on the one thing you did wrong, I'm going to focus on all the things you did right and pretend that you didn't just disobey a direct order."

Alexander nodded, unable to muster a verbal reply. He was still too angry, and he was afraid anything he said at this point would sound insubordinate.

"No apologies necessary," Wilson said, as if he thought Alexander had been about to offer one. "Hopefully you've learned enough from this engagement to make the hard decisions without me having to hold your hand in future. Now it's time to turn the fleet around and set course for Earth in case they need our help mopping up. Stand by to receive new nav inputs."

"Aye." Alexander saluted stiffly as the holo projection faded. He let out a long sigh and switched his focus to more immediate concerns.

"McAdams, what's our status?"

"Lots of minor hull damage still being repaired, but all sections are re-pressurized. Some noncritical systems remain offline, but otherwise we're all green."

"How about the MHD?" he asked, staring at the large, blank screen dead ahead that should have been showing a star-dappled view from the *Lincoln's* bow cameras

"That's one of the noncritical systems, sir."

"Great. Stone, do we have any fighters in the 61st still alive out there?"

"Just one pilot, sir. Should I recall him now?"

"Please. Who is it?"

"Ryder."

Alexander was tempted to smile at that, but then he noticed the ragged gash where Davorian should have been seated. They might have won the war, but victory was bittersweet. They'd all lost a lot. He raised his voice to address the crew. "Good job everyone. The war's over. Time for us to go home."

A few of the crew nodded silently, and others made unenthusiastic comments. Alexander couldn't blame them. They'd been gone so long, what did they even have to go back to? Most of them had lost friends and family in the war, and even those who hadn't, had lost them to the slow march of time and hearts moving on.

Alexander's gaze fell on the back of McAdams' helmet, and he wondered what her plans were now that they didn't technically have to remain in the navy. Maybe it was time he found out. He looked over to Carter, planning to reduce readiness from general quarters to condition yellow and leave Carter with the conn so he could take a break and attend to personal matters, but something about the way his XO was staring fixedly at the blank screen of the MHD made him frown.

"Something on your mind, Carter?"

The man turned to look at him with wide, lifeless blue eyes. He looked haunted. "What have we done?" he asked.

Alexander's frown deepened. Maybe Carter had taken that last act of betrayal harder than Alexander had thought.

"You wouldn't be human if you didn't feel bad, but we took a stand, Commander, so whatever blame there is, it falls squarely on Admiral Wilson's shoulders."

"No, you don't understand. There's still *millions* of Confederate soldiers back on Earth, and if they all decide to become rebels and terrorists, we could be in for a lot of trouble."

"Maybe they'll surrender," Alexander suggested.

"Not after they learn what Admiral Wilson did."

"How would they learn about that?"

"They already have. Admiral Zhang was busy communicating his surrender to the Confederate Chancellor when we destroyed the enemy fleet. President Baker just contacted me from Earth, asking what the hell we were thinking. Previously surrendered Confederate troops back on Earth have begun turning hostile again."

Alexander blinked. "I thought the president was with the fleet."

Carter shook his head. "That was just a rumor we spread to make the Confederates believe we were committed to reaching Wonderland."

"Well… shit. This isn't good."

Carter nodded. "It's going to be a long road to repair the damage Wilson did by pretending to accept Zhang's surrender.

He should have left me to negotiate. That's *my* job, but he barely gave me a chance to speak. Wilson's going to be in for a rude shock when he gets back to Earth. He thinks he's going back to a hero's welcome, but he'll be lucky if the president doesn't court-martial him on the spot."

Alexander grimaced. One bad call was all it took to go from hero to villain. He definitely needed to get out of the navy.

CHAPTER 47

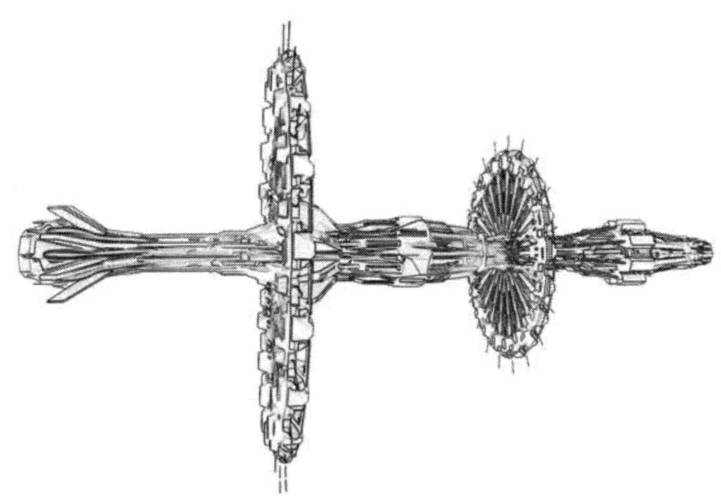

Two Weeks Later - March 6, 2793

Alexander watched their final approach to Earth and Freedom Station on the main holo display. Orbit was already secure thanks to the Alliance's fleet of colony-class destroyers. The planet still looked green, white, and blue, which he thought was a good sign. No doubt they'd see a different story as they flew over the mainland on their way to visit loved ones or pay their respects to the radioactive ruins where they used to live.

"Docking sequence initiated," Alexander announced as he set the autopilot. He kept an eye on their approach vector in case he needed to make manual adjustments. Of all the ships in the fleet, the *Lincoln* had spent the most time away, so they were given first rights to shore leave. And despite the on-going occupation of Confederate territories, officers whose terms of service were up, were actually being allowed to leave the navy.

That meant that this shore leave could be permanent if they

wanted it to.

Alexander wanted nothing more than to get the hell out. He and McAdams had plans to go settle down in a sleepy little town that would never become a target for terrorists. There they planned to bury their heads in the sand and pretend like this hard-won peace wasn't just the start of another type of war.

Alexander sighed, watching as the *Lincoln's* rear airlock made a successful connection to Freedom Station's forward airlock, and gravity resumed it's normal course.

"That's it, everyone!" he announced. "We're home."

A few of the crew cheered and clapped their hands. Everyone unbuckled and went back to their quarters to gather their things. They already had their bags packed, so it didn't take long. On his way out of his quarters, Alexander bumped into McAdams, and she greeted him with a kiss.

Lieutenants Stone and Ryder came striding down the corridor toward them, and Alexander cleared his throat. "That's an unusual way to salute your captain," he said, hoping they hadn't noticed.

McAdams smiled wryly at him. "I had another greeting in mind, but it'll have to wait for a more private setting."

Ryder made no comment as he walked by. Alexander watched him curiously, thinking that it was unusual for him to pass up an opening like that. He was going to need a lot of therapy to get over his survivor's guilt. He'd lost his entire squadron.

Alexander regarded McAdams with a grim smile. "Technically we're still on duty, but remind me about that greeting once we're dirtside."

"Yes, *sir,*" she said, saluting and winking at him as she turned to leave.

He watched her go, his smile more genuine now. A welcome

warmth began seeping through him, and he hurried to catch up.

* * *

"Let me be the first to welcome you and your crew back to Earth, Captain de Leon," President Baker said, reaching out to shake Alexander's hand with both of his. Alexander tried to thank the president, but the deafening report of Anchor Station's saluting guns drowned him out. Then came the steady thunder of applause from several platoons of naval officers—admirals, captains, commanders, and lieutenants—all of them wearing full dress uniforms, standing in formation to one side of Anchor Station's flight deck.

To the other side, standing behind a navy blue velvet rope, was a screaming crowd of reporters, their holo cameras filming and snapping holograms. The spotlights and flashes blinded Alexander in the dim light of dusk.

The president turned to face the press while still gripping Alexander's hand. Alexander took that as his cue to smile for the cameras, all the while his mind raced, trying to come up with an explanation for all the pomp and ceremony surrounding his return to Earth. Why was everyone suddenly so interested in him?

After a moment, the president let go of his hand and gestured for him and the rest of his crew to follow him below decks. The press screamed questions at them as they went, drowning each other out.

Despite the chaos, Alexander did manage to catch a few of the reporters' questions—"Captain de Leon, what made you stand up to Fleet Admiral Wilson? Did you know he was planning to betray the surrender?"

The president's security detail shadowed them down the stairwell from the upper deck of Anchor Station. At the bottom of the stairs they continued on, winding along narrow corridors. After a few minutes of that, the president stopped outside a particular door and asked Alexander and Carter to join him inside. Two of the president's security detail broke away from the group and took up positions to either side of the door. Alexander traded looks with his XO, and then glanced back at the rest of his bridge crew.

"They'll be debriefed separately," the president explained.

Alexander nodded. "Lead the way, sir."

Once they were inside, the president directed them to sit in one of the couches, while he went to sit in an armchair facing them. The room was some type of office, utilitarian, but neat—gray metal walls, beveled metal floors, and a thin brown rug. The couches and chair were old and upholstered in cracked and creased brown vinyl.

Alexander's gaze found the president's, and his brow furrowed in question. Why was the president debriefing them personally, and why was he the only one there for the debriefing?

"Captain de Leon," President Baker said slowly. "You're something of a novelty here on Earth. A warrior with a conscience. Do you know what that makes you?"

Alexander shook his head.

"It makes you a hero. I've got you lined up for at least a dozen different medals and awards. But besides that, there's a big promotion waiting for you."

"I'm not sure I understand, sir."

"You stood up to Admiral Wilson. Not once, but twice. You argued to save the Confederate Colonists, and then you refused to attack the Confederate Fleet after they surrendered."

Alexander shook his head. "The Confederacy was hiding missiles behind their colony ships. If I had gotten my way and we had spared them, we would have taken heavy casualties."

The president frowned and considered that for a long moment. "There are no easy decisions in war, Captain, but Admiral Wilson went a step too far when he betrayed the Confederate Fleet after their surrender. They could have been tried for war crimes, and we could have blamed the deaths of all those colonists on them.

"Instead, they've become martyrs. I was in the process of negotiating the Confederacy's surrender when Chancellor Wang Ping learned of the betrayal. He subsequently ordered all branches of his military to dig in and resist capture at all costs because they could expect no mercy from us. Their people are burning our flags and calling us *the great evil*. Does that sound like they'll be welcoming us with open arms?"

Alexander shook his head.

"We have to prove to them that Admiral Wilson's actions were not sanctioned by our government. He's going to be stripped of rank and publicly tried for crimes against humanity and breach of military law. In fact, he was arrested days ago already, long before he reached Earth."

Alexander caught Max nodding along with that, as if he already knew of those developments.

"I understand, sir," Alexander replied. "But what does any of that have to do with me?"

"It has everything to do with you. We need you to be the poster child for the Alliance's moral character. You have to be a foil for Admiral Wilson and prove that we are not all the same. Prove that we aren't evil."

"You need me to run a PR campaign to spruce up our image."

"Exactly! Commander Carter will use his experience to help you run that campaign."

Alexander saw Max nodding along again, as if he and the president had rehearsed all of this ahead of time. Switching his focus back to the president, Alexander waited for him to go on.

"In addition to Commander Carter, you'll have a whole team of publicists and public relations managers to guide you. You do understand what we're trying to accomplish here, and what's at stake? We're talking about the difference between a peaceful transition of power versus another hundred years of war with an enemy that we can't even find."

"I understand, sir."

"Good. The job comes with a promotion from Captain to Vice Admiral. We're going to hold you up high and push Wilson down low. Hopefully, that will make enough of a statement to repair some of the damage he did."

Alexander pursed his lips, considering the offer. He'd already served his country. He'd done his time. When was he ever going to have a chance to live his life?

"Mr. President, grateful as I am for your offer, I'm going to have to decline. I've been in the navy for too long already, and if I don't settle down soon, I might never get another chance. I already lost my wife thanks to these past two years of extra service." Alexander shook his head. "It's just too much to ask."

"I see. You won't do it for your country then."

"I've already done a lot for my country, sir."

"Agreed, but before you turn down my offer, you might like to know that your wife isn't dead."

"I already know that, sir, but she moved on. I'm happy for her, but not so happy for myself—if you know what I mean."

"Oh. Well, I can't pretend to understand all of what went on between you two, but I was simply referring to the fact that technically she's still missing. Until we find bodies we can't be sure that—"

"Wait—sorry—what do you mean she's *missing?* I received a message from her when we returned from Wonderland. She was living outside Sacramento."

The president shook his head. "That was over six months ago. She joined the colony fleet, Captain. During the fighting her shuttle was damaged and forced to make an emergency water landing in enemy territory. We confirmed that they landed safely via their emergency beacon, but she and the other colonists from that shuttle are all still missing."

Alexander felt his entire body grow cold. He shook his head slowly. "Why would she join the colony fleet?"

The president shrugged. "Maybe she didn't think Earth was safe. Lots of people signed up. It wasn't hard to fill the shuttles."

"You filled them with a lie. You never planned to colonize Wonderland."

"Is that what you think?" the president asked, clearly taken aback. "I'm not sure who told you that, but you're mistaken."

"Then why was the colony fleet *armed?* They're warships, not transports."

"They're both. The Confederacy was sending a fleet, too, so we had to ensure that ours would be able to defend itself once it reached Wonderland."

Alexander's brow furrowed.

"Listen, I understand you're angry that your wife was placed in danger, but she knew what she was getting herself into, and the important thing is that she might still be alive. If you agree to help us, I will allocate more resources to finding the colonists. You can even join the search. In fact, I bet there's some type of angle there that will play well with the rest of our PR campaign."

"That's blackmail," Alexander growled.

"No, it's an incentive. You scratch my back, I scratch yours.

What do you say?"

Alexander gritted his teeth. What *could* he say? Caty might have moved on, but that didn't mean he'd magically stopped caring for her. The thought of her falling into enemy hands…

"With your wife missing in Confederate territory, and possibly captured already, it could help her immeasurably if you can improve our image and defuse the enemy's negative feelings toward us."

"I want to be in charge of the search."

"Done."

"And I want an entire fleet at my disposal."

The president hesitated briefly, but then he nodded. "I suppose an admiral *should* have a fleet. I assume you mean a wet fleet."

"Yes, and I'm only going to renew my commission for another six months, or until my wife is found, if six months isn't enough time."

"Agreed. You drive a hard bargain, Captain de Leon," the president said, standing up and extending his hand for shaking.

Alexander pushed off the couch and accepted the handshake. He intentionally crushed the president's hand in his, and Baker gave him a strained smile, pretending not to notice.

Commander Carter joined them in standing. "I guess we'll be seeing a lot more of each other, Capt—I mean Admiral de Leon. As your PR manager we're going to have to work very closely to defuse the on-going media crisis."

Alexander turned from shaking the president's hand to regard Carter with a thin smile. "I can't wait."

CHAPTER 48

Fleet Admiral John Wilson sat on a springy cot, glaring at the bare metal walls of his cell. Politics had ruined his career—no, his entire life. President Baker was a hypocrite. *If he thinks he's going to get away with burning me in a witch hunt, he has another thing coming.* Wilson knew too much, and he was nothing if not shrewd. He'd known something like this might be coming, and he'd taken the necessary precautions.

Wilson heard a *thunk* issue from the door, the sound of locking bolts sliding away. He had a visitor. Either that, or he was being moved from one cell to another. The brig on Anchor Station was a temporary holding area. They had to move him someplace more public if they wanted to try him for *crimes against humanity.*

What a joke. Since when have crimes against humanity ever applied to the winning side of a war?

The door swung wide and in walked President Baker himself, followed by two secret service men in black suits. "Hello, *sir,*" Wilson said, pouring as much derision into that greeting as he could. "Come to release me?"

The president regarded him with a dubious frown as his

bodyguards approached. Wilson watched them carefully, his heart pounding. One of them produced a set of handcuffs and chained him to his cot.

"Wait for me outside," the president ordered.

Without a word both his bodyguards left the cell and shut the door behind them. It closed with an echoing, metallic *boom,* and then the president turned back to face him, his expression full of disappointment.

"I'm sorry it's come to this, John."

"Likewise, *Ryan,* but you've really lost your mind if you think you can get away with it."

The president cocked his head to one side. "Get away with what?"

"You and I both know that you're even guiltier than I am."

"I don't know what you're talking about, and I would strongly advise you to stop trying to deflect the blame for your actions."

Wilson gritted his teeth and jerked his wrists against his chains with the reflexive need to choke the life out of the president. "All right. I'll play along, you smug bastard. You find some way to release me and have me pardoned from these charges you've trumped up, and I won't vomit your secrets all over the world's news networks."

The president appeared to consider that for a moment, but then he smiled. "You're an excellent bluffer, John."

"It takes one to know one."

"Touché. There's just one problem. You were arrested without warning. You've had no access to any networks, or anyone associated with the press, and to top it all off, I've had you under surveillance since your arrest. I know exactly what you have up your sleeve—*nothing.*"

Wilson deliberately narrowed his eyes. "You think I'm so

stupid that I couldn't see the writing on the wall before I was arrested? I know you. I knew you would try something like this, so I took the necessary precautions. If I don't do something to stop it, Operation Alice will get blown wide open in exactly five days. That should be enough time for you to arrange for my release."

"A dead man's switch. Clever. Assuming I believe your latest bluff, what makes you think people will believe a word you say? I'll discredit you and make you look crazy. It's not going to be an easy sell."

Wilson set his jaw. "The truth never is."

Baker laughed and smiled, his eyes twinkling in the glare of the cell's only light fixture—a naked bulb. "I really am sorry, you know," he said, turning to leave. "I liked you. In another world we might have even been friends."

Wilson felt his heart rate kick it up a notch, beating painfully against his sternum. "Wait! Are you going to release me, or not?"

"Not," the president said, already knocking on the door. Bolts *thunked* once more as they slid aside.

"Even if you don't believe me, think about the trial! It's going to be public. You won't be able to keep me quiet no matter how hard you try. The truth *will* come out!"

The president shook his head sadly as the door swung open. "Goodbye, John."

Wilson watched, mouth agape, as the president left. "Baker!" he roared, spittle flying from his lips, but the president was gone. His bodyguards remained, however. Wilson's eyes widened with horror as they entered his cell. Their faces were impassive, but there was a deadly look in their eyes that gave him warning of what was to come.

Wilson strained against his cuffs and chains, trying frantically to break them. He would sooner break his wrists. The door swung shut, and the bolts *thunked* back into place.

"I'll scream," he warned as one of the president's goons approached.

"Your cell is soundproof," the man replied. "You can spare your dignity."

Wilson glared at him and shook his head. "What you're doing is *wrong*. You can't justify it."

"Sure I can. You killed thousands of innocent people—women, children... *babies*."

"*Confederate* women, children, and babies. You think I'm the only one who's ever killed civilians in war?"

"You can't manipulate your way out of this."

Wilson shook his head, incredulous. Then the man began to undress him, pulling off his pants. Incredulity turned to a new brand of horror. "What the fuck are you doing?" Wilson demanded, aiming a kick at the man's face, but hitting his forearm instead.

Wilson was now sitting on the cot in his underwear.

The man said nothing as he fashioned a noose by tying two pant legs together. Wilson understood. These men were professionals. They would make it look like a suicide.

"Listen to me carefully—" Wilson said. The man, goon number one, didn't even look up. Goon number two uncuffed him so they could remove his shirt and improvise a rope for the noose. Wilson struggled, kicking and screaming for good measure, but the bodyguards were strong and experienced enough to avoid his blows. "When the news breaks, you two are going to follow me and the fucking president straight to hell!"

They slipped the noose over his head, and Wilson struggled for all he was worth, trying to make them strike him in some way that would make foul play a possibility for coroners to investigate, but goon number one held him in an impossibly tight headlock, while they picked him up and stood him on the cot. Wilson could feel himself losing consciousness as he watched goon two tie the end of the shirt rope to the sturdy mounting plate of the light fixture. Darkness seeped in at the edges of his vision. His last conscious thought was *pack your bags, assholes. I'm taking you with me.*

CHAPTER 49

"Is something wrong?" McAdams asked.

"Can I come in? We need to talk," Alexander said.

"Be my guest." McAdams stepped aside and he walked in. Her room aboard Anchor Station was nothing but a bunk, a chair, and a locker with a holoscreen on the wall opposite her bed. Typical fare for a lieutenant. She was actually lucky not to be sharing her quarters with someone else.

Alexander sat at the foot of her bed. She shut the door and crossed over to him, all long legs and lithe curves, her blue eyes bright, but full of concern. He patted the bed next to him, and her lips curved wryly. She stopped in front of him with her arms crossed.

"You don't mess around, Captain. I think maybe I gave you the wrong impression about me. You're at least going to have to take me to dinner first."

"It's admiral, not captain."

"Admir..." McAdams said. Her eyes lit with understanding and promptly narrowed. "I thought you were getting out of the navy."

"I was. The president made me an offer I can't refuse."

"So that's it, they make you an admiral and *bang*—suddenly you're back in it for another ten years? I thought you were sick of the Navy."

"I am. It's not about the promotion. The Confederacy has Caty. Or at least… they might have her."

"Your wife?" McAdams shook her head. "I thought she moved on and had a baby."

Alexander nodded. "Apparently she also joined the colony fleet. Her shuttle went down in enemy waters and the colonists are all missing. I'm going to lead the fleet looking for them."

McAdams looked away. "I don't believe this! Just my luck! I should have known better." She turned back to him, her eyes full of hurt and accusation. "What do you think is going to happen when you find her? You think she's just going to ditch her baby daddy and welcome you back with open arms?"

"No. I don't think that."

"Then what are you doing?" she asked, incredulous.

"I still care about her, Viviana. Maybe she doesn't care about me, and maybe we can't go back to the way things were, but that's not the point. The president needs my help, and in exchange he's willing to allocate an extra fleet to look for the missing colonists."

"You're telling me President Baker is blackmailing you? What could you possibly have to offer him that's worth an entire fleet?"

"I wondered the same thing. Turns out I can help repair the damage Wilson did and make the Alliance look like the good guys again."

McAdams snorted. "You say that like you don't believe that we are the good guys anymore."

"I'm not sure there are any good guys in this war."

"Okay, so you get to go play the hero and rescue your wife.

What about us? How long are you signing on for this time?"

"Six months."

"Better than ten years, but that's still a long time. By then I might have a baby daddy of my own." McAdams fixed him with a penetrating stare. "Are you willing to risk that? You know they have to find those colonists with or without you. She's not the only one missing, and you might not be able to help her even by adding more muscle to the search."

Alexander shrugged. "Maybe, maybe not, but I have to try. When it's over, I'll look you up, and we'll see where we stand."

"Don't bother." McAdams looked away again, wiping her eyes on the backs of her hands. She was crying. Alexander watched her with a growing lump in his throat. She sniffled and said. "With all due respect, *Admiral,* I need to hit the rack, and you're sitting on it."

"Of course." He stood up from the bed and placed a hand on her arm. She flinched, but didn't turn to look at him. "For what it's worth, I'm sorry, Viviana. I would have liked to see where we could go with... us."

Now she did look at him. He saw the bitter curve of her lips and the tears shining in her eyes, and suddenly he wondered if he was making the right decision.

"I know," she said. "Now go find your wife, Admiral."

Alexander nodded. "I will."

* * *

Five Days Later - March 11, 2793

Admiral Alexander de Leon sat on his bed below decks in his quarters aboard the *W.A.S. Hancock,* the flagship of the Seventh Fleet, watching World Alliance News with the volume turned down to a whisper. This was his lullaby. Ever since reaching the Alliance supercarrier *Hancock* four days ago, he'd had to eat sleep and drink the news so that he could respond to it and help improve the Alliance's image.

Meanwhile, the *Hancock* with its two entire wings of drones, fighters, and quadcopters were out searching day and night for Caty and the missing colonists off the coast of West Papau, Indonesia. So far the search hadn't turned up anything, and all they'd manage to accomplish was to engage in land skirmishes with Confederate soldiers who'd taken to hiding in the jungles. Casualties had grown high enough that now they conducted all the searches remotely via land and aerial drones.

Alexander was relatively insulated from the fighting—an admiral in name more than function. He gave broad directions to guide the search, but his real job was to spend every day consulting with Ambassador Carter and his team of PR managers. After that he would sit down in front of World Alliance News reporters and their Confederate counterparts, responding to Confederate rebels' demands, propaganda, threats, and all of the other problems associated with winning the war and occupying enemy territory.

President Baker didn't have the manpower to fight an ongoing land battle with enemy rebels in fully half of the world, so he had to focus on holding key areas and winning over the Confederate people with the sheer nobleness of their goals and conduct.

Without popular support, there was no chance to achieve President Baker's happily-ever-after vision of *one world and one people living in peace and harmony forever*. It didn't help that the Alliance had their fleet standing by in orbit to nuke Confederate cities if they tried anything stupid.

So far no nukes had been fired, but orbital bombardment of enemy oceanic fleets and military bases was ongoing, and the Confederate government was still on the run. Their strategy at this point was guerrilla warfare. So far it was working. Attrition was taking a heavy toll on Alliance forces, and they were only a few weeks into the occupation.

It really was a disaster of global proportions. The enemy government and their entire military had been just about to surrender when they learned of Admiral Wilson's betrayal at the Looking Glass. After that, surrender had been taken off the table.

A public trial for Wilson might have eased some of the bad blood, but then he'd hung himself in his cell before justice could be done. Now getting the Confederacy back to the point of surrender was almost an impossible goal, and Alexander didn't see an end to the fighting in the near future. Maybe war was some indelible part of human nature and world peace would never be achieved, but President Baker was adamant that that should be his legacy.

For his part, Alexander's goals were much less ambitious. The only thing he wanted was to rescue his wife and then leave the navy so that he could get down to the business of living the allied dream that navy recruiters had sold him more than a decade ago. If he was lucky, maybe McAdams would still be available. If not… he was immortal now, so eventually he'd find someone to start a life with.

Alexander sighed and then covered a yawn with one hand. Suddenly the news program playing on the holoscreen at the foot of his bed caught his attention. The headline read, *Breaking News Admiral Wilson's Shocking Confession.*

Alexander frowned, wondering what Wilson had done now. The man was dead, and he was still making headlines. Wilson's face appeared next, with his trademark white hair. Alexander saw his lips moving, but his words were too soft to hear. Alexander was about to gesture at the screen to raise the volume when his comm band trilled with an incoming call.

Frowning, he lifted the band to his lips to accept the call. It was from Captain Tristan of the *Hancock*.

"Admiral!" Tristan breathed, sounding out of breath.

Excitement stirred butterflies to life in Alexander's gut, and suddenly he forgot all about whatever the late Admiral Wilson had to say.

"What is it, Captain?" Alexander asked.

"The colonists. We've found them. We have a platoon of automechs securing their location now. We're about to send the quadcopters to bring them in."

"I'll be right there," Alexander said, already flying out of bed. "Tell them to save a seat for me. I want to be there when they're rescued."

"Sir, I strongly advise against—"

"I wasn't asking for permission, Captain. I'm going."

"Yes, sir."

CHAPTER 50

Alexander reached the flight deck already dressed in a full two hundred pounds of powered combat armor. A dozen quadcopters were on the deck, their rotors spinning with a thunderous *thump-thump-thumping*. Navy SEALs rushed every which way in matching gray combat armor. Drones hovered up and away like a swarm of locusts.

Thanks to his powered armor, Alexander felt his steps light and too fast. It was like stepping off a treadmill after running for an hour—the world went by in a blur. Ambassador Carter ran beside him, huffing and puffing to keep up.

"Admiral, you can't risk yourself like this. You are far too valuable to the Alliance."

"I'm going, Carter. You can't stop me. This was the president's end of the deal, remember?"

"What are you going to accomplish by going with them?" Carter yelled at him to be heard above the noise of rotors and the amplified voices of platoon leaders snapping orders at their troops. "You're not a SEAL! You're a starship captain!"

"This discussion is over," Alexander replied, his voice magnified by the external speakers in his helmet.

"You think the enemy is going to pass up the chance to kill *Alexander, the Lion of Liberty?"*

Alexander rounded on the ambassador and planted an armored palm against the other man's chest. Carter bounced away violently and shot him an angry look. "Watch it! You could have broken my ribs!"

"Then maybe you should get back below decks before you get hurt. You think I don't know how to handle myself on the ground just because I've been sitting in an acceleration couch for the past ten years?"

"You're not trained for this," Carter insisted. "You're—" Carter's comm band trilled with an incoming call and he answered it. "Hello? Mr. President, it's a pleasure to… I see. Yes… I understand. I'll be there as soon as I can. No, one of the jets can take me. It'll be faster. Alexander? I'm here with him now. Yes, I'll tell him."

"What was that about?" Alexander asked, his curiosity piqued.

"You have to come with me. We have a situation developing, and the president needs you to join him immediately."

Alexander snorted and shook his head. "Whatever it is, it can wait."

"It can't."

"Yes, it can. Rescuing my wife was my condition for joining your devil's advocacy program, and if you don't live up to it, I sure as hell won't live up to my end of things. I'll see you when I get back." Alexander turned on his heel and jogged away.

"Admiral!" Carter screamed after him. "You'll be court-martialed for this!"

"Good!" Alexander roared back. "Saves me the trouble of deserting!"

* * *

The quadcopters set down in the middle of a paddy field full of Confederate farmers wearing conical rice hats. Alliance corsair-class automechs stood all around the perimeter of the field, their cannons tracking land and sky.

Inside Alexander's quadcopter, buckles clattered and clacked as the SEALs stepped out of their docking stations. The team commander called out, "Let's go! Let's go! Double time!"

Alexander rushed out the back of his quadcopter amidst the *thump-thump-thumping* of giant rotors. Data streamed into his helmet via comms and colorful heads-up displays. Friendly soldiers were highlighted green, names and ranks floating up above their helmets as they ran out the back of the quadcopter and splashed through the paddy fields. Their armor shimmered, adaptive camouflage changing from gunmetal gray to jungle greens.

"Admiral, please stick close to me," Commander Vargas said over comms. "Your safety and that of the missing colonists is my top priority."

Alexander nodded and commed back, "Roger."

He armed his suit's integrated weapons and set his shoulder-mounted cannons to auto-fire on incoming drones, grenades, and AP rockets. The automechs already had a good perimeter secured, but there was always a chance that something might slip through. Carter might be a pain in the ass, but he was right about one thing—the chance to kill Alexander, *the Lion of Liberty* was too tempting to pass up.

Here's hoping they don't know I'm here, he thought, watching as a dozen platoons rushed out into the paddy field amidst confused and shell-shocked rice farmers.

Alexander ran behind Commander Vargas to the edge of the

field where four jungle-green corsair-class automechs stood waiting to escort them through a tunnel of shattered trees and trampled ground cover. Alexander watched their armor shimmer and appear to liquefy, affording them a wraith-like invisibility.

"Engage stealth mode and step lightly," Commander Vargas said over the comms.

Alexander toggled stealth and he felt his steps slow as his powered armor adapted to keep him from making too much noise. There was no hiding the corsairs' ground-shaking footsteps, but at least that would draw attention away from the ground troops following behind.

Alexander had to resist the urge to run for it. It was torture to think of his wife in enemy territory, not knowing if she was okay or whether she'd been mistreated. But he had to remind himself that she wasn't *his* anymore.

In the distance Alexander heard shouting in a foreign language, followed by the sound of gunfire. A swarm of Allied drones went racing over the treetops. Then came the *thud-thud-thud* of cannon fire and the golden flicker of tracer rounds slashing down.

Comms crackled in Alexander's helmet—Commander Vargas ordering them to get ready for action, followed by an order to adopt a new formation. Ghostly shadows swarmed around Alexander in a protective circle.

The shouting stopped and they came into a smoke-clouded clearing. The jungle was shredded, and burning here and there in smoking clumps of blackened vegetation. In the distance Alexander saw a concrete structure with a rusty steel door. Then Alexander noticed all of the bodies. Asian skin tones mixed with bloody reds. There was a scattering of severed limbs, and a few charred rice hats. None of them appeared to be wearing Confederate uniforms, and Alexander didn't see any weapons lying around the bodies.

"What happened here?" he asked over comms. "These people weren't armed."

"You don't know that," Vargas replied. "They were in the engagement area. If they had good intentions they would have run."

Alexander looked away and tried to keep his eyes on the door, now marked on his HUD as their objective. A pair of SEALs ran out and began cutting the door open with high-powered lasers. Commander Vargas came on the comms snapping orders, all the while Alexander heard the booming footsteps of the Corsairs and the *whirring* of Allied drones racing overhead.

In the distance cannon fire sounded counterpoint to that of smaller handheld weapons. There was fighting going on not far from their location.

The SEALs finished cutting open the door and then kicked it in. Alexander saw a dark tunnel and a staircase leading down below ground. This was some kind of fallout shelter.

What are allied prisoners doing here? Alexander wondered as he reached the door. Vargas and four other SEALs preceded him down the stairs, while the remainder of the team followed. Dust swirled in the yellow beams of ancient lights. The metal rungs echoed and groaned as they marched down the stairway. At the bottom they encountered another metal door and again they were forced to cut through.

Alexander frowned, wondering how they knew the prisoners were here if they hadn't even opened the bunker yet. He got on the comms to Vargas asking exactly that.

The commander replied, "We have a short-ranged tracker implanted in the captain of the shuttle that went missing. His beacon is broadcasting from here."

Alexander grimaced, realizing that meant they didn't know anything about who else might be with him, or even if the captain himself was still alive. Caty might not even be here.

High-powered lasers crackled and hissed. Alexander watched the SEALs trace a molten orange line across the door, and his visor auto-polarized to protect his eyes from the glare. The line became a closed circle and then the SEALs kicked in the door. The piece they'd cut fell inward with a *bang*, and SEALs rushed through the gap.

Vargas called out in an amplified voice, ordering everyone in the bunker to raise their hands and remain calm.

Alexander felt himself carried inside by the press of soldiers behind him. A huddled, bedraggled mass of civilians with dirty faces and tear-streaked cheeks appeared all around the room, all of them highlighted yellow on his HUD to indicate that their friend/foe status was unknown. Then facial recognition took over and began painting them green one by one, until all of them were identified as Alliance citizens.

They'd found the colonists, and apart from how dirty they were, they all appeared to be fine. Alexander saw the soldiers around him relax their guard somewhat. Vargas walked up to one of the civilians, and Alexander saw from the HUD overlay that his name was Captain Fuentes. Scanning the crowd anxiously, Alexander read names in a hurry, trying to find one that read *Catalina de Leon.* She couldn't have changed her name already… unless she'd filed for a divorce in absentia and remarried.

Then he saw her. He didn't even need to read her name to know it was Caty. Blond hair, blue eyes, small nose, full lips—and the baby boy sitting in her lap was added confirmation. Alexander ran toward her, his heart pounding and his veins buzzing with adrenaline. He toggled his external speakers and called out to her. "Caty!"

She looked up suddenly, her eyes wide with shock. She saw him coming at her in full body armor and her surprise turned to fear. She curled protectively around her son. Then he mentally retracted his visor, allowing her to see his face. The smell of sewage and rotting food hit him like a punch in the gut, but he managed to smile for her sake.

"Alex!" she screamed, stumbling to her feet. "Is that you?" Her face scrunched up and she began to cry.

He stopped within arms' reach of her. "Are you okay?" he asked, studying her from head to toe and looking for injuries. He reached out with an armored hand, as if to stroke her cheek, but stopped himself, and looked around suddenly. "Where's… the father?"

She shook her head and bit her lip, her tears coming steadily now. "David didn't go with us. It's a long story."

The boy in her arms began to cry, too, and Alexander regarded him with a sympathetic look. "Come on, we need to get you out of here," he said. "We have air transports waiting."

Caty nodded, and then Commander Vargas reiterated that, saying, "Let's go everyone! If any of you is in need of assistance, check in with Corpsman Torres over there—" Alexander noticed Vargas pointing to where a huddled group of medics were already busy conducting first aid for injured colonists.

People climbed to their feet, trading shell-shocked looks with one another. The reality of their rescue hadn't sunk in yet. Not the welcome he'd expected. Turning back to Caty he asked, "Did they hurt you?"

She shook her head. "No, they've been protecting us."

Alexander's eyebrows floated up. "They who?"

"The rice farmers. They hid us down here to keep Confederate soldiers from finding us."

Alexander remembered the dead farmers in the clearing around the entrance of the bunker and he grimaced. On the one hand the president was trying to convince the Confederate people that the Alliance wasn't evil, and on the other hand, Alliance soldiers and drones were shooting first and asking questions later.

"What's wrong?" Caty asked.

He shook his head. "Nothing." Looking away, he saw the other colonists busy shuffling toward the open door. A bright circle of daylight streamed in from the stairwell, illuminating drifting clouds of dust. Reaching out, he wrapped an armored arm around her shoulders and guided her toward the light. "Come on. It's time to go home."

CHAPTER 51

There was no concealing Caty's shock as they ran back to the quadcopters. The same farmers who had been protecting her and the other colonists had been gunned down without hesitation.

Now sitting in the cockpit of one of the quadcopters, behind the pilot and copilot, Alexander leaned across the aisle between their seats to reassure Caty that everything was going to be okay. It was almost impossible to hear over the noise of the rotors, but their headsets and microphones muffled the noise and enabled them to speak via comms.

"What happened to... David?" Alexander asked, anxious to know why she was alone. "Why didn't he go with you?"

Caty gave him a broken smile and shook her head. The quadcopter hovered up and away amidst an escorting cloud of drones. She began to explain, starting from the message she'd sent to him, where she'd asked him not to contact her again because contact with him was provoking David. Then she explained about the abuse, the alcoholism, and how helpless and trapped she had felt.

Alexander felt himself growing progressively more furious

with every passing second. He was horrified and seeing red. His stomach burned with an acid rage.

He would hunt David down and make him pay if it was the last thing he did.

Then Caty got to the part about joining the colony fleet and going to Wonderland to start a new life. That was when she'd discovered that David was illegal in the northern states and he couldn't go, and that was why he'd never changed despite multiple behavioral adjustments. He didn't have standard gener implants to adjust. The adjustments reports were all forgeries.

That revelation was one too many. The lies, the abuse… it was too much. *David's a dead man,* he thought.

"You're very quiet," Caty said, reaching for his hand.

He was still wearing armor, so he didn't feel her touch.

"Alexander?"

He shook his head, snapping out of it. "I'm so sorry you had to go through that."

"It's okay. I wish you had been there, but I know it's not your fault. You didn't have a choice."

Alexander tried to process all of what she'd said to him, and suddenly he realized that if David wasn't in the picture anymore, there might still be a chance for the two of them. "Caty…" He held her hand loosely in his. "I didn't move on until you contacted me, telling me to stay away. And even after that, I never *really* moved on. I don't know where you're at right now, but if there's any chance that we might still be together, I promise to make up for all those years I was away, and I promise that I'll love Dorian as if he were my own son."

Caty's face crumpled; her blue eyes grew moist and sparkled like the sun shining on the deep blue sea below. Her lower lip trembled. "Oh, Alex." She shook her head. "I must be dreaming."

He smiled back at her.

"You're done with the Navy now, right?"

Alexander hesitated. "I signed on for another six months so that I could look for you."

Some of Caty's excitement faded and she nodded soberly. "And after that?"

"After that I'm a free man."

"You promise?"

"I promise."

Caty unbuckled; leaning across the aisle, she kissed him. Despite the fact that she smelled terrible and her breath was no bouquet of roses, Alexander felt a familiar spark in that kiss, and a warm rush of hope swept away any lingering doubts about him and Caty picking up where they'd left off. She was everything that he'd been missing for so long. Dorian squirmed in her lap and began swatting their faces with his hands.

Alexander withdrew and looked down on him with a wry grin.

"Hey there little guy."

Dorian regarded him with lips parted and eyes wide, as if fascinated by him.

Looking up at Caty, Alexander asked, "How did you get pregnant, if you don't mind me asking?"

"My implant failed," Caty explained.

"And the father didn't have one, so it was bound to happen sooner or later."

"I didn't think of that..." Caty said. "That's true."

"He's going to pay for what he did to you."

Caty's expression became guarded. "What are you going to do?"

Alexander felt a flash of jealousy and anger. Was she trying to protect him? "After what he did to you, what do you care?"

"I care because I know you, and I don't want you to go to jail, Alex. Revenge won't fix anything."

He shook his head. "This isn't about revenge. It's about justice. By law, illegal immigrants are to be conscripted on sight. After that, if a stray bullet hits him in occupied enemy territory, you won't see me crying."

Dorian fussed in his mother's lap, and Alexander turned to look at him, forgetting for a moment to make a baby-friendly face. Dorian took one look at him and started screaming.

"You're scaring him!" Caty said.

"Sorry." Alexander let his anger out in a sigh.

Caty shot him an accusing look. "Let's not talk about this anymore. I'm sure David will get what's coming to him without you hunting him down."

Alexander nodded but said nothing, looking instead out to the horizon. He wasn't going to leave David's fate to chance.

Justice would be done.

* * *

As soon as they reached the *W.A.S. Hancock* Alexander whisked Caty and her son away to his quarters so that they could eat a hot meal and get cleaned up. After they both ate, he had the ship's doctor come up and check them out so that they wouldn't have to wait in line for hours with all of the other colonists.

The doctor gave them a clean bill of health, but injected them both with a booster shot of nanobodies just in case.

Now, as Alexander sat waiting for them to get washed up, there came a knock at the door, followed by a voice over the intercom. "Admiral de Leon, it's Ambassador Carter."

"Come in," he said, already sighing.

The ambassador strode in wearing a heavy frown. "Have you heard?"

Alexander shook his head. "Heard what? I just got back."

"Wilson's confession."

Alexander remembered that had been the breaking news just before he left.

"Right. What was that about?"

"He's claiming—posthumously—that the entire trip to Wonderland was a fake."

"What? That's ridiculous."

"Exactly."

"People aren't actually believing that are they?"

"Even if people don't fully believe it, hearing something like that from the man who used to be in command of the entire Alliance fleet is enough to make them wonder."

"Well..." Alexander considered that for a moment. "If I recall, during the first Cold War, some people claimed that the moon landing was a fake, too, and that was equally ridiculous."

Carter's eyes lit up. "Exactly! I'd forgotten about that."

"There's always going to be a few nutcases claiming some kind of conspiracy."

Carter nodded. "I agree, and since you led the mission to Wonderland you're in a unique position to answer those claims. The president wants you to give testimony to everything you saw and did while you were on Wonderland. We were going to do that stateside, but since you ran off to be the hero, we've lost too much time already. I need you to go meet with the press right now."

Alexander considered that. "And if I say no?"

"Then you'll be court-martialed and tried for treason. You'll go to prison, *Alex*."

Alexander scowled and turned toward the bathroom, where

Caty was still washing up with Dorian. *"Mi amor, este pendejo quiere que me vaya con el para defender la imagen publica de la Alianza. Ahorita vuelvo."*

After a moment, he heard, *"Esta bien. Cuidado con lo que dices. Te amo!"*

"Y yo a ti." Turning back to Carter, he smiled thinly and said, "Let's go."

"I'm an Ambassador. I understand Spanish, and I know what *pendejo* means," Carter said.

Alexander's smile became lop-sided. "I know, but it's not polite to call a man a dumbass in his native language."

Carter glared at him. "We're wasting time. Let's go."

CHAPTER 52

As they left Alexander's quarters, Carter asked him, "You haven't seen the confession yet, have you?"

"No."

"Then you'd better watch it with me now. If you're only hearing about it for the first time when reporters interview you, you might be surprised by something. We need ready answers and confidence, not hesitation. We'll go to my quarters and watch it before we meet with the press."

Alexander nodded. "Lead the way."

Carter's quarters weren't far from Alexander's own—just down the corridor. Carter waved the door open and they breezed inside. "Sit down," he said, pointing to the couch in the living room.

Alexander angled for the couch and sat down facing the room's holo projector while Carter configured it from his comm band. A moment later the lights dimmed, and an image of Wilson's face sprang to life, larger than life, and staring at them with intense blue eyes that contrasted sharply with his military short white hair.

"I'm recording this message in anticipation of the fact that I may be arrested when I return to Earth. I won't try to defend my actions, only to say that they felt like necessary measures at the time. If you are watching this, it's because I have become the Alliance's scapegoat in this war. But if I'm going to be accused of wrongful actions, then it is only fair that the mastermind behind these actions be brought to justice with me. With that I am referring to President Ryan Baker. He was the one who dreamed up Operation Alice in the first place.

"Operation Alice was a manned mission we sent to land on and explore an Earth-type planet on the other side of a traversable Lorentzian Wormhole, code-named the *Looking Glass,* but I'm here to tell you that all of that was a lie."

Alexander blew out an incredulous breath.

Carter sat down beside him. "Wait," he whispered. "It gets better."

The late Admiral Wilson went on, "I was only brought into the president's scheme late in the game, but as all of you know by now, we fought a war over sole access to the wormhole, and many millions of people died in the nuclear strikes that followed. Those people all died for a lie, and that lie was what we showed the Confederacy through leaked intelligence information. We showed them that the wormhole was traversable and that it led to a habitable planet called Wonderland, but the truth is that there is no way through the wormhole and there never was."

"What?" Alexander shook his head, and Carter paused the recording with a gesture. "He lost his mind! We've been there and back again. We have *reams* of data. Even if we *could* fake such a thing, why the hell would we want to?"

Carter nodded gravely. "Listen up." He gestured for the recording to play once more.

Wilson went on, "We lied and intentionally leaked falsified

data to the Confederacy in the hopes that they would just take our word for it and fly headlong through the wormhole with everything they had in an attempt to beat us to colonizing what might be the next Earth. It wasn't reasonable to expect them to do that based on probe data alone, so we organized a manned mission to Wonderland with a team of experts who could realistically invent the data it would take to convince the Confederacy that Wonderland was real. This had to be done without even those experts knowing the truth, because one of them would be a spy, standing ready to leak all of the mission data to the enemy. This crew member was a known enemy agent by the name of Commander Sirena Korbin."

Alexander's eyes narrowed swiftly at that. *They* knew *she was a spy?*

"We also needed a man on the inside to help her and guide everyone else through their virtual reality experience, making sure that no one got suspicious. That man was an Alliance ambassador."

Alexander shot Carter a look, to which the ambassador made a dubious face and shook his head, as if to say that it was news to him.

"Everything, even the time dilation, had to add up. Just over three months passed for the crew while they floated in water-filled tanks to protect them from the forces and radiation in the mouth of the wormhole. Time dilation due to gravity made those three months more than two years back on Earth.

"But in order to give a more realistic length to the wormhole, we had to tell the crew that they would spend more than five months traveling to wonderland and back. As a result, when the mission allegedly *returned,* every clock on board, including the comm bands the crew took with them, was automatically reset to reflect that over five months had passed instead of three."

The mention of that time discrepancy set off fireworks in Alexander's brain, and he tuned Wilson out. It took him a moment to figure out why that time discrepancy was so important, but then he remembered—*the pocket watch.* He had emerged from his G-tank for the last time to find that the mechanical watch Caty had given him showed only a little over three months had passed since leaving Earth, while every other clock on board the *Lincoln* had shown the anticipated time lapse of more than five months. That lined up perfectly with what Wilson was saying. Alexander's entire body went cold, and he could feel the blood draining from his face. He slowly shook his head and forced himself to focus on what Wilson was saying.

"The virtual experience that the crew from Operation Alice shared was generated by an experimental technology code-named *Excelsior.* Using standard neural implants and injected nanites, people's brains are stimulated directly in order to produce sight, sound, and sensation while immersed in an alert dream-like state. It's a more vivid version of a dream, one that can be shared and sculpted by the thoughts and impressions of the people who are experiencing it. Information and observations that participants make about their virtual world are recorded so that the experience has real, invariant characteristics even though it is evolving in a very dynamic way.

"Now, imagine what happens when you put a team of experts from various fields together and have them all participate in the shaping of the same virtual world. The result is that much more convincing, and the data gathered will look to other experts in those fields like it was gathered directly from a *real* world.

"The only noticeable seam in the illusion is that what people see and experience tends to fit their expectations, which brings me to the first article of proof I have to back up my claims. I have multiple reports from the officers sent to Wonderland, making mention of strange coincidences they noted while exploring. I will disclose these reports separately for you to analyze and make up your own minds. Then there's also the fact that no physical samples were brought home from Wonderland. They all mysteriously vanished after the crew emerged from their tanks for the last time, along with all of the ship's internal and external surveillance footage. They assumed that was the work of the spy in their midsts. Then there is the fact that the Confederacy just lost their entire fleet while trying to travel through a wormhole that was never open to begin with. All of that points to one inescapable conclusion—the mission was a fake.

"President Baker's plan worked. The war is over, and we won. Yes, we lost millions of people because of it, and if the enemy hadn't bought our bluff, they would have all died for nothing.

"What I did, betraying the enemy surrender in order to ensure that no remnant of the Confederate fleet survived is perhaps worthy of judgment, but I would argue that the president did something far worse. He tricked an entire colony fleet full of innocent civilians into throwing their lives away for the promise of a better world that doesn't even exist. If you want to point a finger at someone for war crimes, you can start with our commander-in-chief.

"You probably want to know why I'm revealing all of this, since it certainly won't help me to reveal that I was part of a government conspiracy.

"It's simple. This confession was my insurance policy, and if you're watching it, that's because the president didn't believe my threats, or he thought he could stop this information from getting out. Either way, I suppose that makes this more about revenge than coming clean, but you are welcome to ascribe more noble motives to my confession." Admiral Wilson gave the camera a bitter smile and saluted. "Long live the Alliance."

The holo recording ended there and overhead lights swelled to full brightness once more. Alexander was left breathless with horror and shock. He couldn't believe it.

"Now you see what we're up against," Carter said.

Alexander turned to face the other man. He could feel the anger and resentment bubbling over. He'd been played for a fool. They all had.

"It is true?" he demanded.

Carter blinked, taken aback. "Of course not! We went to Wonderland together, or have you forgotten?"

Alexander reached into his pocket and withdrew his pocket watch. He hadn't had the heart to look at it again after Caty had told him she'd moved on, so he hadn't reset the date yet, and just as well. Now he flicked the watch open with his thumb and angled it to face Carter.

The ambassador shook his head, clearly baffled. "If I wanted to know the time, I'd check my comm band."

"This was a gift from my wife."

"What does that have to do with—"

"Let me finish!" Alexander roared. "This is an antique. It's hard to find mechanical watches anymore, but do you know what's special about them?"

Carter said nothing, just stared stonily at the watch.

"They aren't networked, so you have to change the time manually with this little dial here," Alexander said, tapping the cog on the side of the watch. "Do you know how much time my watch said had passed when we returned to Earth?"

Again, no answer. Carter regarded him unblinkingly, waiting for him to finish.

"I'll give you a hint. Admiral Wilson just told us."

Carter's eyes widened fractionally, and Alexander nodded. "That's right. Three months."

"Coincidence—" Carter spluttered.

"Speaking of coincidences—I was one of the ones who wrote about the sheer number of them on Wonderland. I also mentioned the missing samples. If Wilson was lying about all of that, then he's remarkably good at backing his lies with facts. He mentioned you were the president's man on the inside. Is there something you'd like to confess to before I tell everything I just told you to the press?"

"You do that and you won't just be court-martialed, you'll be executed."

"Since when did it become illegal to tell the truth? Besides, after Wilson's confession, I think people might just believe me, don't you? And if that's the case, then it won't be my head on the chopping block—it will be yours, right alongside the president's."

"You fool! Do you have any idea what's at stake here? Even if you were right, stop and *think* for a minute! If a conspiracy like this comes to light, the Alliance will be overturned. Our soldiers will all drop their weapons and desert! We'll be plunged into anarchy. We won't win the war, we'll *lose* it. Millions more people could die, and all the ones who already died will have died for nothing!"

"Maybe, maybe not. Everybody keeps saying that the war is over, but all I see are more bodies. Maybe if we all start telling the truth, people will wake up and realize how stupid we've been."

"Yes, after thousands of years of going to war, humanity will finally see how destructive it is and stop the fighting once and for all. Grow up, Alexander."

"Admit your involvement or I'm going public with what I

know."

Carter gritted his teeth. His face turned red, and veins began pulsing in his forehead and neck. "You want me to admit it? Fine! It was all ruse, one giant bluff that led to victory. In the grand scheme of things, is that really so bad?"

Alexander smiled. "I left my wife alone on Earth because of Operation Alice. She almost died when fighting broke out. She had a son without me, and she ended up being physically abused for years by the boy's father until she finally had enough and decided to join the colonists headed for Wonderland. During the recent fighting in orbit, her shuttle was forced to crash-land in the ocean, and she spent weeks in enemy territory, living in wretched conditions. She was lucky she didn't die in the fighting, or during the crash-landing, or in captivity. By my count that's four times that your lies almost killed her."

"Allegedly," Carter said, backtracking.

Fury overcame him. Alexander's arm snapped out and his fist knocked Carter's perfect jaw out of alignment.

"You hit me!" Carter exclaimed.

Alexander shrugged. "Allegedly." Then he hit Carter again before the ambassador could recover. The plenipotentiary of the Alliance fell off the couch with a *thud* and lay spread-eagled on the deck, unconscious and drooling.

Alexander stood up and shook out his fist. He loomed over Carter with a scowl, waiting for him to get up for another round, but the other man didn't even stir. Watching the diplomat, he felt his hatred and disgust grow. Korbin had been right. The Confederacy wasn't the enemy. The Alliance was.

* * *

Alexander had Ambassador Carter placed under arrest and

then he went to meet with the press alone. Reporters from both World Alliance News and the Confederacy's equivalent, Central News Group, were there. He gave his evidence to corroborate Wilson's confession, and now all of two hours later, he sat in his quarters with Caty and Dorian, watching his face appear all over every news channel in the world. Alexander, *the Lion of Liberty,* denouncing his own government.

World Alliance News showed an aerial view of a large demonstration outside the newly constructed presidential palace. Demonstrators' holo signs called for everything from Bakers' resignation to the death penalty for him and his co-conspirators. The coverage went from there to current investigations into Wilson's death. Previously ruled a suicide, it was now cast into doubt due to the circumstances. Forensic experts from all over the Alliance were coming forward, suggesting that it would have been impossible for Wilson to hang himself in his own cell using nothing but his uniform. Impossible or not, Wilson's confession implied that he had threatened the president, so his subsequent death was highly suspect.

Caty squeezed his hand and turned to him. "Let's turn this off," she said.

Alexander regarded her with a frown. "We need to know what's happening. This could kickstart another war, and if it does, we're sitting right in the middle of an engagement zone. The fate of the entire world is at stake. Don't you want to know the outcome?"

She shook her head. "No, I want to know *our* outcome. We've spent enough of our lives worrying about war. It's time that someone else worried about it for a change. You deserve a break. *We* deserve a break. The world can wait."

Alexander smiled wanly and nodded. He waved absently at the holoscreen to turn it off, and the lights in the room swelled to their normal brightness. Dorian clapped his hands together, as if he thought that was a neat trick. Caty regarded her son with a smile.

"Just six more months," Alexander said.

Caty turned back to him. This time she was frowning. "What if war *does* break out? Can they keep you in the navy?"

He shook his head. "No force on Earth is going to take me away from you again."

She cracked a smile. "You promise?"

He nodded. Leaning toward her, he took her face in his hands and kissed her, long and hard. The taste and smell of his wife intoxicated him, carrying him away on a cloud of hope. Caty was right. They'd spent enough time worrying about the rest of the world, serving their country. It was time to be a little selfish.

The future would take care of itself. *For now it's just the two of us*—Dorian made a noise and he corrected himself—*the three of us,* he thought, smiling against Caty's lips.

"What is it?" she asked, withdrawing just far enough to look him in the eye.

"I was just thinking about us. We got what we always dreamed of—a family. We made it."

"Twelve years late," she reminded him.

"Time is an illusion," Alexander said.

Caty smiled. "And love is the only truth."

Alexander nodded. "Let mine be yours."

"About damn time, Alex," she said, and pulled him in for another kiss.

EPILOGUE

Alexander lay in bed beside Caty, wide awake and watching her sleep. He'd forgotten how beautiful she was.

On her side of the bed Dorian lay in his crib, also sleeping soundly. Alexander had asked a few junior ratings from engineering to fashion that crib for Dorian. Caty was a civilian, so she didn't belong with the fleet, but for now Alexander would rather stretch the rules to have her aboard the *Hancock,* than send her stateside where civil unrest was still in full swing in the aftermath of President Baker's arrest.

Alexander's comm band trilled, interrupting his thoughts. He muttered a curse under his breath and lunged for the end table where he'd left it. Fumbling around in the drawer, he pulled out the device and brought it up to his lips.

"What?" he answered, getting ready to bite the caller's head off.

"It's Captain Tristan, sir."

"What are you doing up at this hour?" he asked in a fierce whisper. He climbed out of bed and went to the office adjoining his quarters so he could speak without waking Caty or Dorian. "No, never mind," he went on as he waved open the door and breezed through to his desk. "What are you doing *calling me* at this hour?"

"It's important, sir."

"I'm listening."

"We received a transmission from a Minister Wang Jun, who is claiming to be the Confederate Chancellor's direct representative. Apparently the Chancellor wants to re-open peace talks."

"Then why isn't he calling Acting President Luther?"

"He wants you to negotiate the treaty. According to Mr. Wang, any man who would rather betray his country than his conscience is a man who can be trusted."

Alexander snorted. "They got it all backward, Captain. I didn't betray my country; my country betrayed me."

"Semantics, Admiral. What would you like me to tell Mr. Wang?"

"They're still waiting for a reply?"

"Yes."

"Tell him I'll be right there to speak with him myself."

"See you soon then, sir."

Going back to his quarters, Alexander crossed over to his locker and pulled out a fresh uniform. He was halfway through getting dressed when Caty woke up to ask what he was doing.

"The Confederacy wants to sign a peace treaty. Apparently I'm the only one they trust enough to negotiate the terms."

"What?" Caty asked, sitting up and rubbing the sleep from her eyes. "Where are you going? It could be a trap, Alex."

"Relax, I'm not going anywhere—" He said while yanking on his boots. "—just to the bridge to answer their transmission. If I do meet with anyone it will be in neutral territory, under tightly-controlled circumstances."

"Okay... but be careful what you agree to."

"I will, darling," he said, now buttoning up his uniform.

Once dressed, he crossed over to her side of the bed and dropped a quick peck on her lips. "Go back to sleep."

"I love you," she said.

"Me, too," he replied as he headed out the door and ran down the corridor to the nearest elevator.

Less than five minutes later, Alexander stepped out of that elevator and onto the bridge.

Captain Tristan stood with his hands clasped behind his back, staring out over the moonlit waters of the Indian Ocean. The rest of the bridge crew sat at their stations, almost too busy to notice his arrival. A petty officer standing guard by the doors announced him—

"Admiral on deck!"

Everyone looked away from their stations to offer a brisk salute.

"As you were," Alexander said. "Report, Captain."

Captain Tristan turned from the view and nodded. "Good to see you, Admiral—Lieutenant Campos, get Minister Wang back on the comms."

"Aye, Captain... connection established. Transmitting."

"On-screen," Tristan replied.

Alexander stopped beside Captain Tristan, and watched as the viewport directly in front of them faded from moonlit waters to the unsmiling face of a Chinese man with narrow, aristocratic features and hawkish light gray eyes.

"It is the lion himself. A pleasure to meet you."

"Good evening, Minister," Alexander replied. "I'm told your government wants to talk terms."

"What's left of my government, yes."

"I'm listening."

"We would like to put an end to the fighting in exchange for amnesty for all our soldiers and all our people, myself and the chancellor included."

"So no one gets to pay for their crimes."

"The victor will always try to pin the blame on their enemy, but ask yourself—did we do anything that your government did not also do? Did our soldiers take more lives than yours? If we keep score to see who committed the greater evil, I am certain that the Alliance will win."

Alexander frowned, unable to argue with that. "Listen, Mr. Wang, I appreciate what you're trying to do, but you're talking to the wrong man. My government has not given me the authority to negotiate a peace treaty, so anything I agree to isn't official."

"We are giving you that authority by insisting that you be the one to communicate our terms to your new president. When you do so, be sure to remind him that we are giving up our way of life, allowing your government to come in and turn everything upside down—if that is what they think is best—and in exchange, all that we ask is that you do not make us the scapegoats for this war. Both sides have done terrible things, but it is time for humanity to put terrible things aside, yes?"

"I couldn't agree more, Minister," Alexander said, nodding. "I'll communicate your terms. I sincerely hope my government accepts them. Is there anything else you would like to add?"

"A word of caution."

"And that is?"

"Our surrender does not guarantee the surrender of all Confederate forces everywhere, or a smooth transition of power. All it means is that you will have created a safe place for as many people as possible to lay down their arms and go on with their lives."

Alexander narrowed his eyes at that. "Either you're double-talking, or your government no longer has the authority to give orders to its troops."

"If I were trying to deceive you, I would not warn you ahead of time. As for how much authority still rests with my government—that remains to be seen. If nothing else, having an official treaty in place will give the appearance of unity. That is a step in the right direction, Admiral."

"Agreed. I'll relay your terms to the president."

"Good."

"How do I reach you again?"

"I'm not going anywhere, but if you or any of your people try to capture me or harm me in any way, this deal is off the table."

"Understood. And how do we know that you have the authority to negotiate for the Chancellor?"

"Because I am his son." The camera shifted sideways, and a more familiar face swept into view. Chancellor Wang Ping had been standing there all along, listening to the entire exchange.

Alexander blinked. "Chancellor..."

"Take our terms to your government. It's time to end this war."

Alexander nodded. "I'll be in touch, Chancellor."

The chancellor nodded, and both he and his son faded from view as the transmission ended. The viewport became transparent once more, and back was the moonlit ocean.

Captain Tristan blew out a breath. "I didn't see *that* coming."

"Neither did I," Alexander replied.

"Let's hope President Luther goes for it."

Alexander nodded, his eyes narrowing on the dark line of the horizon, as if trying to peer into tomorrow. "We'll find out soon enough, Captain. Get me President Luther on the comms."

* * *

Six Months and One Week Later - September 17, 2793

"I'm resigning my commission tomorrow," Alexander said, setting his briefcase down on the kitchen counter as he walked in.

Caty turned from washing carrots in the sink. Her eyes flew wide, and before Alexander knew it, she dropped the carrots and leapt into his arms. He caught her with a grunt and stumbled back a step. She showered him with kisses, and he began to laugh.

She withdrew, suddenly suspicious. "You're not joking, are you?"

He shook his head.

"I thought you said you had some unfinished business to attend to—that's why you were staying an extra week."

"I did, but that's all settled now."

Caty smiled, her eyes sparkling, and went back to kissing him. "Someone's getting lucky tonight," she murmured against his neck as she unbuttoned his uniform.

Alexander's comm band trilled and he caught Caty's wrists in his hands, stopping her from undressing him. "I need to take this."

"Hmmm."

"Don't worry. It won't take long."

"It better not," she said, climbing off him and wagging a finger in his face. She grabbed his face with one hand, smushing his cheeks together. "You're mine now."

He smiled and nodded. In the distance he heard Dorian crying from his crib. Alexander jerked his chin in that direction. "Sounds like someone's calling you, too."

Caty went to check on Dorian, and Alexander turned away

to answer his call.

"Admiral de Leon speaking."

"Admiral, it's Stone—sorry to bother you—just checking to see where you'd like to send our new conscript."

Alexander considered that for a moment. The war had ended six months ago with the signing of the World Peace Treaty of 2793, which Alexander had personally helped to negotiate, but ironically the Alliance needed soldiers now more than ever. Not everyone was content to stop the fighting, and defending the entire planet against random acts of terror was no small task. The military had effectively been co-opted into a kind of heavily-armed police force, and Alexander didn't see the need for soldiers diminishing anytime soon.

"What about Stalingrad?" he said. "Nice and cold, and I hear the Russian Reds are even more formidable than the Chinese ones."

"Are you sure, sir?"

"Something you'd like to get off your chest, Lieutenant?"

"He's your son's father. If he dies, you might catch some heat from that."

"We're not doing anything illegal, Stone. He should have thought about the consequences before he decided to cross state lines without a passport. You think it's fair that he gets a free pass and the rest of us all had to risk life and limb to get here?"

"No, sir."

"Besides, a man who beats a woman is a coward. If he lives out his term of service, at least we can be sure that he won't be one anymore. It's about time he picked a fight with someone who could fight back. You have your orders."

"Yes, sir. Stalingrad it is."

"De Leon out." Alexander ended the comm call and turned to see his wife facing him, arms crossed over her chest, her blue eyes sad and full of disappointment. He started when he saw her and tried to affect a smile, hoping that she hadn't overheard much.

"I hope you know what you're doing, Alex. Dorian is going to ask about him one day."

Alexander felt his expression darken. "Let him ask. I'll tell him that I obeyed the law and his biological father broke it. Whatever happens, it's on David's head, not mine."

Caty shrugged and looked away. "You keep telling yourself that."

"Why shouldn't he pay for what he did?"

"What he did to me, or by breaking the law?"

"Both."

Caty sighed. "I didn't say he shouldn't be punished, just that I didn't want you to get your hands dirty. I don't want our son to blame you someday."

"He can't blame me for something he doesn't know."

"Lies have a way of revealing themselves, Alex. Not even silence can keep them. The truth always comes out."

Alexander walked up behind his wife as she went back to washing vegetables in the sink. He wrapped his arms around her waist and whispered in her ear, "You let me handle that. When the time comes, he'll understand."

"I hope you're right, Alexander."

"I am, but let's not talk about this anymore," he said, turning her to face him. "We should be celebrating. I'm done with the navy!"

Caty cracked a smile. "*We're* done. So now what? What are you going to do for a living? Have you thought about it? Jobs aren't exactly easy to come by."

"I'll find something. Anything. Teach myself a trade if I have to. The sky's the limit, Caty."

"No it isn't."

Alexander regarded her with a curious look.

"You of all people should know that. You've been to space, so the *sky* is clearly not the limit."

"Ha ha," Alexander said, smiling wryly at her. "You know what I meant."

"Do I?"

"I meant that we're only limited by what we can dream or imagine. Anything is possible."

Caty nodded slowly. "After what the Alliance did to you with the Excelsior program, I might actually believe that."

Alexander frowned. "When that technology becomes commercially available, we're going to end up with more virtual worlds than real ones."

"Just so long as you don't trade me for a virtual wife, we'll be okay."

Alexander regarded her with a lopsided grin and grabbed her face in his hands for another kiss. "Never."

He withdrew, allowing a whisper to escape from her lips. "Never is a long time."

"But time is an illusion."

Caty smiled and kissed him again.

READ ON FOR A SNEAK PEEK OF THE SEQUEL

MINDSCAPE

Coming December 2016!

To get a **FREE** *digital* copy of *Mindscape* when it's released, please post an honest review of this book and send it to me by signing up here

(http://files.jaspertscott.com/mindscapefree.html)

Remember, your feedback is important to me and to helping other readers find the books they like!

CHAPTER 1

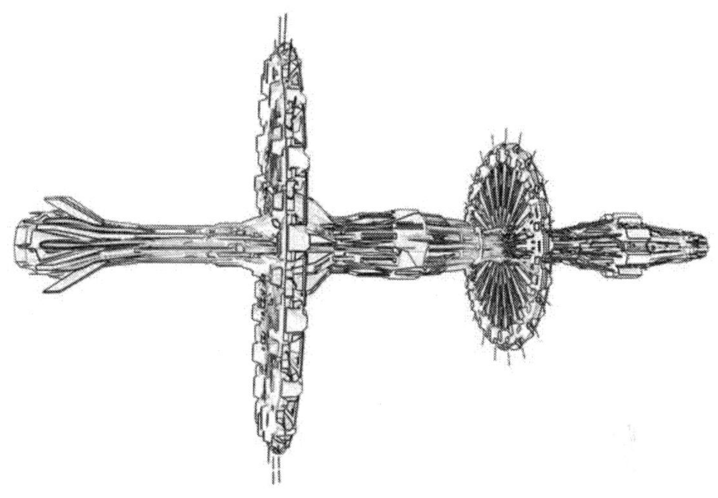

Thirty Years Later…

Alexander rode the elevator down through Freedom Station to the space-facing docking arm. From there he climbed down the ladder through Freedom Station's airlock into the airlock of the *N.W.A.S. Adamantine,* his new command.

But *new* wasn't the right word—this aging battleship was the last of its kind, a relic of a bygone era of war. With a unified government ruling Earth, the only kind of war still being fought was the low-resources kind, in the form of civil unrest and terrorism. The time when whole nations went to war was long since past.

Alexander continued from one ladder to another, passing through the *Adamantine's* airlock, too, and into the elevator waiting on the other side. The *Adamantine's* airlock *swished* shut overhead and Alexander selected the glowing white button marked *Bridge (65)* from the control panel. He braced himself, and the deck suddenly dropped out from under his feet.

The only reason Earth still had a fleet at all was to guard against the now independent colonies in case they tried something stupid. Mars, Titan, and Europa had watched The Last War, and they'd declared their independence soon after it had ended. Amidst the rising cost of occupying unruly Confederate territories on Earth, the colonies couldn't have picked a better time to break away. Their bid for independence had gone largely uncontested. Earth had too many of its own problems to worry about losing its hold over a handful of extraterrestrial settlements, especially when maintaining those settlements was barely better than a break-even proposition. The colonies had enough trouble providing for their basic needs, let alone building fleets and going to war with their ancestral homeworld.

Alexander watched the lights of passing decks flicker through the transparent windows at the top of the elevator doors as he rode *Adamantine's* elevator down to the bridge. This was all too familiar, he thought, looking around at the padded walls of the elevator. He spied handrails for zero-G, exposed conduits here and there (because covered ones were a pain in the ass to get at for repairs). Thirty years ago he'd wanted nothing better than to get the hell out of the navy. Now, what felt like a lifetime later, he was right back where he'd started.

At least this time it was on his own terms—not that those terms were pleasant. His stepson, Dorian, found out what had happened to his biological father, and promptly disowned his parents for keeping that lie. In Alexander's case it was also because he'd hunted Dorian's father down and had him conscripted to fight in a dangerous, war-torn state of the New World Alliance.

Caty blamed Alexander for losing their son, because *he* was the one who had insisted on hunting David down and bringing him to justice. Then she'd left him to go after Dorian.

Alexander would have gone chasing after them both, but every time he thought about it, something stopped him. Maybe it was the thought that after all he'd done, and all he and Caty had been through to be together, she'd *left* him. Clearly she loved Dorian more than she ever loved him, and that told him there really wasn't anything left to go chasing after.

The Mindscape had ruined them, just like it had ruined so many others. It was too addictive. Humanity had upped and disappeared from the real world to rather pour all of its energy into fake ones. Even he, with all his reasons to distrust the Mindscape, had fallen victim to that.

It starts slow.

At first it's this thing you do as a couple, or as a family. You all participate in building a virtual life together in the same mindscape, but then pretty soon you find another one you like better, and each of you splits off into your own private worlds. Temptations abound, good and bad alike. For him and Caty it wasn't any one thing, but it didn't help that one day Alexander went into Caty's mindscape using an alias and an avatar she wouldn't recognize, thinking he'd surprise her, and he'd found her in bed with another man—if it had even been a man. No way to tell with virtual worlds. Something like that happens in the real world and it's pretty clear cut, but when it happens in a virtual one…

Things get a whole lot muddier.

They talked about it, and after a big fight, they made love in the real world for the first time in a very long time. Then they agreed that virtual cheating was still cheating.

Funny, Alexander seemed to recall that had been *Caty's* rule since day one, but he'd been willing to let it go. He hadn't exactly been blameless. When was the last time he'd even *tried* to touch his wife—in any world? He promised to do better.

But they still didn't find more time to be together. In hindsight, Caty leaving him to go look for their son wasn't all that strange. They'd stopped being husband and wife a long time ago.

The elevator stopped with a rusty screech of brakes that set Alexander's teeth on edge. *This ship is falling apart* he thought. The doors opened and he stepped out onto the bridge to see his crew all assembled and waiting.

"Admiral on deck!" someone called out, and a cheer rose from the crew, accompanied by hoots and whistles, and a clapping of hands.

Frowning, Alexander shook his head. *Not the salute I was expecting.* "Settle down everyone. Save the fanfare for someone who deserves it."

One of the crew stepped forward, a familiar face—blond hair, blue eyes, perfect skin, ruby red lips. *McAdams.* Alexander smiled, feeling better already.

"If you don't deserve it, then who does, sir? You're Admiral Alexander de Leon, *the Lion of Liberty.* You negotiated world peace and won a Nobel prize for it, so yes, I think that deserves more than just a salute."

Alexander spied the silver oak-leaf insignia on her uniform. *She's a commander now.* "I thought you left the navy?"

"Likewise, sir."

"Touché. My wife and son left me. What's your excuse?"

The corners of McAdams mouth turned down. "Sorry to hear that, sir."

"I'm not looking for a pity party, just stating the facts."

"Well, I did leave the navy, but I came back about two years ago. Turns out civilian life wasn't for me—Navy jobs are practically the only real ones left. And I'm not the only one who had trouble settling down. I managed to get most of the others transferred here, too."

"The others?"

McAdams nodded and turned. "Lieutenant Commander Stone—" a particularly burly officer with a familiar lumpy face stepped forward and saluted. "—Lieutenant Cardinal—" The *Lincoln's* old weapons officer stepped out of line next. "—and Lieutenant Hayes." The comms officer.

Alexander felt a suspicious warmth leaking from the corner of one eye.

"Gettin' all misty-eyed on us, Admiral?" Stone quipped.

Alexander shook his head. "Having to stare at your ugly mug again is making my eyes burn."

Stone snorted.

McAdams smiled. "Welcome home, Admiral."

Alexander nodded, realizing just how true that was. "Thank you—all of you," he said, his eyes skipping over the group. There were still a few faces he didn't recognize.

"Maybe you'd better finish the introductions, Commander."

"It would be my pleasure, sir."

* * *

Alexander sat in his acceleration couch, staring out at the diamond sparkle of stars. Each of them was another galaxy or solar system that humanity would probably never reach. What else was out there? People had been looking up at the stars and asking that question for as long as humans had walked the Earth, and now that they were flying through space, they were still no closer to answering it.

"Entering lunar orbit," Lieutenant Bishop reported from the helm.

Alexander nodded. "Keep me posted."

"Aye, sir."

Bishop was a gener, like McAdams. Over six feet tall with perfect brown skin, wavy black hair, straight white teeth, and piercing blue eyes. Physical perfection was just one of the hallmarks of his genetically-engineered heritage that set him apart from the natural-borns. There were a lot more geners in the Navy these days, now that there wasn't any real threat of war. But besides that, disillusionment was universal. Gener or not, some people got tired of the Mindscape and went looking for *real* fulfillment. Sooner or later those people all signed up—that, or they became Humanists and joined the Human League, where automata, AI, and the Mindscape were all treated like the plague.

Joining the Navy was a far less extreme way to go.

Alexander watched a dark arc of seeming emptiness rise up under them and sweep away the stars. Then Lunar City appeared, creeping in from the horizon like some luminous spider crouching over the Moon.

"The dark side of the Moon is a lot brighter than I remember it," Alexander said.

"It's been thirty years since you last saw it, Admiral," McAdams said. "You have some catching up to do."

"Admiral, I'm getting a clearer fix on that signal..." Hayes reported from the comms.

"Good, any idea where it's coming from?"

"Still calculating, but I should have an answer for you in about a minute, sir."

Alexander nodded. This mission was the latest in a series of make work projects from fleet command—investigate a mystery signal that Lunar City had reported coming from somewhere out in deep space; help them triangulate it and decrypt it if possible. Alexander sighed. He supposed the fleet had to look busy if they wanted to hang on to what little funding they had left.

"Got it!"

"Give me coordinates."

"It's… that can't be right."

"Start talking, Hayes. Where is it?"

"It's coming from the Looking Glass."

"The wormhole? How can a wormhole be producing a comm signal?"

"I don't think it's the wormhole, sir. It looks like the signal is using an old Confederate encryption."

Alexander's eyes widened. "The Confederacy doesn't have a fleet anymore. It was disbanded in 2793 with the signing of the World Peace Treaty. I should know, I helped negotiate it."

"I'm not arguing with that, sir, just reporting the facts."

"Well, can we decrypt the signal?"

"Sure. Computers have come a long way in the last thirty years. Easy as cracking an egg."

"Then get cracking."

"Aye, sir."

Alexander nodded to McAdams. "What's your take on this?"

She turned to him, blue eyes wide and blinking. "Either someone's spoofing that signal, or some part of the Confederate fleet we sent down the gullet of the wormhole all those years ago actually made it to the other side."

Alexander shook his head. "Try again. We saw their ships get ripped apart with our own eyes. Besides—the wormhole isn't traversable. That's why we tricked the Reds into flying through it in the first place."

McAdams shrugged. "Then what's your theory?"

"Someone's spoofing the signal with a drone that they parked in the mouth of the wormhole."

"Got it!" Hayes announced. "It's audio-visual."

"On-screen, Lieutenant."

"Aye-aye."

"Time to meet our secret admirer," Lieutenant Stone said from his control station.

Alexander saw a snowy image appear. Front and center was a woman of Chinese descent, wearing a stained and torn Confederate uniform. In the background, he recognized the CIC of an ancient-looking warship. Flickering lights revealed floating debris, but for some reason the woman standing in front of the camera wasn't floating. *Magnetic boots,* Alexander decided. "If this is someone's idea of a joke..." he began.

Then he saw the woman's eyes. They were completely black, as if she didn't even have eyes, or else her pupils had dilated to the size of overripe grapes. "What the hell?" Alexander shook his head.

"Hello wretched creatures. We invite you to look upon your legacy." The voice was deep and inflectionless, not a woman's voice at all.

The camera switched from the dilapidated CIC to a darkened space, crammed with floating debris. Alexander sat forward in his couch and peered at the main holo display, trying to decide what he was looking at. Lights flickered between the floating bits of debris as they shifted through the room. Based on the ceiling height and openness of the space, Alexander decided he was looking into some kind of hangar bay or cargo hold.

"Hayes, can you shine some light on the feed?"

"On it, sir. Here comes the sun..."

A second later the darkness peeled away and everything snapped into focus. A few of the crew gasped, and Alexander felt his gut churn.

The debris was bodies, hundreds of them, all floating in zero-G, limbs tangling, mops of hair drifting like seaweed. Fully half of the bodies were children. All of the bodies wore pressure suits emblazoned with a familiar hammer-and-sickle pattern of gold stars—the old Confederate flag.

The scene lingered there a moment longer before cutting back to the woman with the black eyes. "Any race that can do this to its own kind will do worse to others. You have been judged and found guilty. Your sentence will be delivered soon."

The transmission faded to black, and Alexander scowled. "Hayes—analyze that recording."

"What am I looking for, sir?"

"'Scapers tags, signatures—any sign that what we just saw is part of a mindscape, and if possible, some clue that might lead us to the 'scaper who built it."

"On it, sir."

"You don't believe it's real," McAdams said.

Alexander regarded her with eyebrows raised. "Do you?"

"I guess not, but if this was the work of some rogue 'scaper terrorist, why were there no demands?"

"What if someone from the Confederate colony fleet actually made it?" Bishop suggested from the helm.

"Even if that were possible, it would mean that that bit about passing judgment and delivering a sentence was just to make us wet our pants. There's nothing they can do to us from the other side of the wormhole."

"Did anyone notice the woman's voice?" McAdams asked.

"How about her eyes?" Cardinal said from gunnery.

Alexander considered that. "Assuming I believe this signal is real—which I don't—those features could be explained by implants used to repair physical damage after traveling through high radiation and high gravity zones inside the wormhole."

"Well, the language was also off," Hayes added. "She called

us *wretched creatures,* as if she didn't consider herself to be one of us. Then there's that part about how a race that kills its own will do worse to others. It's almost like she was trying to say that she isn't human."

"So what is she then?" Alexander asked. "An alien? She looked human enough."

"Maybe that's what it wanted us to think," Hayes said. "We still don't know who created the wormhole. We've known from the start that it couldn't be naturally occurring."

Alexander shook his head, incredulous. "Come on people—there's a rational explanation here, and we're going to find it. Remember Wonderland? Fool us once, shame on them. Fool us twice—I'll be damned if there's going to be a second time. Things aren't always what they appear to be. Someone, somewhere, wants us jumping at shadows. The question is who, and *why*. It's our job to find out. Hayes—pass that recording back to fleet command, maybe they can make more out of it than we can."

"Aye-aye, sir."

Alexander frowned, and went back to studying the view from the *Adamantine's* bow cameras. Lunar City was now almost directly below them. Alexander absently watched the towering spires, all glittering with lights. He remembered when Lunar City had been nothing but an Alliance naval base. Now it was a bustling city with a population of more than two million.

The day side of the Moon appeared in the distance, a dazzling silver crescent rushing toward them like a tidal wave. *Beautiful...* Alexander saw a ring of stars wink at him.

"Admiral, we've got incoming! Looks like ordnance!" Lieutenant Frost, reported from sensors.

Those weren't stars. A second later the ship's combat computer highlighted them with red target boxes.

"McAdams, sound general quarters! Frost, get me vectors!"

"Aye, sir."

The lights dimmed to a bloody red, and the battle siren screamed out a pair of warning cries before McAdams silenced it.

"Bishop, take evasive action! Ten *G*s to port."

"Wait—" McAdams said. "—the rest of the crew isn't strapped in yet!"

"Tell them to belt in at emergency anchor points. They've got thirty seconds. Bishop, set thrusters to fire in thirty-one."

"Aye, sir."

"Vectors calculated!"

"On screen," Alexander ordered.

An over-sized tactical map came up on the MHD, taking the place of the visual feed from the bow cameras. Ten different red icons appeared dead ahead of the *Adamantine's* tactical icon. Hair-thin vector lines tracked the missiles' trajectories. All of them were converging on...

Lunar City.

"They're not headed for us," McAdams whispered.

"One million klicks and closing... They're moving at relativistic speeds! Over one third *C!*" Frost reported.

"Cardinal, intercept those missiles *now!*" Alexander roared.

"Aye!"

"Hayes—warn Lunar City. They need to get their defenses tracking."

Alexander watched bright golden streams of hypervelocity rounds go streaking out from his ship along the paths of the incoming ordnance. Seven out of ten missiles winked off the tactical with pinpricks of fire. The remaining three sailed on.

"Too late!" McAdams screamed.

Lunar city became a bright smear on the tactical map, and

then it was gone. Alexander gaped at the blank spot on the map where more than two million people used to live.

Alexander slammed his fists against his armrests.

"Incoming transmission—audio only," Hayes reported.

"On-screen!"

The deep, toneless voice was the same as before. It said, "This, is only the beginning."

Alexander turned to his XO. She stared back at him with wide eyes and a furrowed brow.

"Hayes—trace that signal!" Alexander ordered.

"It came from the wormhole again, sir. Same source."

"You don't think *she* fired those missiles, do you?" McAdams asked.

Alexander shook his head. "I don't know *who* fired them, Commander, but whoever it was, they just declared war on Earth."

FREE OFFER

MINDSCAPE

Coming December 2016!

To get a **FREE** *digital* copy of *Mindscape* when it's released, please post an honest review of this book and send it to me by signing up here

(http://files.jaspertscott.com/mindscapefree.html)

Remember, your feedback is important to me and to helping other readers find the books they like!

KEEP IN TOUCH

SUBSCRIBE to my Mailing List and Stay Informed about Upcoming Books and Discounts!

(http://files.jaspertscott.com/mailinglist.html)

Follow me on Twitter:

@JasperTscott

Look me up on Facebook:

Jasper T. Scott

Check out my website:

http://www.JasperTscott.com

Or send me an e-mail:

JasperTscott@gmail.com

ABOUT THE AUTHOR

Jasper T. Scott Jasper Scott is the USA Today best-selling author of more than 13 novels written across various genres. He was born and raised in Canada by South African parents, with a British cultural heritage on his mother's side and German on his father's, to which he has now added Latin culture with his wonderful wife.

Jasper spent years living as a starving artist before finally quitting his various jobs to become a full-time writer. In his spare time he enjoys reading, traveling, going to the gym, and spending time with his family.

Printed in Great Britain
by Amazon